WORMWOOD

MARIE CORELLI, c. 1906.

Photograph by G. Gabell. Kindly provided by
the Shakespeare Birthplace Trust, Stratford-upon-Avon.

WORMWOOD

A Drama of Paris

Marie Corelli

edited by Kirsten MacLeod

broadview editions

National Library of Canada Cataloguing in Publication Data

Corelli, Marie
    Wormwood : a drama of Paris / Marie Corelli ; edited by Kirsten MacLeod.

(Broadview editions)
Includes bibliographical references.
ISBN 1-55111-419-4

I. MacLeod, Kirsten, 1969- II. Title. III. Series.

PR4504.W67 2004   823'.8   C2004-900698-3

Broadview Press Ltd. is an independent, international publishing house, incorporated in 1985. Broadview believes in shared ownership, both with its employees and with the general public; since the year 2000 Broadview shares have traded publicly on the Toronto Venture Exchange under the symbol BDP.

We welcome comments and suggestions regarding any aspect of our publications—please feel free to contact us at the addresses below or at broadview@broadviewpress.com / www.broadviewpress.com

North America
PO Box 1243, Peterborough, Ontario, Canada K9J 7H5
Tel: (705) 743-8990; Fax: (705) 743-8353
email: customerservice@broadviewpress.com
3576 California Road, Orchard Park, NY, USA 14127

UK, Ireland, and continental Europe
NBN Plymbridge
Estover Road
Plymouth PL6 7PY UK
Tel: 44 (0) 1752 202 301
Fax: 44 (0) 1752 202 331
Fax Order Line: 44 (0) 1752 202 333
Customer Service: cservs@nbnplymbridge.com
Orders: orders@nbnplymbridge.com

Australia and New Zealand
UNIREPS, University of New South Wales
Sydney, NSW, 2052
Tel: 61 2 9664 0999; Fax: 61 2 9664 5420
email: info.press@unsw.edu.au

Series editor: Professor L.W. Conolly
Advisory editor for this volume: Professor Eugene Benson

Broadview Press Ltd. gratefully acknowledges the financial support of the Government of Canada through the Book Publishing Industry Development Program for our publishing activities.

PRINTED IN CANADA

Contents

Acknowledgements

I have been helped by a number of people in preparing this edition. I am grateful to the staff at the Beinecke Library, Yale University, for allowing me access to the Marie Corelli Collection, which contains the bulk of her letters to George Bentley. I must also thank Gemey Kelly of the Owens Art Gallery, Mount Allison University, Michael Pantazzi, Assistant Curator of European Art at the National Gallery of Canada, and Anne Koval of the Department of Fine Arts at Mount Allison University for helping me sort out the distinctions between French Academic artists and French Bohemian artists at the end of the nineteenth century. Thanks also to the Social Sciences and Humanities Research Council of Canada which helped fund my research for this project. Without Jo-Ann Wallace's guidance, I might never have taken up work on the fascinating Marie Corelli. Finally, I owe my thanks to Gary Kelly whose encouragement and support have made this edition possible.

Introduction

Marie Corelli was a literary phenomenon for thirty years, from the moment she burst onto the literary scene in 1886 until World War I when her popularity began to wane. Corelli's novels sold more copies than the combined sales of most of her competitors including such popular authors as Arthur Conan Doyle, E.F. Benson, Rudyard Kipling, and H.G. Wells. One could compare her to the best-selling women authors of our own day, writers such as Danielle Steele or Catherine Cookson, but such a comparison would not do justice to the particular hold that Corelli had over the public imagination—a hold that might more fruitfully be compared to that of a major television personality like Oprah Winfrey, a rock star like Madonna, and a religious evangelist like Jerry Falwell. For not only did her admirers voraciously devour her books, they also looked to her for guidance on religious and spiritual matters, on issues of social reform, on the status of women, and on the role of science in modern life; they fought to get near her, trying to kiss the hem of her dress; in America they founded religions based on her writings and named cities after her (Corelli City in Colorado); they named their children after characters in her books (Corelli popularized the names Mavis and Thelma, which had not previously been used in English-speaking nations); they even integrated her name into popular slang (in Cockney rhyming slang a "Corelli" means a "telly" or "television").

Despite Corelli's massive popular appeal she was harshly derided by literary critics and intellectual highbrows who referred to her derisively as "the idol of suburbia," and "the favourite of the common multitude."[1] Q.D. Leavis, for example, declared that "high-level reader[s] of Marie Corelli ... [are] impelled to laugh" at her writing, "so ridiculously inadequate to the issues raised is the equipment of the mind that so resolutely tackles them," while Rebecca West accused Corelli of having an "incurably commonplace mind."[2] Similarly, J.M. Stuart-Young declared that no intelligent reader could enjoy Corelli's books and that her "appeal" was only to the "unthinking classes":

---

[1] A. St. John Adcock, "Marie Corelli: A Record and an Appreciation," *The Bookman* (May 1909): 60.

[2] Q.D. Leavis, *Fiction and the Reading Public* (1932; London: Pimlico, 2000) 66; Rebecca West, *The Strange Necessity: Essays and Reviews* (London: Jonathan Cape, 1928) 321.

She is sentimental, pathetic, mawkish, bitter, tender, and sensuous by turn. The majority of the readers of her books are undoubtedly taken from the members of her own sex, in middle-class society, and from the working classes—shop-girls and young men of the large towns. She is doted on in the drawing-room as well as in the servants' hall. I have a shrewd suspicion that the features that provoke the keenest criticism of men who know how to discriminate, are the features which are the most popular with women and youths. She has the courage of her hysteria and is not afraid to scream.[1]

That Corelli only appealed to the "unthinking," however, is not entirely true. Alfred Lord Tennyson, Poet Laureate of England, and Algernon Charles Swinburne, poet, were admirers, as were some of the leading political, religious, and educational figures of her day including Lord Haldane, William Gladstone, Herbert Asquith, the Deans of Gloucester and Westminster, Dean Wilberforce, Dean Farrar, the Master of Magdalene, and the Rector of St. Andrews University. These were hardly persons to be classed among the "unthinking." Moreover, the claims that Corelli was the "idol of suburbia" are hardly sustainable in view of the fact that her works were translated into French, German, Italian, Swedish, Spanish, Hungarian, Norwegian, Hindustani, Danish, Russian, Dutch, Greek, Japanese, and Persian. As one of her supporters rightly asked, "if this is suburban, which one of our novelists may be regarded as approximately cosmopolitan?"[2] Even her harshest critics could not entirely disguise their awe at the phenomenon that was Marie Corelli. West, for example, praised Corelli's "demoniac vitality" while Stuart-Young stood in awe of the "Corelli cult," acknowledging that her works were "worthy of serious consideration" if only by virtue of the "unique" popularity she had achieved in her time.[3]

Many attempts have been made to account for Corelli's popularity. Typically, Corelli is credited with touching a chord in the hearts of her readers and of capturing the spirit of her age. As John Lucas writes, "her books ... clearly reflect opinions, wishes, likes and dislikes of the nineteenth century and the early years of the twentieth. If you want to know what the man on the Clapham omnibus thought of life during

---

[1] J.M. Stuart-Young, "A Note Upon Marie Corelli by Another Writer of Less Repute," *Westminster Review* 166.6 (1906): 683.

[2] Adcock 60.

[3] Stuart-Young 680.

those years, Marie Corelli's books will help to tell you."[1] A BBC critic similarly acknowledged, "[Corelli] said and did things we would all like to say and do, for we are all of us Marie Corelli under the skin."[2] Corelli herself attributed her success to her ability to serve as a voice for her age: "I can feel the pulse of the people ringing and beating through me as if I were a mere glass bell for it to sound against."[3] But whatever we make of these assessments of Corelli's phenomenal fame—and it must be acknowledged that no one has yet been able to account for her astounding success internationally—there is no doubt that Corelli is a fascinating figure.

No less fascinating than Corelli herself is her novel *Wormwood: A Drama of Paris* (1890), which is a striking example of Corelli's ability to "feel the pulse of the people" and to reflect their "opinions, wishes, likes, and dislikes." *Wormwood* was written at a time when Britain felt its economic and imperial powers threatened by nations such as the United States and Germany and by the social agitation of the working classes and suffragettes closer to home. In the novel, the anxieties of *fin de siècle* Britain take monstrous shape in the form of the corrupt French nation. In this period, France served as a powerful image for Britain in concretizing the nation's more general fear of its own demise. Though there were many British lovers of French culture at this time, notably among the intellectual and artistic milieus, in the main, Britons regarded France as a country characterized by dangerous political radicalism, lax social and moral values, and a corrupt literary and artistic culture. Indeed, many Britons feared that their own nation would be, in their own words, "contaminated" or "poisoned" by pernicious French culture. It is not surprising, then, that a barely disguised Francophobia pervades most of the important social and cultural debates within Britain at this time, in particular literary and artistic debates about Naturalism (also known as Realism), Decadence, and Impressionism. These French literary and artistic schools were beginning to influence British writers and artists and many feared that this influence would lead to the degeneration of British culture. *Wormwood* engages with these debates and exploits British Francophobia to the full in its attack on Realism and Naturalism, Decadence, French art, French bohemian artistic life, French

---

[1] John Lucas, "Marie Corelli," *Great Writers of the English Language: Novelists and Prose Writers*, ed. James Vinson (New York: St. Martin's Press, 1979) 283.

[2] Quoted in Brian Masters, *Now Barabbas Was a Rotter: The Extraordinary Life of Marie Corelli* (London: Hamish Hamilton, 1978) 292.

[3] Quoted in Masters 294.

Catholicism, and, most significantly, French drinking culture and the burgeoning craze for absinthe. Absinthe was a French apéritif with such a high alcohol content that, in terms of its effect on the drinker, it was considered more of a drug than alcohol. It was so popular in France that the traditional end of day drinking hour became known as *l'heure verte* (the green hour), after the colour of absinthe. Generally, the British viewed the French absinthe craze as a confirmation of their suspicion that France was a degenerate nation on a steady course of decline. This view was confirmed by newspaper reports and medical findings that linked absinthism with insanity and criminal behaviour. None of this coverage, however, was as powerful in its representation to the British public of the dangers of absinthe as *Wormwood*, the first treatment of the subject of absinthism in British literature.

In a less explicit fashion, *Wormwood* is also an important reflection of Corelli's personal and professional struggles. Despite her enormous commercial success, Corelli was continually seeking approval from established social and literary institutions as she struggled to deal with the social contradictions of class and gender. Corelli wanted to fit in everywhere—in the homes of the rich and famous, in the cottages of the poor, in the drawing rooms of the middle class, and in the exclusive literary and intellectual London clubs. Her novels of otherworldly transcendence and her many social satires suggest that she never really did find a sense of community in this world. Viewed in the context of its production and reception, *Wormwood* is, in part, the story of Corelli's struggle to find a place for herself in the élite literary circles of her day.

Because Corelli's personal and professional investments figure so strongly in the production of *Wormwood* and because details of her life are not widely known, this introduction provides a detailed account of her personal and professional life and her struggles as a woman and as a woman writer. This biographical account is followed by an equally detailed discussion of the important social and literary debates about Naturalism, Decadence, absinthe, and cultural degeneration. These issues shaped the production and reception of *Wormwood*, a novel that is a fascinating reflection of the interest and fears of late-Victorian Britain by an equally fascinating woman who embodied the contradictions of her age.

Biography

For a woman who would achieve international fame, be lauded on the one hand as a "prophetess" and decried on the other as a "social menace," Corelli's beginnings were inauspicious to say the least.[1] Corelli, whose real name was Mary ("Minnie") Mackay, was born on 1 May 1855, an illegitimate child whose parentage is shrouded in mystery. Most accounts identify her as the illegitimate daughter of Elizabeth Mary Mills (also known as Ellen) and Charles MacKay, a married man and father of four. Mackay eventually married Mills in 1861, but only after observing a year of mourning after the death of his first wife. Corelli herself never publicly acknowledged this version of her origins, claiming instead that Mackay had adopted her. Of the woman who is supposed to have been Corelli's mother, Corelli said next to nothing even though her mother lived until Corelli was twenty. Corelli's own versions of her parentage were many. In one account she claimed that her mother was a Venetian, in another that her mother was Scottish and her father Italian, and in yet another that she was descended from Italian royalty and related to the famous Baroque composer Arcangelo Corelli.

Though Corelli's origins will probably never be fully corroborated, her most recent biographer, Teresa Ransom, offers some interesting speculations which she bases on a poem written by Mackay. In the handwritten copy of the poem, entitled "The Wayside Spring in Alabama," the line "like a little daughter's daughter" is scored out and replaced with "Like a little maiden," leading Ransom to wonder whether Corelli was Mackay's granddaughter rather than his daughter. Mackay, after all, had a daughter who died in Italy the year of Corelli's birth. Was this daughter of Mackay's the Scottish mother Corelli refers to? Did she become pregnant by an Italian, the nationality Corelli claimed was her father's? Did Mackay then marry Mills in order to provide a family environment for his "daughter's daughter"? Was the name Corelli, a name that Corelli claimed was a genuine family name, the name of her real father? And if so, was her father the tenor Signor Corelli who had sung at Her Majesty's theatre in London—a theatre managed by a friend of Mackay's—and who may have returned to Italy when the theatre closed from 1852 to 1856?[2]

Almost as obscure as Corelli's origins are the events of her early child-hood. Though Mackay apparently adopted Corelli when she was three months old, he appears not to have been around in the first six years of

---

[1] *Review of Reviews*, May 1924. Quoted in Teresa Ransom, *The Mysterious Miss Marie Corelli: Queen of Victorian Bestsellers* (Thrupp, Glouscestershire, UK: 1999) 6; Stuart-Young 692.

[2] Ransom 225–31.

her life. During this time, Corelli was raised by Mary Elizabeth ("Ellen") Mills while Mackay travelled in Scotland and America collecting material for his songs, lecturing on poetry and song, and doing journalistic work. In 1861, Mackay returned to England and married Mills. At this time, however, Mackay had no permanent employment and even a literary pension of £100 a year did little to alleviate the financial burden of the newly remarried Mackay. An offer of a posting with the *Times* in New York in 1862 came at an opportune time. Mackay returned to London at the end of 1863 and headed back to New York once more until the end of 1865. From 1866 to1870, no permanent address is recorded for Mackay. It was during these years that Corelli probably attended a convent school either in Paris or Italy (Corelli made different claims at various points in her life). At school, Corelli began to demonstrate her interest in music, writing, and the theatre.

Corelli returned to England around 1870. Home was now Fern Dell Cottage, Box Hill, in Surrey, where the famous writer George Meredith was a neighbour and friend of Mackay's. Here Corelli continued with her singing and piano lessons and took advantage of MacKay's extensive library. She began writing poems and submitted a poem entitled "Sappho" to *Blackwood's Magazine* in 1874. So began fruitless attempts on Corelli's part to publish poems and articles, a task that she undertook with great resolve and persistence despite the many rejections she received. Corelli hounded editors, berating them for not responding to her letters and expressing her disappointment at their rejections. Her attempts to bully editors are amusing but her desperation was real. Mackay was in financial difficulties again and his health was poor, while Marie's "mother," Ellen, was terminally ill. Corelli felt the strain of this situation enormously and took upon herself the responsibility of running the household and of providing for the financially strapped family. Luckily, she had the help of her friend Bertha Vyver who had joined the household when Ellen became ill and who would become Corelli's lifelong companion.

Another addition to the Mackay household at this time was Corelli's step-brother, Eric Mackay. A ne'er-do-well in his mid-forties who had failed in his attempts to establish himself in business, in literature, on the stage, and as an opera singer, Eric was an additional burden on the household. Corelli, however, was dazzled by Eric and did everything in her power to support him. When he determined on a career as a violinist, Corelli bought him a violin and paid for his lessons. Corelli also intervened on his behalf when he wanted to publish a book of his poems, selling her jewellery in order to pay for its publication. The book was a complete failure, its only positive review written by none other than Eric's devoted step-sister who reviewed the work under an assumed name. Unfortunately, Corelli's devotion to Eric was misguided. Eric played up to Corelli but behind her back he disparaged her and, when she began to achieve success as a writer, he claimed that he had written her books.

In June 1883 the situation in the Mackay household became worse. Mackay had a severe stroke in June and the family left Fern Dell to be closer to medical specialists in London. In desperation, Corelli renewed her assault on the *Blackwood's Magazine* editor, presenting herself for the first time as Signorina Marie Corelli of Venice and offering some poems for publication. Receiving no response from *Blackwood's*, Corelli turned to Clement Scott, editor of *Theatre Magazine*, where she met with success. Her poems, written in Shakespearean sonnet style, were published in the magazine in 1883 and 1884. While this achievement delighted Corelli, it brought in little money and Corelli began to focus on music as a career. Her chance to launch herself as a piano *improvisatrice* came when she was invited to give a public concert in the drawing room of a Harley Street doctor in December 1884. Included among the distinguished audience that night were the poet Algernon Charles Swinburne and his friend Theodore Watts-Dunton, critic and man of letters. Swinburne was duly impressed with Corelli's performance and offered her permission to publish her musical arrangement of two of his poems. After this success, Corelli went on to give concerts in London, the provinces, and in Edinburgh but her success did not last. After a few brief months, Corelli abandoned her music career and turned to writing once more. This time she would try her hand at a novel.

In 1885 Corelli's luck began to change for the better. Her successful placement of an article with *Temple Bar* magazine represented the beginning of her profitable association with its editor, George Bentley, who was also the leading publisher of popular novels throughout the Victorian period. Corelli submitted a manuscript to him and, against the advice of all his readers including the popular novelist, Hall Caine, Bentley published it in 1886 under the title *A Romance of Two Worlds*. The novel exploited the popular fascination with mysticism, spiritualism, and with Edison's recent discoveries about electricity. Though the novel was generally not well-received by critics, it caught the attention of the public. Corelli became an overnight sensation and was fêted by prominent artists including Oscar Wilde, William Michael Rossetti, and the actor Wilson Barrett.

No sooner had her first book been published, than Corelli was ready with a second. She sent the manuscript of her next novel, *Vendetta*, to Bentley only two weeks after the publication of *A Romance of Two Worlds*. *Vendetta* (1886) was very different from Corelli's first novel. On the advice of Bentley, Corelli had decided to abandon the supernatural theme for something more dramatic. Corelli came up with a story about a wronged husband's vengeance on his unfaithful wife. Her third novel, *Thelma* (1887), was different yet again, a society novel about an innocent Norwegian girl exposed to the hypocrisies and vices of London society. *Thelma* was a phenomenal success and Corelli, despite her attack on London high society in the novel, found herself on every prominent society hostess' guest list. A fourth novel, *Ardath* (1889), soon followed, winning Corelli the admiration of the Poet Laureate, Alfred Tennyson, William Gladstone, former Prime Minister of Britain, and Queen Victoria, who insisted that she be sent all Corelli's books. Nonetheless, the critical acclaim Corelli so strongly desired continued to elude her.

Flushed with her success—with the public if not with the critics—Corelli was determined to keep surprising people with her artistic virtuosity. "I wish to prove that I am capable of more than *one* style of novel," she wrote Bentley in 1887, "and that the simply sensational will form but a very small part of my future work. In brief I have resolved that no two books of mine shall be in the least alike, so that neither the critics nor the public shall know *what* to expect from me."[1] As Corelli became increasingly aware of the cut-throat nature of the profession that she had chosen, however, her optimism about winning the critical favour of highbrow critics and the literary élite waned. In the male-dominated literary élite of the 1880s and 1890s, women writers fared badly. Accused of being limited in their artistic range and capable only of writing sensationalistic trash for lowbrow audiences, women writers were generally paid less than their male counterparts and were rarely accorded the respect of being considered "artists." Corelli's desire to prove herself "capable of more than *one* style of novel" was, in many respects, a response to this gendered hierarchy of categorization. Corelli believed that by displaying her virtuosity she would force critics to recognize her as an artist.

Corelli was appalled at the harsh competitiveness of the literary world and longed, as she told Bentley, for a "*fraternity* among all the

---

[1]   Marie Corelli, letter to George Bentley, 1 January 1887, Marie Corelli Collection, General Collection, Beinecke Rare Book and Manuscript Library, Yale University. Unless otherwise indicated all cited letters from Corelli to Bentley are from this collection.

followers of Art," and for "a bond of joyous and sympathetic union ... among them."[1] But despite her belief that "no author ought to judge of another," Corelli was herself extremely critical of her peers.[2] In such a "rough-and-tumble" environment, as she would later write, it was either "fight" or "lie down and be walked over."[3] Corelli chose to fight. In letters to Bentley, Corelli railed at the critical acclaim bestowed upon such writers as Rider Haggard and Rudyard Kipling. Of Kipling, for example, she wrote, "Rudyard Kipling is a young mushroom growing on the roots of the Savile Club,—and this is why he is elevated into a sudden 'Genius'—though of genius he has none."[4] Ironically, however, in spite of her rage at the injustices practised upon women authors, her harshest criticism was reserved for women authors. Internalizing the gender bias that dominated the *fin de siècle* literary world, Corelli denigrated the works of "John Strange Winter" (pseudonym of Henrietta Eliza Vaughan Palmer), Rhoda Broughton, Mrs. Humphrey Ward, and Florence Marryat. "John Strange Winter," she told Bentley, was nothing more than a "Shilling Popular" novelist who wrote "deplorable English," and Corelli could not understand why John Ruskin, a highly acclaimed art and social critic of the day, should admire Winter's "inartistic" and "commonplace" writing.[5] Far from feeling solidarity with her sister authors, Corelli did everything in her power to distance herself from them, even going so far to describe her own writing as "masculine." "The principal thing my 'sisters' grudge me," she wrote Bentley, "is the 'man's pen'... I do not write in a 'ladylike' or effeminate way, and for that they hate me. Over and over again I have suffered a great deal in absolute silence,—more sorry for the littleness of my sex than for anything else."[6]

Corelli's bitterness at her treatment at the hands of the literary establishment led her in 1892 to write a biting satire called *Silver Domino, or: Side Whispers, Social and Literary* in which she launched invectives against numerous writers, critics, journalists, publishers (including Bentley), and even political men of the day. She wanted it published anonymously and, once it created a stir, which she was sure it would,

---

[1] See this edition, Appendix D.2.

[2] See this edition, Appendix D.2.

[3] Marie Corelli, "The Happy Life," *The Strand* 28.163 (1904): 74.

[4] Marie Corelli, letter to George Bentley, 30 April 1890.

[5] Marie Corelli, letter to George Bentley, 17 January 1888; Marie Corelli, letter to George Bentley, 21 January 1888.

[6] See this edition, Appendix B.8.

she would reveal herself as the author in order to reap the critical acclaim that would be her due: "I am positively certain it will place me in the front rank of writers, and for the first time people will find out what I am really made of."[1] Corelli offered the manuscript to Bentley on the condition that he take it sight unseen. Ever a cautious publisher and only too well aware of Corelli's talent for venomous criticism, Bentley declined and the book was published by Lamley and Co. Though the book aroused interest, it did not have the intended effect. Far from hailing the author as a genius, the reviews were generally scathing, causing Corelli to change her mind about claiming authorship. Moreover, it destroyed her relationship with her friend, mentor, and publisher, George Bentley, who felt betrayed by Corelli's inclusion of him as a target in her satire.

While Corelli continued to battle with the literary establishment throughout the 1890s, her popular appeal remained unaffected, as did her social appeal. In 1892, Corelli spent time with the Prince of Wales at Homburg where they were both vacationing. The Prince, like his mother, Queen Victoria, was a great admirer of Corelli's work. Though Corelli tried to repair the rift with Bentley by offering him her latest book, *Barabbas*, 1893 would mark the beginning of her long and profitable association with Methuen, a newer and more enterprising firm than Bentley's. *Barabbas* (1893) was a fictionalized account of the thief who, instead of Jesus, receives a reprieve at the hands of the Jews. The novel was Corelli's most popular work to date, going into seven editions in seven months. When the one volume edition came out in 1894 it sold 10,000 copies in a week. Though critical acclaim still eluded her, Corelli had less and less reason to care. She was now firmly established among the top rank of popular writers and, for all her naysayers, she had as many, if not more, ardent and devoted supporters among the British public.

Secure in her virtually unassailable popularity with the public, Corelli determined that she would no longer submit her books to the press for review. In her typically outspoken fashion Corelli made this announcement in a note inserted into her next novel, *The Sorrows of Satan* (1895), declaring that if members of the press wished to obtain a copy of the book, they could do so "in the usual way with the rest of the public, i.e., through the Booksellers and Libraries."[2] With *The*

---

[1]   Quoted in Masters 116.
[2]   Quoted in Peter Keating, Introduction, *The Sorrows of Satan*, by Marie Corelli (Oxford: Oxford UP, 1998) ix.

Sorrows of Satan Corelli outdid herself once again. In terms of its initial sale, the novel outsold all previous English novels, and it has been called the first "best-seller" in English history. In part, the novel's success was helped along by the collapse of the three-volume system in 1894. Throughout the Victorian period and up until 1894, novels were typically first published in an expensive three-volume form, making them inaccessible to all but the wealthiest people and to circulating libraries, which were offered novels at a reduced rate. This form of novel production and distribution fostered a book-borrowing rather than book-buying culture in Britain. Readers would pay a yearly subscription rate to circulating libraries, which enabled them to borrow a volume at a time, more volumes if they paid a higher rate. Whereas under the old system, a sale of as few as five hundred books ensured a profit for the publisher and a sale of over a thousand was very good indeed, the new system, which made books cheaper and enabled readers to buy their own books, opened up the market considerably. The collapse of the three-volume system created the conditions for the emergence of the "best-seller," books that sold in the tens and hundreds of thousands, an almost impossible feat under the old system.

Corelli maintained her "best-seller" status throughout the 1890s and entered a period of high productivity in 1896 and 1897, writing *The Mighty Atom*, *The Murder of Delicia*, *Cameos*, *Ziska*, *Jane*, *The Strange Visitation*, and *The Distant Voice*. Her productivity was halted, however, by severe medical problems. Discovering that she needed a hysterectomy, Corelli insisted on having a female surgeon despite the fact that women doctors, let alone surgeons, were rare at the time and not highly regarded in the male-dominated medical profession. Dr. Mary Scharlieb, who would soon become one of the most famous surgeons in England, performed the operation and, after four months recuperation, Corelli was ready to resume her productive career. Unfortunately, a further tragedy beset her. Her beloved step-brother, Eric Mackay, died of septic pneumonia in June 1898. Perhaps even more traumatic than his death was Corelli's discovery, upon going through his papers, that, despite all the support Corelli had given him, he had been cheating her and denouncing her to their friends and to the press. He had even claimed that he was the author of Corelli's books and may also have been spreading rumors that Bertha and Corelli were lesbian lovers. Distressed at Eric's betrayal, Corelli suffered a relapse and was advised to spend at least two years in the country. Eager to get away from a house that was now tainted with the memory of Eric's treachery, Corelli and Bertha went first to Brighton and then, in May 1899, to Stratford-upon-Avon, where they would spend the rest of their lives.

Corelli's success continued unabated through the pre-war years of the 1900s. She was earning as much as £10,000 per book (roughly 1,000,000 US dollars) and in 1901 she was invited to attend the coronation of Edward VII, who remembered their time together at Homburg in 1892 with fondness. In Stratford-upon-Avon, however, Corelli was making enemies due to what many regarded as her unwanted interference in town affairs. Corelli viewed herself as the defender of the sacred memory of Shakespeare and, in 1900, she voiced strong opposition to the erection of a statue of a prominent Shakespearean actress who had recently died, claiming that the seven-foot statue would overshadow the bust of Shakespeare near which it was to be placed. In another incident, she campaigned against the Stratford-upon-Avon Corporation's refusal to allow a statue of Shakespeare to be erected. She also roused the ire of one of the most prominent Stratford families, the Flowers, by objecting to their plans for a Memorial Theatre, which she regarded as more of a memorial to Charles Flower than to Shakespeare. Corelli's most controversial intervention, however, came in 1903 when she began a crusade against the establishment of a Carnegie free library in Stratford. Corelli objected to plans that involved the destruction of five historic buildings adjacent to Shakespeare's birthplace. This battle drew national attention and though Corelli had many prominent members of the British literary and artistic community on her side, there were equally prominent people on the opposing side. A defamation case relating to the controversy brought by Corelli against the town newspaper and a local resident did much to damage Corelli's reputation. The judge described Corelli's actions as dishonourable and declared the case one that should never have been brought to trial. The defamation case, which was widely reported in the national press, overshadowed the good work that Corelli had done in preserving Stratford-upon-Avon's buildings of historic importance. Corelli's novels throughout this period concerned what were now recognizable as her personal hobbyhorses—political corruption, spiritual faith, social hypocrisy, and her own idiosyncratic scientific beliefs. In *Temporal Power* (1902), Corelli took on contemporary politics and the corruption of politicians, attacking socialism and defending monarchy. *God's Good Man* (1904) was a fictionalized account of the Stratford-upon-Avon controversy, while Corelli's 1906 publication, *The Treasure of Heaven*, a novel which had a record-breaking first-day sale of 100,000 copies, was also notable for its inclusion of the first authorized photograph of Corelli, notorious for her resistance to being photographed.

Towards the end of the decade, Corelli's popularity had begun to decline. The younger generation of readers was turning to writers such as Elinor Glyn, whose stories were more exotic and lurid in their depiction of female sexuality and were free of the moralizing element that dominated even the most sensational of Corelli's romances. During this period, Corelli developed a ten-year passion for Arthur Severn—her only known romantic attachment to a man. Severn, a happily married artist, was flattered by Corelli's attentions and seems to have reciprocated to some degree, though only Corelli's side of their correspondence and a few fragments of his letters remain. Severn, if judged by this correspondence, was quite cruel to Corelli and the relationship ended acrimoniously. A fictionalized account of this tempestuous relationship entitled *Open Confession, to a Man from a Woman* (1925) was published posthumously, likely under Corelli's instruction, by Bertha Vyver.

In the years 1914–18, Corelli became passionately involved in the war effort. She published no books during this period though she wrote numerous articles about the war for which she took no payment. In addition, she offered her home for use as a hospital. But despite her generous efforts, controversy continued to dog Corelli. In 1918, she was convicted of food hoarding for exceeding the sugar restrictions. Though Corelli's stories were in great demand in these early days of film-making she did not care for the film medium. Corelli proved a difficult negotiator, though a number of her novels did become films, notable among them a version of *The Sorrows of Satan* directed by D.W. Griffith (1926) and a version of *The Young Diana* (1922) starring Marion Davies. During her lifetime, at least ten other films were made of her works in Hollywood, England, Denmark, and Italy. Even after her death, film rights were still being sought for *Barabbas* and *The Life Everlasting*.

Marie Corelli wrote three more novels before her death in 1924, *The Young Diana* (1918), *The Secret Power* (1921), and *Love and the Philosopher* (1923), none of which garnered much attention. By the 1920s, her style of writing was deemed old-fashioned and a new brand of popular writer came to the fore. Corelli suffered a heart attack in January 1924 and, though she lived another three months, she never fully recovered. Corelli died on 21 April 1924. Her death sparked a considerable amount of media attention and journalists took the opportunity to speculate about the mystery of Corelli's enormous popular success. There were other mysteries they were interested in as well: notably, the mystery of Corelli's birth and the mysterious nature of her relationship with Bertha Vyver— "the romance of two women" as headlines referred to it. "Romantic" friendships between women—meaning friendships that included almost all aspects of a modern heterosexual love relationship from physical and verbal displays of affection to expressions of jealousy—were not uncommon in the eighteenth and nineteenth centuries. By the early twentieth century, however, perceptions about these relationships were beginning to change. Lillian Faderman has argued that this change may have been brought about by Freud's insistence that such relationships were maladies and by the "discovery" that women could have sexual drives as well.[1] Thus, although the articles that speculated about the relationship between Corelli and Vyver did not explicitly characterize the relationship as sexual, there was clearly a degree of unease around the topic, an unease which points to the changing perceptions about female relationships. Certainly there is evidence that the Corelli/Vyver relationship was "romantic" in the sense described by Faderman, but whether there was a sexual component remains unknown.

After the flurry of interest immediately following Corelli's death, Corelli dwindled into relative obscurity. By 1941, annual royalties on Corelli's books had fallen to under £30. Vyver, who had promised Corelli that she would preserve Mason Croft for posterity, struggled to keep the house going. Vyver died in November 1941 and was buried beside Corelli. After Vyver's death, the Executors of the estate found themselves unable to maintain Mason Croft and in 1943 all the contents of the house were auctioned off. Eventually Mason Croft was taken over by the University of Birmingham to house their Shakespeare Institute, a function it still serves today. Corelli's books continued to sell, with resurgences of interest during the war and again in the 1960s when they gained a following with those interested in New Age philosophy. Corelli also continued to have a few ardent admirers, notably those who enjoyed Corelli's mystical and spiritualist works. Some of these admirers wrote books that they claimed had been dictated posthumously to them by Marie Corelli. These books included *Paulus Antonius: A Tale of Ancient Rome* (1931), through the pen of Marie Elfram, *The Voice of Marie Corelli* (1933), through the pen of Dorothy Agnes, *The Immortal Garden* (1948), through the pen of E.G. Pinnegar and written on a table

---

[1] Lillian Faderman, *Surpassing the Love of Men: Romantic Friendship and Love Between Women from the Renaissance to the Present* (New York: William Morrow, 1981).

formerly owned by Corelli, *Judith* (1950), transcribed by Blanche A. Webb, and *No Matter* (1969) through the pen of C.A. Wild from the dictation of the spirits of Corelli and Lalasal, a Tibetan monk.

Corelli's critical reputation remained as poor in the years after her death as it had been in her life. Analyses of popular fiction in the 1920s and 1930s attributed the success of writers like Corelli to the "immense drop from the highly critical and intelligent society [of early Victorian England] to later Victorian taste" as well as to the emergence, thanks to the Education Acts of the 1870s and 1880s, of a mass readership consisting of what the literary intelligentsia described as poorly educated and undiscriminating readers.[1] While feminist scholars recuperated many neglected women writers of the late Victorian and Edwardian period in the 1960s and 1970s, Corelli was ignored, likely because her particular brand of feminism seemed conservative by the standards of this time. Instead of being recuperated by feminist critics, Corelli found an unlikely supporter in the figure of Henry Miller, a controversial writer famous for his frank treatment of sex. In a 1976 article for the *New York Times Book Review*, Miller called Corelli an "extraordinary writer" and hoped for a revival of interest in her work.[2] Brian Masters also went some way towards reviving this interest in an informative 1978 biography of Corelli, though he is sometimes unnecessarily condescending towards his subject.

Critical and academic interest in Corelli took longer to develop. Apart from a 1974 article by Richard Kowalczyk on Corelli for the *Journal of Popular Culture* and a handful of theses and dissertations on Corelli, she was largely ignored until the 1990s, when "cultural studies," a methodology that privileges popular texts and popular culture, came to the fore in literary criticism.[3] In the first of the 1990s re-evaluations of Corelli, Janet Galligani Casey takes up Corelli's ambiguous relationship to feminism. In an examination of Corelli's views on women, Casey argues that Corelli was neither an advocate of the Victorian ideal of woman—"the angel in the house"—nor of the emerging feminism of the "New Woman." Instead, argues Casey, Corelli was a transitional figure in the development of feminism: "[Corelli] reflects the confusion of an entire generation of women, a generation confronted at once with

---

[1] Leavis 166.

[2] Henry Miller, "Marie Corelli: A Recommendation," *New York Times Book Review* (12 September 1976): 55.

[3] Richard Kowalczyk, "In Vanished Summertime: Marie Corelli and Popular Culture," *Journal of Popular Culture* 7 (1974): 850–63.

the suffragette movement and the decline of the feminine ideal."[1] In her chapter on Corelli in *The Gender of Modernity*, Rita Felski also considers Corelli's particular brand of feminism, though Felski focuses on Corelli's aesthetic mediation between the highly gendered categories of high (male) and popular (female) culture through the medium of what Felski calls "the popular sublime."[2] Like Felski, R.B. Kershner's interests lie in the relationship between high and popular culture in Corelli's work. In "Modernism's Mirror: The Sorrows of Marie Corelli," Kershner argues that the "ideological contradictions" that characterize her treatment of "high" and popular art, science and religion, and materialism and spiritualism, make her something of a "Modernist hybrid."[3] In another article, Kershner discusses Corelli's influence on the high Modernist work of James Joyce.[4]

Approaching Corelli's relation to Modernism in yet another fashion, I have examined Corelli's work in light of the strong resistance in Britain to the emerging Modernist forms of Realism and Naturalism, Impressionism, and Decadence in the late-Victorian period and have linked this resistance to Francophobia and fears of cultural degeneration.[5] Employing yet another approach to Corelli, N.N. Feltes situates Corelli within the context of the transformation of the British publishing industry from a "petty-commodity literary mode of production" to a "patriarchal" and "capitalist literary mode of production." He also examines Corelli's engagement with the gender and class biases that characterized the late-Victorian publishing industry.[6] Finally, in one of the first book-length studies of Corelli, Annette Federico examines both Corelli's life and works, revealing the extent to which Corelli was engaged in many of the central literary, philosophical, and social debates of the late-Victorian and early modern period.[7] Federico's book

---

1   Janet Galligani Casey, "Marie Corelli and Fin de Siècle Feminism," *English Literature in Transition* 35.2 (1992): 164.

2   Rita Felski, *The Gender of Modernity* (Cambridge, MA: Harvard UP, 1995) 119.

3   R.B. Kershner, "Modernism's Mirror: The Sorrows of Marie Corelli," *Transforming Genres: New Approaches to British Fiction in the 1890s* (New York: St. Martin's Press, 1994) 70, 79.

4   R.B. Kershner, "Joyce and Popular Culture: The Case of Corelli." *James Joyce and his Contemporaries*, ed. Diana A. Ben-Merre and Maureen Murphy (New York: Greenwood, 1989) 52–58.

5   Kirsten MacLeod, "Marie Corelli and Fin de Siècle Francophobia: The Absinthe Trail of French Art," *English Literature in Transition* 43.1 (2000): 66–82.

6   N.N. Feltes, *Literary Capital and the Late Victorian Novel* (Madison, WI: U of Wisconsin P, 1993).

7   Annette Federico, *Idol of Suburbia: Marie Corelli and Late-Victorian Literary Culture* (Charlottesville, VA: UP of Virginia, 2000).

contains chapters on Corelli's relationship to the emerging concept of literary celebrity, on Corelli's attempts to mediate between high art and popular culture, on Corelli's attempts to develop a feminist aesthetic, on the relationship between Corelli's religious beliefs and her utopian visions of sexual equality, and on cultural readings of Corelli in the post-Victorian era. Federico's multi-faceted approach to Corelli has indicated the fruitful possibilities of further studies of this fascinating woman whose life and works tell us so much about the main cultural and literary preoccupations of the late-Victorian and Edwardian period.

Wormwood: A Drama of Paris

Corelli began her fifth novel, *Wormwood: A Drama of Paris*, in October 1889. Corelli threw herself into her work with her customary zeal, declaring, as she did with each new project, that this novel was her best to date. Corelli wrote at a furious pace, completing half the manuscript by mid-December. Her progress was interrupted, however, by the death of Dr. Mackay, her adoptive father, on Christmas Eve. Though Corelli took some time to get back on track, her novel was completed by early August 1890 and was published at the end of October of that year.

Wormwood is the first-person account of a promising young *fin de siècle* Parisian man, Gaston Beauvais, who, after being betrayed by his beloved fiancée and his best friend, becomes a prey to the seductive powers of absinthe. The novel traces the consequences on Gaston and those around him of his descent into debauchery and addiction. *Wormwood* was written as a three-volume novel, the dominant form in which novels were published in the Victorian period. This form had a strong impact on the way novels were constructed.[1] The long form was conducive to stories with multiple plots, a profusion of incidents, and narratives in which the development of character was paramount. The prescribed long form of the three-volume novel, however, had certain negative consequences as well. The padding of stories to fill three volumes, for example, was a complaint frequently made by critics who also disliked the often digressive reflections, asides, and meditations on the part of the author that the form encouraged.

Corelli was strongly influenced in her composition of *Wormwood* by the conventions that governed the construction of the three-volume

---

[1]   A thorough analysis of the three-volume novel can be found in Guinevere Griest's *Mudie's Circulating Library and the Three-Volume Novel* (Devon, UK: David and Charles, 1970).

novel plot. The novel has a clear tripartite structure. The first volume (chapters 1 to 12 in this edition) charts what Corelli described to Bentley as the "*respectable* career" of her protagonist,[1] giving the reader a sense of Gaston's youthful promise, his love for Pauline, her betrayal, and ending with his first encounter with the absinthe that will destroy his life. The second volume of the novel (chapters 13 to 24 of this edition) suffers from none of the complaints often made about second volumes, namely that they retarded the progress of the narrative in order to drag out the story to three volumes. Corelli's second volume is full of exciting incident— Gaston's rejection of his unfaithful fiancée at the altar, the death of Pauline's father, the murder of Silvion, and the visit of Gaston and his artist friend André Gessonex to the Paris Morgue. The third volume (chapters 25 to L'Envoi) is also incident-packed as the tragic repercussions of Gaston's addiction unfold. Local colour is provided in a depiction of a *bal-masqué*, Gaston has confrontations with those whose lives he has ruined—his father, Pauline, Héloïse, and Père Vaudron—and there are more deaths as well as a second morgue visit, which parallels that of the second volume. The novel does bear signs of the padding techniques that were a familiar complaint made about the genre.[2] At times, the conversations between characters seem stilted by too much repetition or echoing of phrasing, particularly from the second volume on. In addition, Corelli was also prone to padding her work with digressive reflections, asides, and meditations. These reflections and meditations were a conventional part of Victorian fiction and readers would have been well used to them, though it is true that by the 1880s artistic conventions were changing and these kinds of authorial meditations were beginning to be considered artificial and out of place. Corelli herself, however, believed that *Wormwood* was "a good piece of literary work ... without showiness ... drag or *padding* [and not] short of dramatic interest."[3] For her, the asides and reflections in the novel were an important element in providing the moral and didactic function that she believed literature should serve.

Wormwood: Literary and Social Contexts

Corelli's belief that literature and art ought to serve moral and didactic functions was not unique to her: it was a belief she shared with

---

[1]   See this edition, Appendix B.3.

[2]   Griest 106.

[3]   See this edition, Appendix B.10.

many Victorian novelists of her day. As she conceived it, *Wormwood* was a "novel with a purpose" which represented an important intervention in some of the key literary and social controversies of the day—degeneration, absinthism, and the effects of Naturalist and Decadent literature and art on the British public. But though *Wormwood* was written with the moralistic intention of exposing the dangers of absinthe and of denouncing the corrupting effects of contemporary French literature, the novel is far more than a temperance tract or a treatise of literary criticism. If Corelli was at heart a moralist, she was also a first-rate entertainer who more than provided the spoonful of sugar necessary to help the medicine go down. Corelli's ability to provide narrative excitement *and* moral purpose was an important factor in her success. Corelli's admirers came away from her books with a feeling not only of having been thoroughly entertained but also of having been educated, uplifted, and morally improved. In *Wormwood*, Corelli skilfully employs all the familiar motifs of the popular novels of her day—murder, love, betrayal, bohemian artistic life, suicide, and debauchery—in an effort to engage her readers ultimately in the more serious concerns of absinthe addiction and the corrupting effects of pernicious literature. In the sections that follow, I discuss the literary and social contexts in which *Wormwood* was produced and explain how Corelli engages with these contexts in constructing a novel that she insisted would not only "cause critics to meditate and readers to think" but would also "interest and absorb" her readers.[1]

Literary Naturalism and the School of Zola

Naturalism was a literary movement that began in the 1860s in France and is generally associated with the novelist Émile Zola. Based on a rejection of the Romantic movement and opposing the idea that art ought to represent the ideal, Naturalism drew strongly on the positivist tradition in philosophy, science, and the arts. Naturalists shared with Positivists a suspicion of metaphysics and any phenomena that could not be positively verified by experience and insisted on the importance of scientific observation and objective representation. Naturalists were interested in demonstrating the influence of heredity and the social environment on mankind and their representations of these effects were largely negative. Writers such as Zola and the Goncourt brothers wrote

---

[1]   See this edition Appendix B.4; Marie Corelli, letter to George Bentley, 30 April 1890.

deterministic novels in which characters subject to hereditary taints and adverse social conditions are unable to escape their socio-biological fate.

In Britain, Naturalism, which was often referred to by the more general term "Realism," gained popularity among writers who were trying to counteract what they regarded as the dominance of the "femi-nized" or "effeminate" novel, in particular sentimental romantic stories and society novels.[1] These proponents of Naturalism believed that fiction in Britain catered too much to a predominantly female reader-ship and consequently was unable to treat life frankly. Many aspects of male experience, they felt, could not be treated at all. Writers such as George Moore and Thomas Hardy, for example, wanted to extend the purview of fiction to include aspects of life untreatable in novels read by women and young girls, to create fiction that would address the "cultured" male reader. In contrast to the existing "feminine" or "effeminate" novel, a form they regarded as sentimental, unrealistic, emotional, and commercial, proponents of Naturalism set out to re-"masculinize" the novel with an aesthetic that they regarded as objec-tive, scientific, disciplined, and artistic.

But while Naturalism had high-profile supporters in Britain includ-ing Moore and Hardy, it also had its fair share of detractors—also lead-ing literary figures of the day—including Rider Haggard and W.S. Lilly (see Appendix E). While the supporters of Naturalism were eager to extend the purview of fiction, its opponents greatly feared the effects of such an endeavour. Because Naturalism dealt in a frank and often brutal manner with life and with sexual matters, opponents of Naturalism believed it might have a corrupting effect on certain classes of readers, namely those considered less educated: the working classes, women, and young persons of either sex. Haggard, for example, believed that for those of "average mind," Naturalism was extremely dangerous: "Once start the average mind upon [the subjects treated in Naturalist fiction], and it will go down the slope of itself. It is useless afterwards to turn round and say that, although you cut loose the cords of decent

---

[1] For more about the gendered hierarchical structure of literary life in late-Victorian England see Lyn Pykett, *Engendering Fictions: The English Novel in the Early Twentieth Century* (London: Edward Arnold, 1985); Gaye Tuchman, with Nina Fortin, *Edging Women Out: Victorian Novelists, Publishers and Social Change* (New Haven: Yale UP, 1989); Elaine Showalter, *Sexual Anarchy: Gender and Culture at the Fin de Siècle* (New York: Viking, 1990); Ann Ardis, *New Women, New Novels: Feminism and Early Modernism* (New Brunswick, NJ: Rutgers UP, 1990); Sally Ledger, *The New Woman: Fiction and Feminism at the Fin de Siècle.* (Manchester: Manchester UP, 1997).

reticence which bound the fancy, you intended that it should run *uphill* to the white heights of virtue."[1]

Concerns about the effects of reading Naturalistic fiction were not confined to the literary community. In this period, literature was seen as having a direct influence on society at large. Just as many today worry about the effects of violent films and video games on youth and see a correlation between these media and the increase of violence in society, the Victorians worried about the effects of a corrupting literature on their nation. By 1888, the controversy over Naturalism had reached such a pitch that it came under the scrutiny of the British parliament by way of John Smith, a Member of Parliament who was associated with the National Vigilance Association, an organization determined to stop the spread of what it called "pernicious literature." Quoting from a feature in the *Saturday Review*, Smith described Naturalism in the following manner:

> Realism [i.e. Naturalism], according to latter-day French lights, means nothing short of sheer beastliness; it means going out of the way to dig up foul expressions to embody filthy ideas; it means not only the old insinuation of petty intrigue, but the laying bare of social sores in their most loathesome forms; it means the alteration of the brutal directness of the drunken operative of to-day with the flabby sensuality of Corinth in the past. In a word, it is dirt and horror pure and simple.[2]

For crusaders against "pernicious literature," Naturalism represented a serious threat to British "religious, national, and social life," and its new-found influence in Britain constituted "a gigantic national disaster."[3] The efforts of Smith and the National Vigilance Association resulted in the prosecution of publisher Henry Vizetelly in October 1888 for publishing translations of "obscene" Naturalist works by Émile Zola. Though he got off with a fine on this occasion, Vizetelly was prosecuted again in May 1889 for publishing translations of eight further Zola novels as well as other objectionable translations of Flaubert, Maupassant, and Bourget. This time, Vizetelly was found guilty and sent to prison.

. Corelli's determination to counter Naturalism emerged in the wake of the first Vizetelly trial, though it would take her some months to find

---

[1] See this edition, Appendix E.2.
[2] See this edition, Appendix E.3.
[3] See this edition, Appendix E.3.

the subject matter for her novel. As expressed in letters written to Bentley at this time, Corelli's sympathies in the Naturalist controversy were entirely with its opponents:

> Believe me my dear Bentley, if I could bring myself to write a daring, powerful, absolutely materialistic book, depicting in strong and merciless colouring the most hideous side of human nature à la ... Zola, I should be a fortunate author! as far as reputation and cash could carry me;—for this is what the modern public want ... But so long as I live I will never pander to the taste for atheism and *stage-morality*; if my pen has any power at all it will be used to condemn such abominations till it can write no more.[1]

These sentiments found their way into more public venues as well. Corelli attacked Zola and Naturalism, which she invariably referred to as "Realism," in a number of essays (see Appendix D) as well as in *Wormwood*. In the novel, Corelli's absinthe-addicted narrator, who professes to be offering his readers a "Realist" (i.e., Naturalist) account of his life, describes his story in terms that echo the language of the National Vigilance Association: "you want Realism, do you not?... you want to look at the loathsome worms and unsightly poisonous growths that attend your own decomposition and decay? You want life denuded of all poetical adornment that you may see it as it truly *is*?" In addition, Zola is described as "the literary scavenger of Paris" and as one who "with a sort of pitchfork pen turns up under men's nostrils such literary garbage as loads the very air with stench and mind-malaria!"[2]

But if Corelli deplored the atheistic, anti-idealistic, and positivist school of Naturalism that she regarded as corrupting and immoral, she also recognized the high artistic status accorded it among a certain portion of the late-Victorian literary avant-garde, those like Arthur Symons, critic and poet, to whom she would send a copy of *Wormwood*. Though Corelli had achieved popularity and commercial success in both Britain and America, her novels were attacked savagely by critics who wielded immense power in determining, particularly for the literary community, the artistic merits of writers. Despite her popular success, then, Corelli had little artistic credibility within the largely male-dominated British literary establishment that tended to regard

---

[1]   Marie Corelli, letter to George Bentley, 20 April 1889.
[2]   See this edition page 74, 266, 303.

women writers with contempt. Unhampered by the disadvantage of her sex, Corelli was determined to establish herself among this élite or, at the very least, to earn its respect and to have it acknowledge her as a writer of high literary merit.

Up until this point, Corelli's novels had been of the popular "feminine" kind associated with women readers and writers—mystical romances, society novels, and gothic melodramas—but in tackling Naturalism, Corelli was entering the domain of literary men. Corelli's taking up of Naturalism was risky for a number of reasons. On the one hand, because Naturalism dealt with frank and brutal aspects of life that women were not supposed to know about, Corelli risked displaying that she knew too much. On the other hand, if Corelli failed to present an appropriately objective and scientific Naturalism, Corelli risked exposing herself to ridicule for her limited knowledge of life. That Corelli felt this double-bind of the woman writer engaging with typically "masculine" subject matter is indicated in her introductory note in which she justifies her knowledge of the racy French dance the "cancan," assuring the reader that she received her description second-hand, through overhearing an English tourist's enthusiastic description of the dance. Corelli even indicated to Bentley that she believed *Wormwood* was "work for a man to have done."[1] By taking up what she characterized as man's work and engaging with a "masculine" literary genre, Corelli hoped to earn the respect of the male-dominated literary élite though, as always, she aimed to do so on her own terms. In other words, Corelli, who was always guided by a zealous missionary purpose in her work, hoped to exploit Naturalism in order to reveal the limitations of the school and convince its followers of its evils. As she explained to Bentley, "my next book may suit *even* them [the lovers of Naturalism], though as you may be sure it will not be *their* realism."[2]

After months of contemplating how she would create her own brand of "Realism," Corelli finally hit upon her subject matter in October 1889. Her new novel, she coyly hinted to Bentley, was to be a study of "a strange and terrible phase of the present life of the Paris people."[3] Corelli had settled upon the subject of absinthism, a theme that, to her mind, was linked directly to the problem of pernicious literature and art and, ultimately, to the degeneration of the entire French nation.

---

[1] See this edition, Appendix B. 7.

[2] Marie Corelli, letter to George Bentley, 2 January 1889.

[3] See this edition, Appendix B.1.

Corelli shared the Francophobic sentiments of the National Vigilance Association who claimed that French Naturalist literature was "a poison" responsible for "destroying the whole national life" of France.[1] Corelli, however, traced the cause of French national decay one step further—to absinthism. Absinthism, she claimed in a letter to Bentley, was the main cause of "French *morbidness*, the partial secret of national decay. The absinthe *trail* is over all France,—it helps to make French literature obscene, and French art repulsive."[2] Corelli conceived of a novel with a two-fold purpose. Explicitly the novel targeted the controversial subject of absinthism and the degeneration of the French nation as represented through the tragic decline of the absintheur, a subject that would captivate Corelli's audience and feed the Francophobia prevalent in British culture at that time. The novel would also, however, serve an important moral function in its exposure of the dangers of absinthe by "rous[ing] some few to think of the deterioration they are bringing on themselves and their children," by "lash[ing] the *Paris* people up to a kind of wrath and shame," and by informing people about the "European curse of Absinthe."[3] Implicitly, however, the novel also targeted the Naturalist fiction that Corelli had so fervently wished to denounce when she first conceived of treating what she called a "Realist" theme.

In fashioning her own brand of "Realism," one that would undermine the contemporary Realist school of Naturalism, Corelli modelled herself on an older brand of Realism, that of Honoré de Balzac (1799-1850). Balzac, who was the founder of French Realism, appealed to Corelli because his "realistic" examinations of French society were combined with romantic elements—melodramatic plots, expressions of violent passions, rhetorical passages, and larger-than-life characters. In addition, Balzac's moral stance was explicit in his works in contrast with the work of newer realism of the Naturalist school. Thus, while Corelli took pride in the research she had done for the novel, often comparing the novel in letters to Bentley to contemporary newspaper and medical accounts of absinthism (see Appendix B), she distinguished herself from the scientific and objective Naturalists by referring to herself as an "artist," a "fictionist" and a "romancist." And, though Corelli did claim to be "an observer of men and women as they are"

---

[1] See this edition, Appendix E.3.

[2] See this edition, Appendix B.8.

[3] See this edition, Appendix B.7; Marie Corelli, letter to George Bentley, 30 April 1890; Marie Corelli, letter to George Bentley, 22 August 1890.

and a chronicler of the "truth" in ways that echo the claims of Naturalists, there were clear differences in their respective understandings of what constituted the "truth."[1] While Naturalists, in Corelli's opinion, degraded and corrupted their readers in their representations of life, Corelli's "artists," "romancists," and "fictionists" transcended the base reality of everyday life in their art in order to inspire the reader and effect change. For Corelli's "artists," "romancists," and "fictionists," a sense of the ideal must be present in art. This ideal was, in her opinion, an integral part of the "truth" and was necessary because, even in an age of "infinite weariness and cynicism," the characteristics of an age addicted to "realism," people still yearned "for something higher and more lasting"[2] (for Corelli's ideas on art, see Appendix D).

Given that she had chosen to narrate *Wormwood* from the first-person point of view of the unrepentant absinthe addict, Corelli had more difficulty than usual in characterizing an idea of an ideal of "something higher and more lasting." She even expressed her fear that the novel might be mistaken for a Naturalist novel though she assured a worried Bentley that she would take pains to let her readers know that the views presented in the book "are not *my* thoughts but the *imagined* thoughts of the absintheur."[3] Corelli conveys this distancing from her absinthe-addict narrator in a number of ways, most obviously in an explicit statement in the introductory note: "When an author depicts a character, he is not of necessity that character himself ... I have nothing whatever to do with the wretched 'Gaston Beauvais' beyond the portraiture of him in his own necessarily lurid colours."[4] In addition, other framing materials such as the apocalyptic epigraph from the Book of Revelation and the biting dedication to the absintheurs of Paris help to situate the reader in Corelli's moral universe. This moral universe is also apparent in the narrative itself. The novel, for example, contains many digressions which allow Corelli to comment on the moral laxity of the Parisians and French culture though they are voiced through the intermittently remorseful but more often sarcastic Gaston.

By far Corelli's most important moral force in the novel is Héloïse, who embodies Corelli's idealistic view of life. Héloïse is the archetypal female artist figure who is linked in the novel with a number of mythological and fictional artist figures. Primarily she is a musician whose

---

[1] See this edition, page 63.

[2] See this edition, Appendix B.7.

[3] See this edition, Appendix B.8.

[4] See this edition, page 62.

playing, we are told, is as enchanting as that of Orpheus and as enthralling as the story-telling powers of Scheherazade. In terms of her learnedness and unconventionality, Héloïse is also compared with Corinne, the poetess heroine of Germaine de Staël's romantic novel *Corinne, ou l'Italie* (1807). Héloïse's name and unconventionality also link her with the heroine of Jean-Jacques Rousseau's *Julie, ou la Nouvelle Héloïse* (1761). Like Corelli's own tastes, Héloïse's run to the classics and to poetry and she despises Zola and his school. In many respects, Héloïse is the true heroine of the novel rather than the silly girl-child, Pauline, and it is through Héloïse's eyes that Corelli wishes us to judge the events of the story.

Ultimately, Corelli was satisfied with her ability in *Wormwood* to expose the limits of Naturalism while at the same time producing a novel that was, by her own accounts, a "realistic" depiction of the world as seen through the eyes of an absintheur, a book in which "the sequence of events." was "perfectly natural and as it would inevitably happen."[1] And, more importantly, from her point of view, the novel also served a didactic and moral function, alerting her readers to the dangers of absinthe and degenerate French fiction.

Decadence

No less important than the connection between *Wormwood* and Naturalism is its relation to the literary movement known as Decadence. Like Naturalism, Decadence was a French literary phenomenon of the late-nineteenth century. While both literary movements, from their detractors' point of view, dwelt on the sordid and unseemly aspects of life, and while both were interested in the effects of heredity, society, and the environment on the individual, Naturalism and Decadence differed in significant ways. Where Naturalism emphasized an objective perspective and sought to represent everyday life as it really was, Decadent literature dealt not with the everyday but with the eccentric, the bizarre, the morbid, and the perverse and was more interested in the individual psychology and personal experience of the outsider type—particularly the artist figure—than in analyzing broader social types as Naturalism did. Far from seeing themselves as objective, scientific observers of the human condition, Decadents viewed themselves as misunderstood martyrs to art who wanted to escape from the

---

[1] See this edition, Appendix B.6.

real world into their own artificially created worlds via art, drugs, drink, or through mystical transcendence. Though he wrote well before the Decadent movement emerged in France, Charles Baudelaire, poet and author of *Les Fleurs du mal* (1857), was revered as the "high priest" of Decadents. His work inspired the later generation of Decadents, including Arthur Rimbaud, Paul Verlaine, Joris-Karl Huysmans, Jean Lorrain, and Villiers de l'Isle-Adam. Perhaps the most famous work of French Decadence is Huysmans' *À Rebours* (1884), a novel that Arthur Symons, a writer associated with the English Decadent school, called "the breviary of decadence." *À Rebours* is the story of a rich neurotic named Des Esseintes who, unable to cope with everyday life, retreats into his own private world where he concocts perverse, exotic, and bizarre entertainments for himself.

Like Naturalism, Decadence appealed to certain writers among the British literary élite. George Moore, a supporter of Naturalism, for example, was also a proponent of Decadence and was one of the first to write about French Decadence for an English audience. Havelock Ellis, the famous sexologist, and Arthur Symons, Decadent poet, were also early proponents of Decadence in Britain. The most famous proponent of Decadence, however, was Oscar Wilde, whose sensational story *The Picture of Dorian Gray* brought Decadence beyond the realm of the literary élite and introduced it to the wider public. *The Picture of Dorian Gray* is a story that chronicles the downfall of a young man who, discovering that he can remain youthful forever while his portrait ages and decays, embarks on a life of sin and sensation-seeking. *The Picture of Dorian Gray* was essentially an English *À Rebours* and was heavily modelled on its French counterpart. It caused a sensation in the summer of 1890 when it appeared in *Lippincott's Monthly Magazine* and was denounced viciously in the press. Wilde was accused by reviewers of "air[ing] his cheap research among the garbage of the French *décadents*," of writing a "poisonous book, heavy with the mephitic odours of moral and spiritual putrefaction" that was "spawned from the leprous literature of the French *décadents*."[1] From 1890 on interest in Naturalism was on the wane in England. Writers like Moore and Wilde had decided that Naturalism was not sufficiently artistic as an aesthetic principle. From 1890 to 1895 (when Oscar Wilde's conviction for "acts of gross indecency" dealt a fatal blow to the Decadent movement), Decadence came to the fore as the most influential French literary form amongst

---

[1]   Karl Beckson, ed., *Oscar Wilde: The Critical Heritage* (London: Routledge, 1970) 69, 72, 72.

the British literary avant-garde. At the same time, Decadence replaced Naturalism as the central target of attack for conservatives and moralists who regarded Decadence as an equally pernicious literary French import.

If Corelli had any knowledge of the emerging Decadent movement when she began work on *Wormwood* it is not evident in her letters of this period, which are more immediately concerned with the evils of what she called "realism." Nevertheless, *Wormwood*'s publication six months after Wilde's notorious *The Picture of Dorian Gray* and its treatment of subjects and themes that would increasingly come to be associated with Decadence throughout the 1890s—absinthe and drug addiction, Bohemian artistic life, morbidity, perversion, and eroticized images of death and violence—render the novel fit for an examination of its relationship to Decadence. Ironically, though no Decadent herself, Corelli treated the subject of absinthe in literature even before British Decadents, who were fervent admirers of absinthe, such as Ernest Dowson and Arthur Symons, who wrote poems about absinthe (see Appendix G). She was also among the first to use the subjective form that would become popular with Decadents who wished to portray, at first hand, the psychology of the abnormal personality. In many respects, then, Corelli is prescient about the emergence of Decadence in this novel. Certainly by the time she came to know about it she despised it as much as she had Naturalism. Her hatred of Decadence is hardly surprising given her disdain for French literature and art more broadly, which she found to be predominantly "obscene," "repulsive," and "morbid."[1]

And yet, if *Wormwood*, in its negative depiction of bohemianism, is as fierce a condemnation of Decadence as it is of Naturalism, there are ways in which it is also "the very flower of decadence" and "is completely dependent on decadent tropes."[2] From Corelli's ideas for the design of the cover of the book—pale green, the colour of absinthe with an adder or serpent twisted through the big W of the title—to her presentation of a copy of the novel to Arthur Symons, to her evocative descriptions of the pleasures of absinthe, Corelli is, at the very least, ambivalent about her subject matter.[3] Perhaps most damning of all is Corelli's appreciative citation in the novel of the French Decadent poet Charles Cros. In the novel, Corelli explicitly expresses her admiration of Cros in a footnote, which

---

[1] See this edition, Appendix B.8.
[2] Federico 72, 73.
[3] Federico 72-75.

is in her voice, and not that of her wretched absintheur. Cros was friends with the notorious Arthur Rimbaud and Paul Verlaine, whose Decadent poetry was hardly a match for their decadent lives. Sharing with these poets a love of absinthe, Cros is said to have drunk as many as twenty absinthes day, a habit that led to his untimely death at the age of forty-six. Corelli may not have known about Cros's absinthe addiction and, to be fair, the poetry she cites, though morbid at times, is arguably more Romantic than Decadent. Yet, it is hardly credible that Corelli was ignorant of Cros's love of absinthe when one of the poems she quotes from, "Lendemain," is a tribute to absinthe (see Appendix G). "Conclusion," another Cros poem she cites, ends with the despairing narrator declaring "Je vais mourir soûl, dans un coin" ("I will die drunk in a corner"). In the novel, however, "soûl" is transcribed as "seul," meaning "alone," a change that alters the meaning substantially. Whether she misunderstood the poem, made the change on purpose, or whether it was a typographical error on the part of the printer we cannot know, though Corelli insisted on correcting a number of errors for subsequent editions of the novel and this one was never changed. Whatever she knew or did not know about Cros's lifestyle and whether or not she fully understood his poems, clearly, in her mind, he was exempt from the charges of "vice and indecent vulgarity" that she launched against most French literature. To her, Cros was a kind of Keats figure, "a perished genius" whose "great abilities were never encouraged or recognized in his lifetime."[1]

Federico explains Corelli's fascination with Cros as evidence of her "susceptib[ility] to the myth of 'perished genius,'" an attitude that was not uncommon to the middle classes of this period who were fascinated with artists.[2] The Aesthetic movement, an artistic trend that preceded Decadence and shared with it certain key elements, prompted this interest on the part of the middle classes who were drawn to colourful artistic personalities such as Oscar Wilde and James McNeill Whistler. This interest continued as Decadence emerged, another movement that drew attention to the artist and the lifestyle of the artist. Speculating about this late-Victorian middle-class fascination with the artist figure, Jonathan Freedman writes: "the public could look to these writers and painters to confirm their prejudices about the nature of artists—their excessive and often perverse sexuality, their liberating but nevertheless inefficacious release from the exigencies of work and

---

[1]   See this edition page 109, note 2.
[2]   Federico 75.

marketplace.... [the public was] thereby endowed with a voyeuristic sexual thrill and soupçon of vicarious social rebellion."[1] Corelli, who shared so much in common with her conservative middle-class readers, may well have shared their interest in alienated artist figures, causing her to create a narrative that expresses both fascination with and repulsion at the decadent lifestyles she describes.

If the novel exploits this middle-class fascination, it does little towards depicting anything more than the most sensational aspects of this lifestyle. It hardly matters, for example, that Gaston is a writer, for all the narrative tells us about his writing. When did he get the time to write his sentimental novel and his *feuilletons* while working on a career in banking? How, where, and under what conditions is he working on the account of his own life that the novel represents? Corelli's account of the artistic life of Gaston's friend, André Gessonex, while slightly more detailed, is also somewhat contradictory. On the one hand, Gessonex, in his interest in absinthe, his frequenting of cafés, and in his black and white sketches of dancers, is a perfect embodiment of the French Decadent Bohemian artist of the period. On the other hand, Corelli has Gessonex as an artist of classical subjects associated with the conventional Academic painters of the official Salons. Bohemian and avant-garde painters of this period in France would have had neither the money nor the inclination to produce this kind of commercial art. That being said, Corelli's description of Gessonex's masterpiece—his gloomy study of a priest looking upon the decaying countenance of a dead woman—is certainly evocative of the kind of art produced by real Decadent artists such as Gustave Moreau. All in all, the distinctive features of particular literary and artistic movements are less important to Corelli than her insistence that French art and literature is, almost without exception, morbid and immoral. Such stereotypes of the bohemian artist as Corelli provides in the novel were certainly not uncommon in a period in which novels about artists and artists' lifestyles were so popular with the mass reading public.

Degeneration

One of the reasons literary movements like Naturalism and Decadence were so controversial in this period was that Victorians perceived a link

---

[1] Jonathan Freedman, *Professions of Taste: Henry James, British Aestheticism, and Commodity Culture* (Stanford, CA: Stanford UP, 1990) 54-55.

between the literature and the health of a nation (healthy literature/healthy nation, unhealthy literature/unhealthy nation) where the literature was both a cause and symptom of the state of the nation. In their focus on the baser aspects of human nature, Naturalism and Decadence played on the anxieties of late Victorians who were coming to believe that *fin de siècle* meant *fin du monde* ("the end of the world"). Earlier in the Victorian period, Charles Darwin's theory of evolution, outlined in his 1859 book *The Origin of Species*, had led Victorians to adopt a progressive view of human development—one which proposed that species evolve through a process of natural selection and that the fittest of any species are the ones who ultimately survive. From the 1880s on, however, this progressive theory of evolution began to be questioned. If species could progress, surely they could regress or degenerate also? Out of this doubt grew theories of degeneration and of atavism, theories that argued that species could indeed revert to earlier or more primitive forms. Even Darwin himself began to question the progressive narrative of *The Origin of Species*.

In fact, degeneration theories had existed even prior to Darwin's *The Origin of Species*. In France in 1857 B.A. Morel published *Traité des dégénérescences physiques, intellectuelles et morales de l'espèce humaine* ("Treatise on the physical, mental, and moral degeneration of the human species") in which he traced the degeneration of a family through four generations from a tendency towards "alcoholic excess" in the first generation, to signs of "hereditary drunkenness" in the second, to "delusions of persecutions" in the third and, finally, to "complete idiocy" in the fourth generation.[1] Degeneration theory became popular in Europe in the late-nineteenth century and was applied across a variety of disciplines including medicine, biology, psychiatry and psychology, criminology, anthropology, social science, sexology, and literature and art. As Daniel Pick has argued, "there was no one stable referent to which degeneration applied; instead a fantastic kaleidoscope of concerns and objects through the second half of the century, from cretinism to alcoholism to syphilis, from peasantry to working class, bourgeoisie to aristocracy, madness to theft, individual to crowd, anarchism to feminism, population decline to population increase."[2] Furthermore, these problems ceased to be moral, religious,

---

[1]   As summarized by Henry Maudsley, *Body and Mind* (London: Macmillan, 1870) 45.
[2]   Daniel Pick, *Faces of Degeneration: A European Disorder c. 1848–1918* (Cambridge: Cambridge UP, 1989) 15.

or ethical in nature; instead, they became "empirically demonstrable medical, biological, or physical anthropological fact."[1] Degeneration was used, for example, to argue that some races were more developed than others, that criminals were degenerates identifiable by specific physical features, and that works of art and literature contained within them evidence of the pathological condition of the artist. The connection between degeneration and art became extremely popular when Max Nordau published *Degeneration* (1893; English trans. 1895), in which he provided a detailed analysis of the pathologies of a number of artists and schools of art including Realism (i.e. Naturalism) and Decadence. Nordau's theory was a powerful factor in the prosecution of Oscar Wilde, as the prosecutors in the case based much of their evidence of Wilde's commission of "acts of gross indecency" on Wilde's novel, *The Picture of Dorian Gray*.

In Britain, the "language of degeneration ... informed much wider representations of culture in the late nineteenth and early twentieth centuries" and concepts of degeneration were much less specifically employed in this country than they were in Continental Europe.[2] Also, the theory circulated as a form of common sense in the British context and was used to explain "all the pathologies from which the nation suffered."[3] Corelli's representation of degeneration theory in the novel is typical of the rather diffuse way in which degeneration was taken up by the British. Corelli does not use the term "degeneration" in the novel or in her correspondence with Bentley about the novel, nor does she specifically name any of its major theorists as Bram Stoker would do in his novel *Dracula* seven years later. Still, Corelli is well versed in the kinds of popularized notions of degeneration that were circulating in the 1880s. In *Wormwood*, for example, she alludes to the popular notion that Darwin had not, in his theory of evolution, anticipated the possibility of degeneration: "[Darwin] traced, or thought he could trace man's *ascent* from the monkey,—but he could not calculate man's *descent* to the monkey again."[4]

Corelli exploits popular degeneration theory in the novel most explicitly through her portrayal of André Gessonex's companion, an illiterate beast-like young boy. André's narrative of his friend's life

---

[1] Pick 20.

[2] Pick 5.

[3] Robert A. Nye, *Crime, Madness and Politics in Modern France: The Medical Concept of National Decline* (Princeton: Princeton UP, 1984) 119.

[4] See this edition, page 198–99.

loosely combines the hereditary degeneration theories of B.A. Morel, the criminal degeneration theories of Cesare Lombroso, and the Lombrosian degeneration theories that linked genius and insanity. Firstly, the boy is the grandson of a genius, a man of science whose degeneracy is linked to his atheism and positivism. The end result of his degeneration is madness and suicide. This man's son, the young savage's father, inherits his father's degeneracy and is a worse degenerate than his father. An absinthe addict and dissolute actor he too comes to a tragic end, throttling himself to death in a lunatic asylum. His child, a "product [o]f absinthe and mania," represents an even lower rung on the evolutionary ladder.[1] He is, as André describes, "a type of the Age of Stone" or the "primary Brute-period," unable to talk except for a few words and like a savage beast in his appearance and actions.[2] The boy is "a towzled half-naked creature who sat crouched in one of the darkest corners, biting a crust of bread and snarling over it in very much the fashion of an angry tiger-cat"[3] and his countenance is "brutish, repulsive, terrible in all respects save for the eyes, which were magnificent, jewel-like, clear and cruel as the eyes of a wolf or snake."[4] In addition, his facial structure is primitive: "the chin … is not developed,—the forehead recedes like that of the baboon ancestor,—the nose has not yet received its full intellectual prominence,—but the eyes are perfectly formed."[5] These descriptions of the boy are in keeping with the medical and psychiatric discourses of degeneration and atavism. Both Henry Maudsley and Cesare Lombroso frequently characterized criminals, idiots, and the insane as bestial both in terms of their physiology and their behaviour. Though Corelli differs from Lombroso and Maudsley in the type of physical characteristics she attributes to the atavistic person, the underlying principle remains the same. The savage boy's idiocy and degeneracy are marked on his body.

Corelli also draws on the degeneration theories of criminal anthropology in her depiction of Gaston. Gaston's degeneration is not attributed to heredity as the savage boy's is, but rather to his absinthism, which ultimately makes a degenerate criminal of him. Corelli is not, however, as deterministic in her representation of Gaston as were many

---

[1] See this edition, page 253.
[2] See this edition, page 253, 255.
[3] See this edition, page 250.
[4] See this edition, page 250.
[5] See this edition, page 250.

of the criminal anthropologists of her day. Gaston is not Lombroso's "born criminal," born with the physical markers of his predetermined degeneracy already inscribed on his body. On the contrary, as he himself tells us, his youthful physiognomy was one of "promising intelligence."[1] It is only once launched on his downward course of absinthism and crime that his physiognomy takes on a different aspect and he becomes "a slinking, shuffling beast, half monkey, half man, whose aspect is so vile, whose body is so shaken with delirium, whose eyes are so murderous, that if you met me by chance in the day-time, you would probably shriek for sheer alarm."[2]

Francophobia

If Corelli draws on criminal anthropology in her depiction of Gaston, she also draws on more traditional anthropology in linking his degeneracy to the broader degeneracy of the French nation. Gaston is not an exceptional case, Corelli tells us, but rather "a very ordinary type of a large and ever-increasing class ... to be met with every day in Paris."[3] In characterizing Gaston as "an ordinary type," Corelli invites us to read Gaston as the modern French Everyman with his story serving as an allegory for the decline of a once great nation. In her generalizations about France and the French people through the degenerate Gaston, Corelli exposes the Francophobia that was prevalent in Britain at this time.

This Francophobia must be understood as part of a broader fear about the decline of European civilization and degeneration theory helped to perpetuate these fears. In the new science of anthropology, anthropologists approached the study of other cultures with the preconception that non-European cultures were primitive cultures beyond which civilized Europeans had progressed. While these anthropological studies sustained and justified the imperialist ambitions of many European countries, degeneration theory also raised the frightening possibility that European nations might revert back to the savagery that Europeans associated with Asian and African races. In fact, the issue of whether European civilization was in a state of decline or progress, was becoming less civilized, more civilized, or perhaps even over-civilized became a dominant concern of the period. European nations watched

---

[1]   See this edition, page 76.
[2]   See this edition, page 363.
[3]   See this edition, page 61.

their neighbours with suspicion. In England, there was a belief that Celtic neighbours, particularly the Irish, were more primitive than the Anglo-Saxons of England.

An object of even greater suspicion from the British point of view, however, was France, a country whose turbulent past hundred years of revolution, wars, and civil unrest were regarded by the British as sure signs of a nation in decline. Francophobia was prevalent in Britain in the 1880s and 1890s even in educated quarters. Articles in highbrow periodicals, for example, often discussed the decline of France. One such example was "The Decadence of Thought in France," an article in which the writer commented on the prevalence of "moral and intellectual epileptics" in contemporary France.[1] The degenerate state of France was even a subject of discussion in the House of Commons debate over pernicious literature: "Were [the British] to wait [to ban pernicious literature]," asked Mr. Smith, MP for Flintshire, "until the moral fibre of the English race was eaten out, as that of the French was almost? Look what such literature had done for France. It overspread the nation like a torrent, and its poison was destroying the whole national life.... Such garbage was simply death to a nation. Were they to wait until this poison spread itself over English soil and killed the life of this great and noble people?"[2]

Corelli's rampant attack on France in her introductory note, then, was not unusual given the broader context of anti-French sentiment in Britain. Though her language is more hyperbolic than that used in the highbrow quarterlies, it is on a par with Mr. Smith's. Corelli writes:

> The morbidness of the modern French mind is well known and universally admitted, even by the French themselves; the open atheism, heartlessness, flippancy, and flagrant immorality of the whole modern French school of thought is unquestioned. If a crime of more than usual cold-blooded atrocity is committed, it generally dates from Paris, or near it;—if a book or a picture is produced that is confessedly obscene, the author or artist is, in nine cases out of ten, discovered to be a Frenchman. The shop-windows and bookstalls of Paris are of themselves sufficient witnesses of the national taste in art and literature,—a national

---

[1] Madame Blaze de Bury, "The Decadence of Thought in France," *Fortnightly Review* (March 1889): 401.

[2] See this edition, Appendix E.3.

taste for vice and indecent vulgarity which cannot be too sincerely and compassionately deplored.[1]

While this passage must strike the early twenty-first century reader as a blatant instance of racism, such rhetoric, as I have argued, was far from unusual in the period. This Francophobia and indeed other forms of racism were enabled by the legitimate "scientific" discourse of degeneration theory. As William Greenslade has argued, degeneration theory was a means "by which the conventional and respectable classes could justify and articulate their hostility to the deviant, the diseased, and the subversive."[2]

Underlying the British Francophobia of this period was a strong fear of contamination. Indeed Francophobic discourse is often structured around references to disease and contamination. Certainly Corelli worried about the apparent popularity of so many French things in Britain, including "French habits," "French fashions," "French books," "French pictures," and "French drug-drinking," fearing the pernicious influence of France's degenerate culture on Britain.[3] Corelli was not alone in this fear. From the campaigners against French Naturalism to those who worried about the influence of French visual arts on young English artists (such as the artists in the Francophilic New English Art Club), many Britons feared that their nation would eventually be "infected by the disease of [these] French school[s]."[4]

Absinthe

In *Wormwood*, Corelli attributes the main cause of France's degeneration to absinthe, a bitter anise-flavoured liquor, pale green in colour and made from the wormwood plant. Though absinthe existed in some form in Ancient Greece, absinthe, as we have come to know it, owes its origins to Pierre Ordinaire, a Frenchman who settled in Switzerland in 1790 and gained renown as a physician. One of the medicines he produced was absinthe, which he prescribed as a cure for stomach ailments. It was around this time that absinthe became known by its familiar nickname, "the green fairy." Absinthe would subsequently

---

[1] See this edition, page 61.
[2] William Greenslade, *Degeneration, Culture and the Novel 1880–1940* (Cambridge: Cambridge UP, 1994) 2.
[3] See this edition, page 62.
[4] John Trevor, *French Art and English Morals* (London: Swann Sonnenschein, 1886) 43.

acquire many more nicknames: "the green muse," "the green menace," "the green fiend," "the green goddess," and "the green curse." By the early nineteenth century, absinthe began to be commercially manufactured by Major Dubied and his son and son-in-law, Henry-Louis Pernod. At first absinthe was expensive and its consumption was restricted mainly to the French middle classes and certain artistic groups who enjoyed its hallucinatory effects. A series of phylloxera (plant lice) outbreaks in the vineyards in the 1870s and 1880s, however, led to a decrease in the price of absinthe. Absinthe producers had been, until this point, dependent on wine alcohol to produce absinthe but, with the shortage of wine caused by the lice outbreaks, they began to turn to cheaper beet and grain alcohol. Consequently absinthe could be sold at much cheaper prices. Frenchmen of all classes were now drinking absinthe and, by the 1880s, it was the most popular apéritif among the French who customarily consumed a distilled alcoholic drink before eating dinner. Absinthe was consumed during *l'heure de l'apéritif* (apéritif hour) or what became more widely known as *l'heure verte* (the green hour) after the colour of absinthe. Absinthe was such a prevalent part of French café life that the streets of Montmartre were said to reek of "the sickly odour of absinthe."[1]

Though popular among all classes of people, absinthe was most strongly associated with the bohemian world of literary men and artists. Alfred de Musset, Henri de Toulouse-Lautrec, Paul Verlaine, Arthur Rimbaud, Edgar Allan Poe, Oscar Wilde, Ernest Dowson, Arthur Symons, Vincent Van Gogh, and Picasso all enjoyed absinthe and created works under its inspiration. Writers and artists attributed near magical powers to absinthe, citing it as an important source of their creative powers and through them absinthe acquired a legendary romantic mystique that continues to this day. Oscar Wilde, for example, described the third stage of absinthe drinking as one in which "you see things that you *want* to see, wonderful, curious things."[2] Dowson wrote of absinthe, "Whiskey and beer are for fools; absinthe for poets; absinthe has the power of the magicians; it can wipe out or renew the past, and annul or foretell the future."[3] Richard Le Gallienne, a poet and contemporary of Wilde's, was more ambivalent about the "green fairy," saying

---

[1] Barnaby Conrad, *Absinthe: History in a Bottle* (San Francisco: Chronicle Books, 1988) 44.

[2] Quoted in Conrad ix.

[3] Ernest Dowson, *Letters of Ernest Dowson*, ed. Desmond Flower and Henry Maas (London: Cassell, 1967) 441.

of his first encounter with it, "I had just heard of it, as a drink mysteriously sophisticated and even Satanic. To me it had the sound of hellebore or mandragora.... [i]n the [18]90s it was spoken of with a self-conscious sense of one's being desperately wicked, suggesting diabolism and nameless iniquity."[1] For some writers and artists, however, such as Verlaine who described absinthe as the "source of folly and crime, of idiocy and shame," absinthe contributed significantly to the diminishing of their creative powers.[2] Even Wilde, who had once so lyrically rhapsodized about absinthe, acknowledged its less attractive aspects in a statement that contradicts his assertion that one sees "wonderful things" when drinking absinthe: "After the first glass you see things as you wish they were. After the second, you see things as they are not. Finally you see things as they really are, and that is the most horrible thing in the world."[3]

Though absinthe was often advertised as a health tonic, many people were seriously concerned about its potential dangers. Absinthe has a much higher alcohol content than wine or other apéritifs (fifty to seventy-five and sometimes as high as ninety per cent) and was therefore regarded by many doctors as more dangerous than other kinds of alcohol. Certainly its effects were quite different, effects which one medical expert described in the following way:

> you seem to lose your feet, and you mount to a boundless realm without a horizon. You probably imagine that you are going in the direction of the infinite, whereas you are simply drifting into the incoherent. Absinthe affects the brain unlike any other stimulant; it produces neither the heavy drunkenness of beer, the furious inebriation of brandy, nor the exhilarant intoxication of wine. It is an ignoble poison, destroying life not until it has more or less brutalized its votaries, and made drivelling idiots of them.[4]

Doctors soon defined absinthism as a distinctive form of alcoholism. They noted a significant difference, for example, between the "delirium tremens" of the normal alcoholic and what were described as more serious epileptic convulsions suffered by absinthe drinkers. Doctors also

[1]   Richard Le Gallienne, *The Romantic 90s* (London: G.P. Putnam's Sons, 1926) 142.
[2]   Quoted in Conrad 36.
[3]   Quoted in Conrad 37.
[4]   "Absinthe," (London) *Times* (4 May 1868): 12.

identified in absinthe drinkers a strong tendency towards automatism, amnesia, fits of violence, and hallucinations.

The British watched the growing absinthe problem in France with concern throughout the latter part of the nineteenth century. In September 1889, just before Corelli began writing *Wormwood*, the London *Times* reported: "The effects of general and unrestrained absinthe drinking in France are coming to be recognized as forming the basis of one of the gravest dangers that now threaten the physical and moral welfare of the people."[1] Corelli's adoptive father, Dr. Mackay, had even written of the dangers of absinthe in an article that he submitted to *Blackwood's Magazine* in October 1889, shortly before his death.[2] The intensified concerns over absinthe in England in the late 1880s can no doubt be attributed to the fear that absinthe might soon pose a threat on home soil. British visitors to France, artists and writers in particular, were bringing back with them a taste for absinthe and many British establishments were beginning to serve absinthe to meet the demands of their customers. It was to bars like the Cock in Shaftesbury Avenue, the Café Royale in Regent Street, the Crown in Charing Cross Road—all favourite haunts of the British Francophile absinthe-drinking bohemian set—that Corelli was referring to when she complained of "the many French *cafés* and restaurants which have recently sprung up in London" where "absinthe is always to be obtained at its customary low price."[3]

While absinthe-drinking, as it turns out, never did become as popular in Britain as it was in France, consumption in France mounted steadily in the late nineteenth and early twentieth century. Whereas in 1874 the French had consumed 700,000 litres of absinthe, that figure rose to 36,000,000 by 1910. Though temperance movements were not very popular in a country with a strong cultural tradition of drinking, the rapid increase in absinthe consumption alarmed many. Absinthe was being held accountable for many social ills, not least of which was that it was thought to be contributing significantly to the "physical, mental, and moral degeneration of the French race," a belief that Corelli would have strongly endorsed.[4] Absinthe consumption was linked to the declining birth rate, the high rate of tuberculosis, as well as to the

---

[1] "Manufacture of Absinthe in France," (London) *Times* (19 September 1889): 6.
[2] Ransom 58. This article does not appear to have been published.
[3] See this edition, page 62.
[4] P.E. Prestwich, "Temperance in France: The Curious Case of Absinth [*sic*]," *Historical Reflections* 6 (1979): 307.

increase in violent crime, suicide, and insanity. As P.E. Prestwich argues, these fears were, to a large degree, alarmist, with absinthe being blamed for "social problems that today would be considered typical of a modern industrial society."[1] Though attempts to ban absinthe in France in 1907 failed, the onset of World War I raised anxieties about the fitness of French men, as up to twenty per cent of French conscripts failed to pass basic medical exams. Finally, on March 16, 1915, a law went into effect banning the production, circulation, and sale of absinthe. It had already been banned in Holland, Belgium, Brazil, Switzerland, Italy, and in the United States where it was popular in cosmopolitan centres like New York, New Orleans, Chicago, and San Francisco.

After the war, the French found other things to drink, though absinthe held a certain allure for members of the rich and Bohemian sets, particularly American expatriate and British artists and writers of the 1920s. Ernest Hemingway, Evelyn and Alec Waugh, William Somerset Maugham, and Harry Crosby all enjoyed the pleasures of absinthe and in the 1920s absinthe cocktails were extremely popular. Absinthe was still being produced legally in Spain and Holland and illegally in France. These countries supplied absinthe to Britain, where the controversial liquor had never been banned. In 1930 absinthe was once again a cause of concern in Britain when the British medical journal, *The Lancet*, declared that absinthe-drinking, even if not yet widespread in Britain, was even more insidious than cocaine or heroin use:

> To argue that, because a comparatively small quantity of this deadly liquor is consumed at the present time, the importation of absinthe may be ignored, is as dangerous as to suggest a similar course in regard to heroin or cocaine, and with less reason, because these alkaloids have their legitimate uses, whereas in the considered opinion of many eminent physicians in France and Switzerland, absinthe is not only valueless, but is also a menace to the public health and the prosperity of the country.[2]

Again, this apparent menace proved benign. Absinthe lapsed into obscurity again in the 1930s but is now, once again, undergoing a revival in Britain and North America. This revival was initiated in the late 1990s

---

[1]   Prestwich 307.
[2]   C.W.J. Brasher, "Absinthe and Absinthe Drinking in England," *The Lancet* (26 April 1930): 946.

by a firm called the "Green Bohemians" consisting of John Moore, formerly of the 1980s alternative band The Jesus and Mary Chain and currently in a band called Black Box Recorder, Tom Hodgkinson and Gavin Pretor-Pinney of the hip British magazine the *Idler*, and British liquor importer George Rowley. Discovering that absinthe had never been banned in England, the "Green Bohemians" decided to import absinthe from the Czech Republic. The drink caught on in Britain, no doubt aided by the Millennium fever of the late 1990s and the renewed interest in Decadence and decadent lifestyles. Nostalgia for the decadent 1890s, the previous *fin de siècle*, was rampant, and absinthes of various kinds flooded the market, all of them appealing to their buyer's desire for a piece of decadent bohemia. Recently, Moore and his cohorts (now calling themselves "Green Utopia") have introduced La Fée Absinthe to the market, an absinthe which claims to capture the genuine flavour of original absinthe and which has earned the stamp of approval of Marie-Claude Delahaye, an absinthe expert who runs the absinthe museum in Paris. Though now available in parts of Canada where, as in Britain, absinthe was never banned, absinthe is still illegal in the United States where there is nevertheless a strong underground interest in the drink. Numerous websites exist that perpetuate the romantic image of absinthe and offer advice on how to concoct homemade absinthe.

While in France absinthe was a drink enjoyed by all classes from the last quarter of the nineteenth century and on, in Britain absinthe-drinking was in Corelli's time and is again today a means of distinguishing oneself from mainstream culture. In the *fin de siècle* of the last century, the Wildes, Dowsons, Symonses and others of the British Decadent circle thought of themselves as a sophisticated élite counter-cultural group. Similarly today, those who have taken up an interest in absinthe in Britain consider themselves a cultural élite. Tom Hodgkinson, one of the "Green Bohemians" responsible for reintroducing absinthe to Britain, describes those interested in absinthe as "literary hedonists, or people aspiring to that ... People like myself, who like to imagine they're talking with Oscar Wilde in a Parisian cafe."[1] Absinthe is more than just a drink, then. It is a symbol of cultural sophistication, of élite status, and of a rejection of what the Decadents would have called "philistine" culture. In her day, Corelli fought against these counter-cultural groups

---

[1] Gemma Tarlach, "Absinthe makes a comeback: Powerful liqueur has been banned almost worldwide," *South Coast Today*. http://www.s-t.com/daily/03-99/03-03-99/b04li210.htm. Accessed on 14 February 2003.

for whom she had no sympathy. For her, the Decadents' markers of artistry—from their absinthe-drinking and eccentric dress and lifestyles to their claims to economic disinterestedness and hatred of the masses—were shams that she wished to expose. In their place, she wished that her own ideas of the artist might prevail: industrious, possessed of strong moral and ethical values, and serving as a voice of and for the people. Thus, while *Wormwood* is in part a temperance tract to warn her readers of the dangers of absinthe, it is also, on a symbolic level, an account of the battle for cultural domination in which absinthe is made to stand for a range of what were, in Corelli's mind, debased social values.

The Reception of *Wormwood*

Though Bentley had no doubt that Corelli's "public" would be captivated by the "extraordinary power" of her new novel, he warned Corelli against being over-eager about its reception, as he believed that the press and Corelli's "sister" authors would react harshly to her "repulsive" subject.[1] Not all the reviews were unfavourable, however. *Wormwood* received high praise in popular middle-class women's magazines such as *Kensington Society* and the *County Gentlewoman*, in popular newspapers such as the *Graphic*, and in more mainstream literary magazines such as the *Literary World*. The *Kensington Society* reviewer, carried away by the sensationalist aspects of the novel, waxed rhapsodic about Corelli's "eloquently vigorous language" and launched into a florid description of the effects of the novel on the reader in a pseudo-Corellian style: "The reader is whirled about like a leaflet amidst lurid flashes and wild gusts of maddened invective, almost blinded by the efforts he or she makes to realize the tempest which rages through the man possessed of the 'liquid fire.'"[2] Other reviewers, though equally complimentary about the novel, were more restrained. These reviewers were not struck by the melodramatic sensational aspects that had appealed to the *Kensington Society* reviewer. On the contrary, they found the novel to be extremely realistic. "Never before," remarked the reviewer for the *County Gentlewoman*, "has the subject of absinthe-drinking in Paris been gone into so thoroughly and all its effects laid bare."[3] For these reviewers, Corelli had succeeded in her attempt to

---

[1]   See this edition, Appendix B.8 and B.9.
[2]   See this edition, Appendix C.5.
[3]   See this edition, Appendix C.9.

create a moralized realism à la Balzac to undermine the contemporary realist school of Naturalism. As the reviewer for the *Literary World* noted, "This strong romance ... is a study—extremely realistic, yet saved by the honest and clean mind of the author from needless offence—of the horrible demoralization and the reversion to brute types of the modern Parisians, caused by the absinthe habit."[1] For this reviewer who, like Corelli, was wary of French Naturalism, Corelli had "employ[ed] to a worthy end" the tenets of this morally questionable literature. Similarly, the reviewer for the *Graphic* found that Corelli's "frantic" style was extremely well suited to the portrayal of the "homicidal maniac" who served as her protagonist.[2]

But while these reviews no doubt pleased Corelli, they were not the reviews that would be read by those among the literary élite by whom she so longed to be accepted. The *Academy*, the *Athenaeum*, the *Spectator*, the *Times*, and the *Pall Mall Gazette*—these were the periodicals in which critical praise for a new novel counted. Of these five, the *Times* and the *Pall Mall Gazette* were the most vicious about *Wormwood*. The reviews in these periodicals are characteristic of the kinds of criticisms that were so often launched against female novelists by the largely male-dominated literary élite. Lacking access to the kinds of life experience that their male counterparts enjoyed, women writers were often mocked for their sentimental, unrealistic, and morally didactic stories. The reviewers for the *Times* and the *Pall Mall Gazette*, for example, mocked Corelli's pretensions to "Realism" (i.e., Naturalism) mercilessly, both using as their starting point the following lines from Corelli's prefatory note in which she makes a claim for her particular brand of romantic realism as "truth":

> The fictionist need never torture his brain for stories, either of adventure or spectral horror. Life itself, as it is lived among ourselves in all countries, is so amazing, swift, varied, wonderful, terrible, ghastly, beautiful, dreadful, and withal so wildly inconsistent and changeful, that whosoever desires to write romances has only to closely and patiently observe men and women as they are—not as they seem—and then take pen in hand and write—"the truth."[3]

---

1   See this edition, Appendix C.6.
2   See this edition, Appendix C.3.
3   See this edition, page 63.

Disparaging Corelli's efforts at "Realism," the *Pall Mall Gazette* reviewer declared that Corelli's "theory differs wildly from her practice," condemning the novel as "wildly inconsistent and changeful."[1] Even more brutal in his commentary is the *Times* reviewer who ridiculed Corelli's claims to be a "Realist" writer when, as she herself admits in the introductory note, she has no first-hand knowledge of many of the events she describes in the novel.

> But ought a "fictionist" who deals in nothing but verities to palm off upon her readers lurid descriptions of a *café-chantant* orgy without having been there? It is not a trifle shabby to father her glowing picture upon a respectable English tourist, whom the "fictionist" (*vide* again the preface) perceived from his dress to be "of some religious persuasion," and whom she overheard enthusiastically commending the can-can to a younger companion, yet did not withdraw suffused with blushes, but "took calm note thereof for literary use thereafter?" At first, we felt inclined to say, with a Sheffielder in a certain play, "I know that tourist!" But upon other evidence we have decided to exonerate Marie Corelli from a suspicion which, one would have thought, a student of life as it is lived would have been in no hurry to repel. The evidence which satisfies us that Marie Corelli has never set foot in one of these naughty places is comprised in a single sentence:—"There are lovely women at the *cafés-chantants*; ... women as delicate as nymphs, and dainty as flowers."[2]

In addition to mocking her pretensions to "realism," the reviewers for the *Pall Mall Gazette* and the *Times* also criticized her writing style and grammar in an equally patronizing manner. The *Times* reviewer condemns her "feminine redundancy of adjectives,"[3] while the *Pall Mall Gazette* reviewer provides a detailed criticism of her grammar and mocks Corelli's use of an elementary French vocabulary:

> Gaston Beauvais, "the unhappy hero," tells his own story in hysterical prose, and we are gradually shown how his desire for love begot desire for absinthe.... None of the characters are real, or

---

[1] See this edition, Appendix C.2.
[2] See this edition, Appendix C.7.
[3] See this edition, Appendix C.7.

interesting, or pleasant.... A Frenchman with a taste for absinthe should be forgiven much in the way of bad words, so if Gaston writes "dumbfoundered," "dumbly," "favorite," "overwhelment," and even "frissonement," of course it is not Miss Corelli's fault. Nor can we reasonably rebuke her for such a piece of simmering stuff as this: "She looked at me straightly, her eyes full of a mournful exaltation, her breath coming and going rapidly between her parted lips. I met her glance with an amazed scorn—and hurled the bitter truth like pellets of ice upon the amorous heat of her impetuous avowal." As the book is "a drama of Paris," such untranslatable expressions as *mon ami, bon jour, allons, vraiment, au revoir*, abound, but, with the aid of Ollendorff [a popular foreign language manual], no doubt the patient reader will master them.[1]

Thus, just as women writers were accused of writing sentimental and unrealistic stories, so too they were often criticized for their faulty style, florid writing, and bad syntax. While to some degree such writing was an effect of the lack of access women writers had to the kinds of education available to their male peers, differing notions of literary and artistic value also account for the styles of writing adopted by various authors in the period. While Corelli's language was, in the words of the *Kensington Society* reviewer, "eloquently vigorous," to the *Times* reviewer and the male-dominated literary élite whose opinions he represented, Corelli's writing was faulty for its "feminine redundancy of adjectives." So too, the reviewer takes advantage of the fact that, as a woman writer, Corelli felt compelled to account for her knowledge of *café-chantants*— the kind of place no "respectable" woman would be found in—by insisting that it is second-hand knowledge, overheard in conversation.

Not all the reviews in prominent journals were so scathing. The *Academy* and the *Athenaeum*, the two leading literary periodicals of the day, were at least polite, if not overly enthusiastic, about *Wormwood*. For Corelli, however, these reviews were, in many respects, an instance of damning with faint praise. Commenting on the *Athenaeum* review to Bentley, Corelli wrote, "I saw the 'critique' in the *Athenaeum*;—it struck me as a strange one—and a more or less useless one, purposely arranged so *as to be* useless."[2] Though Corelli claimed to be indifferent to the negative reviews, her bitterness at the novel's reception is plain in her

---

[1]   See this edition, Appendix C.2
[2]   See this edition, Appendix B.10.

letters to Bentley as is her sense of injustice as a female writer in a male-dominated field:

> I feel that it is impossible for a woman writer to receive justice from *men*-critics, more particularly if she chance to show masculine power. If any *man* had written *Wormwood* there would have been a grand shouting over it both in the French and English press. I think it is not unnatural that one should feel disheartened at times; ... when I *know* and *feel* in my secret conscience that I have done a good piece of literary work, in pure nervous language, without showiness, without drag or *padding* or short of dramatic interest, I feel it a trifle hard that when others who do less good work can get high praise, that I should not also win a trifle of honest *recognition*."[1]

But if Corelli was disappointed by *Wormwood*'s lack of success among the literary élite, she had nothing to complain of in terms of its popular success. The first print run sold out in ten days and it was translated into German, Italian, and Swedish within months of its publication. Throughout the winter of 1890-91, Corelli, by her own accounts, was inundated with offers from publishers who wanted to publish a cheap edition of the novel and who were willing to offer her very generous terms for the privilege. She stayed true to Bentley, however, and by early 1891 *Wormwood* was issued in a cheap one-volume edition. Though *Wormwood* was not among the most popular of Corelli's novels, it continued to sell well throughout her lifetime. Corelli's absinthe novel was still popular enough eight years later to be mentioned in *The Hypocrite* by Ranger Gull, in which a character jokingly dismisses the idea of becoming an absintheur because of the bad name Corelli had given this practice.[2] In 1915, a silent film based on the novel was released[3] and in 1924, at the time of Corelli's death, the novel was in its twenty-third edition. Editions of the novel continued to be published after her death and in 1962 it was in its twenty-seventh edition. In 1967, *Wormwood* was translated into Thai and in 1987 it was translated into Urdu and published in India where Corelli has long been popular.

---

[1] See this edition, Appendix B.10.
[2] Anonymous [Ranger Gull], *The Hypocrite* (London: Greening and Co., 1898) 95.
[3] *Wormwood*, dir. Marshal Farnum, perf. John St. Polis, Charles Arthur, Lillian Dilworth, and Philip Hahn, 1915.

Wormwood has had some attention paid to it in the recent critical recuperation of Corelli and her work. Annette Federico, for example, argues for the novel's importance in demonstrating Corelli's engagement with some of the most important literary trends of the 1880s and 1890s, while I have argued that it is a central text in understanding the prevalence and circulation of Francophobic discourse in the British *fin de siècle*. Like Federico, I also see *Wormwood* as an important intervention in the main literary and cultural debates of the 1880s and 1890s. Though not an explicitly feminist novel, once viewed in the context of its production and Corelli's position as a woman writer in a male-dominated elitist literary milieu, *Wormwood* takes on a new meaning. If at its most explicit level *Wormwood* is a tract against absinthism and the degenerate French, it is also a novel which, in the context of its production and reception, registers the tensions and contradictions of being a woman writer in a man's field and those of being a popular writer trying to create "high" art. Despite the disparagement of her male avant-garde contemporaries and despite her own feelings about absinthe, Corelli must be credited with having created one of the most compelling accounts of absinthe drinking. Taken out of context, some of her descriptions of absinthe drinking glamorize the practice, ironically making her an important figurehead in the revival of interest in absinthe. *Wormwood* is mentioned on virtually all the websites that promote absinthe. Most notably, excerpts from *Wormwood* form the basis of two musical pieces in a collaboration between the American underground band Blood Axis and the French band Les Joyaux de la Princesse on a CD called *Absinthe, La Folie Verte* (2001).[1] On this CD, excerpts from *Wormwood* take their place alongside musical tributes to Ernest Dowson's and Charles Cros's poems about absinthe. If Corelli has not achieved the kind of posterity she desired, neither has she been erased from cultural memory entirely, as her opponents thought she would be. The current academic and critical interest is continuing to grow and, if only for writing a novel about absinthe, Corelli is gaining a new following among popular sub-cultural groups following our own fin de siècle.

---

[1] Blood Axis/Les Joyaux de la Princesse, *Absinthe, La Folie Verte*, Athanor, 2001.

Marie Corelli: A Brief Chronology

1855   Corelli born Mary ("Minnie") Mackay on May 1.
Parentage obscure, possibly the illegitimate child of Dr.
Charles Mackay, journalist and song-writer, and his
mistress Elizabeth Mary Mills.

1861   Dr. Mackay marries Elizabeth Mary Mills.

1862-63   Dr. Mackay goes to America where he works as a
reporter.

1866-70   Corelli attends convent school in Paris or Italy.

1870   Family moves to Fern Dell, Box Hill, Surrey; George
Meredith is a neighbour.

1874   Submits a poem and an article to *Blackwood's Magazine*.
Both are rejected. Turns attention to music, concentrating
on piano and singing in an effort to become a
professional musician.

1875-76   Mother becomes ill. Bertha Vyver, Corelli's life-long
friend, comes to live with the Mackays. Mother dies in
February 1876.

1881   Offers five sonnets to *Blackwood's Magazine*. Rejected
again. Eric Mackay, Corelli's step-brother, comes to live
with the family.

1883   Dr. Mackay suffers heart attack and his health declines.
The family, including Bertha Vyver, move to London.
Corelli again submits poems to *Blackwood's* under the
name Signorina Marie Corelli. Corelli again ignored by
Blackwood's but her poems published in *Theatre Magazine*.

1884   As Signorina Marie Corelli, Corelli stages a well-received
public piano concert in December. Among those
attending is poet Algernon Charles Swinburne.

1885   Publisher George Bentley publishes an article by Corelli
in *Temple Bar* in July. Corelli submits manuscript for *A
Romance of Two Worlds* to Bentley.

1886   *A Romance of Two Worlds* published in February. Her
second novel, *Vendetta*, published later that year. Corelli
begins work on third novel, *Thelma*.

1887   *Thelma* published. Corelli meets Oscar Wilde who
admires her work.

1889   *Ardath* published. William Gladstone, former Prime
        Minister of Britain and an admirer of Corelli's work, visits
        Corelli. Dr. Mackay dies in December.

1890   Church founded in America on the doctrines of *A
        Romance of Two Worlds*. A town in Colorado is named after
        her. *Wormwood* is published in October.

1891   Queen Victoria asks that all Corelli's books be sent to her.

1892   *Soul of Lilith* published. Corelli invited to a private dinner
        with the Prince of Wales during a summer vacation in
        Homburg. In October scandal erupts over *Silver Domino*,
        an anonymous satirical work penned by Corelli. Relations
        with Bentley are strained.

1893   *Barabbas* published by Corelli's new publisher, Methuen.

1895   Corelli's *The Sorrows of Satan* is one of the first best-sellers
        and the most talked about book of 1895. Corelli ceases
        sending her books out to reviewers.

1896-97 Productive period in which Corelli produces *The Mighty
        Atom*, *The Murder of Delicia*, *Cameos*, *Ziska*, *Jane*, *The
        Strange Visitation*, and *The Distant Voice*.

1897   Corelli has hysterectomy. Insists on being operated on by
        female surgeon.

1898   Corelli's step-brother Eric Mackay dies.

1899   Corelli and Bertha Vyver leave London to settle in
        Stratford-upon-Avon.

1900   *Boy* and *The Master Christian* published.

1901   Corelli and Vyver move into Mason Croft in Stratford-
        upon-Avon. Queen Victoria dies. Corelli invited to attend
        the coronation of Edward VII.

1903   Corelli embroiled in controversy over establishment of a
        Carnegie free library in Stratford. Corelli vehemently
        opposes the desecration of important historical sites.
        Corelli wins defamation case relating to the Shakespeare
        controversy but is awarded the paltry sum of one
        farthing damages.

1906   *The Treasure of Heaven* published. Camera-shy Corelli
        finally sits for a portrait which appears as frontispiece to
        the novel. Photograph is altered to make Corelli appear
        much younger than her fifty years. Meets and falls in love
        with the married artist Arthur Severn.

1908   *Holy Orders* published.

1911   Corelli returns to the mystical themes of her earlier work in *The Life Everlasting*.

1914-18   Becomes passionately involved in the war effort, writing numerous articles for which she took no payment. Relationship with Severn comes to an end.

1918   Corelli charged with food hoarding which, because of the shortage of food, was illegal during the war. *The Young Diana*, her first book in a number of years, is published.

1921   *The Secret Power*, Corelli's last major novel, is published.

1924   Corelli dies on April 21. Corelli's companion, Bertha Vyver, lives until 1942.

A Note on the Text

This edition is based on the original 1890 three-volume edition of *Wormwood*. I have made some editorial emendations where obvious typographical errors exist. These are listed below. I have also made some alterations in the italicizing of French words and phrases in the text, a feature that was not consistent in the first edition.

71: animalism] animalisme
76: Royale] Royal
76: boulvardier] boulevardier
87: crêche] crèche
97: frissonement] frissonnement
112: talons!] talons!'"
113: he his proud privilege] be his proud
118: 'le pauvre clerc, mademoiselle] 'le pauvre clerc,' mademoiselle
118: etrennes] étrennes
119: marrons glacées] marrons glacés
129: made] make
130: stedfastly] steadfastly
133: '"Mieux que la] 'Mieux que la
165: centered] centred
167: Gessenex] Gessonex
177: hien] hein
178: "Margot, you are cross'] "Margot, you are cross"
186: boulvardier] boulevardier
187: cure] curé
206: fanfarronade] fanfaronade
206: rose early] I rose early
208: tête-à-téte] tête-à-tête
230: Comtess] Comtesse
244: stedfastly] steadfastly
251: chèf] chef
254: sobriquèt] sobriquet
270: Opèra] Opéra
276: "There!] "There!"
277: Lêve] lève
291: agressively] aggressively

291: Elyseés] Elysées
344: cortége] cortège
358: beautous] beauteous
360: Hélàs] Hélas

Corelli's Introductory Note

The unhappy hero of the following *drame*[1] is presented to English readers, not as an example of what is exceptionally tragic and uncommon,
but simply as a very ordinary type of a large and ever-increasing class.
Men such as 'Gaston Beauvais' are to be met with every day in Paris,—
and not only in Paris, but in every part of the Continent where the Curse,
which forms the subject of this story, has any sort of sway. The morbidness of the modern French mind is well known and universally admitted, even by the French themselves; the open atheism, heartlessness,
flippancy, and flagrant immorality of the whole modern French school
of thought is unquestioned. If a crime of more than usual cold-blooded
atrocity is committed, it generally dates from Paris, or near it;—if a book
or a picture is produced that is confessedly obscene, the author or artist
is, in nine cases out of ten, discovered to be a Frenchman. The shop-
windows and bookstalls of Paris are of themselves sufficient witnesses of
the national taste in art and literature,—a national taste for vice and indecent vulgarity which cannot be too sincerely and compassionately
deplored. There are, no doubt, many causes for the wretchedly low stan-
dard of moral responsibility and fine feeling displayed by the Parisians of
to-day,—but I do not hesitate to say that one of those causes is undoubtedly the reckless Absinthe-mania, which pervades all classes, rich and poor
alike. Every one knows that in Paris the men have certain hours set apart
for the indulgence of this fatal craze as religiously as Mussulmans[2] have
their hours for prayer,—and in a very short time the love of the hideous
poison clings so closely to their blood and system that it becomes an
absolute necessity of existence. The effects of its rapid working on the
human brain are beyond all imagination horrible and incurable, and no
romancist can exaggerate the terrific reality of the evil. If any of my readers are disposed to doubt the possibility of the incidents in my story or
to think the details exaggerated, let such make due inquiries of any leading member of the French medical faculty as to the actual meaning of
ABSINTHISM, and the measured statement of the physician will seem
wilder than the wildest tragedy. Moreover, it is not as if this dreadful frenzy
affected a few individuals merely,—it has crept into the brain of France

---

[1] French word for "drama," or "tragedy."
[2] Muslims.

as a nation, and there breeds perpetual mischief,—and from France it has spread, and is still spreading, over the entire Continent of Europe. It must also be remembered that in the many French *cafés*[1] and restaurants which have recently sprung up in London, Absinthe is always to be obtained at its customary low price,—French habits, French fashions, French books, French pictures, are particularly favoured by the English, and who can predict that French drug-drinking shall not also become *à la mode*[2] in Britain?—particularly at a period when our medical men are bound to admit that the love of Morphia[3] is fast becoming almost a mania with hundreds of English women!

In the present story I have, as I say, selected a merely ordinary Parisian type; there are of course infinitely worse examples who have not even the shadow of a love-disappointment to excuse them for their self-indulgence. All I ask of my readers and critics is that they will kindly refrain from setting down my hero's opinions on men and things to *me* personally, as they were unwise enough to do in the case of a previous novel of mine entitled "Vendetta!" When an author depicts a character, he is not of necessity that character himself; it would have been somewhat unfair to Balzac, for example, to have endowed him when a living man, with the extraordinary ideas and outrageous principles of his matchless artistic creation 'Père Goriot.'[4] I have nothing whatever to do with the wretched 'Gaston Beauvais' beyond the portraiture of him in his own necessarily lurid colours;—while for the description of the low-class "*bal masqué*"[5] in Paris, I am in a great measure indebted to a very respectable-looking English tourist, who by his dress was

---

1 Cafés, which serve alcohol as well as coffee, were and continue to be a prominent feature of French cultural life where people meet friends, read newspapers, play cards and billiards, or simply watch the passers-by on the street. The 1889 *Baedeker* guide to Paris described them as "one of the specialities of Paris," allowing one a glimpse of "Parisian life in all its phases" (5).

2 French expression meaning "fashionable."

3 Morphine.

4 Honoré de Balzac (1799-1850). French novelist, generally regarded as the father of the Realist movement in literature. *Père Goriot* (1835) was one of the key novels of Balzac's *La Comédie Humaine*, a series of novels in which Balzac sought to present a comprehensive social history of France. The character Père Goriot is an overly affectionate father who gives up his wealth to his ungrateful daughters.

5 Masked ball. These were popular entertainments in Paris in the 1880s and 1890s. Respectable masked balls were given weekly during Lent at grand establishments like the Paris Opera House and were attended by gentlemen and ladies. The low-class balls Corelli refers to were held year-round in public dancing halls, which were known to be frequented by prostitutes.

evidently of some religious persuasion, and whom I overheard talking to a younger man, on board a steamer going from Thun to Interlaken. It was evidently the worthy creature's first trip abroad,—he had visited the French capital, and he detailed to his friend, a very hilarious individual, certain of his most lively experiences there. I, sitting close by in a corner unobserved, listened with a good deal of surprise as well as amusement to his enthusiastic eulogy of the "*can-can*"[1] as he had seen it danced in some peculiar haunt of questionable entertainment, and I took calm note thereof, for literary use hereafter. The most delicate feelings can hardly be ruffled by an honest (and pious) Britisher's raptures,—and as I have included these raptures in my story, I beg to tender my thanks to the unknown individual who so unconsciously furnished me with a glowing description of what I have never seen and never wish to see!

For the rest, my 'drama' is a true phase of the modern life of Paris; one scene out of the countless tragedies that take place every day and everywhere in these our present times. There is no necessity to invent fables nowadays,—the fictionist need never torture his brain for stories either of adventure or spectral horror. Life itself as it is lived among ourselves in all countries, is so amazing, swift, varied, wonderful, terrible, ghastly, beautiful, dreadful, and, withal, so wildly inconsistent and changeful, that whosoever desires to write romances has only to closely and patiently observe men and women as they *are*, not as they *seem*,— and then take pen in hand and write—the TRUTH.

MARIE CORELLI.
CLARENS, LAKE LEMAN, SWITZERLAND,
September, 1890.

---

[1] High-kicking dance considered scandalous in the nineteenth century because legs and petticoats were exposed to public view.

WORMWOOD

A Drama of Paris

"And the name of the star is called WORMWOOD; and the third part of the waters became *wormwood*; and many men died of the waters, because they were made bitter."

—REVELATION viii. 11.

"Et le nom de cette étoile était ABSINTHE: et la troisième partie des eaux fut changée en *absinthe*; et elles firent mourir un grand nombre d'hommes parce qu'elles étaient devenues amères."

—REVELATION viii. 11
(Nouveau Testament Français).

À Messieurs
Les absintheurs de Paris
Ces fanfarons du vice
Qui sont
La honte et le désespoir de leur patrie[1]

---

[1] To the gentlemen, the *absintheurs* of Paris, those who brag of their corruption and who are the shame and despair of their country.

CHAPTER 1

Silence,—silence! It is the hour of the deepest hush of night; the invisible intangible clouds of sleep brood over the brilliant city. Sleep! What is it? Forgetfulness? A sweet unconsciousness of dreamless rest? Aye! it must be so, if I remember rightly; but I cannot be quite sure, for it seems a century since I slept well. But what of that? Does any one sleep well nowadays, save children and hard-worked diggers of the soil? We who *think*—oh, the entanglements and perplexities of this perpetual Thought!—we have no space or time wherein to slumber; between the small hours of midnight and morning we rest on our pillows for mere form's sake, and doze and dream,—but we do not *sleep*.

Stay! let me consider. What am I doing here so late? why am I not at home? Why do I stand alone on this bridge, gazing down into the cold sparkling water of the Seine[1]—water that, to my mind, resembles a glittering glass screen, through which I see faces peering up at me, white and aghast with a frozen wonder? How they stare, how they smile, all those drowned women and men! Some are beautiful, all are mournful. I am not sorry for them, no! but I am sure they must have died with half their griefs unspoken, to look so wildly even in death! Is it my fancy, or do they want something of me? I feel impelled towards them—they draw me downwards by a deadly fascination; I must go on, or else——

With a violent effort I tear myself away, and, leaving the bridge, I wander slowly homeward.

The city sleeps, did I say? Oh no! Paris is not so clean of conscience or so pure of heart that its inhabitants should compose themselves to rest simply because it is midnight. There are hosts of people about and stirring; rich aristocrats for instance, whose names are blazoned on the lists of honour and *la haute noblesse*,[2] can be met at every turn, stalking abroad like beasts in search of prey; there are the painted and bedizened outcasts who draw their silken skirts scornfully aside from any chance of contact with the soiled and ragged garments worn by the wretched and starving members of the same deplorable sisterhood; and every now and again the flashing of lamps in a passing carriage, containing some redoubtable princess of the *demi-monde*,[3] assures the beholder of the fact

---

[1] One of the chief rivers of France.
[2] French phrase meaning "the nobility."
[3] French term for those engaged in activity of doubtful or twilight legality.

that, however soundly virtue may slumber, vice is awake and rampant. But what am I that I should talk of vice or virtue? What business has a wreck cast on the shores of ruin to concern itself with the distant sailing of the gaudy ships bound for the same disastrous end!

How my brain reels! The hot pavements scorch my tired feet, and the round white moon looks at me from the sky like the foolish ghost of herself in a dream. Street after street I pass, scarcely conscious of sight or sense: I hardly know whither I am bound, and it is by mere mechanical instinct alone that I finally reach my destination.

Home at last! I recognize the dim and dirty alley,—the tumbledown miserable lodging-house in which, of all the wretched rooms it holds, the wretchedest is the garret I call mine. That gaunt cat is always on the doorstep,—always tearing some horrible offal she has found, with claws and teeth—yet savage as hunger has made her, she is afraid of *me*, and bounds stealthily aside and away as I cross the threshold. Two men, my drunken landlord and his no less drunken brother, are quarrelling furiously in the passage; I shrink past them unobserved, and make my way up the dark foul-smelling staircase to my narrow den, where, on entering, I jealously lock myself in, eager to be alone. Alone, alone—always alone! I approach the window and fling it wide open; I rest my arms on the sill and look out drearily at the vast deep star-besprinkled heaven.

They were cruel to me to-night at the *café*, particularly that young curly-haired student. Who is he, and what is he? I hate him, I know not why! except that he reminds me of one who is dead. "Do not drink that," he said gravely, touching the glass I held. "It will drive you mad some day!" Drive me mad! Good, very good! That is what a great many people have told me,—croakers all! Who is mad, and who is sane? It is not easy to decide. The world has various ways of defining insanity in different individuals. The genius who has grand ideas and imagines he can carry them out is "mad;" the priest who, like Saint Damien,[1] sacrifices himself for others is "mad," the hero who, like the English Gordon,[2] perishes at his post instead of running away to save his own skin, is "mad," and only the comfortable tradesman or financier who

---

[1] Corelli probably means Father Damien who was not beatified until 1994. Father Damien went to Moloka'i in Hawaii to care for the patients in a leper settlement where he eventually contracted leprosy. Father Damien is famous for having made an enormous personal sacrifice in his zeal to help those whom no one would help. He died in 1889 and was much in the news when Corelli was working on *Wormwood*.

[2] Charles George Gordon (1833–85). British soldier and colonial administrator renowned for his bravery. He was killed in 1885 during the siege of Khartoum by the Mahdi.

amasses millions by systematically cheating his fellows, is "sane." Excellent! Let me be mad, then, by all means! mad with the madness of *Absinthe*,[1] the wildest, most luxurious madness in the world! *Vive la folie! Vive l'amour! Vive l'animalisme! Vive le Diable!*[2] Live everybody, and everything that *can* live without a conscience, for conscience is at a discount in this age, and honesty cannot keep pace with our modern progress! The times are as we make them; and we have made ours those of realism; the old idyllic days of faith and sentiment are past.

Those cold and quiet stars! What innumerable multitudes of them there are! Why were they created? Through countless centuries bewildered mankind has gazed at them and asked the same question,—a question never to be answered,—a problem never to be solved. The mind soon grows fatigued with pondering. It is better not to think. Yet one good thing has lately come out of the subtle and incessant workings of intellect; and that is that we need not trouble ourselves about God any more. Nothing in all the vast mechanism of the universe can actually prove a Deity to be existent; and no one is called upon to believe in what cannot be proved. I am glad of this, very glad; for if I thought there were a God in heaven—a Supreme Justice enthroned in some far-off Sphere of life unseen yet eternal, I think—I do not know, but I think—I should be afraid! Afraid of the day, afraid of the night; afraid of the glassy river, with its thousands of drowned eyes below; afraid, perchance, of my own hovering shadow; and still more darkly dimly afraid of creatures that might await me in lands invisible beyond the grave—phantom creatures that I have wronged as much and haply more than they in their time wronged me!

Yet, after all, I am a coward; for why should I fear God, supposing a God should, notwithstanding our denial of Him, positively exist? If He is the Author of Creation, He is answerable for every atom within it, even for me. I have done evil. What then? Am I the only one? If I have sinned more, I have also suffered more; and plenty of scientists and physiologists could be found to prove that my faults are those of temperament and brain-construction, and that I cannot help them if I would. Ah, how consoling are these advanced doctrines! No criminal ought, in strict justice, to be punished at all, seeing that it is his inborn nature

---

[1] An extremely strong, bitter anise-tasting alcoholic drink, pale green in colour. It was popular in *fin de siècle* France but was eventually banned in 1915. See the entry on "Absinthe" in the introduction to this edition.

[2] Long live insanity! Long live love! Long live animalism! Long live the Devil!

to commit crime, and that he cannot alter that nature even if he tried! Only a canting priest would dare to ask him to try; and, in France at least, we have done with priestcraft.

Well, we live in a great and wonderful era, and we have great and wonderful needs—needs which must be supplied! One of our chief requirements is that we should know everything—even things that used for honour and decency's sake to be concealed. Wise and pure and beautiful things we have had enough of. They belong to the old classic days of Greece and Rome, the ages of idyll and allegory; and we find them on the whole rather *ennuyant*.[1] We have developed different tastes. We want the ugly truths of life, not the pretty fables. We like ugly truths. We find them piquant and palatable, like the hot sauce poured on fish to give it a flavour. For example, the story of "Paul et Virginie"[2] is very charming, but also very tame and foolish. It suited the literary spirit of the time in which it was written; but to us in the present day there is something far more *entraînant*[3] in a novel which faithfully describes the love-making of Jeanne the washer-woman with Jacques the rag-picker.[4] We prefer their coarse *amours*[5] to Virginie's tearful sentiment—*autres temps, autres moeurs*.[6] I thought of this yesterday, when, strolling aimlessly across the Pont Neuf,[7] I glanced at the various titles of the books for sale on the open-air counters, and saw Realism[8] represented to the last dregs of Reality. And then I began to consider what the story of *my* life would

---

[1] French word for "boring" or "tiresome."

[2] A popular romance by Bernardin de Saint-Pierre first published in 1787 and translated into many languages. It is a sentimental tale which contrasts the beauty and innocence of nature with corrupt society.

[3] French word meaning "engaging."

[4] Corelli is making a general reference here to the subject matter of the French Realist novels of writers like Emile Zola, contrasting these novels which present a more cynical view of humanity with those like *Paul et Virginie* which are more idealistic.

[5] French word meaning "love affairs."

[6] French expression roughly translating as "Other days, other ways."

[7] The oldest bridge in Paris connecting the 1st arrondissment to the Ile de la Cité and the Ile de la Cité to the 6th arrondissment.

[8] Originally a philosophical term denoting that which was opposed to idealism, realism emerged as an important artistic and literary category in the mid-nineteenth century. Literary Realism is concerned with the depiction of everyday, ordinary lives, especially of working-class people and insists on a factual quasi-journalistic approach to its subject matter. In the French tradition, Stendhal, Balzac, Flaubert, and Zola have been described as Realists. In Britain, Realism was most strongly associated with the works of Zola (more properly a Naturalist writer) and many British people, including Corelli, regarded it as a pernicious literary trend. For more on Realism see the entry on "Literary Naturalism and the School of Zola" in the introduction to this edition.

look like when written, and what people would think of it if they read it. This idea has haunted me all last night and to-day. I have turned it over and over again in my mind with a certain savage amusement. Dear old world! dear Society! will you believe me if I tell you what I am? No, I am sure you will not! You will shudder a little, perhaps; but it is far more likely that you will scoff and sneer. It is so easy to make light of a fellow-creature's downfall. Moreover, your critics will assure you that the whole narrative is a tissue of absurd improbabilities, that such and such events never could and never would happen under any sort of circumstances whatever, and that a disordered imagination alone has to do with the weaving of a drama as wild as mine!

But, think what you will, say what you choose, I am resolved you shall know me. It is well you should learn what manner of man is in your midst: a man as pitiless as pestilence, as fierce as flame; one dangerous to himself, and still more dangerous to the community at large; and yet—remember this, I pray you!—a man who is, after all, only one example out of a thousand; a thousand? ay, more than a thousand like him, who in this very city are possessed by the same seductive delirium, and are pressing on swiftly to the same predestined end!

However, my concern is not with others, but solely with myself. I care little for the fact that perhaps nearly half the population of France is with me in my frenzy: what is France to me or I to France, *now*? Time was when I loved my country; when I would have shed every drop of blood in my body gladly for her defence; but now—now,—*enfin!*[1] I see the folly of patriotism; and to speak frankly, I would rather drown like a dog in the Seine than undergo the troublesome fatigues of war. I was not always so indifferent, I confess; I came to it by degrees as others have done, and as others are doing who live as I live. I tell you there are hundreds of men in Paris to-day who are quite as apathetic on the subject of national honour or disgrace as I am,—who, thanks to the pale-green draught we drain in our *cafés* night after night with unabated zest and never-satiated craving, have nigh forgotten their country's bitter defeat,[2]—or if they have not forgotten, have certainly ceased to care. True, they talk,—we all talk,—of taking the Rhine and storming Berlin, just as children babble of their toy castles and tin soldiers, but *we are not in earnest*! No, no! not we! We are wise in our generation, we *absintheurs*;

---

[1]   French word meaning "finally."

[2]   In 1870-71 France and Prussia were at war in the Franco-Prussian war. France suffered a humiliating defeat at the hands of Prussia and was forced to give up Alsace and part of Lorraine.

life is so worthless that we grudge making any sort of exertion to prolong it, and it is probable that if the enemy were at our very doors we should scarcely stir a finger to repel attack. Do the Germans know this, I wonder? Very likely! and, knowing it, bide their time! But let them come. Why not? One authority is as good as another, to me, at any rate,—for I have no prejudices and no principles. The whole wide earth is the same to me,—a mere Grave to bury nations in.

Well! I have done many strange things in my day, and what I choose to do now is perhaps the strangest of all—to write the history of my life and thought; to strip my soul naked, as it were, to the wind of the world's contempt. World's contempt! A bagatelle![1] the world can have no more contempt for me, than I have contempt for the world!

Dear people of Paris, you want Realism, do you not? Realism in art, realism in literature, realism in everything? You, Frenchmen and Frenchwomen, dancing on the edge of your own sepulchre—for the time is coming fast when France will no more be accounted a nation— you want to look at the loathsome worms and unsightly poisonous growths that attend your own decomposition and decay? You want life denuded of all poetical adornment that you may see it as it truly *is*? Well, so you shall, as far as I am concerned! I will hide nothing from you! I will tear out the very fibres of my being and lay them on your modern dissecting-table; nay, I will even assist you in the probing-work of the mental scalpel. Like you, I hate all mysticism and sublime ideal things; we need them as little, or as much, as we need God!

Perhaps it is not often that you chance upon a human subject who is entirely callous? A creature in whose nerves you can thrust your steel hooks of inquisitorial research without his uttering so much as a smoth- ered sob of pain? a being hard as flint, impressionless as adamant, and totally impervious to past, present, or future misery? Yet I am such an one! Perchance you may find me a strange, even an interesting study!

Consider me well! My heart has turned to stone, my brain to fire; I am conscious of no emotion whatever, save an all devouring dreadful curiosity—curiosity to know dark things forbidden to all but madmen,—things that society, afraid of its own wickedness, hastily covers up and hides from the light of day, feebly pretending they have no existence; things that make weak souls shudder and cry and wrestle with their mythical God in useless prayer,—these are the things I love; the things I drag out from the obscure corners and murky recesses of

---

[1]   A trifle.

life, and examine and gloat upon, till I have learnt from them all they can teach me. But I never know enough; search as I may into the minutest details of our complex being, there is always something that escapes me; some link that I lose; some clue that I fancy might explain much that seems incomprehensible. I suppose others have missed this little unnameable something also, and that may be the reason why they have found it necessary to invent a God. But enough! I am here to confess myself, not as a conscience-stricken penitent confesses to a priest, but as a man may confess himself to his fellow-men. Let human nature judge me! I am too proud to make appeal to an unproven Divinity. Already I have passed judgment on myself; what can you say for, or against me, O world, that will alter or strengthen my own self-wrought condemnation and doom? I have lived fast, what then? Is it not the way to die quickly?

CHAPTER 2

It is a familiar business to me, this taking up of the pen and writing down of thought. Long ago, when I was quite a young man, I used to scribble *feuilletons*[1] and stray articles for the Paris papers and gain a few extra francs[2] thereby. Once, too, I wrote a novel,—very high-flown in style and full of romantic sentiment. It was about a girl all innocence, and a man all nobleness, who were interrupted in the progress of their *amours* by the usual sort of villain so useful to the authors of melodrama. I saw the book for sale at a stall near the Palais Royal[3] the other day, and should probably have bought it for mere idle curiosity's sake, but that it cost two francs, and I could not spare the money. I stood and looked at it instead, thinking how droll it was that I should ever have written it! And, little by little, I began to remember what I had been like at that time—the portrait of myself emerged out of the nebulous grey mist that always more or less obscures my vision, and I saw my face as it had appeared in youth,—clear-complexioned, dark-eyed, and smiling—such a face as

---

[1] French term for "serial stories."

[2] A franc is a unit of French money.

[3] Formerly a palace of the royal family, occupied by Louis XIV's brother, the Duke of Orleans. At the time the story is set, the Palais housed the Conseil d'état and was not open to the public but the gardens and the galleries with shops were popular Parisian gathering places.

may be seen more frequently in Provence or Southern Italy than in the streets of Paris; a face that many were complaisant enough to call handsome, and that assuredly by none would have been deemed positively ill-looking. There was a promising intelligence, I believe, in my physiognomy; a certain deceptive earnestness and animation that led my over-sanguine relatives and friends to expect wonders of me—a few enthusiasts expressing their firm (and foolish) conviction that I should be a great man some day. Great! I? I laugh to think of it. I can see my own features as I write, in a cracked and blurred mirror opposite; I note the dim and sunken eyes, the discoloured skin, the dishevelled hair—a villainous reflection truly! I might be sixty from my looks—yet I am barely forty. Hard living? Well no—not what the practised *boulevardier*[1] would understand by that term. I do not frequent places of amusement, I am not the boon companion of ballet-dancers and *café-chanteuses*;[2] I am too poor for that sort of revelry, inasmuch as I can seldom afford to dine. Yet I might have been rich, I might have been respectable, I might even have been famous—imagine it! for I know I once had a few glimmerings of the swift lightning called genius in me, and that my thoughts were not precisely like those of everyday men and women. But chance was against me, chance or fate; both terms are synonymous. Let none talk to me of opposing one's self to fate; that is simply impossible. Fight as we may, we cannot alter an evil destiny, or reverse a lucky one.

Resist temptation! cry the preachers. Very good! but suppose you *cannot* resist? Suppose you see no object whatever in making resistance? For example, point out to me if you can, what use it would be to any one living that I should reform my ways? Not a soul would care! I should starve on just as I starve now, only without any sort of comfort; I should seek help, work, sympathy, and find none; and I should perish in the end just as surely and as friendlessly as I shall perish now. We know how the honest poor are treated in this best of worlds—pushed to the wall and trampled upon to make room for the rich to ride by. We also know what the much-prated-of rewards of virtue are; the grudging thanks and reluctant praise of a few obscure individuals who

---

[1] French term for a frequenter of Parisian boulevards.

[2] Female singers at café-chantants. Café-chantants were places where popular musical entertainment was provided. The Baedeker for Paris of 1889 characterizes these cafés as generally disreputable places: "The music and singing at these establishments ... is never of a high class, while the audience is of a mixed character. The entertainments, however, are often amusing, and sometimes consist of vaudevilles, operettas, and farces" (Karl Baedeker, *Baedeker's Paris and its Environs* 33-34).

make haste to forget you as soon as you are dead; think you that such reward is worth the trouble of winning? In the present advanced condition of things it is really all one whether we are virtuous or vicious, for who cares very much about morality in this age? Morality has always seemed to me such an ambiguous term! I asked my father to define it once, and he answered me thus—

"Morality is a full and sensible recognition of the responsibilities of one's being, and a steadfast obedience to the laws of God and one's country."

Exactly! but how does this definition work, when by the merest chance you discover that you have *no* actual responsibilities, and that it does not matter in the least what becomes of you? Again, that the laws of God and country are drawn up, after much violent dispute and petty wrangling, by a few human individuals nearly, if not quite, as capricious and unreasonable as yourself? What of morality, then? Does it not resolve itself into a myth, like the Creed the churches live by?

A truce, I say, to such fair-seeming hypocritical shows of good, in a world which is evil to its very core! Let us know ourselves truly for what we are; let us not deceive our minds with phantasms of what we cannot be. We are mere animals—we shall never be angels—neither here nor hereafter. As for me, I have done with romances; love, friendship, ambition, fame; in past days it is true I set some store by these airy cheats—these vaporous visions; but now—now they count to me as naught, I possess a dearer joy, more real, more lasting than them all!

Would you learn what thing it is that holds me, wretched as I seem, to life? what link binds my frail body and frailer soul together? and why, with no friends and no fortune, I still contrive to beat back death as long as possible? Would you know the single craving of my blood—the craving that burns in me more fiercely than hunger in a starving beast of prey—the one desire, to gratify which I would desperately dare and defy all men? Listen, then! A nectar, bitter-sweet—like the last kiss on the lips of a discarded mistress—is the secret charm of my existence; green as the moon's light on a forest pool it glimmers in my glass!— eagerly I quaff it, and, as I drink, I dream! Not of foolish things. No! Not of dull saints and smooth landscapes in heaven and wearisome prudish maids; but of glittering bacchantes, nude nymphs in a dance of hell, flashing torrents and dazzling mountain-peaks, of storm and terror, of lightning and rain, of horses galloping, of flags flying, of armies marching, of haste and uproar and confusion and death! Aye! even at times I have heard the trumpets blare on the field of battle, and the shout "*La revanche! la revanche!*"[1] echoing wildly in my ears; and I have waded deep in the blood of our enemies, and wrested back from their grasp Alsace-Lorraine!...

Ah, fool that I am! What! raving again? I torture myself with absurd delusions; did I not but lately say I loved France no longer?... France! Do I *not* love thee? Not now! Oh, not now let my words be accepted concerning thee; not now, but later on, when this heavy weight is lifted from my heart; when this hot pulsation is stilled in my brain; when the bonds of living are cut asunder and I wander released, a shadow among shades; then, it may be, I shall find tears to shed: tears of passionate tenderness and wild remorse above thy grave, poor France, thou beaten and discrowned fair empress of nations; thou whom I, and others such as I am, might yet help to rescue and re-invest with glory if—if only we could be roused—roused to swift action in time, before it is too late!...

There! the agony is over, and I am calm once more. I do not often yield to my own fancies; I know their power, how they drag at me, and strive to seize and possess me with regrets for the past; but they shall not succeed. No wise man stops to consider his by-gone possibilities. The land of Might-Have-Been is, after all, nothing but a blurred prospect; a sort of dim and distant landscape, where the dull clouds rain perpetual tears!

Of course the beginning of my history is—love. It is the beginning of every man and every woman's history, if they are only frank enough to admit it. Before that period, life is a mere series of smooth and small events, monotonously agreeable or disagreeable, according to our surroundings, a time in which we learn a few useful things and a great many useless ones, and are for the most part in a half-awakened pleasing state of uncertainty and wonder about the world in general. Love lights upon us suddenly like a flame, and lo! we are transformed; we are for the first time alive, and conscious of our beating pulses, our warm and hurrying blood; we feel; we know; we gain a wisdom wider and sweeter than any to be found in books, and we climb step by step up the height of ecstasy, till we stand in so lofty an altitude that we seem to ourselves to dominate both earth and heaven! It is only a fool's paradise we stumble into, after all; but, then, everything is more or less foolish in this world; if we wish to avoid folly we must seek a different planet.

---

[1]   "Revenge! Revenge!" The battle-cry of the French who sought vengeance on Germany and who wanted to reclaim Alsace-Lorraine, which the French had lost in the Franco-Prussian war.

Let me think; where did I see her first? At her mother's house, it must have been. Yes! the picture floats back to me across a hazy sea of memories, and suspends itself, mirage-like, before my half-bewildered gaze. She had just returned to Paris from her school at Lausanne in Switzerland. The Swiss wild-roses had left their delicate hues on her cheeks, the Alpine blue gentians had lost their little hearts in her eyes. She was dressed that night in quaint Empire fashion—a simple garb of purest white silk, with a broad sash drawn closely under the bosom—her rich curls of dark brown hair were caught up in high masses and tied with a golden ribbon. A small party was being held in honour of her home-coming. Her father, the Comte de Charmilles, a stern old royalist[1] whose allegiance to the Orleans family was only equalled by his fanatical devotion to the Church, led her through the rooms leaning gracefully on his arm, and formally introduced her, in his stately old-fashioned way, to all the guests assembled. I was among the last of these, yet not the least, for my father and the Comte had been friends from boyhood, and there was an especially marked kindness in his voice and manner, when, pausing at my side, he thus addressed me—

"Monsieur Beauvais, permit me to present to you my daughter Pauline. Pauline, my child, this is M. Gaston Beauvais, the son of our excellent friend M. Charles Beauvais, the banker, who has the beautiful house at Neuilly,[2] and who used to give thee so many *marrons glacés*[3] when thou wert a small, dear, greedy baby; dost thou remember?"

A charming smile parted her lovely lips, and she returned my profound bow with the prettiest sweeping curtsey imaginable.

"*Hélas!*"[4] she said, playfully, shrugging her shoulders. "I must confess that the days of the *marrons glacés* are not yet past! I am a greedy baby still, am I not, my good papa? Can you believe it, Monsieur Beauvais, those *marrons glacés* were the first luxuries I asked for when I came home! they are so good! everything is so good in Paris! My dear, beautiful Paris! I am so glad to be back again! You cannot imagine how dull it is at Lausanne! A pretty place? Oh yes! but so very dull! There are no good *bon-bons*, no *délices*[5] of any kind, and the people are so stupid they do not even know how to make an *éclair*[6] properly! Ah, how I used to

---

[1] A supporter of the restoration of the French monarchy and also often supporters of the Catholic church.
[2] Suburb of Paris, north of the Bois de Boulogne.
[3] French for "sugar-coated chestnuts."
[4] French expression meaning "Alas."
[5] French for "delights."
[6] A finger-shaped pastry made with chocolate and cream.

long for *éclairs*! I saw some, one afternoon, in a little shop-window, and went in to try what they were like; *mon Dieu!*[1] they were so very bad, they tasted of cheese! Yes, truly! so many things in Switzerland taste of cheese, I think! *Par exemple,*[2] have you ever been to Vevey? No? ah! when you do go there, you will taste cheese in the very air!"

She laughed, and heaved a comical little sigh over the one serious inconvenience and unforgettable disadvantage of her past school-life, namely, the lack of delectable *éclairs* and *marrons glacés*, while I, who had been absorbed in a fascinated study of her eyes, her hair, her pretty figure, her small hand that every now and then waved a white fan to and fro with a lazy grace that reminded me of the flashing of a sea-bird's pinion, thought to myself what a mere child she was for all the dignity of her eighteen years, a child as innocent and fresh as a flower just bursting into bloom, with no knowledge of the world into which she was entering, and with certainly no idea of the power of her own beauty to rouse the passions of men. I listened to her soft and trifling chatter with far deeper interest than I should probably have felt in the conversation of the most astute diplomast[3] or learned philosopher, and as soon as I saw my opportunity I made haste to offer her my arm, first, however, as in duty bound, glancing expressively at her father for permission to do so—permission which he instantly and smilingly accorded. Old fool! why did he throw us together? Why did he not place obstacles in the way of our intercourse? Because, royalist and devotee as he was, he understood the practical side of life as well, if not better than any shrewd republican[4] going; he knew that my father was rich, and that I was his only heir, and he laid his plans accordingly. He was like all French fathers; yet why should I specify French fathers so particularly? English fathers are the same; all fathers of all nations nowadays look to the practical-utility advantages of marriage for their children—and quite right too! One cannot live on air-bubbles of sentiment.

Pauline de Charmilles was not a shy girl, but by this I do not mean it to be in the least imagined that she was bold. On the contrary, she had

[1] French for "My God."
[2] French phrase meaning "for example."
[3] Possibly Corelli means "diplomat" or "diplomatist."
[4] French Republicans of the nineteenth century supported the idea of France as a democratic republic. Unlike Royalists, Republicans were opposed to the monarchy as well as to the Catholic clergy of France whom they believed possessed too much political power. France was a republic at the time the events of the novel take place. France had rid itself of its last monarch in 1871 at the end of the Franco-Prussian war, establishing the Third Republic which lasted until World War II.

merely that quick brightness and *esprit*[1] which is the happy heritage of so many Frenchwomen, none of whom think it necessary to practice or assume the chilly touch-me-not diffidence and unbecoming constraint which makes the young English "*mees*" such a tame and tiresome companion to men of sense and humour. She was soon perfectly at her ease with me, and became prettily garrulous and confidential, telling me stories of her life at Lausanne, describing the loveliness of the scenery on Lake Leman, and drawing word-portraits of her teachers and school-mates, with a facile directness and point that brought them at once before the mind's eye as though they were actually present. We sat together for some time on a window-seat from which we could command a charm-ing little glimpse of the Bois de Boulogne,[2] for M. de Charmilles would not live far away from this, his favourite promenade in all weathers, and talked of many things, particularly of life in Paris, and the gaieties that were foretold for the approaching winter season. Réunions,[3] balls, recep-tions, operas, theatres, all such festivities as these, this ingenuous worship-per of the "*marron glacé*" looked forward to with singular vivacity, and it was only after she had babbled sweetly about fashion and society for several minutes that she suddenly turned upon me with a marvellously brilliant penetrating glance of her dark blue eyes, a glance such as I after-wards found out was common to her, but which then startled me as much as an unexpected flash of lightning might have done, and said—

"And you? What are *you* going to do? How do you amuse yourself?"

"Mademoiselle, I work!"

"Ah yes! You are in your father's business."

"I am his partner."

"You have difficult things to think about? You labour *all* the day?"

I laughed—she looked so charmingly compassionate.

"No, not *all* the day, but for several hours of it. We are bankers, you know; and the taking charge of other people's money, mademoiselle, is a very serious business!"

"Oh, that I can quite imagine! But you must rest sometimes,—you must visit your friends and be gay—is it not so?"

"Assuredly! But perhaps I do not take my rest precisely like other people,—I read a great deal, and I write also,—occasionally."

---

[1] French word for "sprightliness" or "wit."

[2] Park area in Paris bordered by the fortifications of Paris on the East, the Seine on the West, Boulogne and the Boulevard d'Auteuil on the South, and Neuilly on the North. It was a popular and fashionable promenade for Parisians.

[3] French word for "parties."

"Books?" she exclaimed, her lovely eyes opening wide with eager interest. "You write books?"

"I *have* written one or two," I admitted modestly.

"Oh, *do* tell me the titles of them!" she entreated. "I shall be so interested! I read every story I can get hold of, especially love-stories, you know! I *adore* love stories! I always cry over them, and——"

Here our conversation was abruptly broken off. Madame la Comtesse de Charmilles, a dignified *grande dame*[1] clad in richest black silk, with diamonds gleaming here and there upon her handsome person, sailed up to us from a remote corner of the room where she had no doubt been watching us with the speculative observation of the match-making matron, and said—

"Pauline, my child, the Marquis de Guiscard desires the honour of taking you in to supper. Monsieur Beauvais will have the amiability to escort your cousin. My niece, Mademoiselle St. Cyr—Monsieur Gaston Beauvais." And thereupon she presented me to a pale serious-looking girl, who merely acknowledged my formal salute by the slightest perceptible bend of her head, and whom I scarcely glanced at, so great was my chagrin to see the fascinating Pauline carried off on the arm of De Guiscard, a battered beau of sixty, grizzled as a bear, and wrinkled as old parchment. I suppose my vexation was distinctly visible in my face, for Madame de Charmilles smiled a little as she saw me march stiffly past her into the supper-room, without condescending to say a word to my pale partner, whom I considered at the moment positively ugly. To my comfort, however, I found Pauline seated next to me at table, and I made amends for my previous disappointment by conversing with her all the time, to the complete vanquishment and discomfiture of old De Guiscard. Not that he really cared, I think, seeing he was so entirely absorbed in eating. We talked of books and pictures. I sought and obtained the permission to send her two of my own literary productions, the two which I myself judged as my best efforts; one a critical study of Alfred de Musset,[2] the other the high-flown sentimental novel before mentioned, which at that time had only just been published. I spoke to her of the great geniuses reigning in the musical world—of the unrivalled Sarasate,[3] of Rubinstein,[4] of Verdi,[5] of the child-pianist, Otto

---

[1]   French term for a "great lady."

[2]   French Romantic poet, novelist, and dramatist (1810-57).

[3]   Pablo Martin Meliton de Sarasate y Navescues, Spanish violinist (1844-1908).

[4]   Anton Grigorovich Rubinstein, Russian pianist (1829-94).

[5]   Guiseppe Fortunino Francesco Verdi, Italian composer (1813-1901).

Hegner;[1] then, skimming down from the empyrean of music to the lower level of the histrionic art, I described to her the various qualities of talent displayed by the several actors and actresses who were ranked among the most popular of the passing hour. And so we chatted on, happily engrossed with one another, and forgetful of all else. As for the pale cousin, whose name I afterwards learned was Héloïse, I never gave her a second thought. She sat on the other side of me, and that was all I knew of her *then*; but afterwards!——No matter! she is dead, quite dead, and I only dream I see her still!

The hours fled by on golden wings, and before that evening ended—before I pressed her two small white hands in my own at parting, I felt that I *loved* Pauline de Charmilles—loved her as I should never love any other woman. An overwhelming passion seized me; I was no longer master of my own destiny; Pauline was my fate. What was her fascination? How was it that she, a girl fresh from school, a mere baby in thought, fond of *bon-bons* and foolish trifles, should suddenly ravish my soul by surprise and enslave and dominate it utterly? I cannot tell; put the question to the physiologists and scientists who explain everything, and they will answer you. She was beautiful—that I can positively affirm, for I have studied every detail of her loveliness as few could have done. And I suppose her beauty allured me. Men never fall in love at first with a woman's mind; only with her body. They may learn to admire the mind afterwards, if it prove worth admiration, but it is always a secondary thing. This may be called a rough truth, but it is true for all that. Who marries a woman of intellect by choice? No one, and if some unhappy man does it by accident, he generally regrets it. A stupid beauty is the most comfortable sort of housekeeper going, believe me—she will be strict with the children, scold the servants, and make herself look as ornamental as she can, till age and fat render ornament superfluous. But a woman of genius, with that strange subtle attraction about her which is yet not actual beauty,—she is the person to be avoided if you would have peace; if you would escape reproach; if you would elude the fixed and melancholy watchfulness of a pair of eyes haunting you in the night. Eyes such I see always—always, and shudderingly wonder at!—eyes full of unshed tears—will those tears never fall?—large, soft, serious eyes, like those of Pauline's pale cousin Héloïse!

---

[1] Swiss child prodigy of the piano (1876-1907).

CHAPTER 3

I may as well speak of this woman Héloïse St. Cyr, before I go on any further. I say this woman; I could never call her a girl, though she was young enough—only twenty. But she was so pale and quiet, and so concentrated within the mystic circle of her own thoughts, that she never seemed to me like others of her sex and age. At first I took a strong dislike to her; she had such fair bright hair, and I hated golden-haired women. I suppose this was because writers—poets especially—have sung their praises of golden hair till the world is wearied,—and also because so many females of the *demi-monde* have dyed their coarse tresses to such hideous straw-tints in order to be in accordance with the prevailing fashion and sentiment. However, the abundant locks of Héloïse were, in their way, of a matchless hue; a singularly pale gold, brightening here and there into flecks of reddish auburn close to the smooth nape of her neck, where they grew in soft small curls like the delicate fluff under a young bird's wing. I often caught myself staring at these little warm rings of sun-colour on the milky whiteness of her skin, when she sat in a window-corner apart from myself and Pauline, reading some great volume of history or poetry, entirely absorbed, and apparently unconscious of our presence. Her uncle told me she was a wonderful scholar; that she had numberless romances in her head, and all the poets in her heart. I remember I thought at the time that he was exaggerating her gifts out of mere affectionate *complaisance*,[1] for I never quite believed in woman's real aptitude for learning. I could quite understand a certain surface-brilliancy of attainment in the female mind, but I would never admit that such knowledge went deep enough to last. I was mistaken of course; since then I have realized that a woman's genius if great and true, equals and often surpasses that of the most gifted man. I used however to look upon Héloïse St. Cyr with a certain condescension, only allowing her, in my opinion, to be about one degree in advance beyond the ordinary feminine intelligence. I had, as I said, a vague dislike to her, which was not lessened when, after reading my novel—*the* novel I was so proud of having written—she smiled at the woes of my sentimental heroine, and told me very gently that I did not yet understand women. Not understand women! I, a born and bred Parisian of five-and-twenty! Absurd! Now Pauline "adored" my book. She read and re-read it many times, and I gave her much more credit for

---

[1]   French word for "obligingness."

good taste in literature than the pale woman-student who was for ever mooning over Homer and Plato.[1] I could not understand Pauline's almost passionate reverence for this quiet, sad-eyed cousin of hers—never were two creatures more utterly opposed to each other in character and sentiment. But, strange to say, love for Héloïse seemed the one really serious part of Pauline's nature, while Héloïse's affection for her, though not so openly displayed, was evidently strong and deeply rooted. Mademoiselle St. Cyr was poor, so I understood; her parents resided in some obscure town in Normandy, and had hard work to keep a decent roof above their heads, for which reason the Comtesse de Charmilles had undertaken the care of this eldest girl of her brother's family, promising to do her best for her, and, if possible, to marry her well. But Héloïse showed no inclination for marriage; she was dull and *distraite*[2] in the company of men, and seemed bored by their conversation rather than pleased. Nevertheless, she possessed her own fascination: what it was I never could see, not *then*— a fascination sufficient to win the devoted attachment of both her aunt and uncle, to whom she became a positive necessity in the household. I soon found out that nothing was done without Héloïse being first consulted,—that in any domestic difficulty or *contretemps*,[3] everybody washed their hands of trouble and transferred it to Héloïse; that when her uncle, to gratify his extreme love of fresh air and exercise, cantered into the Bois[4] every morning at six o'clock, she rode with him on a spirited mare that the very groom was afraid of; that *she* put the finishing touches to her aunt's toilette and tied the last little decorative knot of ribbon in Pauline's luxuriant hair, and that she was generally useful to every one. This fact of itself made me consider her with a sort of faint contempt;— practical-utility persons were never attractive to me, though I reluctantly owned the advisability of their existence. And then I never half believed what I heard about her; her talents and virtues seemed to me to be always over-rated. *I* never saw her occupied otherwise than with a book. She was for ever reading,—she was, I decided, going to develop herself into a "femme savante,"[5] a character I detested. So I paid her very little attention, and when I did speak to her on any subject it was always with that particularly condescending carelessness which a wise man of five-and-

---

[1] Homer, an Ionian poet, author of the famous epic tales the *Iliad* and the *Odyssey*; Plato (c. 427–c. 338), Greek philosopher and prose writer.

[2] French word for "distracted" or "inattentive."

[3] French word for "mishap."

[4] Bois de Boulogne.

[5] French phrase meaning "learned woman."

twenty who has written books, may bestow on a vastly inferior type of humanity.

In a very short time I became a frequent and intimate visitor at the house of the De Charmilles, and my intentions there were pretty well guessed by all the members of the family. Nothing to the purport of marriage, however, had yet been said. I had not even dared to whisper to Pauline my growing love for her. I was aware of her father's old-fashioned sentiments on etiquette, and knew that in strict accordance with what he deemed honour, I was bound, before paying any serious addresses to his daughter, to go through the formality of asking his permission. But I was in no hurry to do this; it was a sufficient delight to me for the present to see my heart's enchantress occasionally, to bring her flowers or *bon-bons*, to hear her sing and play—for she was a graceful proficient in music—and to make one of the family party at supper, and argue politics good-humouredly with the old Royalist Count, whose contempt for the Republic was beyond all bounds, and who was anxious to convert me to his way of thinking. Often on these occasions my father, an excellent man, though apt to be rather prosy when he yielded to his weakness for telling anecdotes, would join us, bringing with him one of his special friends, the little fat Curé[1] of our parish, whose *bon-mots*[2] were prover-bial; and many a pleasant evening we passed all together, seated round the large table in the oak-panelled dining-room, from whose walls the stiffly painted portraits of the ancestral De Charmilles seemed to frown or smile upon us, according to the way in which the lamp-light flickered or fell. And as the days flew on and November began to rustle by in a shroud of dead autumn leaves, it seemed to my adoring eyes that Pauline grew love-lier than ever. Her gaiety increased; she invested herself with a thousand new fascinations, a thousand fresh coquetries. Every dress she wore appeared to become her more perfectly than the last. She fluttered here and there like a beautiful butterfly in a garden of roses, and I, who had loved her half-timidly before, now grew mad for her! mad with a passion of longing that I could hardly restrain—a passion that consumed me hotly like a fever and would scarcely let me sleep. Whenever I fell, out of the sheer exhaustion of my thoughts, into a restless slumber, I saw her in my dreams—a flitting, dancing sylph on rainbow-coloured clouds—her voice rang in my ears, her arms would wave and beckon me. "Pauline! Pauline!" I would cry aloud, and, starting from my pillow, I would rise and pace

---

[1] Term for a parish priest in France.
[2] French term for "witticisms."

my room to and fro, to and fro, like a chafing prisoner in a cell till morning dawned. During all this self-torment which I half enjoyed, it being a more delicious than painful experience, I might have spoken to the Comte de Charmilles; but I refrained, determining to wait till after the feast of Noël. I was sure of his consent. I felt convinced that he and my father had already spoken together on the subject, and as for Pauline herself—ah! if looks had eloquence, if the secret pressure of a hand, the sudden smile, the quick blush, meant anything at all, then surely she loved me! There were no obstacles in the way of our union, and it was impossible to invent any; all was smooth sailing, fair skies above, calm seas below; and we, out of all the people in the world, should probably be the happiest living. So I thought; and I made many pleasant plans, never considering for a moment how foolish it is to make plans beforehand for anything; but, remember, I was very young, and Héloïse St. Cyr was quite right when she said I did not yet understand women.

We lived alone, my father and I, at Neuilly, in a large old quaint mansion, part of which had been standing at the time of the famous Reign of Terror.[1] The rooms were full of antique furniture such as would have been the joy of connoisseurs, and everything, even to the smallest trifle, was kept in the exact order in which my mother had left it seventeen years previously, when she died giving birth to a girl-child who survived her but a few hours. One of the earliest impressions of my life is that of the hush of death in the house, the soft stepping to and fro of the servants, the drawn blinds, the smell of incense and burning candles; and I remember how, with a beating heart, I, as a little fellow, stopped outside the door of the closed room and whispered, "*Maman! petite maman!*"[2] in a voice rendered so weak by fright that I myself could scarcely hear it. And then, how, on a sudden impulse, I entered the mysteriously darkened chamber and saw a strange, white, beautiful figure lying on the bed with lilies in its hair, a figure that held encircled in one arm a tiny waxen creature that looked as pretty and gentle as the little Jésus in the church *crèche*[3] at Christmas-time; and how, after staring at this sight bewildered for a minute's space, I became aware of my father kneeling at the bedside, his strong frame shaken with such convulsive sobs as were terrible to hear; so terrible, that I, breaking into childish

---

[1] Extremely violent period of the French Revolution lasting from 1793 to 1794.

[2] "Petite," the French for "little" can also be used as a term of affection meaning "dear," as is done here.

[3] Model of the manger scene at Bethlehem.

wailing, fled to his arms for shelter, and stayed there shuddering, clasped to his heart and feeling his hot tears raining on my hair. That was a long, long while ago! It is odd that I should recollect every detail of that scene so well at this distance of time!

I have said that my father had a special friend with whom he loved to talk and argue on all the political and philosophical questions that came up for discussion, namely, Monsieur Vaudron, the Curé of our parish. He was a good man—perfectly unaffected, simple-hearted, and *honest*. Imagine, an honest priest! It is a sufficient rarity in France. He was in earnest, too. He believed in Our Lady[1] and his patron saint with unflinching fervour and tenacity. It was no use bringing the heavy batteries of advanced science to storm *his* little citadel. He stood firm.

"Talk as you will," he would say, "there is always something left that you cannot understand. No! neither you nor M. Renan,[2] nor any other overwise theorist living, and for me that Something is Everything. When you can explain away that little inexplicable—why then, who knows!—I may go as far and even further than any heretic of the age"—here he would smile and rub his hands complacently—"but *till* then———" An expressive gesture would complete the sentence, and both my father and I liked and respected him too well to carry on any ultra-positive views on religion in his presence.

One evening late in November, M. Vaudron called upon us, as it was often his custom to do, after supper, with an expression of countenance that betokened some vexation and anxiety.

"To speak truly, I am worried," he said at last, in answer to my father's repeated inquiries as to whether anything was wrong with him. "And I am full of uncomfortable doubts and presentiments. I am to have an unexpected addition to my poor household in the person of my nephew, who is studying to be a priest. You never heard of my nephew? No. I never thought I should have occasion to speak of him. He is the only son of my only sister, who married a respectable, somewhat wealthy farmer possessing house and lands in Brittany.[3] They settled in that province, and have never left it; and this boy—I suppose he must be about twenty-two—has seen no other city larger than the town of

---

[1]   Term for the Virgin Mary.

[2]   Ernest Renan (1823-92). French critic and writer. Renan was a relativist, believing that no one system of scientific, religious, or historical knowledge could lay claim to absolute truth.

[3]   Northern province and duchy of France. Bretons are a Celtic people whose ancestors came over from Britain in the fifth and sixth centuries. Bretons have their own distinctive customs and language—*Brezhoneg* or Breton.

Rennes,[1] where he began and has since carried on his studies. Now, his parents wish him to see Paris, and continue his probation with me; this is all very well, but you know how I live, and you can imagine how my old Margot will look upon such an unexpected invasion!"

We smiled. Margot was the good Curé's cook, housekeeper, and domestic tyrant; a withered little woman, something like a dried apple, one of those apples that you have to cut into pretty deeply before you find the sweetness that lurks at its core. She had a sharp tongue, too, had Margot, and however much the Curé might believe in his priestly power to exorcise the devil, it was certain he could never exorcise his old cook's love of scolding out of her. He was ludicrously afraid of her wrath, and he surveyed us now as he spoke with a most whimsical air of timidity and supplication.

"You see, *mon ami*,"[2] he continued, addressing my father who, smoking comfortably, glanced at him with a keen yet friendly amusement, "this nephew, whom I do not know, may be troublesome."

"Assuredly he may!" agreed my father solemnly, yet with a twinkle in his eye. "Young men are proverbially difficult to manage."

"They are—they are! I am sure of that!" and the Curé shook his head in a desponding manner. "But still I cannot refuse the request of my only sister, the first request she has ever made of me since her marriage! Besides, if I would refuse, it is too late; the boy is on his way—he will be here to-morrow, and I must break the news somehow to Margot; it will be difficult—*mon Dieu!* it will be very difficult!—but it must be done!"

And he heaved such a profound sigh, that I, who had been glancing up and down the flimsy columns of the "Petit Journal,"[3] to avoid interrupting the conversation of my elders, suddenly gave way to irresistible laughter. My merriment was contagious; the picture of M. Vaudron trembling like an aspen-leaf before the little waspish Margot, and faltering forth the news that henceforth, for a time at least, she would have to wait upon two men instead of one, and proffering his mild apologies for the same, struck us all with an overwhelming sense of the ridiculous, even the Curé himself, whose laughter was as loud and long as my father's or mine.

"Ah well!" he said at last, wiping away the drops of mirth from his eyes. "I know I am an old fool, and that I allow Margot to have her own way a little too much—but then she is a good soul, a very good soul!

---

[1] Town in Brittany.
[2] French for "my friend."
[3] Popular French daily newspaper.

and truly she takes care of me as I never could take care of myself. And how well she washes the church linen! Could anything be more spotlessly white and fit for holy service! She is an excellent woman—I assure you, excellent! but regarding this nephew——"

"Ah, that is a serious question!" murmured my father, who seemed mischievously determined not to help him out with any solution of his difficulty. "He is coming, you say, to-morrow?"

"He is—he is, without a doubt!" replied poor M. Vaudron, with another forlorn shake of his head. "And as he will probably arrive before noon, there is very little time to prepare Margot for his arrival. You see I would not wish to blame my good sister for the world, but I think—I *think* she has been a little hasty in this matter. She has given me no chance of refusal, not that I could have refused her, but I might have arranged better, had more time been given me. However, I suppose I must do my utmost for the boy."

Here he broke off and rubbed his nose perplexedly.

"What is he like, this nephew of yours?" I put in suddenly. "Have you any idea?"

"Truly, not much," he replied thoughtfully. "I never saw him but once, and then he was only three years old, a fine child, if I remember rightly. If one is to believe in his mother's description of him (but that, of course, cannot be done) he is an intellectual marvel; a positive prodigy of good looks and wisdom combined; there never was such a youth born into this planet before, according to her account, poor dear soul! Ah! good mothers are all alike; God has made their hearts the tenderest in the world!"

My father sighed a little. I knew he was thinking of the dead; of his fair lost love, with whom had perished all mother's tenderness for me, at any rate. He rose, knocked the ashes out of his pipe and put it by, then looked round with a smile at the still perplexed and musing Curé.

"Come, *mon cher!*"[1] he said cheerfully, "I know what you want as well as possible! You want me to go round with you and help smooth this affair over with your old Margot. Is it not so? Speak truly!"

"Ah, *mon ami!*" cried poor M. Vaudron, rising from his chair in an ecstasy. "If you would but do me this favour! She will listen to you! she has the profoundest admiration for you, and she will understand reason from your lips! You really will accompany me? ah, what it is to have so excellent a friend! I shall owe you a thousand obligations for

---

[1] French for "my dear."

this kindness! there will no longer be any difficulty, and I shall be once more at ease! But you are sure it is no trouble?"

While he thus spoke, my father had stepped into the hall and put on his coat and hat, and he now stood equipped for walking, his stalwart form and refined, rather melancholy face, offering a great contrast to the round dumpy figure and plump clean-shaven countenance of the good little Curé.

"*Allons!*"[1] he said mirthfully. "We will start before it grows any later, and take Madame Margot by surprise. She is in love with me, that old Margot of thine! I warn thee, Vaudron, that she has designs upon me! She will need one of thy exordiums after mass next Sunday; for I will so confuse her with compliments on her house-management, and on the excellent way in which she will certainly purpose attending to thy nephew, that she will almost believe herself to be young and marriage-able once more!"

He laughed, so did the Curé, and they prepared to leave the house together. I accompanied them to the street-door, and on the threshold my father turned round to me, saying—

"Amuse thyself well, Gaston! Art thou going to see the pretty Pauline this evening?"

The hot colour surged to my brows; but I made a pretence of indifference, and answered in the negative.

"Ah well! One night more or less in the week, will not make much difference to thy feelings, or to hers. See, what a bright moon! Thou canst play Romeo with real scenery; is there no balcony to thy Juliet's window?"

And with this sort of *badinage*,[2] mingled with laughter, the two elderly gentlemen descended the steps, and crossing the road arm-in-arm were soon lost to sight in an opposite avenue of trees. I stayed a minute or two at the open door, looking after them, and puffing slowly at my half-finished cigarette. They knew—they guessed, my love for Pauline; it was probable every one knew or guessed it. I might as well speak openly and at once to the Comte de Charmilles; why not to-morrow? Yes, to-morrow! I resolved I would do so. And to-morrow then,—ah, God!—I should be free to clasp my darling in my arms unre-proved, to tell her how I had thought of her every minute of the day and night; how I adored her; how I worshipped her; I should be allowed to kiss those soft sweet lips, and touch those lovely curls of loose brown

---

[1] French word meaning "let's go."
[2] French for "banter."

hair! she would be mine, betrothed to me! The very thought made me tremble with my own eagerness and ecstasy, and, to calm myself, I went abruptly indoors, and began to busy my brain with certain financial calculations and reports which demanded the closest attention. And while I was thus engaged, softly whistling a tune as I worked for pure lightness of heart, the moon soared high up like a great beacon, flooding the room in which I sat, with strange ghostly beams of silver and green, one green ray falling right across the paper on which I was scribbling, and shining with such a conspicuous brilliancy that it almost dimmed the brightness of the lit lamp over my head. I stopped writing to look at it; it flickered with a liquid pale radiance like the lustre of an emerald, or *the colour of absinthe.* It moved away after a while, and I went on with my work. But I well remember the weird, almost spectral loveliness of the skies that night, the weather was so calm and frostily clear. When my father came back in about an hour's time, after having been triumphantly successful as intermediator between the Curé and his old Margot, he remarked to me, as we went upstairs to our bedrooms—

"The unexpected nephew of M. Vaudron will have fine weather for his journey!"

"Excellent!" I agreed, stifling a yawn, for I was rather sleepy. "By the way, what is the unexpected nephew's name?"

"Silvion Guidèl."

I stopped on the stairs.

"Silvion Guidèl! A strange name, surely?"

"It sounds strange, yes! but 'Guidèl' is an old Brittany name, so Vaudron tells me; 'Silvion' is certainly not so common as 'Sylvain,' yet they are very nearly alike."

"True!" and I said no more. But I thought several times, at odd waking moments during the night, of that name—Silvion Guidèl—and wondered what sort of being he was that bore it. He was studying to be a priest, so it was not likely that *I* should see much of him. However, a curious sense of irritation grew up in me that this fellow from Brittany should be coming to Paris at all. I disliked him already, even while admitting to myself that such a dislike was altogether foolish and unreasonable. And the name, 'Silvion Guidèl' haunted me then, even as it haunts me now; only *then* it suggested nothing, save a faint inexplicable sense of aversion; but *now?*—now it is written before me in letters of fire! it stares at me from every clear blank space of wall, it writes itself beneath my feet on the ground, and above me in the heavens; I never lose the accursed sight of it!—I never shall!—never, never! until I die!

CHAPTER 4

The next day I carried out my previous night's resolution to ask the Comte de Charmilles for his daughter's hand in marriage. As I expected, I was met with entire favour, and when I left the old aristocrat's library, after about an hour's satisfactory conversation, I had his full parental permission to go straightway to Pauline and tell her of my passion. How my heart beat, how my pulses galloped, as I stepped swiftly along the corridor in search of my soul's idol! She usually sat with her cousin in a small boudoir fronting on the garden; and she was generally at home at this early hour of the afternoon; but for once I could not find her. Where was she, I wondered? Perhaps in the large drawing-room, though she seldom went there, that apartment being only used occasionally for the reception of visitors. However, I turned in that direction, and was just crossing the passage, when I was brought to an abrupt stand-still by the sound of music; such music as might have been played by Orpheus to charm his lost bride out of hell.[1] I listened amazed and entranced; it was a violin that discoursed such wild melody; some one was playing it with so much *verve* and fire and feeling, that it seemed as though every throbbing note were a burning thing alive, with wings to carry it to and fro in the air for ever. I pushed open the door of the drawing-room suddenly, and stared at its solitary inmate dumfounded; why, it was that pale and quiet Héloïse St. Cyr who stood there, her bow lifted, her features alit with enthusiasm, her bright hair ruffled, and her large eyes ablaze! What a face! what an attitude! she was actually beautiful, this woman, and I had never perceived it before! When she saw me she started; then, in a moment, regained her self-possession, laid down her bow, and, still holding the violin, advanced a little.

"You want Pauline?" she asked, slightly smiling. "She will be down directly. She is upstairs changing her dress; she and my aunt have just returned from a drive in the Bois—they found it very cold."

I looked at her, feeling stupid and tongue-tied. I wanted to say something about her marvellous playing, but at the moment could find no words. Her eyes met mine steadily, the faint smile still lurking in their clear depths, and after a brief pause she spoke again.

---

[1] In Greek mythology, the musician husband of Eurydice who descended to Hades to recover her after her death. He charmed Dis and Persephone with his music in order to induce them to allow Eurydice to leave Hades.

"I was practising." And placing the violin against her slim white throat, she ran her fingers dumbly up and down the strings. "I seldom have the chance of a couple of hours all to myself, but this afternoon I managed to escape from the drive. My aunt went to call at the house of M. Vaudron, in order to leave her card for his nephew, who has just arrived."

I was considerably surprised at this, and very quickly found voice to remonstrate.

"Surely Madame la Comtesse has been almost too courteous in this regard?" I said. "The young man is a perfect stranger, the mere son of a farmer in Brittany——"

"*Pardon!*"[1] interrupted Héloïse. "He is already highly distinguished for learning and scholarship, and a special letter of introduction and recommendation concerning him came by last night's post for my uncle from the Prior of St. Xavier's monastery at Rennes. The Prior is one of my uncle's dearest and oldest friends, thus, you see, it is quite *en règle*[2] that this Monsieur Guidèl should receive his first welcome from the house of De Charmilles."

Again she ran her delicate fingers up and down the strings of her violin, and again that unreasonable sense of irritation which had possessed me during the past night possessed me now. All things seemed to conspire together to make this Breton fellow actually one of our intimate circle!

"Will Mademoiselle Pauline be long, do you think?" I asked rather crossly. "I am anxious to see her; I have her father's permission to speak to her in private."

What a curious change passed over her face as I said these words! She evidently guessed my errand, and there was something in her expression that was perplexing and difficult to decipher. She looked startled, sorry, vaguely troubled, and I wondered why. Presently, laying down her violin, she came towards me and touched my arm gently, almost pleadingly.

"Do not be in a hurry, Monsieur Beauvais!" she said very earnestly. "I think—indeed I am sure—I know what you are going to say to Pauline! But, give her time to think—plenty of time! she is so very young, she scarcely knows her own mind. Oh, do not be angry with me; indeed I speak for the best! I have lived with my cousin so long,—in truth, I have seldom been away from her, except when she went to her finishing school in Switzerland three years ago; but before that we were both educated at

---

[1]   French word meaning "I beg your pardon."
[2]   French term meaning "in order."

the Convent of the Sacré Coeur[1] together. I know her nature thoroughly! She is sweet, she is good, she is a little angel of beauty; but she does not understand what love is, she cannot even translate the passing emotions of her own heart. You must be very patient with her! give her time to be quite sure of herself, for now she is not sure; she cannot be sure!"

Her voice thrilled with quite a plaintive cadence, and her strange eyes, which I now noticed were a sort of grey-green colour like the tint of the sea before a storm, filled with tears. But I was extremely angry; angry with her for speaking to me at all on the subject of my *amour*,[2] it was none of her business! She had her doubts, this pale, serious, cold woman, as to the possibility of Pauline's having any real love for me, that was evident. Well, she should find out her mistake! She should soon see how fondly and truly my darling returned my passion!

"Mademoiselle," I said frigidly, "you are exceedingly good to concern yourself so deeply with the question of your cousin's happiness! I am grateful to you, I assure you, as grateful perhaps as even she herself can be; but at present I think the matter is best left in my hands. You may be quite certain that I shall urge nothing upon Mademoiselle de Charmilles that will be in any way distressing to her, my sole desire being to make her life, so far as I am able, one of perfect felicity. As for the comprehension of love, I think that comes instinctively to all women of marriageable age. Surely you yourself"—and I spoke in a more bantering tone—"cannot be ignorant of its meaning! If you loved any one, you would not require much time to think about it?"

"Yes, indeed I should!" she replied slowly. "I should need time to commune with my own heart; to ask it if all this panting passion, this restless fever, *would last?* Whether it were but a fancy of the moment, a dream of the hour, or the never-to-be-quenched fire of love indeed— love in its perfect strength and changeless fidelity—love absolutely unselfish, pure, and deathless! I should need time to know myself and my lover, and to feel that our two spirits merged into one as harmoniously as the two notes in this perfect chord!"

And taking up her violin, she drew the bow across the strings. A sweet and solemn sound, organ-like in tone, floated through the room with such a penetrating richness that the very air seemed to pulsate

---

[1] The Society of the Sacred Heart, established in France in 1800, was strongly committed to the education of girls. Throughout the nineteenth century they established schools for girls throughout Europe.

[2] French word for "love."

around me in faint yet soothing echoes. What a strange creature she was, I thought! and a quick sigh escaped my lips unconsciously.

"I did not know you played the violin, Mademoiselle," I began hastily, and with a touch of embarrassment.

"*Vraiment!*"[1] and she smiled. "But that is not surprising! You do not know, and it is probable you never *will* know anything at all about me! I am a very uninteresting person; it is not worth any one's while to study me. Listen!"—and she held up her finger as a clear voice rang through the house carolling a lively strain from one of the operettas popular at the time—"there is Pauline; she is coming this way. One word more, M. Beauvais"—and she turned swiftly upon me with an air of almost imperial dignity—"If you are modest and wise, you will remember what I have said to you; if you are conceited and foolish, you will forget! *Au revoir!*"[2]

And before I had time to answer her, she had vanished, taking her violin with her, and leaving me in a state of mingled perplexity and vague annoyance. However, as I have before stated, I never paid much attention to Héloïse St. Cyr, or attached any great importance to her opinions; and on this occasion I soon dismissed her from my mind, for in another minute an ethereal vision clad in soft pink and white draperies, with a curly dark head and a pair of laughing deep blue eyes, appeared at the open door of the room, and Pauline herself entering, stretched out both her hands in gay greeting.

"*Bon jour,*[3] *Monsieur Gaston!* How long have you been here, making love to Héloïse? Ah, *méchant!*[4] I know how very bad you are! What? you come to see *me*—only me? Oh yes, that is a very pretty way to excuse yourself! Then why was Héloïse crying as she passed me? You have vexed her, and I shall not forgive you, for I love her dearly!"

"Crying!" I stammered in amazement. "Mademoiselle St. Cyr? Why, she was as bright as possible just now; she has been playing her violin——"

"Yes; she plays it only when she is sad," and Pauline nodded her head sagely, "never when she is happy. So that I know something is not well with her; and who am I to blame for it? It must be your fault! I shall blame *you.*"

---

[1] French exclamation meaning "Really!"
[2] French phrase meaning "goodbye."
[3] French for "hello."
[4] French for "naughty boy."

"*Me!*" I stared helplessly, then smiled, for I at once perceived she was only jesting, and I watched her with my heart beating quick hammer-strokes, as she sank lazily down in a cushioned ottoman near the fire, and held out her little hands to the warmth of the red glow.

"We have been driving in the Bois, mamma and I, and it was *so* cold!" she said, with a delicate *frissonnement*[1] of her pretty figure. "Héloïse was wise to remain at home. Only she missed seeing Monsieur Antinous[2] from Brittany!"

Engrossed as I was with my own thoughts and the contemplation of her beauty—for I was wondering how I should begin my declaration of love—this last sentence of hers impressed me unpleasantly.

"Do you mean the nephew of M. Vaudron?" I inquired, with, no doubt, a touch of annoyance in my accents which she, woman-like, was quick to notice.

"Yes, truly! I *do* mean the nephew of M. Vaudron!" she replied, a little sparkle of malicious mirth lighting up her lovely eyes. "He has arrived. *Oh, qu'il est beau!*[3] He is a savage from Brittany—a forest philosopher—very wise, very serious, very good! Ah, *so* good! He is going to be a priest, you know, and he looks so grave and tranquil that one feels quite wicked in his presence. Ah, you frown!" and, laughing, she clapped her hands gaily. "You are jealous—jealous because I say M. Silvion Guidèl is handsome!"

"Jealous!" I exclaimed, with some heat, "I? Why should I be? I know nothing about the young man—*I* have not seen him yet! When I do I will tell you frankly what I think of him. Meanwhile"—here I gathered my hesitating courage together—"Pauline, I want to speak to you; will you be serious for a moment and listen to me?"

"Serious?" and a surprised look flitted over her face. Then, as I fixed my ardent gaze upon her, a deep blush coloured her fair cheeks and brow, and she quickly rose from her chair with a sudden movement of fear or timidity, making as though she would have fled from the room. But I caught her hands and held her fast, and all the pent-up longing of my soul found utterance in words. Her beauty, her irresistible sweetness, my deep and deathless love, the happiness we would enjoy when once united,—these were the themes on which I discoursed with the fiery eloquence and pleading of a troubadour; though, truly, I scarcely knew what I said,

---

[1]   French word for "shivering."

[2]   Page of the Roman Emperor Hadrian; a model of manly beauty.

[3]   French phrase meaning "Oh, how handsome he is."

so overwhelming was the released tide of my excitement and ardour. And she? She trembled a little at first, but soon grew very quiet, and, still allowing me to hold her hands, looked up with an innocent vague wonder.

"You really want to marry me, Monsieur Gaston?" she asked, a faint smile parting her lips. "Soon?"

"Soon?" I echoed passionately. "Would I might claim you to-morrow as my bride, Pauline! then should I be the happiest of men! But you have not answered me, *mon ange!*"[1] And now I ventured to put my arm about her and draw her to my breast, while I adopted the endearing "thou" of more familiar speech. "Dost thou love me, Pauline—even as I love thee?"

She did not answer at once, and a cold dread seized my heart; was Héloïse St. Cyr right after all, and was she not sure of herself? A meditative expression darkened her eyes into lovelier hues; she seemed to consider; and I watched her in an agonized suspense that almost stopped my breath. Then, with a swift action, as though she threw all reflection to the winds, she laughed, and nestled her pretty head confidingly against my shoulder.

"*Oui, mon Gaston!*[2] I love thee! Thou art good and kind; papa is pleased with thee, mama also; we shall be very, very happy! *Oh, quel baiser!*"[3] for I had in the relief and ecstasy of the moment pressed my first love-kiss on her sweet mouth. "Must we always kiss each other now? Is it necessary?"

"Not necessary to thee, perhaps!" I whispered tenderly, kissing her again. "But it is to me!"

With an impulsive half-petulant movement, she drew herself suddenly away from my embrace; then, apparently regretting the hastiness of this action, she came once more towards me, and, folding her hands in demure fashion on my arm, looked at me searchingly, as though she sought to read my very soul.

"*Pauvre garçon!*"[4] she sighed softly, "thou dost truly love me? Very, very dearly?"

More dearly, I assured her, than my own life!

"It is very kind of thee," she said, with a pretty plaintiveness, "for I am very stupid, and every one says thou art such a clever man! It is good for us to marry, is it not, Gaston? Thou art sure?"

---

[1] French for "my angel."
[2] French for "Yes, my Gaston."
[3] French for "Oh, what a kiss."
[4] French for "Poor boy."

"If we love each other—yes, my Pauline! Of course it is good for us to marry!" I answered eagerly, a vague fear arising in my mind lest she should retract or hesitate. She waited with downcast eyes for a minute, and then glanced up at me radiantly smiling.

"Then we *will* marry!" she said. "We will live at Neuilly, and papa and mama will visit us, and Héloïse will come and see us, and we shall please everybody! *C'est fini!* So!"—and she dropped me a mischievous little curtsey. "*Me voici, Monsieur Gaston! votre jolie petite fiancée, —à votre service!*"[1]

She looked so ravishingly pretty and enchanting that I was about to snatch her in my arms and kiss her again and yet again, when the door opened and the discreet Comtesse de Charmilles entered with a serene and gracious kindliness of manner that plainly evinced her knowledge and approval of the situation. She glanced smilingly from her daughter to me, and from me back to her daughter, and straightway comprehended that all was well.

"*Bon jour, mon fils!*"[2] she said gently, laying a slight emphasis on the affectionate title, and adopting the *tutoyer*[3] form of address without further ceremony. "Thou art very welcome! Thou wilt stay and dine this evening? M. de Charmilles has gone to persuade thy father to join us, and M. Vaudron is coming also, with his nephew, M. Silvion Guidèl."

CHAPTER 5

I have forgotten many things. Many circumstances that I might otherwise have remembered, are now, thanks to the merciful Elixir I love, effaced from my brain as utterly as though they had been burnt out with fire; but that one night in my life—the night of my betrothal to Pauline de Charmilles—remains a fixture in my memory, a sting implanted there to irritate and torture me when I would fain lose my very sense of being in the depths of oblivion. It was a marked evening in many respects; marked, not only by my triumph as Pauline's accepted lover, but also by the astonishing and bewildering presence of the man, Silvion Guidèl. I say astonishing and bewildering, because that was the

---

[1] French for "That's the end of it.... Here I am, Monsieur Gaston! Your pretty little fiancée at your service!"

[2] French meaning "Good day, my son."

[3] To address someone in French using the informal "*tu*" rather than the formal "*vous.*"

first effect his singular beauty made upon the most prejudiced and casual observer. It was not that he was in the first flush of youth, and that his features still had all the fine transparency and glow of boyhood upon them; it was not that his eyes, grey-black and fiery, seemed full of some potent magnetic force which compelled the beholder's fascinated gaze; no; it was the expression of the whole countenance that was so extraordinarily interesting; an expression such as an inspired painter might strive to convey into the visage of some ideal seraph of patience and wisdom supernal. I, like every one else at the house of the De Charmilles that night, found myself attracted against my will by the graceful demeanour and refined courtesy of this son of a Brittany farmer; this mere provincial, whose face and figure would have done honour to the most brilliant aristocratic assemblage. The former instinctive aversion I had felt with regard to him subsided for the time being, and I listened as attentively as any one at table, whenever his voice, melodious as a bell, chimed in with our conversation. I was perfectly happy myself, for in a few brief words, simple and suited to the occasion, the Comte de Charmilles had announced to all present the news of his daughter's engagement to me. When he did so I glanced quickly at Héloïse St. Cyr, but though she looked even paler than usual she gave no sign either of surprise or pleasure. My father had then, in his turn, proposed the health of the "chers fiancés,"[1] which was drunk with readiness by all except Silvion Guidèl, who never touched wine. He apologized for this lack of *bonne camaraderie*,[2] and was about to raise a glass of water to his lips, in order to join in the toast, when Héloïse spoke across the table in swift eager accents.

"Do not drink my cousin's health in water, M. Guidèl!" she said. "It is unlucky, and your wishes may prove fatal to them both!"

He smiled, and at once set down the glass.

"You are superstitious, mademoiselle!" he replied, gently bending his handsome head towards her. "But I will not try to combat your feeling. I will content myself with a silent prayer in my heart for your cousin's happiness, a prayer which, though it may not find expression in words, is none the less sincere."

His voice was so serious and soft and full of emotion, that it left an impression of gravity upon us; that vague subdued sensation that comes across the mind when the little bell rings at mass, and the people kneel

---

[1]   French for "dear fiancés."
[2]   French term meaning "good companionship."

before the Host unveiled. And then I saw the meditative eyes of Héloïse rest upon the Breton stranger with a curiously searching earnestness in their grey-green depths, a look that seemed to be silently indicative of a desire to know more of his character, life, and aims. The dinner went on, and we were all conversing more or less merrily on various desultory matters, when she quite suddenly asked him the question—

"Are you really going to be a priest, Monsieur Guidèl?"

He turned his dark picturesque face in her direction.

"I hope so, God willing! As my revered uncle will tell you, I have studied solely for the priesthood."

"Yes, that may be," returned Héloïse, a faint colour creeping through the soft pallor of her cheeks. "But, pardon me! you seem also to have studied many things not necessary to religion. For instance——"

"Now, Héloïse, *petite femme Socrate!*"[1] exclaimed the Comte de Charmilles good-naturedly. "What art thou going to say out of thy stores of wisdom? You must understand, M. Guidèl"—and he turned to the person he addressed—"my niece is a great student of the classics, and is well versed in the literature of many nations, so that she often puts me to shame by her knowledge of the strange and wonderful works, done by men of genius in this world for the benefit of the ignorant. Excuse her, therefore, if she trespasses on *your* ground of learning; I have often told her that she studies like a man."

Silvion Guidèl bowed courteously, and looked towards Héloïse with renewed interest.

"I am proud to have the honour of being addressed by one who has the air of a Corinne,[2] and is no doubt the possessor of more than Corinne's admirable qualities!" he said suavely. "You were observing, mademoiselle, that I seem to have studied things not altogether necessary to religion. In what way do you consider this proved?"

Héloïse met his gaze very fixedly.

"I heard you speaking with my uncle some minutes ago, of science," she answered. "Of modern science in particular, and its various wonderful discoveries. Now do you not find something in *that* branch of study, which confutes much of the legendary doctrine of the Church?"

"Much that *seems* to confute it, yes," he returned quietly, "but which, if pursued far enough, would, I am fully persuaded, strengthen our belief

---

[1] French for "little Socratic lady." Socrates was a Greek philosopher (c. 470-399 BC).

[2] In the novel *Corinne, or Italy* (1807) by Germaine de Staël, Corinne is a famous poetess. She is both a learned and unconventional woman.

instead of weakening it. I am not afraid of science, mademoiselle; my faith is firm!"

Here he raised his magnificent eyes with the expression of a rapt saint, and again we felt that embarrassed gravity stealing over us, as if we were in church instead of at dinner. M.Vaudron, good-hearted man, was profoundly touched.

"Well said, Silvion, *mon garçon!*"[1] he said with tender seriousness. "When the good God has once drawn our hearts to the love of His Holy service, it matters little what the learning or the philosophy of the world can teach us. The world and the things of the world are always on the surface, but the faith of a servant of the Church is implanted deep in the soul!"

He nodded his head several times with pious sedateness, then, relapsing into smiles, added, "Not that even I can boast of such strong faith as my old Margot after all! She has a favourite saint, St. Francis of Assisi;[2] she has made a petticoat for his image which she keeps in her sleeping-chamber, and whenever she wishes to obtain any special favour she sticks a pin in the petticoat, with the most absolute belief that the saint noticing that pin, will straightway remember what he has to do for her, without any further reminder!"

We laughed,—I say *we*, but Silvion Guidèl did not laugh.

"It is very touching and very beautiful," he said, "that quaint faith of the lower classes concerning special intercession. I have never been able to see anything ridiculous in the superstition which is born of ignorance:—as well blame an innocent child for believing in the pretty fancies taken from fairy-tales, as scoff at the poor peasant for trusting that one or other of the saints will have a special care of his vineyard or field of corn. I love the ignorant!—they are our flock, our 'little ones,' whom we are to guide and instruct; if all were wise in the world——"

"There would be no necessity for churches or priests!" I put in hastily.

My father frowned warningly; and I at once perceived I had ruffled the devout feelings of the Comte de Charmilles, who, nevertheless, remembering that I was the excellent match he had just secured for his daughter, refrained from allowing any angry observation to escape him. Silvion Guidèl however, looked straight at me, and as his brilliant eyes flashed on mine, the aversion I had felt for him before I ever saw him sprang up afresh in my mind.

---

[1]   French for "my boy."
[2]   Founder of the Franciscan order (AD 1181 or 1182–1226).

"Monsieur is of the new school of France?" he inquired with the faintest little curl of mockery dividing his delicate lips. "He possibly entertains—as so many do—the progressive principles of atheist and republican?"

The blood rushed to my face; his manner angered me, and I should have answered him with a good deal of heat and impatience, had I not felt a soft little hand suddenly steal into mine and press my fingers appealingly. It was Pauline's hand; she was a timid creature, and she dreaded any sort of argument, lest it might lead to high words and general unpleasantness. But whatever I might have said was forestalled by M. Vaudron, who addressed his nephew gently, yet with a touch of severity too.

"*Tais-toi—tais-toi, mon garz!*"[1] he said, using the old Breton term of endearment, "Monsieur Gaston Beauvais is a young man like thee, and in all probability he is no more certain of his principles than thou art! It takes a long while to ripen a man's sense of right and honour into a fixed guiding-rule for life. Those who are republicans in the flush of their impetuous youth may be Royalists or Imperialists[2] when they arrive at mature manhood; those who are atheists when they first commence their career, may become devout servants of heaven before they have reached the middle of their course. Patience for all and prejudice for none!—otherwise we, as followers of Christ, lay ourselves open to just blame. You are boys—both you and Monsieur Gaston; as boys you must be judged by your elders, till time and experience give you the right to be considered as men."

This little homily was evidently very satisfactory to both my father and the Comte de Charmilles. Silvion Guidèl bowed respectfully, as he always did whenever his uncle spoke to him, and the conversation again drifted into more or less desultory channels. When the ladies left the dinner-table for the drawing-room, Guidèl crossed over and took Pauline's vacated seat next to mine.

"I must ask you to pardon me!" he said softly, under cover of a discussion on finance which was being carried on by the other gentlemen. "I feel that I spoke to you rudely and roughly, and I am quite ashamed. Will you forget it and be friends?"

He extended his hand. There was a soft caressing grace about him that was indescribably fascinating,—his beautiful countenance was like

---

[1] French meaning "Be quiet—be quiet, my boy." "Garz" is the Breton spelling of the French "gars" meaning "boy."

[2] Advocates of the practice by nations of acquiring colonies and dependencies in order to extend the acquiring nation's influence.

that of a pleading angel, his eyes were bright with warmth and sympathy. I could do no less than take his proffered hand in my own, and assure him of my esteem, and though my words were brief and scarcely enthusiastic, he seemed quite satisfied.

"How lovely she is!" he then said in the same confidential tone, leaning back in his chair and smiling a little. "How like a fairy dream! It is impossible to imagine a more enchanting creature!"

I looked at him, surprised. I had got the very foolish idea into my head that the devotees of religion never perceived a woman's beauty.

"You mean——" I began.

"I mean your lovely *fiancée*, Mademoiselle de Charmilles! Ah! you are indeed to be congratulated! She is like some fair saint in a sculptured niche where the light falls through rose-coloured windows; her eyes have so pure a radiance in them!—an innocence such as is seen in the eyes of birds! She would infuse into the dullest mind gleams of inspired thought; she is the very model of what we might imagine Our Lady to have been before the Annunciation!"[1]

"You are more likely to be a poet than a priest!" I said, amazed and vaguely vexed at his enthusiasm.

He smiled. "*Mon ami*, religion is poetry—poetry is religion. The worship of beauty is as holy a service as the worship of the beauty-creating Divinity. There is a great deal of harm done to the Church by bigotry—the priesthood are too fond of sack-cloth and ashes, penitence and prayer. They should look out upon the mirror of the world, and see life reflected there in all its varying dark and brilliant colours; then, raising their thoughts to heaven, they should appeal for grace to understand these wonders and explain them to the less enlightened multitude. The duty of a priest is, to my thinking, to preach of happiness and hope, not sorrow and death. If ever I become an ordained servant of Christ"—here he raised his eyes devoutly and made almost imperceptibly the sign of the Cross—"I shall make it my province to preach joy! I shall speak of the flowers, the birds and trees, of the stars and their inexhaustible marvels, of the great rivers and greater oceans, of the blessedness of life, of everything that is fair and gracious and suggestive of promise!"

"Would you take the beauty of woman as a text, for example?" I asked incredulously.

"Why not?" he answered calmly. "The beauty of woman is one of the gifts of God to gladden our eyes;—it is not to be rejected or

---

[1]   The angel Gabriel's announcement of the Virgin Mary's conception of Christ.

deemed unsacred. I should love to preach of beautiful women! they are the reflexes of beautiful souls!"

"Not always!" I said drily, and with a slight scorn for his ignorance. "You have not lived in Paris, M. Guidèl! There are lovely women at the *cafés-chantants*;[1] and also at other places not mentionable to the ears of a student of religion; women delicate as nymphs and dainty as flowers, who possess not a shred of character, and who have been veritable harpies of vice from their earliest years!"

A sudden interest flashed into his face. I noticed it with surprise, and he saw that I did, for a rich wave of colour rushed up to his brows, and he avoided my gaze. Then an idea seemed to strike him, and he uttered it directly, with that faint tinge of mockery that once before had marked his accents when addressing me.

"Ah! *you* have had a wider experience!" he said softly, "you have met these—these *harpies?*"

I was indescribably irritated at this. What business had he to cast even the suspicion of such a slur on my manner of conduct? I controlled my annoyance with difficulty, and replied curtly—

"You mistake! No *gentleman* who cares a straw for his good reputation visits such low and despicable haunts as they inhabit. What I have told you I know by hearsay."

"Indeed!" and he sighed gently. "But one should always prove the truth of things before believing in an ill report. Virtue is so very easily calumniated!"

I laughed aloud. "Perhaps *you* would like to meet the harpies in question?" I said half jestingly.

He was not offended. He looked at me with the utmost seriousness.

"I should!" he admitted quite frankly. "If they have fallen, they can be raised up; our Divine Lord never turned away in scorn from even a sinful woman!"

I uttered an impatient exclamation—but said no more, as just then the Comte de Charmilles rose from table, my father and the Curé following his example, and we all made our entrance into the drawing-room where the ladies awaited us, and where coffee was already prepared. I took instant advantage of my newly gained privileges as Pauline's *fiancé* to ensconce myself by her side, and, drawing a chair to where she sat toying with some delicate embroidery, I conversed with her in that dulcet *sotto-voce*,[2] which,

---

[1]   See note for café-chanteuses, page 76, note 2.
[2]   Latin phrase meaning "in an undertone."

though very delightful and convenient to the lovers concerned, is often peculiarly provoking to those left out in the cold. Once or twice I saw the would-be priest Guidèl glance at us with a singular flashing light in his eyes, as though he had become suddenly conscious that there were pleasanter things to be done than the chanting of masses, droning of "offices"[1] and counting of rosary-beads; but he was for the most part very reserved and quiet, only now and then joining in conversation with the Comte de Charmilles, yet proving himself, whenever he *did* speak, to be unquestionably a man of rare intellectual endowment and splendid scholarship. I noticed that Héloïse St. Cyr watched him with the deepest interest, and I jestingly called Pauline's attention to the fact.

"Thy cousin is becoming enamoured of the handsome Breton!" I said. "Who knows but that she may not lead him altogether aside from his holier intentions!"

She looked at me, with a sudden rosy flush of colour in her face.

"Oh no!" she murmured hastily, and there was, or so I then fancied, a touch of petulance in her accents. "That is impossible! Héloïse loves no one; she *will* love no one but—but me!"

I smiled, and taking her little hand in mine, studied all its pretty dimples and rose-tinted finger-tips.

"Not yet, perhaps!" I answered softly. "But a time for love will come to her, Pauline, even as to thee!"

"Are you sure it has come for me?" she asked half timidly, half mischievously. "Are you so vain, Gaston, as to think that I—I—*worship* you, for instance?"

I raised my eyes to hers, and saw that she was smiling.

"'Worship' is a strong word, my sweetest," I replied. "It is for *me* to worship! not for you! And I do worship the fairest angel under heaven!"

And I furtively kissed the little hand I held.

"Yes," she said, with a meditative air. "But, sometimes, a woman *may* worship a man, may she not? She may love him so much, that he may seem to her mind almost more than God?"

"Assuredly she may!" I rejoined slowly, and in some surprise, for she had spoken with unusual seriousness and passion; "but, Pauline, such excess of love is rare, moreover, it is not likely to last; it is too violent and headstrong; it is always unwise and often dangerous; and the priests would tell you it is wicked!"

"Yes, I am sure it *is* wicked!" she acquiesced, sighing a little. "Dreadfully

---

[1] Daily public prayers which priests and some clerics are bound by duty to recite.

wicked! and—and, as you say, dangerous." She paused; the pensiveness passed from her bright face like a passing cloud from a star, and she laughed, a little low laugh of perfect contentment. "Well, be satisfied, Gaston! I do not worship *thee*, so *I* am not wicked! I am thy very good little *fiancée*, who is very, very fond of thee, and happy in thy company, *voilà tout!*"[1]

And, bending towards me, she took a rose from her *bouquet-de-corsage*,[2] and fastened it in my button-hole, while I, enchanted by her sweet manner and coquettish grace, attached not the least importance to what she had just been saying. I remembered her words afterwards—afterwards, when I learnt the fact that a woman can indeed "worship" a man with such idolatrous fervour, that she will allow herself to be set down in the dust of contempt for his sake, aye! and be torn and tortured to the very death rather than cease to adore! Women are strange folk! Some are cruel, some frivolous, some faithless; but I believe they are nearly all alike in their immense, their boundless capacity for loving. Find me a woman who has never loved anything or anybody, and you will have found the one, the only marvel of the centuries!

CHAPTER 6

That same evening,—the evening of Silvion Guidèl's introduction into our midst,—Héloïse St. Cyr suddenly invested herself with the powers of an Arabian Nights' enchantress,[3] and transferred us all whither she would, on the magic swing of her violin-bow. As a general rule, so her aunt told me, she never would exhibit her rare talent before any listeners that were not of her own family, so her behaviour on this occasion was altogether exceptional. It was Pauline who asked her to play, and probably the fact that it was her little cousin's betrothal-night, induced her to accede to the eager request. Any way, she made no difficulty about it, but consented at once, without the least hesitation. Pauline accompanied her on the piano, being careful to subdue her part of the performance to a delicate softness, so that we might hear, to its full splendour of tone and utmost fineness of

---

[1]   French expression meaning "that is all!"
[2]   French term for an arrangement of flowers worn on the bodice.
[3]   Reference to Scheherazade, one of the many wives of the Sultan Schahriah. Scheherazade avoids the fate of the Sultan's other wives—who are executed because the Sultan believes all women to be unfaithful—by enchanting her husband with fascinating stories night after night, always leaving off at a climactic moment in the story.

silver sound, the marvellous music this strange, pale, golden-haired woman flung out on the air in such wild throbs of passion that our very hearts beat faster as we listened. While she played, she was in herself a fit study for an artist; she stood within the arched embrasure of a window, where the fall of the close-drawn rose silken curtains provided a lustrous background for her figure; clad in a plain straight white gown, without a flower to relieve its classical severity, her rounded arm had a snowy gleam, like that of marble, contrasted with the golden-brown hue of her Amati violin.[1] To and fro, with unerring grace and exquisite precision, swept that wand-like bow, with the ease and lightness of a willow-branch waving in the wind, and yet with a force and nerve-power that were absolutely astonishing in a woman-performer. Grand pleading notes came quivering to us from the sensitive fibre of the fourth string; delicate harmonies flew over our heads like fine foam-bells, breaking from a wave of tune; we caught faint whispers of the sweetest spiritual confessions, prayers and aspirations; we listened to the airy dancing of winged sylphs on golden floors of melody; we heard the rustle of the nightingale's brown wings against cool green leaves, followed by a torrent of "full-throated" song; and when the player finally ceased, with a rich chord that seemed to divide the air like the harmonious roll of a dividing billow, we broke into a spontaneous round of enthusiastic applause. I sprang up from where I had been sitting, rapt in a silent ecstasy of attention, and poured out the praise which, being unpremeditated and heartfelt, was no mere flattery. She heard me, and smiled, a strange little wistful smile.

"So you love music, Monsieur Gaston!" she said. "Does it teach you anything, I wonder?"

"Teach me anything?" I echoed. "Are you proposing enigmas, mademoiselle?"

Pauline looked round from the piano with a half-perplexed expression on her lovely features.

"That is one of Héloïse's funny ideas," she declared. "Music teaches *her*, so she says, all sorts of things, not only beautiful, but terrible. Now *I* can see nothing terrible in music!"

Héloïse bent over her swiftly, and kissed her curls.

"No, *chérie*; because you have never thought of anything sad. Even so may it always be!"

"Of course sorrow is expressed in music," said Silvion Guidèl, who, almost unobserved, had joined our little group near the window, and

---

[1] Violin of high quality made by the Amati family of Cremona from 1550 to 1700.

now stood leaning one arm on the piano, regarding Pauline as he spoke, "sorrow and joy alternately; but when sorrow and joy deepen into darker and more tragic colours, I doubt whether music can adequately denote absolute horror, frenzy, or remorse. A tragedy in sound seems to me almost impossible."

"Yet language is sound," replied Héloïse; "even as music is, and music is often able to go on with a story when language breaks off and fails. You would have your mind tuned to a tragic key, M. Guidèl? Well, then, listen! There is no greater tragedy than the ever-recurring one of love and death; and this is a sad legend of both. Do not play, Pauline, *ma douce!*[1] I will be an independent soloist this time!"

We all gazed at her in vague admiration as she took up her violin once more, and began to play a delicate prelude, more like the rippling of a brook than the sound of a stringed instrument. The thread of melody seemed to wander in and out through tufts of moss and budding violets; and all at once, while we were still drinking in these dulcet notes, she ceased abruptly, and still holding the violin in position, recited aloud in a voice harmonious as music itself—

"Elle avait de beaux cheveux, blonds[2]
Comme une moisson d'aôut, si longs
Qu'ils lui tombaient jusqu'au talons.

"Elle avait une voix étrange,
Musicale, de fée ou d'ange;
Des yeux verts sous leur noire frange."[3]

Here the bow moved caressingly upwards, and a plaintively wild tune that seemed born of high mountains and dense forests floated softly

---

[1] French expression meaning "my sweet."

[2] [Corelli's note] This exquisite poem, entitled "L'Archet," here quoted in full, was written by one CHARLES CROS, a French poet, whose distinctly great abilities were never encouraged or recognized in his lifetime. Young still and full of promise, he died quite recently in Paris, surrounded by the very saddest circumstances of suffering, poverty, and neglect. The grass has scarcely had time to grow long or rank enough over his grave; when it has, the critics of his country will possibly take up his book, "Le Coffret de Santal," and call the attention of France to his perished genius. At present he is only very slightly remembered by a set of playful verses, entitled "Le Hareng Saur," written merely for the amusement of children; and yet the "Rendez-vous" exists—a poem almost as beautiful and weird as Keats's "Belle dame sans Merci."

3 Corelli cites Cros's poem in full over the next two pages. A full translation of the poem appears in Appendix A.1.

through the room. And above it, the player's voice still rose and fell—

> "Lui, ne craignait pas de rival,
> Quand il traversait mont ou val,
> En l'emportant sur son cheval.

> "Car, pour tous ceux de la contrée
> Altière elle s'était montrée
> Jusqu'au jour qu'il l'eut rencontrée."

The music changed to a shuddering minor key, and a sobbing wail broke from the strings.

> "L'amour la prit si fort au coeur,
> Que pour un sourire moqueur,
> Il lui vint un mal de langueur.

> "Et dans ses dernières caresses:
> 'Fais un archet avec mes tresses,
> Pour charmer tes autres maîtresses!'

> "Puis, dans un long baiser nerveaux
> Elle mourut!"

And here we distinctly heard the solemn beat of a funeral march underlying the pathetic minor melody—

> "Suivant ses voeux
> Il fit l'archet de ses cheveux!"

There was a half pause, then all suddenly, clamorous chords echoed upon our ears like the passionate exclamations of an almost incoherent despair.

> "Comme un aveugle qui marmonne,
> Sur un violon de Crémone
> Il jouait, demandant l'aumône.

> "Tous avaient d'enivrants frissons,
> A l'écouter. Car dans ces sons
> Vivaient la morte et ses chansons.

"Le roi, charmé, fit sa fortune.
Lui, sut plaire à la reine brune,
Et l'enlever au clair de lune.

"Mais, chaque fois qu'il y touchait
Pour plaire à la reine, l'archet
Tristement le lui reprochait!"

Oh, the unutterable sadness, the wailing melancholy of that wandering wild tune! Tears filled Pauline's eyes; she clasped her little hands in her lap and looked at her cousin in awe and wonder; and I saw Guidèl's colour come and go with the excess of emotion the mingled music and poetry aroused in him, for all his quiet demeanour. Héloïse continued—

"Au son du funèbre langage
Ils moururent à mi-voyage.
Et la morte reprit son gage.

"Elle reprit ses cheveux, blonds
Comme une moisson d'aôut, si longs
Qu'ils lui tombaient jusqu'au talons!"

A long-drawn sigh of sound, and all was still! So deeply fascinated were we with this recitation and violin-music combined, that we sat silent as though under a spell, till we became gradually conscious that Héloïse was surveying us with a slight smile, and a little more colour in her cheeks than usual. Then we surrounded her with acclamations, Pauline moving up to her, and hiding her tear-wet eyes in her breast.

"You are a genius, mademoiselle!" said Silvion Guidèl, bowing profoundly to her as he spoke. "Your gifts are heaven-born and marvellous!"

"That is true!—that is true!" declared the good Curé, coughing away a suspicious little huskiness of voice. "It is astonishing! I have never heard anything like it! It is enough to make a whole congregation of sinners weep!"

Héloïse laughed. "Or else take to sinning afresh!" she said, with that slight touch of sarcasm which sometimes distinguished her. "There is nothing in 'l'Archet,' *mon père*,[1] to incline the refractory to penitence."

---

[1] French for "my father," in this instance a priest.

"Perhaps not, perhaps not!"—and M. Vaudron rubbed his nose very hard—"but it moves the heart, my child; such poetry and such music move the heart to *something*, that is evident. And the influence *must* be good; it cannot possibly be bad!"

"That depends entirely on the temperament of the listener," replied Héloïse quietly, as she put back her violin in its case, despite our entreaties that she would play something else. The servant had just brought in a tray of wine and biscuits, and she prepared to dispense these with her ordinary "practical-utility" manner, thus waiving aside any further conversation on her own musical talents. The Comte and Comtesse de Charmilles were accepting with much pleased complacence, my father's warm and admiring praise of their niece,—and presently the talk became general, exclusive of myself and Pauline, whom I kept beside me in a little corner apart from the others, so that I might say my lingering good night to her with all the tenderness and pride I felt in my new position as her accepted future husband.

"I shall come and see you to-morrow," I whispered. "You will be glad, Pauline?"

She smiled. "Oh yes! you will come every day now, I suppose?"

"Would it please you if I did?" I asked.

"Would it please *you*?" she inquired, evading the question.

Whereupon I launched forth once more into passionate protestations which she listened to, with, as I fancied, the least little touch of weariness. I stopped short abruptly.

"You are tired, *ma chérie*!"[1] I said tenderly. "I am sure you are tired!"

"Yes, I am," she confessed, smothering a little yawn, and giving a careless upward stretch of her lovely rounded arms, much to my secret admiration. "I think my cousin's music exhausted me! Do you know"—and she turned her sweet blue eyes upon me with a wistful expression—"it frightened me! It must be terrible to love like that!"

"Like what?" I asked playfully, rather amused by the tragic earnestness of her tone.

She glanced up quickly, and, seeing that I smiled, gave a little petulant shrug of her shoulders.

"Like the lady with the '*cheveux si longs, qu'ils lui tombaient jusqu'au talons!*'"[2] she answered. "But you laugh at me, so it does not matter!"

---

[1] French for "my beloved."
[2] French for "Hair so long that it reached her heels."

"It was all a fable, *ma mie!*"[1] I said coaxingly. "It should affect you no more than a fairy-tale!"

"Yet there may be a *soupçon*[2] of truth even in fables!" she said, with that sudden seriousness which I had once or twice before remarked in her. "But tell me, Gaston,—remember you promised to tell me!—what do you think of M. Silvion Guidèl?"

I looked across the room to where he stood, not drinking wine as the others were doing, but leaning slightly against the mantelpiece, conversing with the Comtesse de Charmilles.

"He is very handsome!" I admitted. "Too handsome for a man—he should have been a woman."

"And clever?" persisted Pauline. "Do you think he is clever?"

"There can be no doubt of that!" I answered curtly. "I fancy he will be rather out of his element as a priest."

"Oh, but he is *good!*" said my *fiancée* earnestly, opening her blue eyes very wide.

"So he may be!" I laughed; "but all good men need not become priests! *Par exemple,* you would not call *me* very bad; but I am not going to be such a fool as to take the vow of celibacy—I am going to marry *you.*"

"And you imagine that will be very fortunate?" she said, with a bright saucy smile.

"The only fortune I desire!" I replied, kissing her hand.

She blushed prettily; then rising, moved away towards where the rest of the party stood, and joined in their conversation. I followed her example, and after a little more chat, the last good-nights were said, and we—that is, myself and my father, the Curé and his nephew—took our leave. We all four walked part of the way home together, the talk between us turning for the most part on the interesting subject of my engagement to Pauline; and many were the congratulations showered upon me by good old Vaudron, who earnestly expressed the hope that it might be his proud privilege to perform for us the Church ceremony of marriage. My father was in high spirits; such a match was precisely what he had always wished for me. He was a rank Republican, and, with the usual Republican tendency, had a great weakness for unblemished aristocratic lineage, such as the De Charmilles undoubtedly possessed. Silvion Guidèl was the most silent of us all,—he walked beside me, and seemed so absorbed in his own reflections that he started

---

[1]   French expression meaning "my beloved."

[2]   French word for "a small amount."

as though from a dream, when, at a particular turning in the road, we stopped to part company.

"I hope I shall see more of you, M. Gaston," he then said, suddenly proffering me his slim delicate-looking hand. "I have had very few friends of my own age; I trust I may claim you as one?"

"Why, of course you may!" interposed my father cheerily, "though Gaston is not very religious, I fear! Still he is a genial lad, though I say it that should not; he will show you some of the fine sights of Paris, and make the time spin by pleasantly. Come and see us whenever you like; your uncle knows that my house is as free to him as his own."

With these and various other friendly expressions, we went each on our several ways; the Curé and his nephew going to the left, my father and I continuing the road straight onwards. We lit our cigars and walked for some minutes without speaking; then my father broke silence.

"A remarkably handsome fellow, that Guidèl!" he said. "Dangerously so, for a priest! It is fortunate that his lady-penitents will not be able to see him very distinctly through the confessional-gratings, else who knows what might happen! He has a wonderful gift of eloquence too; dost thou like him, Gaston?"

"No!" I replied frankly, and at once, "I cannot say I do!"

My father looked surprised.

"But why?"

"Impossible to tell, *mon père*.[1] He is fascinating, he is agreeable, he is brilliant; but there is something in him that I mistrust!"

"Tut-tut!" and my father took my arm good-humouredly. "Now thou art an engaged man, Gaston, thou must put thy prejudices in thy pocket! Thou art too much like me in thy chronic suspicion of all priest-craft. Remember, this beautiful youth is not a priest yet, and I would not mind wagering that he never will be."

"If he has been trained for the priesthood, what else is he fit for?" I asked, rather irritably.

"What else? He is fit for anything, *mon choux!*[2] A diplomat, a states-man, a writer of astonishing books! He has *genius*; and genius is like the Greek Proteus,[3] it can take all manner of forms and be great in any one of them! Aye!" and my father nodded his head sagaciously. "Take my word for it, Gaston, there is something in this young man Guidèl that is

---

1   French for "my father."
2   French term of endearment meaning "my darling."
3   In mythology, Proteus was Poseidon's herdsman who was able to assume different shapes at will.

altogether exceptional and remarkable; he is one of the world's inspired dreamers, and to my notion he is more likely to aid in overturning priest-craft, than to place himself in its ranks as a bulwark of defence.

I murmured something unintelligible by way of reply: my father's praise of the Breton stranger was not so very pleasing to me that I should wish to encourage him in its continuance. We soon reached our own door, and, bidding each other good-night, retired at once to rest. But all through my sleep I was haunted by fragments of the violin music played by Héloïse St. Cyr, and scraps of the verses she had recited. At one time, between midnight and morning, I dreamt I saw her standing in my room, robed in a white shroud-like garment; she fixed her eyes on mine, and, as I looked, her lips parted, and she said, "*Elle mourût!*"[1] and I thought she meant that Pauline was dead. Struggling to escape from the horror of this impression, I cried, "No, no! she lives! She is mine!" and, making a violent effort, I fancied I had awakened, when lo! the curtain at my window seemed to move slowly and stealthily back, and the beautiful calm face of Silvion Guidèl stared full at me, pallidly illuminated by the moon! Again I started, and cried out, and this time awoke myself thoroughly. I sprang out of bed, and dashed back the window-draperies; I threw open the closed shutters; the night was one of sparkling frosty splendour; the stars twinkled in their glorious millions above my head; there was not a sound anywhere, not a living soul to be seen! I returned to my tossed and tumbled couch, with a smile at my own absurd visionary fancies, and in my heart blaming Héloïse St. Cyr and her weird violin for having conjured them up in my usually clear and evenly-balanced brain.

CHAPTER 7

On the far horizon of my line of life there shines a waving, ever-dimin-ishing gleam of brightness; I know it to be the hazy reflection of my bygone glad days and sweet memories, and when I shut my eyes close and send my thoughts backward, I am almost able to count those little dazzling points of sunshine sparkling through the gloom that now encompasses my soul. But though brilliant they were brief—brief as the few stray flashes of lightning that cross the skies on a hot summer's

---

[1] French phrase meaning "She died."

evening. My inward vision aches to look at them!—let them be swallowed up in blackness, I say, and let me never more remember that once I was happy! For remembrance is very bitter, and very useless as well; to play out one's part bravely in the world, I have said one should have no conscience; but it is far more necessary to have no memory! Are there any poor souls wearing on forlornly towards the grave, and monotonously performing the daily routine of life without either heart or zest in living? Let such look back to the time when the world first opened out before their inexperienced gaze like a brilliant arena of fair fortune, wherein they fancied they might win the chiefest prize, and then they will understand the meaning of spiritual torture! Then will the mind be stretched on a wrenching rack of thought!—then will the futile tears fill the tired eyes; then will the passionate craving for death become more and more clamorous—death, and utter, blessed forgetfulness! Ah! if one could only be sure that we *do* forget when we die!—but that is just what I, for one, cannot count upon. The uncertainty fills me with horror! I dare not allow myself to dwell upon the idea that perhaps I may sink drowningly from the dull shores of life into a tideless ocean of eternal remembrance! I dare not, else I should indeed be mad, more mad than I am now! For even now I am haunted by faces I would fain forget; by voices, by pleading eyes, by praying hands; and anon, by stark rigid forms, dead and white as marble, with the awful frozen smile of death's unutterable secret carved on their stiff set lips! And yet they are but the phantoms of my own drugged brain; I ought to know that by this time! Let me strive to banish them; let me lose sight of them for a little, while I try to knot together the broken threads of my torn Past.

During the two or three months immediately following my betrothal to Pauline de Charmilles, I think I must have been the proudest, most contented, perfectly light-hearted man in France. No cloud marred my joy; no bitterness nauseated my cup of felicity. All things smiled upon me, and in the warm expansion of my nature, I had at last even admitted Silvion Guidèl to a share in my affections. Truth to tell, it was difficult to resist him; his frank friendliness of behaviour towards me made me feel ashamed of my former captiousness and instinctive dislike of him; and by degrees, we became as close intimates as it was possible for two young men to be who were following such widely different professions. He was a great favourite with the De Charmilles, and was frequently invited to their house, though I was of course the more constant visitor; and when, after spending the evening there, we took our leave, we always walked part of the way home together. I was particularly pleased with the extreme deference and almost fastidious reserve of his manner to Pauline; he seemed rather to avoid her than otherwise, and to consider the fact of her engagement to me as a sort of title to command his greater respect. He was not half so constrained with Héloïse St. Cyr; he talked to her freely, led her into arguments on literature and music, in which I was often astonished to observe how brilliantly she shone; lent her rare old books now and then, and wrote down for her from memory fragments of old Breton songs and ballads, airs which she afterwards rendered on her violin with surpassing pathos and skill. One touching little unrhymed ditty, which she recited to her own improvised accompaniment, I remember was called "Le Pauvre Clerc," and ran as follows:—[1]

"J'ai perdu mes sabots et déchiré mes pauvres pieds,
À suivre ma douce dans les champs, dans les bois;
La pluie, le grésil, et la glace,
Ne sont point un obstacle à l'amour!

"Ma douce est jeune comme moi,
Elle n'a pas encore vingt ans;
Elle est fraiche et jolie
Ses regards sont pleins de feu!
Ses paroles charmantes!
Elle est une prison
Où j'ai enfermé mon coeur!

"Je ne saurais à quoi la comparer;
Sera-ce à la petite rose blanche qu'on appelle Rose-Marie?
Petite perle des jeunes filles;
Fleur de lis entre les fleurs;
Elle s'ouvre aujourd'hui, et elle se fermera demain

"En vous faisant la cour, ma douce, j'ai ressemblé
Au rossignol perché sur le rameau d'aubépine;

---

[1] This song can be found in Hersart de la Villemarqué's *Barzaz-Breiz Chants Populaires de la Bretagne*, Villemarqué's French translations of popular Breton songs which was published frequently from the 1840s on in French and in English translations. Corelli's French version differs in slight respects from Villemarqué's version. A translation of Corelli's version appears in Appendix A.2.

Quand il veut s'endormir, les épines le piquent, alors
Il s'élève à la cime de l'arbre et se met à chanter!

"Mon étoile est fatale,
Mon état est contre nature,
Je n'ai eu dans ce monde
Que des peines à endurer,
Je suis comme une âme dans les flammes du purgatoire,
Nul chrétien sur la terre qui me veuille du bien!

"Il n'y a personne qui ait eu autant à souffrir
À votre sujet que moi depuis ma naissance;
Aussi je vous supplie à deux genoux
Et au nom de Dieu d'avoir pitié de votre clerc!"

It was exceedingly simple and yet peculiarly mournful; so much so, that the first time we heard Héloïse's rendering of it, I saw, somewhat to my concern, big tears welling up in my pretty Pauline's eyes and falling one by one on her clasped hands. Guidèl was standing near her at the time, and he too seemed sincerely troubled by her emotion. Bending towards her, he said, with a faint smile—

"Are you crying for 'le pauvre clerc,' mademoiselle? Surely he is not worth such tears!"

I smiled also, and took my betrothed's unresisting hand tenderly in my own.

"She is very sensitive," I said gently. "She is a little angel-harp that responds sympathetically to everything."

But here Pauline hastily dried her eyes, pressed my hand, and went quietly away, and when she came back again, she was radiant and bright as ever.

The Feast of Noël and the gay *Jour de l'An*[1] had been marked to Pauline by the very large number of valuable presents and floral souvenirs she received. All her friends knew she was "*fiancée*," and countless congratulations and "*étrennes*"[2] were poured upon her. But she had grown either slightly *blasée*[3] or philosophical, for she evinced none of her former child-like delight at the big baskets and boxes of

---

[1] French for "New Year's Day."
[2] French word meaning "New Year's gifts."
[3] French word meaning "indifferent."

bon-bons given to her;—even a goodly round hamper of gilded wicker-work, wreathed with violets and packed close with her once-adored "*marrons glacés*," failed to excite her to any great enthusiasm. On the morning of the *Jour de l'An*, I had sent her a fancifully-designed osier gondola full of roses, and a necklace of pearls; and of all her gifts this had seemed to please her most, much to my delight. Silvion Guidèl had contented himself with simply wishing her happiness in his usual serious and earnest fashion, and for the New Year he had offered her no token save a large and spotless cluster of the lilies of St. John. She had shown me these, with rather a wistful look, so I fancied, and had asked me whether it would not be well to place them in a vase near the Virgin's statue in her own little private oratory? I agreed; I never attached importance to the girlishly-romantic notions I knew she had on the subject of religion; in fact, I thought with her, that such pure, white, sacred-looking blossoms were much more fitted for an altar than a drawing-room. And so she put them there, and I encouraged and approved the act—like a fool! Those lilies were allowed to occupy the most honoured place in her sleeping-chamber—to send out their odours to mingle with every breath she drew—to instil their insidious message through her maiden-dreams!—ah God!—if I had only known!

With the passing of the worst part of winter, just towards the close of March, Héloïse St. Cyr was summoned to see her mother who was thought to be dangerously ill. The night before she left for Normandy, I was spending a couple of hours at the De Charmilles'—there was no visitor that evening but myself, and I was now accounted almost one of the family. I thought she looked very weary and anxious, but attributed this solely to the bad news she had received from her native home. I was therefore rather surprised, when, taking advantage of Pauline's absence from the room for a few moments, she came hurriedly up to me and sat down by my side.

"I want to speak to you, Monsieur Gaston," she said, with an odd hesitation and flattered nervousness of manner. "You cannot imagine how unhappy I am at being obliged to leave Pauline just now!"

"Indeed, I can quite understand it!" I replied quickly, for I entirely sympathized in *such* a grief, which to me would have been insupportable. "But let us hope you will not be absent long."

"I hope not—I fervently hope not!" she murmured, her voice trembling a little. "But, M. Gaston, you will not let Pauline be too much alone? You will visit her every day, and see her as often as possible?"

I smiled. "You may rely upon that!" I answered. "Do not be afraid,

Héloïse!"—for I called her Héloïse now, as the others did—"I am not likely to neglect her!"

"No, of course not!" she said, in the same low nervous accents. "Yet, she is not quite herself just now, I fancy; a little morbid perhaps and unstrung. She often sheds tears for—for nothing, you know, and I think she gives way to too much religion. Oh, you laugh!" for I had been unable to resist a smile at this suggestion of my little darling's excess of devotion. I knew the reason, I thought!—she was praying for me! "But I do not think it is natural in one so young, and I would give anything to be able to stay with her, and watch over her a little, instead of going to Normandy! She used not to be so over-particular about her religious duties—and now she never misses early mass; she is up and out of doors while I am yet asleep, and she is quite cross if we try to keep her away from Benediction.[1] And it is not necessary for her to attend M. Vaudron's church *always*; do you think so?"

She looked full at me; but I could perceive no under-drift of meaning in her words. To my mind everything Pauline did or chose to do was perfection.

"She is fond of good old Vaudron," I replied; "we are all fond of him; and if you ask me frankly, I think I would rather she went to his church than to any other. You are over-anxious, Héloïse—the news of your mother's illness has quite unstrung you. Don't be nervous, Pauline is the idol of our hearts; we shall all take extra care of her while you are absent."

"I hope you *will* take extra care!" she said, with strange, almost passionate earnestness. "I pray to God you will!"

Her words impressed me very unpleasantly for the moment; what an uncomfortable creature she was, I thought, with her great, flashing grey-green eyes, and pale classic features, on which the light of a burning inward genius sent a weird unearthly glow! Just then Pauline came back, so she broke off her conversation with me abruptly, and on the following morning she had gone.

Some few days after her departure I jestingly broached the subject of this "too much religion" to my young *fiancée*.

"So you go to mass every morning, like a good little girl?" I said merrily, twisting one of her rich brown curls round my finger as I spoke.

She started. "How did you know that?"

"Héloïse told me, before she went away. Why, you don't mind my

---

[1]   Special Roman Catholic ritual.

knowing it, do you? It is very right of you and very proper; but doesn't it make you get up too early?"

"No; I never sleep much after daybreak," she answered, her face flushing a little.

"Like the daisy, awake at sunrise!" I said laughingly. "Well, I must reform, and be good too. Shall I meet you at church to-morrow for instance?"

"If you wish!" she replied quietly.

She was so very serious about it that I did not like to pursue the question further; some of her parents' religious scruples were no doubt her heritage, I thought, and I had no inclination to offend them by any undue levity. Religion is becoming to a woman; a beautiful girl praying, is the only idea the world can give of what God's angels may be.

The morrow came, and I did not go to church as I had intended, having overslept myself. But in the course of the day, I happened to meet M. Vaudron, and to him I mentioned Pauline's regular attendance at his early mass. The good man's brow clouded, and he looked exceedingly puzzled.

"That is strange!—very strange!" he remarked musingly. "I must be getting very short-sighted, or else the dear child must keep very much in the background of the church, for I never see her except on Sundays, when she comes with her father and mother. Early mass, you say? There are several:—the first one is at six o'clock, when my nephew assists me as deacon; the next at seven, when I have the usual attendant to help me officiate, for at that time Silvion goes for a long walk. He is accustomed to a great deal of exercise in Brittany, and he does not get enough of it here. It must be at seven that the pretty one slips in to pray; she would hardly come earlier. Ah well; it is easy for my old eyes to miss her then, for my sacred duties take up all my attention. She is a good child,—a sweet and virtuous one; thou should'st be very proud of her, Gaston!"

"And am I not so?" I responded laughingly. "I should love her and be proud of her, even—do not be shocked, *mon père!*—even if she never went to mass at all!"

He shook his head with much pious severity at this audacious declaration, but could not quite repress a kindly smile all the same; then we shook hands cordially and parted.

The next day I did manage to rouse myself in time for the seven o'clock mass, and I arrived at the little church in a pleasurable state of excitement, thinking what a surprise my appearance would be to Pauline. To my intense disappointment, however, she was not there! There were very few people present, two or three market-women and an old widow in the deepest mourning, being the most conspicuous members of the congregation. Immediately after the Elevation of the Host,[1] I slipped out, and, hurrying home, wrote a little note to my truant betrothed, telling her how I had been to mass hoping to meet her, and how I had missed her after all. Later in the day I called to see her, and found her in one of her radiant laughing moods.

"*Pauvre garçon!*" she playfully exclaimed, throwing her arms about me. "What a dreadful thing for thee to have risen so early, all for nothing! I did not go to church at all; I stayed in bed for I was sleepy; in fact, I am getting very lazy again, and once lazy, *hélas!*—I shall cease to be religious!"

She sighed, and assumed a demurely penitent air; I laughed, and kissed her, and soon, in the charm of her conversation and the fascination of her company, forgot my little disappointment of the morning. When I left her, I was convinced that her fancy for attending early mass regularly had passed, like all the passing fancies of a very young imaginative girl, and I thought no more about the matter.

Just about this time my father was suddenly compelled to go to London on business connected with certain large financial speculations, in which our firm was concerned, both for ourselves and others. He calculated on being absent about a fortnight or three weeks, with the natural and inevitable result, that, while he was away, all the work of superintending our Paris banking-house, fell entirely on my hands. I was busy from morning until night; I had indeed so little leisure of my own, that I could seldom spare more than the Sunday afternoon and evening for the uninterrupted enjoyment of Pauline's society. I had such rare and brief glimpses of her that I was quite restless and wretched about it; the more so, as Héloïse St. Cyr's parting words often recurred to me with uncomfortable persistency; but nevertheless, my work had to be done, and, after all, each time I did visit my beautiful betrothed, I found her in such blithe, almost wild spirits, and always looking so lovely and brilliant, that I blamed myself for giving way to any anxiety on her behalf. Besides, we were to be married at the beginning of June, and it was now close on the end of April. The Comtesse de Charmilles was pleasantly occupied with the ordering and preparing of the marriage-trousseaux, and a few stray wedding-gifts had already arrived. I was mounting securely upwards to the very summit of joy, so I thought!—I little imagined I was on the brink of ruin!

---

[1] Part of the Communion service occurring after the Host (bread/body of Christ) has been consecrated.

During this period I saw a great deal of Silvion Guidèl. He used to call for me at our Bank of an afternoon and walk home with me; and as I was rather lonely in the big old house at Neuilly, now that my father was absent, he would give me many an occasional hour of his company, talking on various subjects such as he knew were interesting to my particular turn of mind. He had the most vivid and intellectual comprehension of art, science, and literature, and his conversation had always that brilliancy and point which makes spoken language almost as fascinating as the neatly turned and witty phrases written by some author, whose style is his chief charm. And sometimes, when I was obliged to turn to my work and absorb myself in hard and dry calculations, Guidèl would still remain with me, quite silent, sitting in a chair near the window, his head leaning back, and his eyes fixed dreamily on the delicate spring-time leafage of the trees outside. I would often glance up and see him thus, gravely engrossed in his own thoughts, with that serious musing smile on his lips, that was like the smile of some youthful poet who contemplates how to evolve

> "*Beautiful things made new*
> *For the delight of the sky-children!*"[1]

And, worst confession of all, I think, that I have to make, I learnt to love him! I—even I! A peculiar sense of revering tenderness stirred me whenever he, with his beautiful calm face and saintly expression, came into the room where I sat alone, fagged out with the day's labour, and laying his two hands affectionately on my shoulders, said—

"Still working hard, Beauvais! What a thing it is to be so absolutely conscientious! Rest, *mon ami!*—rest a little, if not for your own sake, then for the sake of your fair *fiancée*, who will grieve to see you overwearied!"

I used to feel quite touched by such friendly solicitude on his part; and not only touched, but grateful as well, for the ready manner in which he seemed at once to comprehend and enter into my feelings. I was a sensitive sort of fellow in those days, quick to respond to kindness, and equally quick to resent injustice. But it was I who had been unjust in the case of Silvion Guidèl, I thought; I had disliked him at first without any cause, and now I frequently reproached myself for this, and wondered how I could ever have been so unreasonable! Yet, though first

---

[1] The quotation is from John Keats's 'Hyperion,' Book 1, lines 132–33. Corelli misquotes the second line which should read "For the surprise of the sky children."

impressions are sometimes erroneous, I believe there is a balance in favour of their correctness. If a singular antipathy seizes you for a particular person at first sight, no matter how foolish it may seem, you may be almost sure that there is something in your two natures that is destined to remain in constant opposition. You may conquer it for a time; it may even change, as it did in my case, to profound affection; but, sooner or later, it will spring up again with tenfold strength and deadliness; the reason of your first aversion will be made painfully manifest, and the end of it all will be doubly bitter because of the love that for a brief while sweetened it. I say I loved Silvion Guidèl!—and in proportion to the sincerity of that love, I afterwards measured the intensity of my hate!

CHAPTER 8

A brilliant May had begun in Paris; the foliage was all in its young beauty of pale-green sprouting leaf; the Champs Elysées[1] were bright with flowers, and the gay city looked its loveliest. My father was still delayed by his affairs in England; but I knew he would not remain away much longer now, as he was good-naturedly anxious to relieve me of some of the more onerous cares of business before the time for my marriage came too close at hand. Héloïse St. Cyr was also expected back daily; her mother had recovered, and she had, therefore, nothing to detain her any longer in Normandy. Pauline told me this news; and I noticed that she did not seem at all over-enthusiastic concerning her cousin's return. Like a fool, I flattered myself that this was because I had now become the first in her affections, and that, as a perfectly natural consequence, the once-adored Héloïse was bound to occupy a lower and vastly inferior place. I was full of my own joy, my own triumph; and I was blind to anything else but these. True, I did remark on one or two occasions, during my visits to her, that my *fiancée* was sometimes not quite so brilliant as usual; that there was a certain transparency and ethereal delicacy about her features that was suggestive of hidden suffering; that her deep blue eyes seemed larger than they used to be—larger, darker, and more intense in their wistfulness of expression; that now and then her lips quivered pathetically when I kissed her, and that there were moments when she appeared to be on the verge of tears. But I attributed all these signs of subdued emotion to

---

[1] Fashionable Parisian avenue.

the nervous excitement a young girl would naturally feel at the swift hourly approach of her marriage-day. I knew she was exceedingly sensitive; and for this reason I rather looked forward to the return of Héloïse, as I felt certain that she, with her womanly tact, quiet ways, and strong tenderness for Pauline would, by her very presence in the house, do much to soothe my little betrothed's highly-strung and over-wrought condition, and would also take a great deal of the fatigue of preparation for the wedding off her hands. Still, I did not really think very deeply about it any way; and I was rather taken by surprise one afternoon, when, on calling to leave some flowers for Pauline *en passant*,[1] the servant begged me to enter and wait in the drawing-room for a few minutes, as the Comtesse de Charmilles had expressed a particular wish to see me alone on a matter of importance. I crossed the familiar threshold I remember that day with a strange dull sensation at my heart; and as the doors of the great *salon*[2] were thrown open for me, a shiver seized me as though it were winter instead of spring. The room looked bare and blank in spite of its rich furniture and adornment. No Pauline came tripping in to greet me, and I stood, hat in hand, leaning against the edge of the grand piano, gazing blankly through the window, and wondering foolishly to myself why the gardener, usually so neat, had left a heap of the past winter's dead leaves in one corner of the outside gravel-path! There they were, an ugly brown pile of them; and every now and then the light May wind fluttered them, blowing two or three off to whirl like dark blots against the clear blue sky. I was still monotonously meditating on this trifle, and comparing those swept-up emblems of decay with the cluster of rich dewy red roses I had just brought for my *fiancée*, and which I had laid carefully down on a side table near me, when the door was opened softly and closed again with equal care, and the Comtesse de Charmilles approached. She looked worn and anxious, and there was a puzzled pain and sorrow in her eyes that filled me with alarm. I caught my breath.

"Pauline—is she ill?" I faltered, dreading I knew not what.

"She is not well," began the Comtesse gently, then paused.

My heart beat violently.

"It is something dangerous? You have sent for a physician? You——" Here my attempted self-control gave way, and I exclaimed, "Let me see her! I must—I will! Madame, I have the right to see her! Why do you hinder me?"

---

[1] French expression meaning "in passing."
[2] French term for "drawing room."

The Comtesse laid her hand on my arm in a pacifying manner, and smiled a little forcedly.

"Be tranquil, Gaston. There is nothing serious the matter. To-day, it is true, she is not well; she has been weeping violently, *pauvre enfant!*[1]— such tears!"— and the mother's voice quivered slightly as she spoke— "I have asked her a hundred times the cause of her distress, and she assures me it is nothing—always nothing. But I think there must be some reason; she, who is generally so bright and happy, would scarcely weep so long and piteously without cause,—and this is why I wished to speak to you, *mon fils*,[2]—to ask you,—is the love between you both as great as ever?"

I stared at her, amazed. What a silly woman she was, I thought, to make such an odd and altogether unnecessary inquiry!

"Most assuredly it is, madame!" I replied, with emphatic earnestness. "It is even greater on *my* part,—and of *her* tenderness I have never had a moment's occasion to doubt. That she sheds tears at all is of itself distressing news to me,—but nevertheless, it is true that girls will often weep for nothing, especially when they are a little over-strung and unduly excited, as Pauline may be at the present time. She probably reflects,—with a very natural regret, for which I should be the last to blame her,—that very soon she will have to leave her home and your fostering care;—the change from girlhood to marriage is a very serious one,—and being sensitive, she has perhaps thought more deeply about it than we imagine"—here I paused, embarrassed and concerned, for I saw two big drops roll slowly down the mother's cheeks, and glisten in the folds of her rich silk robe.

"Yes, it may be that,"—she said, in low tremulous accents. "I have thought so myself;—yet every now and then I have had the idea—a very foolish one no doubt,—that perhaps the child is secretly unhappy! But if you assure me that all is well between you, then I must be mistaken. Pardon my anxiety!" and she extended her hand, which I took and kissed respectfully—"we have all had too much to do, I fancy, while our dear Héloïse has been away, and"—here she smiled more readily— "it is possible we are all morbid in consequence! At any rate, next time you are alone with Pauline, will you ask her to confide in you, if indeed there is anything vexing her usually sweet and serene nature? Some mere trifle may have put her out,—a trifle exaggerated by her fancy,

---

[1]   French phrase meaning "poor child."
[2]   French term for "my son."

which we, knowing of, may be able to set right instantly—and surely that would be well!"

The generally dignified and rather austere looking lady was quite softened into plaintiveness by her eager and tender maternal solicitude, and I admired her for it. Kissing her hand again, I promised to do as she asked.

"But cannot I see Pauline to-day?" I inquired.

"No, Gaston,—it is better not!" she answered. "The poor little thing is quite worn out with crying,—she is exhausted, and is now upon her bed asleep. I will give her those roses when she wakes,—they are for her, are they not?"

I assented eagerly, and brought them to her,—she took them, and bade me "*au revoir!*"

"To-morrow come and see Pauline," she said. "I will tell her to expect thee. We will prepare a pretty '*thé à l'Anglaise*'[1] in the little morning-room,—and thou wilt be able to discover the cause of her trouble."

"If there *is* any trouble!" I rejoined, half smiling.

"True! If there *is*! If there is not, then thou must tell her she is a foolish little girl, and frightens us all without reason. *À demain!*[2]"

Carefully carrying the roses I had brought, she left the room with a kindly nod of farewell,—and I went home to get through some work I was bound to finish before the next morning. I found Silvion Guidèl awaiting me, and I hailed his presence with a sense of relief, for my own thoughts harassed me; and, just to unburden my mind, I told him all about Pauline and her tears. He moved away to the window while I was speaking—we were in my father's library—and looked out at the trees in front of the house. As he had deliberately turned his back to me, I took his action as a sign of indifference.

"Are you listening?" I asked, with some testiness.

"Listening? With both ears and with the very spirit of attention!" he replied, changing his attitude abruptly and confronting me. "What the devil would you have me do?"

I almost bounced out of my chair, so startled was I at this sort of language from *his* lips! Meeting my surprised gaze, he laughed aloud,— a ringing laugh which, though clear, seemed to me to have a touch of wildness in it.

"Don't look so thunderstruck, Beauvais! I said, 'the devil'!—and why should I *not* say it? The devil is as important a personage as the Creator

---

[1] French term meaning "tea, English-style."
[2] French phrase for "until tomorrow."

in our perpetual *Divina Commedia*.[1] The world, the flesh, and the devil![2] Three good things, Beauvais!—three positively existent tempting things!—no chimeras!—three fightable enemies that we have to wrestle with and grapple at the throats of till we get them down under our feet and kill them!—aye, even if we kill ourselves in the struggle! The world, the flesh, and the devil! *Mon dieu!* I wonder which is the strongest of the three!"

I could not answer him for a moment, I was so completely taken aback by his strange manner. The soft grey light of the deepening dusk fell on his face, mingling with the warmer glow of the shaded lamp above our heads,—and I saw to my wonder and concern that he looked as if he were undergoing some poignant physical sufferings,—that there were dark lines under his eyes,—and that there was a preternaturally brilliant flush on his cheeks which seemed to me to denote fever.

"Do you know, Guidèl, you are talking very oddly?" I said at last, watching him narrowly. "You are not yourself at all! What's the matter? Are you ill?"

"Ill? *Ma foi!*[3]—not I! I am well, *mon ami,*—well, and in astonishingly cheerful spirits! Don't you see that I am? Don't you see that I am almost too merry for—for a *priest*? Listen, Beauvais!"—and, approaching me, he laid his two hands on my shoulders,—such burning hands!—I felt more than ever certain that he must be going to have some feverish malady—"I have a secret!—and I will confide it to you! It is this,—Paris is making a fool of me! I have got the city's madness into my veins!—I am learning to love light and colour and gay music and song and dance,—and the wildly beautiful eyes of women!—eyes that are blue and passionate and pleading and that make one's heart ache for unuttered and unutterable joys! You stare at me amazed!—but is there anything so wonderful in the fact that I, young, strong, and full of life,—should all at once feel myself turning renegade to the vocation I have been trained to adopt? Do you know—can you imagine, Beauvais, what it is to be a priest?—to meditate on things that human sight can never see, and human ears never hear,—to shut oneself out utterly from the sweet ways of the less devout existence,—to consecrate one's entire body and soul to a vast Invisible that never speaks, that never answers,

---

[1] Italian for "Divine Comedy." An allusion to Dante's *Divine Comedy*.

[2] From the Litany in the *Book of Common Prayer*: "from all the deceits of the world, the flesh, and the devil, / good Lord, deliver us."

[3] French for "really!" or "to be sure!"

that gives no sign of either refusal or acquiescence to the most passion-ate prayers,—to resign a thousand actual joys for the far-off dream of heaven,—to sternly put away the touch of loving lips, the clasp of loving hands,—to cut all natural affections down at one blow, as a reaper cuts a sheaf of corn,—to become a human tomb for one's own buried soul,—to die to the world and to live for God! But,—the world is *here*, Beauvais!—and God is—Where?"

His words touched me most profoundly,—I understood—or I thought I understood—his condition of mind, and I certainly could not deem it unnatural. A man such as he was, not only in the early prime of life, but gifted with rare intellectual ability far above the ordinary calibre, needs must wake up at one time or another to the fact that the vocation of priest was at its best but a melancholy and limited career. So this was what troubled him!—this was the chagrin that secretly fret-ted his soul, and gave this touch of wildness to his behaviour! I hastened to sympathize with him;—and, taking his hands from my shoulders, pressed them cordially in my own.

"*Mon cher*, if these are your real feelings on the subject"—I said earnestly—"why not make a frank confession of them, not only to me, but to everybody concerned? Your uncle, for instance, is far too sensi-ble and broad-minded a man to wish to persuade you into the Church against your true inclinations,—and if Paris has, as you say, worked a change in you, depend upon it, it is all for the best! You are destined for greater things than the preaching of old doctrines to people, who, in these days of advanced thought, will, no matter how eloquent you are, never believe half of what you say. Shake off your shackles, Guidèl, and be a free man;—shape your own future!—with such splendid capabil-ities as yours, it needs must be a fair and prosperous one!"

He looked at me steadily and smiled.

"You are very kind, Beauvais!" he said softly—"as kind and good a fellow as ever I have met! I wish—I wish to God I had your cleanness of conscience!"

I was a little puzzled at this remark. Had he been frequenting low company, and disporting himself with the painted harridans in the common dancing-saloons of Paris?—and was he tormenting himself with scruples born of his strict education and religious discipline? Whatever the reason, it was evident he was very ill at ease. Suddenly, as though making a resolved end of his mental perplexity, he exclaimed—

"Bah! what nonsense I have been talking! It is a foolish frenzy that has seized me, Beauvais,—nothing more! I *must* be a priest! I look it, so people say;—my mother has set her heart upon it,—my father stakes his eternal welfare on my sanctification!—the prior of St. Xavier's at Rennes has written of me to the Holy Father as one of the most promising scions of the Church;—all this preparation must not go for naught, *mon ami*! If I know myself to be a whited sepulchre, what then? There are many like me,—what should I do with a conscience?"

These words pained me infinitely.

"Guidèl, you are indeed much changed!" I said, rather reproachfully—"I cannot bear to hear you talk in this reckless fashion! Priest or no priest, be faithful to whatever principles you finally take up. If you can believe in nothing, why then, believe in nothing steadfastly to the end,—if, on the contrary, you elect to fasten your faith to *something*, then win the respect of every one as our good Père[1] Vaudron does, by clinging to that something till death relaxes your hold of it. No matter what a man does, he should at least be consistent. If you feel you cannot conscientiously fulfil the calling of a priest, you ought to die rather than become one!"

"*Tiens!*"[2] he murmured,—he had thrown himself back in a chair and closed his eyes—"That is easy!"

His voice had a touch of deep pathos in it, and my heart ached for him. There could be no doubt that he was suffering greatly,—some acute unhappiness had him on the rack,—and perhaps he did not tell me all, or even half his griefs. I drew up my own chair to the table, where a large bundle of financial reports awaited my attention,—I was quite accustomed to have him often sitting in the same room with me while I worked, so that his presence did not disturb me in the least,—and I paid no heed to him for several minutes. All at once, though my head was bent down over my writing, I became instinctively aware that he was looking intently at me,—and, lifting my gaze to meet his, was exceedingly sorry to see what a strange expression of positive agony there was in his beautiful dark eyes,—eyes that were formerly so serene and untroubled as to be almost angelic. I laid down my pen and surveyed him anxiously.

"Silvion, *mon ami*," I said gently—"there is something else on your mind, more than this feeling about the priesthood. You have not told me everything!"

He frowned. "What else should there be to tell!" he answered, with a certain quick *brusquerie*,[3]—then in milder accents he added,—"My

---

[1] French for "father" in the ecclesiastical sense.
[2] French interjection translating in this instance as "Indeed!"
[3] French word meaning "abruptness."

dear Beauvais, don't you know a man may have a thousand infinitesimal worries all mingled together in such confusion that he may be absolutely unable to dissever or distinguish them separately? That is my case! I cannot tell you plainly what is the matter with me,—for I hardly know myself."

"Miserable for nothing, then!" I laughed, scribbling away again. "Just like my little Pauline! It must be in the air, this malady!"

There was a pause, during which the clock seemed to tick with an almost aggressive loudness. Then Guidèl spoke.

"Is she indeed miserable, do you think?" he asked, in accents so hoarse and tremulous that I scarcely recognized them as his. "She, that bright child of joy?—the little 'Sainte Vièrge'[1] as I have sometimes called her?—Oh, my God!"

This last exclamation broke from him like a groan of actual physical torture, and seeing him cover his face with his hands, I sprang to his side in haste and alarm.

"Guidèl, you are ill! I know you are! You must either stay here the night with me, or let me walk home with you,—you are not fit to be alone!"

He drew away his hands from his eyes, and looked at me very strangely.

"You are right, Beauvais! I am not fit to be alone! Only the straight-minded and pure of heart are fit for solitude,—there being *no* solitude anywhere! No solitude!—for every inch of space is occupied by some eyed germ of life,—and none can tell how, or by whom our most secret deeds are watched and chronicled! To be alone, simply means to be confronted with God's invisible, silent cloud of witnesses,—and you say truly, Beauvais, I am not fit *thus* to be alone!" He rose from his chair and stood up, resting one hand on my arm. "All the same"—he continued, forcing a faint smile—"I will not bore you any longer with my present dismal humour! Do not bestow another thought on me, *mon ami*,—I am going! No!—positively I cannot allow you to come home with me;— I am not ill, Beauvais, I assure you!—I am only—*miserable*. The malady of misery may be, as you say, 'in the air!'" He laughed drearily, and I watched him with increasing concern and wonder. "Really I do believe there *are* strange influences in the air sometimes; like seeds of plants blown by the wind to places where they may best take root and fructify; so the unseen yet living organic infusions of hatred—or love,—joy or sorrow, may be, for all we know, broadcast in the seemingly clear ether,

---

[1] French term for the Blessed Virgin Mary.

ready to sink sooner or later into the human hearts prepared to receive and germinate them. It is a wonderful Universe!—and wonderful things come of it!" He paused again, and then held out his hand. "Forgive my spleen, Beauvais! Good night!"

"Good night!" I answered, feeling somewhat saddened myself by his utter dejection. "But I wish you would let me accompany you part of the way!"

"On the contrary, you will oblige me, *mon cher*, by sticking to your work, and allowing me to saunter home in my own desultory fashion. I want to think out a difficulty, and I must be by myself to do it."

He walked across the room, I following him, and had nearly reached the door when he turned sharply round and confronted me.

"Supposing I had sinned greatly and irretrievably, Beauvais, could you forgive me?"

I stared at him, astonished.

"Sinned? *You?* Greatly and irretrievably? Nonsense! One might as well expect sin from the arch-angel Raphael!"[1]

He broke into a laugh, forced, harsh, and bitter.

"*Milles remerciements!*[2] Upon my word, Beauvais, you flatter me! If *I* am like the arch-angel Raphael, then Raphael has deserted Heaven for Hell quite recently! But you do not answer my question. Could you forgive me?"

His feverishly brilliant eyes seemed to probe my very soul, and I hesitated before replying, for, strange to say, the old inexplicable sense of distrust and aversion rose up in me anew, and seemed not only to throw a sudden cloud over his beauty, but also in part to quench my friendly sympathy.

"I do not think I have a malicious nature"—I said at last doubtfully—"and I have never borne any one a lasting grudge that I can remember. I do not profess particularly Christian principles either, because, like many of my countrymen of to-day, I rather adhere to the doctrines of a new Universal Religion springing solely out of Human Social Unity,—but I think I could forgive everything except——"

"Except what?" he asked eagerly.

"Deliberate deceit," I answered, "wilful betrayal of trust,—insidious tampering with honour,—this sort of thing I do not fancy I could ever pardon."

---

[1] One of the seven archangels who stand in the presence of God who is said to have healed the earth when it was defiled by the sins of the fallen angels.

[2] French phrase meaning "a thousand thanks."

"And suppose *I* deceived you in a great and important matter?" persisted Guidèl, still looking at me. I met his gaze fixedly, and spoke out the blunt truth as I then felt it.

"Frankly,—I should never forgive you!"

He laughed again, rather boisterously this time, and once more shook hands.

"Well said, Beauvais! I honour you for the sturdy courage of your opinions! Never put up with deceit! A spoken lie is bad enough,—but a wilfully acted lie is worse! And yet, alas!—what a false world we live in!—how full of the most gracefully performed lying! The pity of it is that when truth *is* spoken, no one can be got to believe it. You know the pretty song which says—

"Mieux que la réalité
Vaut un beau mensonge!" [1]

Oddly enough, the least strophe of poetry always reminds me of that clever Mademoiselle St. Cyr! She returns to Paris soon, I suppose?"

"She is expected every day," I replied, glad of a more commonplace turn to the conversation. "She may be home to-morrow."

"Indeed! I shall be glad to see her again!"

"So shall I!" I agreed emphatically. "Pauline will soon recover her good spirits in her cousin's company."

"No doubt,—no doubt!" And he looked preoccupied and thoughtful, then, with a sudden start, he exclaimed, "My good Beauvais! I forgot! Your marriage takes place almost immediately, does it not?"

"At the beginning of next month," I answered, smiling.

He seized me by both hands enthusiastically.

"Ah! *Voilà le bonheur qui vient vite!"* [2] And his eyes flashed radiance into mine,—"I am ashamed, Beauvais!—positively ashamed to have darkened your threshold with the shadow of myself in an ill-humour! A thousand pardons! I will go home and get to bed—with to-morrow's sun I shall probably rise a wiser and more cheerful man! Think no more of my peevishness; we all grumble at fate now and then. *Au revoir, cher ami!* [3] and may your dreams be rose-lit with the glory of love and the face of—Pauline!"

---

[1] French phrase meaning "A beautiful lie is worth more than reality." Proverbial.

[2] French phrase meaning "There's happiness that comes quickly."

[3] French phrase meaning "Goodbye, dear friend."

With a bright smile, more dazzling than usual by contrast with his previous gloom, he left me,—and I watched him from the street-door as he strode swiftly across the road and turned in the direction of his uncle's residence. His behaviour was certainly strange for one who was usually the very quintessence of saintly serenity and studious reserve;— I was puzzled by it, and could not make him out at all. However, after a little cogitation with myself, I came to the conclusion that matters were truly as he had said,—that Paris had unsettled him, and that he was beginning to have serious doubts as to whether after all it was his true vocation to be a priest. I myself had doubted it ever since I had come to know him intimately,—he was too fond of science and philosophy,—too clever, too handsome, and too young to resign all life's splendid opportunities for the service of a narrow and cramping religion. I could thoroughly understand the difficulty in which he was placed,—and I wished him well out of bondage into the liberty of the free. That night I was busy at my work up to the small hours of the morning; and when I did get to bed at last, my slumber was not very refreshing. I continued my task of adding up figures throughout my dreams, without ever arriving at any precise conclusion. I tried in the usual futile visionary way to come to some result of all these distressful and anxious calculations, but in vain,—the arithmetical jumble refused to clear itself up in any sort of fashion, and bothered me all night long, though now and then it dispersed itself out of numbers into words, and became a monotonous refrain of the lines—

"*Mieux que la réalité*
Vaut un beau mensonge!"

CHAPTER 9

On the following afternoon, between four and five o'clock, I went to see Pauline, as I had promised her mother I would,—a promise I myself was only too eager to fulfil. Remembering her extreme fondness for flowers, I bought a basket of lilies-of-the-valley at the establishment of a famous horticulturist, noted for his exquisite taste in floral designs,— it was tied with loops of white and palest pink ribbon;—and the delicate blossoms loved by Christ of old, were softly shaded over by the fine fronds of the prettiest fern known, the dainty maiden-hair. Armed with this fragrant trophy of love, I entered the little morning-room where

the "thé à l'Anglaise" was already prepared, and found Pauline awaiting me, looking a perfect fairy vision of youthful grace, mirth, and loveliness! She sprang forward to greet me,—she took the lilies from my
hands and kissed them,—she threw her arms round my neck and
thanked me with the same child-like rapture and enthusiasm that had
distinguished her on the night I first met her, when she had talked so
ecstatically about the "*marrons glacés*." I held her in my close embrace,
and studied her features with all a lover's passionate scrutiny,—but I
could discover no traces of tears in her eyes,—no touch of pallid grief
upon her rose-flushed cheeks;—her smiles were radiant as a June morning, and I inwardly rejoiced to find her so full of her old sparkling
animation and vivacity. Drawing a comfortable chair up to the table,
she made me sit down while she prepared the tea, and I watched her
with almost dazzled eyes of love and admiration, as she flitted about the
room like a sylph on wings.

"I was told that you were ill yesterday, Pauline!"—I said presently—
"That you were crying,—that you were unhappy. Was that true?"

She looked up laughing.

"Oh yes, quite true!" she answered, with a droll little gesture of self-
disdain. "So many tears, Gaston! I almost floated away on an ocean of
them! So many dreadful gasps and ugly sobs! *Tiens!*[1] I am sure I have a
red nose still, is it not so?" And, kneeling down beside me, she raised
her fair face to mine in mirthful inquiry. Kissing her, I told her she had
never looked lovelier, which was true,—whereupon she sprang up and
curtsied demurely.

"I am glad I am pretty still!" she said,—then all at once a darkness
crossed her brows like the shadow of a cloud. "How horrible it would
be to grow ugly, Gaston!—to get worn and thin and old, with great black
rings like spectacles round the eyes,—to lose all the gloss out of one's
hair,—and to be so weary, so weary, that the feet will hardly bear one
along! Ah!—I saw a woman like that the other day,—she sat on one of
the seats in the Bois, quite, quite alone,—with no one to pity her. Her
eyes said despair, despair!—always despair!—and my heart ached for her!"

"But you must not think about these things, my darling," I said,
taking her hand and drawing her towards me. "There are many such
sad sights in Paris and in all large cities,—but *you* must not dwell upon
them. And as for getting ugly!"—I laughed—"you need have no fear
of that!—you are growing more beautiful every day!"

---

[1]   French interjection translating in this instance as "Look!"

"You think so?" she queried with a coquettish inquisitiveness. "That is well! I am pleased,—for I wish to be beautiful."

"You *are* beautiful!" I re-asserted emphatically.

"Not as beautiful as I should like to be!" she murmured musingly. "There are some people,—even men,—who are possessed of beauty that can never be matched,—that is quite unique, like the beauty of the sculptured god-heroes, and then it is indeed wonderful!" She paused,— then rousing herself with a slight start, she went on more gaily. "Come, Gaston, we will have tea! We will be like the good people in England,—we will sip hot stuff and talk a little scandal between the sips. That is the proper way! Now there is your cup,—here is mine. *Bien!*[1]— Whom shall we abuse?"

I laughed,—she looked so pretty and mischievous.

"Wait a little," I said, "you have not told me yet *why* you cried so much yesterday, Pauline? You admit that you *did* cry,—well!—what was the reason?"

She shrugged her shoulders.

"*Qui sait!*[2] I cannot tell! It was pleasant—it did me good!"

"Pleasant to cry?" I queried amusedly.

"*Very* pleasant!" she answered. "Something was in my heart, you know,—something strange, like a bird that wished to sing and fly far far away!—but it was caged,—and so it fluttered and fluttered a little and teased me,—but when the tears came it was quite still. And now it remains quite still!—I do not think it will try to sing or to fly any more!"

There was a quaint touch of pathos in these words that moved me uneasily. I put down my as yet untasted cup of tea, and stretched out my hand.

"Come here, Pauline!"

She came obediently.

I sat her, like a little child, on my knee, and looked earnestly into her face.

"Tell me, my darling," I said, with tender seriousness, "is there anything that is troubling you? Have you some unhappiness that you conceal from every one?—and, if so, may *I* not be your confidant? Surely you can trust me! You know how truly and ardently I love you!—you know that I would do anything in the world for you,—you might set me any task, however difficult, and I would somehow manage

---

[1] French word meaning "well."
[2] French for "who knows?"

to perform it! My whole life is yours, my dearest!—will you not confide your griefs to me,—if you *have* griefs,—and let me not only share them, but lift the burden of them altogether from your mind, which ought to be as bright and untroubled as a midsummer sky!"

She met my searching gaze openly,—her breathing was a little quicker than usual, but she gave no other sign of disquietude.

"I have no griefs, Gaston," she said, in a low, rather tremulous voice; "none at least that I can give words to. I think—perhaps,—I am a little tired!—and—I have missed Héloïse——"

"Is *that* your trouble!" and I smiled. "But what will you do without Héloïse when you are married?"

"I—I do not know!" she faltered timidly. "I shall have *you* then!" I kissed her. "And you are very, very kind to me, Gaston! and I promise you——".

"What?" I asked eagerly.

She hesitated a moment, then went on—"I promise you I will tell you if I get sad again—yes!—I will tell you everything!—and you will be good and gentle with me, and comfort me, will you not?"

"Indeed I will, my darling, my angel!" I said, fondly caressing her pretty hair. "Who should console you in any sorrow if not I? I shall be quite jealous of Héloïse if she is to have the largest share of your confidence."

"But she will not have it," interrupted Pauline quite suddenly. "I could never tell her any—any *dreadful* trouble!"

I laughed. "Let us hope you will never know what any 'dreadful' trouble is!" I rejoined earnestly. "But why could you not tell Héloïse?"

She mused a little before replying,—then said, speaking slowly and thoughtfully—

"Because she is so great and grand and far above me in everything! Ah, you smile as if you did not believe me, Gaston,—but you do not know her! Héloïse is *divine*!—her goodness seems to me quite unearthly! I have caught her sometimes at her prayers—and it is beautiful to see her face looking as pure and sweet as an angel's!—and her lovely closed eyelids just like shut-up shells,—and she has such long lashes, Gaston!—longer than mine! She reminds me of a picture that used to hang in one of the chapels at the Convent of the Sacré Coeur,—Santa Filomena it was, crowned with thorns and lilies.[1] And she is so very very good in every way, that I know I should never have courage to tell her if—if I had been wicked!"

---

[1] Martyred Christian virgin widely venerated in the nineteenth century though not included in the official register of Christian martyrs. In art, Saint Philomena is depicted as a maiden with a lily or anchor and three arrows. She may also hold a palm and scourge.

Here she lowered her eyes, and a hot blush wavered across her face.

"But you have *not* been wicked, child!" I exclaimed, still somewhat puzzled by her manner. "You could not be wicked, if you tried!"

"You think not?" she returned softly, raising her eyes again to mine, and I observed that she was now as pale as she had a minute before been flushed. "Dear Gaston! You are so fond of me!—and always kind! I am very very grateful!"

Nestling down, she laid her head against my breast for a second,— then springing up again, pushed back her rich curls, and laughingly remonstrated with me for not drinking my tea.

"It is cold now,—I will pour you out some more," she said, suiting the action to the word. "Don't let us talk of disagreeable things, Gaston,—of my crying, and all that nonsense! It was very stupid of me to cry,—you must forget it,—for to-day I am quite well and merry,— and—and—oh, *do* let us be happy while we can!"

Whereupon she seated herself opposite to me, and began chatting away, just in her old bright fashion, of all sorts of things,—of her parents,—of the extra dainty luxuries 'Maman' had recently added to her *trousseau;*—and with feminine tact, she managed to draw together such an inexhaustible number of brilliant trifles in her conversation, that, charmed by her vivacity, I ceased to remember that she could ever have been sad, even for an hour. But, before I left her, I was made miserable again by a very untoward circumstance. Just when I was about to say good-bye,—for the excess of my work would not allow me to stay with her longer,—I alluded once more to her past depression, and said—

"You are such a bright fairy now, Pauline, that I think you must try and put our friend Guidèl in better spirits when next you see him. He seems in a very melancholy frame of mind! Oddly enough, yesterday, when *you* were so sad, he was with me, giving utterance to the most lugubrious sentiments. In fact, I thought he was ill"—Pauline was about to fasten a flower in my coat, but here she dropped it, and stooped down on the floor to find it—"so ill," I continued, "that I was for going home with him to see that he got there all right; but he assured me it was only a *maladie de tristesse.*[1] I fancy he doesn't want to be a priest after all"—here Pauline found the fallen blossom she was searching for, and began to pin it in my button-hole with such shaking fingers that I became alarmed.

"Why, you are shivering, my darling! Are you cold?"

"A little!" she murmured. "I—I——" The sentence died on her lips,

---

[1] French phrase meaning "melancholy."

and with a helpless swaying movement she fell in a sudden swoon at my feet!

Wild with fright, I caught her up in my arms, and rang the bell furiously,—the Comtesse de Charmilles came hurrying in, and, in obedience to her rapid instructions, I laid my pretty little one down on a sofa, and looked on in rigid anxiety, while her mother bathed her hands and forehead with eau-de-cologne.

"She has fainted like this once before," said the Comtesse, in a low tone. "Do not be alarmed, Gaston,—she will be all right in a minute or two. Did you ask her what I told you?"

I nodded in the affirmative. I could not take my eyes off the lovely little face that lay so pale and quiet on the sofa-pillows near me.

"And did she say anything?"

"Nothing!" I answered with a sigh. "Nothing, except that she was quite well, and quite happy, and that she had no grief whatever. And she promised that if ever she felt sad again, she would come to me and tell me everything!"

A look of evident relief brightened the mother's watchful face, and she smiled.

"That is well!" she said gently. "I am glad she promised that! As for this little *malaise*,[1] I attach no importance to it. Young and over-excitable girls often faint in this foolish little way. There!—she is better now—see!—she is looking at you!"

And indeed the sweet blue eyes, that were heaven's own light to my soul, had opened, and were fixed wistfully upon me. Eagerly I bent over her couch.

"Is that you, Gaston?" she faintly inquired.

For all answer I kissed her.

"Thank you!" she said, with a pretty plaintiveness. "Now you will go away, will you not?—and let mamma take care of me. My head aches—but that is nothing. I shall be quite well again soon!" She smiled, and the warm colour came back to her cheeks. "*Au revoir*, Gaston! Kiss me once more,—it comforts me to think how good and true and kind you are!"

With what reverential tenderness I pressed my lips to hers, Heaven only knows!—I little imagined it was the last time I should ever touch that sweet mouth with the passionate sign of love's dearest benediction! She closed her eyes again then,—and the Comtesse told me in a soft undertone, that she would now in all probability fall asleep and slumber

---

[1] French word for "indisposition."

away her temporary weakness,—so, making my whispered adieux to the gentle and patiently absorbed mother, I stole on tip-toe from the room, and in another minute or two, had left the house.

Once out in the open air, however, I became a prey to the most extraordinary and violent anxiety. Everything to my mind looked suddenly overcast with gloom, I knew not why. Certainly the sun had set, and the dusk was deepening,—but the closing-in of the evening shadows did not, as a rule, affect my spirits with such a sense of indefinable dreariness. I walked home mechanically, brooding on Pauline's fainting-fit, and exaggerating it more and more in my thoughts till it assumed the proportion of an ominous symptom of approaching death. I worked myself up into such a morbid condition of mind, that the very trees, covered with their young green and bursting buds, merely suggested the trees in cemeteries, that were also looking heartlessly gay, because it was Spring, regardless of the dead in the ground below them. And, occupied with my miserable musings, I nearly ran up against Silvion Guidèl, who was coming in an opposite direction,—he looked like the ghost of a fair lost god, I thought,—so wan and wild-eyed yet beautiful was he. He caught my hands eagerly.

"Where are you going, Beauvais? You look as if you were stumbling along in a dream!"

I forced a smile. "I dare say I do,—I feel like it! Pauline is very ill, Guidèl!—she fainted at my feet to-day!"

He turned sharply round as though he suddenly perceived some one he knew,—then hurriedly apologized.

"I thought I saw my old *chiffonier*,"[1] he said lightly. "A friend and pensioner of mine, to whom for my soul's sake I give many an odd sou.[2] Mademoiselle de Charmilles fainted, you say? Oh, but that is not a very alarming symptom!"

I considered that he treated the case with undue levity, and told him so rather vexedly. He laughed a little.

"*Mon cher*, I will not encourage you in your morbid humour any more than you encouraged me last night in mine. You are—like all lovers—inclined to exaggerate, every trifling ailment affecting the well-being of the person loved. If *I* loved,—if I could love,—I suppose I should be the same! But I have the hollow heart of a perpetual celibate, *mon ami*!"—and he laughed again—"so I can be merry and wise, both

---

[1] French word for "ragman."
[2] French unit of money worth five centimes.

together. And out of my mirth—which is great,—and my wisdom—which is even greater!—I would advise you not to dwell with such melancholy profoundness on the slight indisposition of your fair *fiancée.* To faint is nothing,—many a school-girl faints at early mass, and the teachers think it of very little import."

But I was too full of my own view of the matter to listen.

"All in one minute"—I persisted morosely—"the dear child fell in a dead swoon,—and I had just been speaking to her about *you!*"

"About me!" and he bit his lips hard. "*Mon Dieu!*—what an uninteresting subject of conversation."

"I had been telling her"—I went on—"that you seemed to be ill last night,—ill and sad; and I had even suggested that she, out of her own brightness, should try to put you in better spirits the next time she saw you,——Really, Guidèl, you are horribly brusque to-day!"

For he had seized my hand, shaken it, and was actually rushing off!

"A thousand pardons, *mon cher!*" he said, in quick, rather hoarse accents; "I am bound on an errand of charity—I must fulfil it!—it is getting late, and I have very little time! *Au revoir!* I will see you later on!"

And away he went, walking at an unusually rapid rate,—and for the moment I was quite hurt at the entire want of sympathy he had shown with regard to Pauline's illness. But I presently came to the conclusion that of course *he* could not be expected to feel as *I* felt about it,—and I resumed the nursing of my own dismal mood in unrelieved despondency till I reached home, where the work I had to do in part distracted me from my sadder thoughts. No one interrupted me. Silvion Guidèl did not come "later on" as he had said, and I saw him no more that night. Towards bed-time I got a telegram from my father, announcing that he would return home on the next day but one. This news was some slight consolation to me,—as, with his arrival, I knew I should be released from many onerous duties at the bank,—and so have more time to spend in Pauline's company. Yet, nevertheless, I remained in the same state of mental dejection, mingled with a certain vague and superstitious morbidness,—for when I went up to my bedroom, and looked out at the skies before shutting the shutters, I saw a dense black rain-cloud creeping up from the western horizon, and I at once took it as an ill omen to my own fortunes. I watched it darkening the heavens slowly and blotting out the stars; and, as I heard the wind beginning to moan softly among the near branches, I murmured to myself almost unconsciously—

"Les âmes dont j'aurais besoin
Et les étoiles sont trop loin!
Je vais mourir seul—dans un coin!"[1]

These lines worried me,—I could not imagine how they had managed to fix themselves in my memory. I put them down to Héloïse and her bizarre recitations,—but all the same they made me inexplicably wretched. Shivering with the chill the approaching storm was already sending through the air, I closed my window, went to bed, and slept soundly, peacefully, and deliciously;—I remember it thus particularly because it was the last time I experienced the blessing of sleep. The last,—the very last time I say! I have not slept at all since then,—I have only dreamed!

CHAPTER 10

With the morrow's daybreak came a complete change in the weather,—a change that was infinitely dismal and dreary. The bright sunshine, that had been like God's best blessing on the world for the past two weeks, disappeared as though it had never shone, and rain fell in torrents. A wild wind blew round and round the city in sweeping gusts, tearing off the delicate young leaves from their parent branches, and making pitiful havoc of all the sweet-scented gaily-coloured spring blossoms. It was a miserable morning,—but in spite of wind and rain I started rather earlier than usual for the bank, as, my father having now signified the next day as the one of his certain return, I was anxious he should find everything in the most absolute order on his arrival, and thus be assured of my value not only as a good son, but also as a thoroughly reliable partner. We were all up to our ears in work that day,— a great deal of extra business came in, and the hours flew on so rapidly that it was past six o'clock in the afternoon before I was released from my office bondage,—and, even then, I still had a good many matters to attend to when I got back to my own house. I had no leisure to call at

---

[1] "The souls that I would need / And the stars are too far! / I will die alone—in a corner." The last stanza of "Conclusion" in Charles Cros's *Le Coffret de santal* (1873). Corelli's version differs in one significant respect from that of the original—where she has "seul," meaning alone, Cros has "soûl," meaning drunk. In the original version, then, the narrator of the poem dies "drunk in a corner."

the De Charmilles', though I longed to know how Pauline was,—but I did not fret myself so greatly about that now as previously, knowing that by the next noon my father would have arrived, and that I should then have my time very much more at my own disposal. The rain still continued pouring fiercely,—very few people were abroad in the streets,—and though I took the omnibus part of the way home, the few steps that remained between that vehicle and my own door, were sufficient to drench me through. As soon as I got in, I changed my clothes, had my solitary dinner, and ordered a small wood fire to be lit in the library, whither I presently repaired with my papers and account books, and was soon so busily engrossed that I almost forgot the angry storm that was raging without, save in the intervals of work, when I heard the rain beat in gusty clamour at the windows, and the trees groan as they rustled and swayed backwards and forwards in the increasing fury of the gale. Presently, from the antique time-piece, that stood on an equally antique *secrétaire*[1] just behind me, nine o'clock struck with a loud and brazen clang,—and as it ceased I laid down my pen for a moment and listened to the deepening snarl of the savage elements.

"What a night!" I thought. "A night for demons to stalk abroad, and witches to ride through the air on broomsticks! *Dieu!*[2] how dull it is! One must smoke to keep the damp away."

And I opened my cigar-case. I was just about to strike a light, when I fancied I heard something like a faint, very faint attempt to ring the street-door bell. I listened,—the same sound was repeated. It was much too feeble to attract the attention of the servants below,—and as the library windows jutted on the street, and as I could, by drawing aside the curtain a little, generally see whosoever might ascend our steps, I peeped cautiously out. At first I could perceive nothing, the night was so wet and dark; but presently I discerned a slight shadowy figure huddled against the door as though sheltering itself from the pitiless rain.

"Some poor starving soul," I soliloquized, "who perhaps does not know where to turn in all Paris for bread. I'll see who it is."

And, acting on the impulse that moved me to be charitable to any unhappy creature benighted in such a hurricane, I crossed the passage softly and opened the door wide. As I did so, the figure started back in apparent fear,—it was a veiled woman,—and through the veil I felt her eyes looking at me.

---

[1] French word for a "writing desk."

[2] French word for "God."

"What is it?" I asked, as gently as I could. "What do you want?"

For all answer, two hands were stretched towards me in wild appeal, and a sobbing voice cried—

"Gaston!"

"My God! *Pauline!*"

Seized by a mortal terror, and with a convulsive effort as though I were dragging forth some drowning creature from the sea, I caught her in my arms and almost lifted her across the threshold; how I supported her, whether I carried her or led her, I never knew,—my senses were all in a whirl, and I realized nothing distinctly till I had reached the library once more, and placed her, a shuddering, drooping little creature, in the arm-chair I had but just vacated near the fire. Then my dazed brain righted itself, and I flung myself at her feet in an agony of alarm and suspense.

"Pauline, Pauline!" I whispered, "what is this?—why have you come here? In such a storm of rain and wind too! See!"—and I took up the end of her dress and wrung it in my hands—"you are wet through! My darling, you frighten me!—Are you ill?—has any one been unkind to you?"

She lifted her head and tremblingly put back the close veil she wore,—and I uttered a stifled cry at the pale misery imprinted on her fair, fair young face.

"No one has been unkind," she said, in a faint plaintive voice, like the voice of one weakened by long physical suffering; "and—I am not ill! I want to speak to you, Gaston!—I promised you that if I was very sad and troubled, I would tell you everything,—and you said you would be gentle with me and would comfort me,—you remember? Well, now I have come!—to tell you something that must be told,—and to-night is my only chance,—for they have gone,—papa and mamma—to the theatre, and I am all alone. They wanted me to go with them, but I begged them to leave me at home,—I felt that I must see you quite by yourself,—and tell you,—yes!—tell you everything!"

A long shivering sigh escaped her lips; and frozen to the very soul by a dim fear that I could not analyze, I rose from my kneeling position at her side, and stood stiffly upright. At first my only thought was for her. A young girl coming alone to the house of her lover at night in a city like Paris, exposed herself, consciously or unconsciously, to the direst slander, and it was with this idea that I was chiefly occupied as I looked at her crouching form in the chair beside me. I hastily considered the only possible risk she at present incurred,—namely, that of being seen by our servants and made the subject of their idle gossip, and I determined to circumvent this at any rate.

"Pauline, my little one," I said gravely, "whatever it is you wish to tell me, could you not have waited till I came to see you in the usual way? You ought not to have flown hither so recklessly, little bird! you expose yourself to scandal."

"Scandal!" she echoed, looking at me with a feverish light in her blue eyes. "It cannot say more evil of me than I deserve!—and I could not wait!—I have waited already far too long!"

A great heaviness fell on my heart at these words,—my very lips grew cold, and a tremor ran through me. But, nevertheless, I resolved to carry out the notion I had preconceived of keeping this nocturnal flight of hers a profound secret.

"Stay here," I said, as calmly as I could for the shaking dread that possessed me. "Try to get warm,—I will bring you some wine. Take that wet cloak off and be quite quiet,—I will return immediately."

She looked after me with a sort of beseeching wonderment as I left her,—but I dared not meet her eyes—there was an expression in them that terrified me! I went, as in a dream, to the dining-room; got some wine and a glass,—carefully turned out the lights, and then proceeded to the head of the basement stairs and called our man-servant.

"Dunois!"

"*Oui, m'sieu!*"[1]

"Tell them all down there that they can go to bed,—you can do the same. I shall want nothing more to-night. I have locked the street-door, and the lamps are out in the dining-room. My father will be home to-morrow,—so you will all have to be up early—call me about seven. Do you hear?"

"*Oui, m'sieu!* Good night!"

Dunois responded,—and I listened breathlessly while he repeated my orders to the other servants. I waited yet a few minutes and presently heard them preparing to ascend their own private stairway to the top of the house, where they each had their several rooms. They were hard workers, and were always glad of extra rest;—they would soon be sound asleep, thank Heaven!—they need know nothing. Satisfied that so far, all was safe, I stepped noiselessly back to the library, and, entering, closed and locked the door. Pauline was sitting exactly in the same position,— her wet cloak still clinging round her,—her veil flung back, her hands

---

[1]   French phrase meaning "Yes, sir."

clasped, and her eyes fixed on the red embers of the fire. Approaching, I, without a word, loosened her cloak and took it off, and methodically hung it on the back of two chairs to dry,—I removed the little rain-soaked hat from her tumbled curls, and pouring out a glass of wine, held it to her lips with a firm hand enough, though God knows my heart was beating as though it would burst its fleshly prison.

"Drink this, Pauline," I said authoritatively. "Come, you *must* drink it,—you are as cold as ice. When you have taken it, I will listen to—to whatever you wish to say."

She obeyed me mechanically, and managed to swallow half the contents of the glass,—then she put it away from her with a faint gesture of aversion.

"I cannot drink it, Gaston!" she faltered,—"it seems to suffocate me!"

I set it aside, and looked at her, waiting for her next words. But no words came. She fixed her large soft eyes upon me with the wistful entreaty of a hunted fawn,—then suddenly the tears welled up into them and brimmed over, and, covering her face, she broke into piteous and passionate sobbing. Every nerve in my body seemed to be wrenched and tortured by the sound!—I could not bear to see her in such grief, and, kneeling down beside her once more, I put my arms round her and pressed her pretty head against my breast. But I did not kiss her; some strange instinct held me back from that!

"Do not cry, Pauline!—do not cry!" I implored, rocking her to and fro as if she were a little tired child. "Do not, my darling!—it breaks my heart! Tell me what is the matter,—you are not afraid of me, *mon ange,* —are you? Hush, hush! To see you in such unhappiness quite distracts me, Pauline!—it unmans me,—do try to be calm! You are quite safe with me,—no one will come near us,—no one knows you are here,— and I will take you home myself as soon as you are more tranquil. There!—now you shall speak to me as long as you like,—you shall tell me everything—everything, except that you do not love me any more!"

With a faint exclamation and a sudden movement, she loosened my arms from her waist and drew herself apart.

"Oh, poor Gaston!—but that is just what I *must* tell you!" she sobbed. "Oh, forgive me—forgive me! I have done you great wrong,—I have deceived you wickedly,—but oh, do not be cruel to me, though I am so cruel to you! Do not be cruel,—I cannot bear it!—it will kill me! I ought to have told you long ago,—but I was a coward,—I was afraid,— I am afraid still!—but I dare not hide the truth from you,—you must know everything. I—I do not love you, Gaston! I have never loved you as you ought to be loved; I never knew the meaning of love till now!"

Till now! What did these words imply? I gazed at her in dumb blank amazement,—my brain seemed frozen. I could not think, I could not speak,—I only knew, in a sort of dim indistinct way, that she had removed herself from my embrace, and that perhaps——perhaps it was, under the circumstances, embarrassing to her to see me kneeling at her feet in such devout, adoring fashion, when, ... *when she no longer loved me!* She no longer loved me!—I could not realize it;—and still less could I realize that she never *had* loved me! I got up slowly and stood beside her, resting one arm on the mantelpiece,—my limbs shook and my head swam round stupidly,—and yet, through all my bewilderment, I was still conscious of *her* misery,—conscious of her tear-spoilt eyes,—her white face and quivering lips,—and of the unutterable despair that made even her youthful features look drawn and old,—and out of very pity for her woe-begone aspect, I tried to master the sudden shock of unexpected wretchedness that overwhelmed my soul. I tried to speak,—my voice seemed gone,—and it was only after one or two efforts that I managed to regain command of language.

"This is strange news!" I then said, in hoarse unsteady accents. "Very strange news, Pauline! You no longer love me? You have never loved me? You never knew the meaning of love till now?—*Till now!*—Pardon me if I do not understand,—I am, no doubt, dull of comprehension,—but such words from your lips sound terrible to me,—unreal, impossible! I must have been dreaming all this while, for—for you have *seemed* to love me—till now, as you say—*till now!*"

She sprang from her chair and confronted me, her hands extended as though in an agony of supplication.

"Oh, there is my worst sin, Gaston!" she wailed. "There is the treachery to you of which I have been guilty! I have *seemed* to love you—yes! and it was wicked of me,—wicked—wicked!—but I have been blind and desperate and mad,—and I could see no way out of the evil I have brought upon myself,—no way but this—to tell you all before it is too late,—to throw myself at your feet—so!"—and she flung herself wildly down before me—"to pray to you, as I would pray to God,—to ask you to pardon me, to have mercy upon me,—and, above all other things, to generously break the tie between us,—to break it now—at once!—and to let me feel that at least I am no longer wronging your trust, or injuring your future by my fault of love for one who has grown dearer to me than you could ever be,—dearer than life itself,—dearer than honour,—dearer than my own soul's safety—dearer than God!"

She spoke with an almost tempestuous intensity of passion,—and I looked at her where she crouched on the ground,—looked at her in a dull, sick wonderment. This child—this playful pretty trifler with time and the things of time, was transformed;—from a mere charming gracefully frivolous girl, she had developed into a wild tragedy queen; and the change had been effected by—what? Love! Love for what,—for whom? Not for me!—not for me—no!—for some one else! *Who* was that some one else? This question gradually asserted itself in my straying stupefied thoughts as the chief thing to be answered,—the vital poison of the whole bitter draught,—the final stab that was to complete the murder. As I considered it, a new and awful instinct rose up within me,—the thirst for revenge that lurks in the soul of every man and beast,—the silently concentrated fury of the tiger that has lain so long in waiting for its prey that its brute patience is well-nigh exhausted,—and involuntarily I clenched my hands and bit my lips hard in the sudden and insatiate eagerness that possessed me, to know the name of my rival! Again I looked down on Pauline's slight shuddering figure, and became hazily conscious that she ought not to kneel there as a suppliant to me, and,—stooping a little, I held out my hand, which she caught and kissed impulsively. Ah, Heaven! how I trembled at that caressing touch!

"Rise, Pauline!" I said, trying to keep my voice steady. "Rise,—do not be afraid!—I—I think I understand,—I shall realize it all better presently. Perhaps you have never quite known how ardently I have loved you,—with what passionate fervour,—with what adoring tenderness!—and what you say to me now is a shock, Pauline!—a cruel blow that will numb and incapacitate my whole life! But one man's pain does not matter much, does it?—come, rise, I beg of you, and let me strive to get some clearer knowledge of this sad and unexpected change in your feelings. You do not love me, so you tell me,—and you never have loved me. You own to having played the part of loving me,—but now you ask me to break the solemn tie between us, because you love some one else,—have I understood you thus far correctly?"

She had sunk back again in the chair near the fire, and her pale lips whispered a faint affirmative. I waited a minute,—then I asked—

"And who, Pauline,—who is that some one else?"

"Oh, why should you know!" she exclaimed, the tears filling her eyes again. "Why should you even *wish* to know! It is not needful,—it would only add to your unhappiness! I cannot tell you, Gaston!—I will not!"

I laughed,—a low laugh of exceeding bitterness. The notion of her keeping such a secret from *me*, amused me in a vague dull way. In my present humour, I felt that I could have ransacked not only earth, but heaven and hell together for that one name which would henceforth be to me the most hateful in the whole world! But I forced myself to be gentle with her; I even tried to persuade myself into the idea that she was perhaps exaggerating a mere transient foolish flirtation into the tragic height of a serious love-affair,—and I was under the influence of this impression when I spoke again.

"Listen, Pauline! You must not play with me any longer,—if you *have* played with me, I can endure no more of it! I *must* know who it is that has usurped my rightful place in your affections. Do not try to conceal it from me,—it will only be doing an injury to yourself and to—*him*! Is it some one you have met lately? And is your love for him a mere sudden freak of fancy?—because if so, Pauline, let me tell you, it is not likely to last! And so great and deep is my tenderness for you, dear, that I could even find it in my heart to have patience with this cruel caprice of your woman's nature,—to have patience to the extent of waiting till it passes, as pass it *must*, Pauline!—no love of lasting value was ever kindled with such volcanic suddenness as this fickle fantasy of yours! Had the famous lovers of Verona[1] not died, they must have quarrelled! Your words, your manner, all spring from impulse, not conviction,—and I should be wronging you,—yes! actually wronging your better nature, if I were to hastily yield to your strange request and end the engagement between us. Why should I end it? for a wandering fitful fancy of yours, that will no doubt die of itself as rapidly as it came into being? No, Pauline!—our contract is too solemn and too binding to be broken for a mere girlish whim!"

"But it *must* be broken!" she cried, springing to her feet and confronting me with a pale majesty of despair that moved me to vague awe. "It must be broken if I die to break it! Whim!—fancy!—caprice!—Do I look as if I were led by a freak? Can you not—will you not understand me, Gaston? Oh, God! I thought you were more merciful!—I have looked upon you as my only friend;—I knew you were the very soul of generosity—and I have clung to the thought of your tenderness as my only chance of rescue! I cannot—I dare not, tell them at home,—I am even afraid to meet Héloïse! Oh, Gaston! only *you* can shield me from disgrace,—you can release me if you will, and give me the chance

---

[1] Reference to Shakespeare's young, star-crossed lovers, Romeo and Juliet.

of freedom in which to retrieve my fault!—Gaston, you can!—you can do everything for me!—you can save me by one generous act,—break off our engagement and say to all the world that it is by our own mutual desire! Oh, surely you can understand now!—you will not force me to confess all my shame—all my dishonour!"

Shame!—*dishonour!*—Those two words, and—Pauline! The air grew suddenly black around me,—black as blackest night,—then bright red rings swam giddily before my eyes, and I caught at something, I know not what, to save myself from falling. A cold dew broke out on my brow and hands, and I struggled for breath in deep panting gasps, conscious of nothing for the moment, except that *she* was there, and that her wild eyes were fixed in wide affright upon me. Presently I heard her voice as in a dream, cry out wailingly—

"Gaston! Gaston! Do not look like that! Oh, God, forgive me! what have I done!—what have I done!"

Slowly the black mists cleared from my sight,—and I seemed to reel uncertainly back to a sense of being.

"What have you done?" I muttered hoarsely. "What have you done, Pauline?—Why—nothing!—but this,—you have fallen from virtue to vileness!—and—you have killed *me*!—that is all! *That* is what you have done,—*that*, at last, I understand,—at last!"

She broke into a piteous sobbing,—but her tears had ceased to move me. I sprang to her side,—I seized her arm.

"Now—now—quick!" I said, the furious passion in my voice jarring it to rough discord —"quick!—I can wait no longer! The name—the name of your seducer!"

She raised her eyes full of speechless alarm,—her lips moved, but no sound issued from them. There was a suffocating tightness in my throat,—my heart leaped to and fro in my breast like a savage bird in a cage,—the wrath that possessed me was so strong and terrible that it made me for the moment a veritable madman.

"Oh speak!" I cried, my grasp tightening on her arm. "Frail, false, fallen woman, speak!—or I shall murder you! The name!—the name!"

Half swooning with the excess of her terror, she vainly strove to disengage herself from my hold,—her head drooped on her bosom— her eyes closed in the very languor of fear,—and her answering whisper stole on my strained sense of hearing like the last sigh of the dying—

"*Silvion Guidèl!*"

Silvion Guidèl!—God! I burst into wild laughter, and flung her from me with a gesture of fierce disdain. Silvion Guidèl!—the saint!—the angel!—the would-be priest!—the man with the face divine! Silvion Guidèl! Detestable hypocrite!—accursed liar!—smiling devil! Priest or no priest, he should cross swords with me, and thereby probe a great mystery presently!—not a church-mystery, but a God-mystery—the mystery of death! He should die, I swore, if I in fair fight could kill him! Silvion Guidèl!—*my* friend!—the "good" fellow I had actually revered!—he—he had made of Pauline the wrecked thing she was!—Ah, Heaven! A wild impulse seized me to rush out of the house and find him wherever he might be,—to drag him from the very church altar if he dared to pollute such a place by his traitorous presence,—and make him then and there answer with his life for the evil he had done! My face must have expressed my raging thoughts,—for suddenly a vision crossed my dazed and aching sight—the figure of Pauline grown stately, terrible, imperial, as any ruined queen.

"You shall not harm him!" she said in low thrilling tones of suppressed passion and fear. "You shall not touch a hair of his head to do him wrong! *I* will prevent you!—I! I would give my life to shield him from a moment's pain!—and you dare—you dare to think of injuring him! Oh yes! I read you through and through;—you have reason, I know, to be cruel—and you may kill *me* if you like,—but not him! Have I not told you that I love him?—Love him?—I adore him! I have sacrificed everything for his sake,—and could I sacrifice more than everything I would do it!—I would burn in hell for ever, could I be sure that he was safe and happy in heaven!"

She looked at me straightly,—her eyes full of a mournful exaltation,—her breath coming and going rapidly between her parted lips. I met her glance with an amazed scorn,—and hurled the bitter truth like pellets of ice upon the amorous heat of her impetuous avowal.

"Oh, spare me your protestations!" I cried,—"and spare yourself some shred of shame! Do not boast of your iniquity as though it were virtue!—do not blazon forth your criminal passion as though it were a glory! Heaven and Hell of which you talk so lightly, may be positive and awful facts after all, and not mere names to swear by!—and to one or the other of them your lover shall go, be assured!—and that speedily! He shall die for his treachery!—he shall die, I say!—if the sword of honour can rid the world of so perfidious and dastardly a liar!"

CHAPTER 11

As I uttered these words sternly and resolvedly, a change passed over her face,—she seemed for the moment to grow rigid with the sudden excess of her fear. Then she threw herself once more on her knees at my feet.

"Gaston, Gaston!—have a little mercy!" she implored. "Think of my deep,—my utter humiliation! Is it so much that I ask of you after all?—to break an engagement with a wretched sinful girl who has proved herself unworthy of you? Oh, for God's sake set me free!—and we will go away from Paris, I and Silvion—far, far away to some distant land where we shall be forgotten,—where the memory of us need trouble you no more! Listen, Gaston! Silvion trusts to your noble nature and generous heart, even as I have done—he believes that you will have pity upon us both! We loved each other from the first,—could we help that love, Gaston?—could we help it? I told you I never knew what love was till now, and that is true!—I was so young!—I never thought I *should* know such desperate joy, such terrible misery, such madness, such reck-lessness, such despair! It seems that I have fallen into some great resist-less river that carries me along with it against my will, I know not where!—I have deceived you, I know, and I pray your pardon for that deceit—but oh, be pitiful, Gaston!—be pitiful!—it cannot hurt you to be generous! If you ever loved me, Gaston, try to forgive me now!"

I looked down upon her in silence. There was a dull aching in my brows,—a cold chill at my heart. She seemed removed from me by immeasurable distance;—she, the once innocent child—the pretty graceful girl, all sweetness and purity,—what was she now? Nothing but—the toy of Silvion Guidèl! No more!—she had entered the melan-choly ranks of the ruined sisterhood,—even she, Pauline de Charmilles, only daughter of one of the proudest aristocrats in France! I shud-dered,—and an involuntary groan escaped my lips. Clasping her hands, she raised them to me in fresh entreaty.

"You will be gentle, Gaston!—you will have mercy?"

The tension of my nerves relaxed,—the scalding moisture of unfalling tears blinded my eyes—and I gave vent to a long and bitter sigh.

"Give me time, Pauline!" I answered huskily. "Give me time! you ask much of me,—and I have never—like your lover—played the part of saint or angel. I am nothing but a man, with all a man's passions roused to their deadliest sense of wrong,—do not expect from me more than man's strength is capable of! And I have loved you!—my God!—how I have loved you!—far far more deeply than you ever guessed! Pauline, Pauline!—my love was honourably set upon you!—I would not have wronged you by so much as one unruly thought! You were to me more sacred than the Virgin's statue in her golden nook at incense-time; you were my God's light on earth,—my lily of heaven,—my queen—my life—my eternity—my all! Pauline, Pauline!"—and my voice trembled more and more as she hid her face in her hands and wept convulsively. "Alas, you cannot realize what you have done—not yet! You cannot in the blindness of your passion see how the world will slowly close upon you like a dark prison wherein to expiate in tears and pain your sin,— you do not yet comprehend how the kindly faces you have known from childhood will turn from you in grief and scorn,—how friends will shrink from and avoid you,—and how desolate your days will be,—too desolate, Pauline, for even your betrayer's love to cheer! For love that begins in crime ends in destruction,—its evil recoils on the heads of those that have yielded to its insidious tempting,—and thinking of this, Pauline, I *can* pity you!—pity you more—aye, a thousand times more than I should pity you if you were dead! I would rather you had died, unhappy child, than lived to be dishonoured!"

She made no reply, but still covered her face, and still wept on,—and, steadying my nerves, I bent down and raised her by gentle force from the ground. The clock struck eleven as I did so,—she had been two hours with me,—it was full time she should return as quickly as possible to her home. Acting promptly on this idea, I gave her her hat and cloak.

"Put these on!" I said.

She removed her hands from her eyes—such woeful eyes!—all swollen and red with weeping,—and tremblingly obeyed me,—her breast heaving with the sobs she could not restrain.

"Now come with me,—softly!" And I took her ice-cold hand in mine and led her out of the room and across the darkened passage, where, stopping a moment to hastily don my overcoat and hat, I cautiously opened the street-door without making the least noise. The strong wind blew gusts of rain in our faces,—and I strove to shelter the shivering girl as best I could with my own body, as I closed the door again behind us as quietly as I had opened it. Then I turned to her with formal courtesy.

"You must walk a little way, I am afraid,—it will not be wise to call a carriage up to this very house,—your departure might be noticed."

She came down the steps at once like a blind creature, seeming scarcely to feel her way, and as I observed her feebleness, and the tottering swaying movement of her limbs, my own wretchedness was suddenly submerged in an overwhelming wave of intense compassion for her fate. Involuntarily I stretched out my hand to save her from stumbling, and, in the very extremity of my anguish, I cried—

"Oh, Pauline! oh, poor little pretty Pauline!"

At this she looked up wildly—and with a low shuddering wail fled to my arms and clung there like a scared bird, panting for breath. I held her to my heart for one despairing minute—then,—remembering all,—I strove for fresh mastery over my feelings, and, putting her gently yet firmly away from my embrace, I supported her with one arm as we walked some little distance along the flooded pavement in the full opposing force of the wind. As soon as I saw a disengaged close carriage, I hailed its driver, and, assisting Pauline into the vehicle, I took my own place beside her. We were soon borne along rapidly in the direction of the Comte de Charmilles' residence; and then my trembling half-weeping companion seemed to awake to new fears.

"What are you going to do, Gaston?" she asked, in a nervous whisper.

"Nothing!"

"Nothing?" she echoed, her white face gleaming like the face of a ghost, in the yellow glare of the carriage lamps.

"Nothing—except to see you home in safety,—and afterwards to return home myself."

"But—Silvion——" she faltered.

"Do not be alarmed, mademoiselle!" I said, my wrath rousing itself anew at bare mention of his name. "I shall not seek him to-night at any rate. It is too late to arrange the scores between us!"

"Gaston!" she murmured sobbingly. "I have asked you to have mercy!"

"And I have said that you must give me time," I responded. "I must think out what will be best for me to do. Meanwhile—for the immediate present—your secret is safe with me,—I shall tell no one of your—your——" I could not finish the sentence—the word 'dishonour' choked me in the utterance.

"But you will break off our engagement, will you not?" she implored anxiously. "You will tell them all that we have changed our minds?—that we cannot be married?"

I regarded her fixedly.

"I do not know that I shall put it in that way," I answered. "To justify my own conduct in breaking off our marriage, I shall of course find it necessary to tell your father the cause of the rupture."

She shuddered back into the corner of the carriage.

"Oh, it will kill him!" she moaned. "It will kill him, I am sure!"

"One murder more or less scarcely matters in such a wholesale slaughter of true tenderness," I said coldly. "You have chosen your own fate, Pauline—and you must abide by it. Will your lover marry you, do you think, when you are free?"

She looked up quickly, her eyes lightened by a sudden hope.

"Yes; he will—he must! He has sworn it!"

"Then bid him fulfil his oath at once," I rejoined. "Bid him set you right as far as he can in the eyes of the world before it is too late. If this is done, your difficulty is almost dispensed with,—you need trouble yourself no more about *me* or my life's ruin! The fact of a private marriage having been consummated between you and M. Guidèl will put an end to all discussion, so far as *I* am concerned!"

A weary puzzled expression crossed her features,—and I smiled bitterly. I knew—I felt instinctively that he—after the fashion of all trai- tor-seducers of women,—would not be in very eager haste to marry his victim!

Just then we turned into the broad beautiful avenue where the Comte de Charmilles had his stately, but now (alas! had he but known it!) ruined home.

"Listen!" I said, bending towards her and emphasizing my words impressively. "I will release you from your engagement to me if Silvion Guidèl consents to wed you immediately, without a day's delay! Failing this, I must, as I told you, have time to consider as to what will be the wisest and best course of action for all in this terrible affair."

The carriage stopped; we descended,—and I paid and dismissed the driver. Murmuring feebly that she would go through the garden and enter the house by the large French window of the morning-room through which she had secretly made her exit, Pauline wrapped her mantle closely round her, and there in the storm and rain, raised her sorrowful blue eyes once more to mine in passionate appeal.

"Pity me, Gaston!" she said—"Pity me! Think of my shame and misery!—and think, oh think, Gaston, that you *can* save me if you will! God make you kind to me!"

And, with a faint sobbing sigh, she waved her hand feebly in farewell, and entering the great armorial gates, glided round among the trees of the garden, and, like a flitting phantom, disappeared.

Left alone, I stood on the pavement like one in a dazed dream. The icy rain beat upon me, the wild gale tore at me,—and I was not clearly conscious of either sleet or wind. Once I stared up at the black sky where the scurrying clouds were chasing each other in mountainous heaps of rapid and dark confusion,—and in that one glance, the light-ning-truth seemed to flash upon me with more deadly vividness than ever,—the truth that for me the world was at an end! Life, and the joys and hopes and ambitions that make life desirable, all these were over— there was nothing left for me to do but to drag on in sick and dull monotony the mechanical business of the daily routine of waking, eating, drinking, sleeping,—a mere preservation of existence when exis-tence had for ever lost its charm! I was roused from my stupefied condi-tion by the noise of wheels, and, looking up, saw the Comte de Charmilles' carriage coming,—he and his wife were returning from the theatre,—and in case they should perceive me outside their house, where I still lingered, I strode swiftly away, neither knowing nor caring in which direction I bent my steps. Presently I found myself on the familiar route of the Champs Elysées,—the trees there were tossing their branches wildly and groaning at the pitiless destruction wreaked upon their tender spring frondage by the cruel blast,—and, weary in body and mind, I sat down on one of the more sheltered seats, utterly regardless of the fact that I was wet through and shivering, and tried to come to some sort of understanding with myself concerning the disas-ter that had befallen me. And as I thought, one by one, of the various dreams of ecstasy, bright moments and love-enraptured days that had lately been mine, I am not ashamed to say that I shed tears. A man may weep when he is alone surely!—and I wept for the bitterest loss the human soul can ever know,—the loss of love, and the loss of good faith in the honour of men and women. The slow drops that blinded my sight were hot as fire,—they burned my eyes as they welled forth, and my throat ached with the pain of them,—but in a certain measure they helped to clear and calm my brain,—the storm of wrath and sorrow in my mind quieted itself by degrees,—and I was able to realize not only the extent of my own cureless grief, but also that of the unhappy girl whom over and over again I had sworn I would die to serve!

Poor, poor Pauline! How ill she looked,—how pale—how sad! Poor little child!—for she was not much more than a child;—and thinking of her youth, her impulsiveness, and her unutterable misery, my heart softened more and more towards her. She loved Silvion Guidèl— Silvion Guidèl loved her;—they were both young, both beautiful,— and they had not been strong enough to resist the insidious attraction of each other's fairness. They had sinned,—they had fallen,—they were ashamed,—they repented;—they sought my pardon,—and I—should

I withhold it?—or should I, like a brave man, make light of my own wrong, my own suffering, and heap coals of fire upon their heads by my free forgiveness,—my magnanimous aid to help them out of the evil plight into which they had wilfully wandered? I asked myself this question many times. I now understood the strange demeanour of Guidèl on that night when he had asked me whether I could forgive him if he had sinned greatly! His conscience had tormented him all through,—he had surely suffered as well as sinned!

Pressing one hand hard over my eyes, and choking back those foolish tears of mine, I strove manfully to consider the whole wretched story from the most merciful point of view possible to my nature. I had been brought up under my father's vigilant care, on lines of broad thought, strict honour, and practical, not theoretical, philosophy,—his chief idea of living nobly being this,—to do good always when good could be done, and when not, at any rate to refrain from doing evil. If I believed in these precepts at all, now, surely, was the time to act upon them. I could never win back Pauline's love,—that had been stolen, or else had gone of its own free will to my rival,—but I had it in my power to make her happy and respected once more. How? Nothing was easier. In the first place I would go to the good Père Vaudron, and tell him all the truth, in confidence;—I would ask him to see that the civic rite of marriage was performed at once between his nephew and Pauline secretly;—I would aid the wedded lovers with money, should they require it, to leave Paris immediately,—and when once their departure was safely assured, I would break the whole thing to the Comte de Charmilles, and accept whatever wrath he chose to display, on my own devoted head. Thus, I should win Pauline's eternal gratitude,—her parents would in time become reconciled to their change of a son-in-law,—and all would be well. I,—only I would be the lasting sufferer!—but should not a true man be ready and willing to sacrifice himself, if by so doing, he can render the one woman he loves in all the world, happy? Still,—on the other hand, there was the more natural plan of vengeance,—one word to Pauline's father, and she would be shamed and disgraced beyond recall,—I could then challenge Silvion Guidèl and do my best to kill him, in which effort I should most probably succeed, and so bring misery on poor old Vaudron and his simple folk in Brittany,—I could do all this, and yet, after all was done, I myself should be as wretched as ever! I thought and thought,—I pondered till my brows ached,—the good and the evil side of my nature fought desperately together, while my consciousness, like a separate watchful person apart, seemed totally unable to decide which would win. It was a sore contest!—the struggle of the elements around me was not more fierce than the struggle in my own tormented soul,—but through all, the plaintive voice of Pauline,—Pauline whom I still loved, alas!—rang in my ears with that last sobbing cry—"Pity me, Gaston! God make you kind to me!"—till gradually, very gradually, I won the mastery over my darker passions,—won it with a sense of warm triumph such as none can understand save him who has been tempted and has steadily overcome temptation. I resolved that I would save Pauline from the consequences of her rash blind error,—and so, at any rate, be at peace with the Eternal Witness of Heaven and my own conscience! This I decided, finally and fixedly,—determining to pursue my plan for the re-establishment of the honour and safety of the woman who trusted me, the very first thing the next day,—and I would say nothing to any one, not even to my father,—till my work of forgiveness and help was carried out and completed beyond recall!

Here let me pause. Do you understand, you, whosoever you are, that read these pages,—do you thoroughly understand my meaning? If not, let me impress it upon you plainly, once and for all,—for I would not have the dullest wits misjudge me at this turning-point of time! I had absolutely made up my mind,—mark you!—to do my best for her who had played me false! Absolutely and unflinchingly. For I loved her in spite of her treachery!—I cared to be remembered in her prayers!—I who, in the hot fervour of my adoration for her beauty, had declared that I would die for her, was now willing to carry out that vow,—to die spiritually,—to crush all my own clamorous affections and desires for *her* sake, that all might be well with her in days present and to come! Remember, I was willing—and not only willing, but ready! Not because I seek pity from you, do I ask it,—world's pity is a weak thing that none but cowards need. I only want justice,—aye! if it be but the mere glimmering justice of your slowest, sleepiest comprehension,— give me enough of it to grasp this one fact—namely, that on the night of the bitterest suffering of my life—the night on which I learned my own betrayal, I had prepared myself to *forgive* the unhappy child who had wronged me,—as freely, as entirely, as I then hoped, before God, to be, in my turn, forgiven!

CHAPTER 12

I do not know how long I sat on that seat in the Champs Elysées, with the tempestuous rain beating down upon me,—the desperate conflict I had had with my own worser self had rendered me insensible to the flight of time. So numbed was I with outward cold and inward misery,—so utterly blind to all external surroundings, that I was as startled as though a pistol-shot had been fired close to me when a hand fell on my shoulder, and a harsh, half-laughing voice exclaimed—

"Gaston Beauvais, by all the gods and goddesses! Gaston Beauvais, drenched as a caught rat in a relentless housekeeper's pail! What the devil are you doing here at this time of night, *mon beau riche*?[1] You, with limitless francs at your command, and good luck showering its honey-dew persistently on your selected fortunate head,—what may be your object in thus fraternizing with the elements, and striving to match them groan for groan, scowl for scowl? By my faith!—I can hardly believe that this soaked and dripping bundle of good clothes spoilt is actually yourself!"

I looked up, forced a smile, and held out my hand. I recognized the speaker,—indeed he was too remarkable a character in his way to be for an instant mistaken. All Paris knew André Gessonex,—a poor wretch of an artist, who painted pictures that were too extraordinary and *risqué* for any respectable householder to buy, and who eked out a bare living by his *décolleté*[2] sketches, in black and white, of all the noted *danseuses*[3] and burlesque actresses in the city. His bizarre figure, clad in its threadbare and nondescript garb, was familiar to every frequenter of the Boulevards,—and, in truth, it was eccentric enough to attract the most casual stranger's attention. His pinched and shrunken legs were covered with the narrowest possible trousers, which by frequent turning up to make the best of the worn ends, had now become so short for him that they left almost a quarter of a yard of flaring red sock exposed to view,—his thin jacket, the only one he had for both winter and summer, was buttoned tightly across his chest to conceal the lack of the long-ago pawned waistcoat,—a collar with very large, unstarched soiled ends, flapped round his skinny throat, relieved by a brilliant strip

---

[1] French expression meaning "my handsome rich man."
[2] Gessonex's sketches exhibit women with low-cut or revealing necklines.
[3] French word for "dancers."

of red flannel which served as tie,—he kept his hair long in strict adherence to true artistic tradition, and on these bushy, half grey, always disordered locks he wore a very battered hat of the "brigand" shape, which had been many times inked over to hide its antique rustiness, and which he took the greatest pains to set airily on one side, to suggest, as he once explained, indifference to the world, and gay carelessness as to the world's opinions. Unlucky devil!—I had always pitied him from my heart,—and many a twenty-franc piece of mine had found its way into his pocket. A cruel fate had bestowed on him genius without common-sense, and the perfectly natural result of such an endowment was, that he starved. He was full of good and even fine ideas,—there were times when he seemed to sparkle all over with felicity of wit and poetry of expression,—many men liked him, and not only liked him, but strove to assist him substantially, without ever succeeding in their charitable endeavours. For André was one of Creation's incurables,—neither money nor advice ever benefited him one iota. Give him the commission to paint a picture,—and he would produce a Titanesque[1] canvas, too big for anything but a cathedral, and on that canvas he would depict the airiest nude personages disporting themselves in such a frankly indelicate manner, that the intending purchaser withdrew his patronage in shuddering haste and alarm, and fled without leaving so much as the odour of a franc behind. Thus the poor fellow was always unfortunate, and when taken to task and told that his ill-luck was entirely his own fault, he would assume an air of the most naive bewilderment.

"You amaze me!" he would say. "You really amaze me! I am not to blame if these people who want to buy pictures have no taste! I cannot paint Dutch interiors,—the carrot waiting to be peeled on the table—the fat old woman cutting onions for the *pot-au-feu*,[2]—the centenarian gentleman with a perpetual cold in his head, who bends over a brazier to warm his aged nose, while a dog and two kittens gazed up confidingly at his wrinkled hands,—this is not in my line![3] I can only produce grand art!—classical subjects,—Danäe in her brazen tower,[4]—Theseus and

---

[1] The Titans were a gigantic race, hence titanesque meaning huge.

[2] French term for "a stew of meat and vegetables."

[3] Reference to "genre" painting or the painting of scenes of everyday life which stood low in the hierarchy of artistic genres at the time.

[4] Danäe was imprisoned by her father in a tower because an oracle declared that he would be killed by a son of hers. Zeus, disguised as a shower of gold, visited and impregnated her. This subject was very popular among Renaissance painters including Titian and Correggio.

Ariadne[1]—the *amours* of Cybele with Atys[2]—or the triumphs of Venus;[3] —I cannot descend to the level of ordinary vulgar minds! Let me be poor—let me starve—but let me keep my artistic conscience! A grateful posterity may recognize what this frivolous age condemns!"

Such was the man who now stood before me like a gaunt spectre in the rain, his dull peering eyes brightening into a faint interest as he fixed them on mine. His face betokened the liveliest surprise and curiosity at meeting me out there at night and in such weather, and I could not at once master my voice sufficiently to answer him. He waited one or two minutes, and then clapped me again on the shoulder.

"Have you lost your speech, Beauvais, or your strength, or your courage, or what? You look alarmingly ill!—will you take my arm?"

There was a friendly solicitude about him that touched me,—another time I might have hesitated to be seen with such an incongruous figure as he was,—he, whose mock-tragic manner and jaunty style of walk had been mimicked and hooted at by all the little *gamins*[4] of Paris, but the hour was late, and I felt so utterly wretched, so thrown out, as it were, from all sympathy, so destitute of all hope, that I was glad of even this forlorn starveling's company, and I, therefore, took his proffered arm,—an arm the very bone of which I could feel sharply protruding through the thin worn sleeve.

"I *am* rather out of my usual line!" I then said, striving to make light of my condition. "Sitting out in the rain on a dreary night like this is certainly not amusing. But—when one is in trouble——"

"Trouble!—Ah!" exclaimed Gessonex, lifting his disengaged hand, clenching it, and shaking it at the frowning sky with a defiant air. "Trouble is the fishing-net of the amiable Deity up yonder, whom none of us can see, and whom few of us want to know! Down it drops, that big black net, out of the clouds, quite unexpectedly, and we are all dragged into it, struggling and sprawling for dear life, just like the helpless fish we ourselves delight to catch and kill and cook and devour! We are all little gods down here, each in our own way,—and the great One above (if there *is* one!) can only be an enlarged pattern of our personalities,— for according to the Bible, 'He made us in His own image!'[5] And so *you* are

---

1   Athenian national hero and daughter of King Minos of Crete, lovers who killed the minotaur. They then ran off together but Theseus eventually abandoned Ariadne.

2   Cybele was the mother-goddess of Phrygia and Atys was her youthful lover who castrated himself in a religious frenzy and became the leader of Cybele's eunuch priests.

3   Goddess of love in Roman mythology, much depicted in Western art.

4   French term for "street urchins."

5   A reference to Genesis 1.25 in the Old Testament of the Bible.

caught, *mon ami*? That is bad!—but let me not forget to mention, that there are a few large holes in the net through which those that have gold about them, can easily slip and escape scot free!"

Poor Gessonex! He, like all hungry folk, imagined money to be a cure for every evil.

"My good fellow," I said gently, "there are some griefs that can follow and persecute to the very death even Croesus[1] among his bags of bullion. I begin to think poverty is one of the least of human misfortunes."

"Absolutely you are right!" declared Gessonex, with an air of triumph. "It is a sort of thing you so soon get accustomed to! It sits upon one easily, like an old coat! You cease to desire a dinner if you never have it!—it is quite extraordinary how the appetite suits itself to circumstances, and puts up with a cigar at twenty centimes[2] instead of a *filet* for one franc!—the *filet* is actually not missed! And what a number of remarkable cases we have had shown to us lately in the field of science, of men existing for a long period of time, without any nourishment save water! I have been deeply interested in that subject,—I believe in the system thoroughly,—I have tried it, (for my own amusement of course!) Yes!—I have tried it for several days together! I find it answers very well!—it is apt to make one feel quite light upon one's feet,—almost aerial in fact, and ready to fly, as if one were disembodied!—most curious and charming!"

My heart smote me,—the man was starving and my purse was full. I pressed his meagre arm more closely, and for the time forgot my own sorrows in consideration for his needs.

"Let us go and sup somewhere," I said hastily. "Any place near at hand will do. A basin of hot soup will take off the chill of this down-pour,—I am positively wet through!"

"You are, *mon ami*,—that is a lamentable fact!" rejoined Gessonex affably—"and,—apart from the condition of those excellent clothes of yours, which are ruined, I regret to observe,—you will most likely wake up to-morrow with a violent cold. And a cold is not becoming—it spoils the face of even a pretty woman. So that if you really believe the hot soup will be beneficial to you,—(as far as I am concerned, I find the cold water nourishment singularly agreeable!) why, I will escort you to a very decent restaurant, where you can procure a really superb *bouillon*[3]—superb, I assure you!—I have often inhaled the odour of it *en passant*!"[4]

---

1   Extremely wealthy sixth-century king of Lydia.
2   A centime is a French unit of money, 1/100th of a franc.
3   French word for "broth."
4   French expression meaning "by the way," but in this context, "as I passed by."

And, quickening his steps unconsciously, out of the mere natural impulse of the hungry craving he could not quite repress, he walked with me out of the Champs Elysées and across the Place de la Concorde,—thence over one of the bridges spanning the Seine,[1] and so on, till we reached a dingy little building in a side street, over which, in faded paint, was inscribed "GRAND CAFÉ BONHOMME. RESTAURANT POUR TOUT LE MONDE."[2] The glass doors were shut, and draped with red curtains, through which the interior lights flung a comfortable glow on the sloppy roadway; and Gessonex pointed to this with the most fervent admiration.

"What a charm there is about the colour red!" he exclaimed enthusiastically. "It is so suggestive of warmth and brilliancy! It is positively fascinating!—and in my great picture of Apollo chasing Daphne,[3] I should be almost tempted to use folds of red drapery were it not for the strict necessity of keeping the figures nude. But the idea of a garmented god fills me with horror!—as well paint Adam and Eve decorously adorned with fig-leaves *before* the fall!—that is what a contemporary of mine has just done,—ha ha! Fig-leaves *before* the fall! Excellent!—ah, very amusing!"

Opening the *café* doors he beckoned me to follow. I did so half mechanically, my only idea for the moment being that he, Gessonex, should get a good meal for once,—I knew that I myself would not be able to taste anything. There were only two or three people in the place;—a solitary waiter, whom I had perceived combing his hair carefully in the background, came forward to receive instructions, and cleared a table for us in a rather retired corner where we at once sat down. I then ordered soup, and whatever else was ready to be had hot and savoury, while André gingerly lifted his brigand hat and placed it on a convenient nail above him, using so much precaution in this action, that I suppose he feared it might come to pieces in his hands. Then, running his fingers through his matted locks, he rested his elbows comfortably on the table, and surveyed me smilingly.

"*Mon cher* Beauvais," he said, "I feel as if there were a mystical new

---

[1] A large public square located between the Champs Elysées and the Jardin des Tuileries. Gessonex and Beauvais are making their way from the fashionable right bank area around the Champs Elysées and crossing over to the Bohemian Left Bank of Paris, a district frequented by students and artists.

[2] Restaurant for everybody.

[3] Daphne was a Greek mountain nymph who was turned into a tree by mother earth in order that she might escape the clutches of Apollo, her pursuer.

bond between us! I always liked you, as you know,—but you were removed from me by an immense gulf of difference,—this difference being that you were never in trouble, and I, as you must be aware, always *was* and always *am*! But do not imagine that it is pleasant to me to see you wriggling fish-like on the *bon Dieu's*[1] disagreeably sharp hook of calamity—*au contraire,*[2] it infinitely distresses me,—but still, if anything can make men brothers, it is surely a joint partnership in woe! All the same, Beauvais"—and he lowered his voice a little—"I am sincerely sorry to find you so cast down!"

I made a mute sign of gratitude,—he was looking at me intently, stroking his peaked beard the while.

"Nothing financially wrong?" he hinted delicately, after a pause.

"My good André!—Nothing!"

"I am glad of that!" he rejoined sedately, "for naturally I could be no sort of service to you in any question of cash. A money difficulty always appeals to me in vain! But for any private vexation of a purely emotional and yet excessively irritating nature, I think I know a cure!"

I forced a smile. "Indeed!"

He nodded gravely, and his eyes dilated with a certain peculiar bright limpidness that I and others had often noticed in them whenever the "mad painter," as he was sometimes called, was about to be more than usually eloquent.

"For the heart's wide wounds which bleed internally;—for the grief of a lost love which can never be regained," he said slowly and dreamily; "for the sting of remorse, and the teazing persecutions of conscience,—for all these, and more than these, I can find a remedy! For the poison of memory I can provide an antidote,—a blessed balm that soothes the wronged spirit into total forgetfulness of its injury, and opens before the mind a fresh and wondrous field of vision, where are found glories that the world knows nothing of, and for the enjoyment of which a man might be well content to starve and suffer, and sacrifice everything—even love!"

His harsh voice had grown musical,—a faint smile rested on his thin pale lips,—and I gazed at him in vague surprise and curiosity.

"What are you poetizing about now, Gessonex?" I asked half banteringly. "What magic Elixir Vitae[3] thus excites your enthusiasm?"

---

1   French for "good God's."
2   French phrase meaning "on the contrary."
3   Latin phrase meaning "elixir of life," a potion said to prolong life indefinitely.

He made no answer, as just then the supper arrived, and, rousing himself quickly as from a reverie, his eyes lost their preternatural light, and all his interest became centred in the food before him. Poor fellow!—how daintily he ate, feigning reluctance, yet lingering over every morsel! How he rated the waiter for not bringing him a damask serviette,—how haughtily he complained of the wine being corked,—and how thoroughly he enjoyed playing the part of a fastidious epicure and fine gentleman! My share in the repast was a mere pretence, and he perceived this, though he refrained from any comment upon my behaviour while the meal was yet in progress. But as soon as it was ended, and he was smoking the cigarette I had offered him, he leaned across the table and addressed me once more in a low confidential tone.

"Beauvais, you have eaten nothing!"

I sighed impatiently. "*Mon cher*, I have no appetite."

"Yet you are wet through,—you shiver?"

I shrugged my shoulders. "*Soit!*"[1]

"You will not even smoke?"

"To oblige you, I will,"—and I opened my case of cigarettes and lit one forthwith, hoping by this *complaisance* to satisfy his anxiety on my behalf. But he rose suddenly, saying no word to me, and crossing over to where the waiter stood, talked with him very earnestly and emphatically for a minute or two. Then he returned leisurely to his seat opposite me, and I looked at him inquiringly.

"What have you been ordering? A cognac?"

"No."

"What then?"

"Oh, nothing! only—*absinthe*."

"Absinthe!" I echoed. "Do you like that stuff?"

His eyes opened wide, and flashed a strangely piercing glance at me.

"Like it? I *love* it! And you?"

"I have never tasted it."

"Never tasted it!" exclaimed Gessonex amazedly. "*Mon Dieu!* You, a born and bred Parisian, have never tasted absinthe?"

I smiled at his excitement.

"Never! I have seen others drinking it often,—but I have not liked the look of it somehow. A repulsive colour to me,—that medicinal green!"

He laughed a trifle nervously, and his hand trembled. But he gave no

---

[1]   French word meaning "So be it."

immediate reply, for at that moment the waiter placed a *flacon*[1] of the drink in question on the table, together with the usual supply of water and tumblers. Carefully preparing and stirring the opaline mixture, Gessonex filled the glasses to the brim, and pushed one across to me. I made a faint sign of rejection. He laughed again, in apparent amusement at my hesitation.

"By Venus and Cupid, and all the dear old heathen deities who are such remarkably convenient myths to take one's oath upon," he said, "I hope you will not compel me to consider you a fool, Beauvais! What an idea that is of yours,—'medicinal green'! Think of melted emeralds instead! There, beside you, you have the most marvellous cordial in all the world,—drink and you will find your sorrows transmuted—yourself transformed! Even if no better result be obtained than escaping from the chill you have incurred in this night's heavy drenching, that is surely something! Life without absinthe!—I cannot imagine it! For me it would be impossible! I should hang, drown, or shoot myself into infinitude, out of sheer rage at the continued cruelty and injustice of the world,—but with this divine nectar of Olympus[2] I can defy misfortune and laugh at poverty, as though these were the merest *bagatelles*! Come!—to your health, *mon brave*![3] Drink with me!"

He raised his glass glimmering pallidly in the light,—his words, his manner, fascinated me, and a curious thrill ran through my veins. There was something spectral in his expression too, as though the skeleton of the man had become suddenly visible beneath its fleshly covering,—as though Death had for a moment peered through the veil of Life. I fixed my eyes doubtingly on the pale-green liquid whose praises he thus sang—had it indeed such a potent charm? Would it still the dull aching at my heart,—the throbbing in my temples,—the sick weariness and contempt of living, that had laid hold upon me like a fever since I knew Pauline was no longer my own? Would it give me a brief respite from the inner fret of tormenting thought? It might!—and, slowly lifting the glass to my lips, I tasted it. It was very bitter and nauseous,—and I made a wry face of disgust as I set it down. The watchful Gessonex touched my arm.

"Again!" he whispered eagerly, with a strange smile. "Once again! It is like vengeance,—bitter at first, but sweet at last! *Mon cher*, if you were not,—as I see you are,—a prey to affliction, I would not offer you the

---

[1]   French for "bottle."
[2]   The highest mountain in Greece, believed to be the home of the Gods.
[3]   French phrase meaning "my brave man."

knowledge of this sure consolation,—for he that is not sad needs no comfort. But supposing—I only guess, of course!—supposing your mind to be chafed by the ever present memory of some wrong,—some injury—some treachery—even some love-betrayal,—why then, I fail to see why you should continue to suffer when the remedy for all such suffering is *here*!" And he sipped the contents of his own glass with an air of almost inspired ecstasy.

I looked at him fixedly. An odd tingling sensation was in my blood, as though it had been suddenly touched by an inward fire.

"You mean to tell me," I said incredulously, "that Absinthe,—which I have heard spoken of as the curse of Paris,—is a cure for all human ills? That it will not only ward off physical cold from the body, but keep out haunting trouble from the mind? *Mon ami*, you rave!—such a thing is not possible! If it could quench mad passion,—if it could kill love!—if it could make of my heart a stone, instead of a tortured, palpitating sentient substance—there!—forgive me! I am talking at random of I know not what,—I have been cruelly betrayed, Gessonex! and I wish to God I could forget my betrayal!"

My words had broken from me involuntarily, and he heard them with an attentive expression of amiable half-melancholy solicitude. But in reply he pointed to the glass beside me.

"Drink!" he said.

Drink!—Well, why not? I could see no earthly reason for hesitating over such a trifle,—I would taste the nauseous fluid again, I thought, if only to satisfy my companion,—and I at once did so. Heavens!—it was now delicious to my palate—exquisitely fine and delicate as balm,—and in my pleasurable amazement I swallowed half the tumbler-full readily, conscious of a new and indescribably delightful sense of restorative warmth and comfort pervading my whole system. I felt that Gessonex observed me intently, and, meeting his gaze, I smiled.

"You are quite right, André!" I told him. "The second trial is the test of flavour. It is excellent!"

And without taking any more thought as to what I was doing, I finished the entire draught, re-lit my cigarette which had gone out, and began to smoke contentedly, while Gessonex re-filled my glass.

"Now you will soon be a man again!" he exclaimed joyously. "To the devil with all the botherations of life, say I! You are too well off in this world's goods, *mon cher*, to allow yourself to be seriously worried about anything,—and I am truly glad I have persuaded you to try my favourite remedy for the kicks of fortune, because I like you! Moreover, to speak frankly, I owe you several excellent dinners,—the one of to-night being particularly welcome, in spite of what I said in favour of the cold water nourishment,—and the only good I can possibly do you in return for your many acts of friendship is to introduce you to the 'Fairy with the Green Eyes'—as this exquisite nectar has been poetically termed. It is a charming fairy!—one wave of the opal wand, and sorrow is conveniently guillotined!"

I let him run on uninterruptedly,—I myself was too drowsily comfortable to speak. I watched the smoke of my cigarette curling up to the ceiling in little dusky wreaths,—they seemed to take phosphorescent gleams of colour as they twisted round and round and melted away. A magical period of sudden and complete repose had been granted to me,—I had ceased to think of Pauline,—of Silvion Guidèl—or of any one incident of my life or surroundings,—all my interest was centred in those rising and disappearing smoky rings! I drank two more tumblers-full of absinthe, with increasing satisfaction and avidity,—previous to tasting it I had been faint and cold and shivering,—now I was thoroughly warm, agreeably languid, and a trifle sleepy. I heard Gessonex talking to me now and then,—there were moments when he seemed to become eloquently energetic in his denunciations of something or somebody,—but by-and-by his voice sounded far off, like a voice in a dream, and I paid very little heed to him, only nodding occasionally whenever he appeared to expect an answer. I was in that hazy condition of mind common to certain phases of intoxication, when the drunkard is apt to think he is thinking,—though really no distinctly comprehensible thought is possible to his befogged and stupefied brain. Yet I understood well enough what Gessonex said about love; he got on that subject, heaven knows how, and launched against it an arrowy shower of cynicism.

"What a fool a man is," he exclaimed, "to let himself be made a slave for life, all for the sake of a pretty face that in time is bound to grow old and ugly! Love is only a hot impulse of the blood, and like any other fever can be cooled and kept down easily if one tries. It is a starving sort of ailment too,—one does not get fat on it. Love emaciates both soul and body—but hate, on the contrary, feeds! I must confess that, for my own part, I have no sympathy with a lover,—but I adore a good hater! To hate well is the most manly of attributes, for there is so much in the world that merits hatred—so little that is worthy of love! As for women—bah! We begin our lives by believing them to be angels,—but we soon find out what painted, bedizened, falsely-smiling courtesans they all are at heart,—at least all *I* have ever met. *Pardieu!*[1] I swear to you, Beauvais, I have never known a good woman!"

"*Hélas!*" I sighed gently, and smiled. "*Pauvre* Gessonex!"[2]

"And you?" he demanded eagerly.

A vision of a pure, pale, proud face, set like a classic cameo, in a frame of golden hair, and lightened into life by the steady brilliancy of two calm star-splendid eyes, flashed suddenly across my mind almost against my will, and I replied, half dreamily—

"One woman I know both fair and wise, and also—I think—good."

"You *think!*" laughed Gessonex, with a touch of wildness in his manner. "You only think!—you do not *fear!* Yes!—I say *fear!* Fear her, *mon ami*, if she is truly good,—for as sure as death the time will come when she will shame you! There is no man pure enough to look upon the face of an innocent woman, and not know himself to be at heart a villain!"

I smiled again. What foolish fancies the fellow had to be sure! He rambled on more or less incoherently,—while I sank deeper and deeper into a maze of indolent reverie. I was roused at last, however, by the respectful appeals of the tired *garçon*,[3] who mildly suggested that we should now take our leave, as it was past midnight, and they were desirous of closing the *café*. I got up sleepily, paid the reckoning, tipped our yawning attendant handsomely, and walked, or rather reeled out of the place arm in arm with my companion, who, as soon as he found himself in the open street exposed once more to the furious rain which poured down as incessantly as ever, fell to rating the elements in the most abusive terms.

"*Sacré diable!*"[4] he exclaimed. "What abominable weather!—Entirely unsuited to the constitution of a gentleman! Only rats, cats, and toads should be abroad on such a night,—and yet I—I, André Gessonex, the only painter in France with any genius, am actually compelled to walk home! What vile injustice! You, *mon cher* Beauvais, are more fortunate— God, or the gods, will permit you to drive! The *fiacre*[5] is at your service for one franc, twenty centimes,—the *voiture de place*[6] for two francs fifty! Which will you choose?—though the hour is so late that it is possible the *brave cocher*[7] may not be forthcoming even when called."

---

1   French expression meaning "By God."
2   French word for "poor."
3   French term for "waiter."
4   French expression meaning "bloody devil."
5   French word for a kind of coach.
6   French term for a kind of coach, superior to the *fiacre.*
7   French for "good cabman" or "good coachman."

And he swaggered jauntily to the edge of the curbstone and looked up and down the nearly deserted street, I watching him curiously the while. An odd calmness possessed me,—some previously active motion in my brain seemed suddenly stopped,—and I was vaguely interested in trifles. For instance, there was a little pool in a hollow of the pavement at my feet, and I found myself dreamily counting the big raindrops that plashed into it with the force of small falling pebbles;—then, a certain change in the face of Gessonex excited my listless attention,— his eyes were so feverishly brilliant that for the moment their lustre gave him a sort of haggard dare-devil beauty, which though wild and starved and faded, was yet strangely picturesque. I studied him coldly for a little space,—then moved close up to him and slipped a twenty-franc piece into his hand. His fingers closed on it instantly.

"Drive home yourself, *mon cher*, if you can get a carriage," I said. "As for me, I shall walk."

"Let the rich man trudge while the beggar rides!" laughed Gessonex, pocketing his gold coin without remark,—he would have considered any expression of gratitude in the worst possible taste. "That is exactly what all the disappointed folk here below expect to do after death, Beauvais!— to ride in coaches-and-six[1] round Heaven and look down at their enemies walking the brimstone miles in Hell! What a truly Christian hope, is it not? And so you will positively invite another drenching? *Bien!*—so then will I,—I can change my clothes when I get home!"

Unfortunate devil!—he had no clothes to change,—I knew that well enough! His road lay in an entirely different direction from mine, so I bade him good night.

"You are a different man now, Beauvais, are you not?" he said, as he shook hands. "The 'green fairy' has cured you of your mind's distemper?"

"Was my mind distempered?" I queried indifferently, wondering as I spoke why the lately incessant pulsation in my brain was now so stunned and still.

"I forget!—but I suppose it was! Anyhow, whatever was the matter with me, I am now quite myself again."

He laughed wildly.

"Good! I am glad of that! As for me, I am never myself,—I am always somebody else! Droll, is it not? The fact is"—and he lowered his voice to a confidential whisper—"I have had a singular experience in my life,—altogether rare and remarkable. I have killed myself and

---

[1]   Coaches that are drawn by six horses.

attended my own funeral! Yes, truly! Candles, priests, black draperies, well-fed long-tailed horses,—*toute la baraque,*[1]—no sparing of expense, you understand? My corpse was in an open shell—I have a curious objection to shut-up coffins—open to the night it lay, with the stars staring down upon it—it had a young face then,—and one might easily believe that it had also had fine eyes. I chose white violets for the wreath just over the heart,—they are charming flowers, full of delicately suggestive odour, do you not find?—and the long procession to the grave was followed by the weeping crowds of Paris. 'Dead!' they cried. 'Our Gessonex! the Raphael[2] of France!' Oh, it was a rare sight, *mon ami!*—Never was there such grief in a land before,—I wept myself for sympathy with my lamenting countrymen! I drew aside till all the flowers had been thrown into the open grave,—for I was the sexton, you must remember!—I waited till the cemetery was deserted and in darkness—and then I made haste to bury myself—piling the earth over my dead youth close and fast, levelling it well, and treading it down! The Raphael of France!—There he lay, I thought—and there he might remain, so far as I was concerned—he was only a genius, and as such was no earthly use to anybody. Good-bye and good riddance, I said, as I hurried away from that graveyard and became from henceforth somebody else! And do you know I infinitely prefer to be somebody else?— it is so much less troublesome!"

These strange, incoherent sentences coursed off his lips with impetuous rapidity,—his voice had a strained piteous pathos in it mingled with scorn,—and the intense light in his eyes deepened to a sort of fiery fury from which I involuntarily recoiled. The appellation of "mad" painter never seemed so entirely suited to him as now. But, mad or not mad, he was quick enough to perceive the instinctive shrinking movement I made, and laughing again, he again shook my hand cordially, lifted his battered hat with an assumption of excessive gentility, and breaking into the most high-flown expressions of French courtesy, bade me once more farewell. I watched him walking along in his customary half-jaunty, half-tragic style till he had disappeared round a corner like a fantastic spectre vanishing in a nightmare, and then—then, as though a flash of blinding fire had crossed my sight, it suddenly became clear to my mind—*what he had done for me!* As I realized it I could have shouted aloud in the semi-delirium of feverish intoxication that burnt my brain!

---

[1]   French expression, roughly translating, in this instance, to "the whole bag of tricks."
[2]   Italian Renaissance painter (1483-1520).

That subtle flavour clinging to my palate—that insidious fluid creeping drop by drop through my veins—I knew what it was at last!—the
first infiltration of another life—the slow but sure transfusion of a
strange and deadly bitterness into my blood, which once absorbed, must
and would cling to me for ever! *Absintheur*! I had heard the name used,
sometimes contemptuously, sometimes compassionately,—it meant,—
oh! so much!—and, like charity, covered such a multitude of sins! On
what a fine hair's-breadth of chance or opportunity one's destiny hangs
after all! To think of that miserable André Gessonex being an instrument of Fate seemed absurd!—a starved *vaurien*[1] and reprobate—a mere
crazed fool!—and yet—yet—my casual meeting with him had been
fore-doomed!—it had given the Devil time to do good work,—to
consume virtue in a breath and conjure up vice from the dead ashes—
to turn a feeling heart to stone—and to make of a man a fiend!

END OF VOLUME I

---

[1]   French word meaning "a good-for-nothing person."

CHAPTER 13

I went home that night, not to sleep but to dream,—to dream, with eyes wide open and senses acutely conscious. I knew I was in my own room and on my own bed,—I could almost count the little gradations of light in the pale glow flung by the flickering night-lamp against the wall and ceiling,—I could hear the muffled "tick-tick" of the clock in my father's chamber next to mine,—but though these every-day impressions were distinct and fully recognizable, I was still away from them all,—far far away in a shadowy land of strange surprises and miraculous events,—a land where beauty and terror, ecstasy and horror, · divided the time between them. I was a prey to the most singular physical sensations;—that curious numbed stillness in my brain, which I had previously felt without being able to analyze, had given place to a busy, swift palpitating motion like the beat of a rapid pendulum,—and by degrees, as this *something* swung to and fro, its vibrations seemed to enter into and possess every part of my body. My heart bounded to the same quick time, my nerves throbbed,—my blood hurled itself, so to speak, through my veins like a fierce torrent,—and I lay staring at the white ceiling above me, and vaguely wondering at all the sights I saw, and the scenes in which I, like a sort of disembodied personality, took active part without stirring! Here, for instance, was a field of scarlet poppies,—I walked knee-deep among them, inhaling the strong opium-odour of their fragile leaves,—they blazed vividly against the sky, and nodded drowsily to and fro in the languid wind. And between their brilliant clusters lay the dead!—bodies of men with ghastly wounds in their hearts, and fragments of swords and guns in their stiffening hands, while round about them were strewn torn flags and broken spears. A battle has been lately fought, I mused as I passed,—this is what some folks call the "field of honour," and Might has gotten the victory over Right, as it ever does and as it ever will! And the poppies wave, and the birds sing,—and the men who have given their lives for truth and loyalty's sake lie here to fester in the earth, forgotten,—and so the world wags on from day to day and hour to hour, and yet people prate of a God of Justice!... What next in the moving panorama of vision?—what next? The sound of a sweet song sung at midnight!—and lo! the moon is there, full, round, and warm!—grand grey towers and palaces rise about me on all sides,—and out on that yellow-glittering water rests one solitary gondola, black as a floating hearse, yet holding light! She, that fair siren in white robes, with bosom bare to the amorous moon-rays,—she, with her wicked laughing eyes and jewel-wreathed tresses,—is she not a beautiful wanton enough for at least one hour's joy? Hark!—she sings,—and the tremulous richness of her silver-toned mandoline quivers in accord with her voice across the bright dividing wave!

> "*Que mon dernier souffle, emporté*
> *Dans les parfums du vent d'été*
> *Soit un soupir de volupté!*
> *Qu'il vole, papillon charmé*
> *Par l'attrait des roses de mai*
> *Sur les lèvres du bien-aimé!*"[1]

I listen in dumb rapt ecstasy,—when all at once the moon vanishes,—a loud clap of thunder reverberates through earth and heaven,—the lightning glitters aloft, and I am alone in darkness and in storm. Alone,—yet not alone,—for there, gliding before me in aeriel phantom-shape, I see Pauline!—her thin garments wet,—her dark locks dank and dripping,—her blue eyes fixed and lustreless—but yet, she smiles!—A strange sad smile!—she waves her hand and passes;—I strive to follow, but some imperative force holds me back,—I can only look after her and wonder why those drops of moisture cling so heavily to her gown and hair! She disappears!—good!—Now I am at peace again,—I can watch to my heart's content those little leaping flames that sparkle round me in lambent wreathes of exquisitely brilliant green,—I can *think*!...

No sooner did this idea of *thought* force itself upon me than it became an urgent and paramount necessity—and I strove to steady that whirling, buzzing wheel in my brain, and compass it to some fixed end, but it was like a perpetually shaken kaleidoscope, always forming itself into a new pattern before I had time to resolve the first. Though this was odd and in a manner confusing, it did not distress me at all,—I patiently endeavoured to set my wits in order with that peculiar pleasure many persons find in arranging a scientific puzzle,—and by degrees

---

[1] "May my last breath, carried away/ in the perfumes of the summer wind / be a sigh of pleasure! / May it fly, like a butterfly charmed / By the lure of the roses of May / Onto the lips of my beloved." From the poem "Nocturne" in *Le Coffret de santal* by Charles Cros. The poem tells the story of a woman who drowns herself after being abandoned by her lover. The lines cited are the woman's last thoughts as she abandons herself to the water.

I arrived at a clear understanding with myself and gained a full comprehension of my own intentions. And now my intelligent perception became as exact and methodical as it had been before erratic and confused,—I found I had acquired new force,—new logic,—new views of principle,—and I was able to turn over quite quietly in my mind Pauline de Charmilles' dishonour. Yes!—dishonour was the word—there was no other—and for her sin she had not the shadow of an excuse. And Silvion Guidèl was a liar and traitor,—he justly merited the punishment due to such *canaille*.[1] What a fool I had been to entertain for a moment the idea of forgiveness!—what a piece of wretched effeminacy it would be on my part, to actually put up with my own betrayal and aid to make my betrayers happy! Such an act might suit the *rôle* of a saint,—but it would not suit *me*. I was no saint,—I was a deeply wronged man,—and was I to have no redress for my wrong? The more I dwelt upon this sense of deadly injury, the more my inward resentment asserted itself and gathered strength, and I laughed aloud as I remembered what a soft-hearted weakling I had been before,—*before I had learned the wisdom of absinthe*! Oh, wonderful elixir!—it had given me courage, ferocity, stern resolve, relentless justice!—and the silly plan I had previously devised for the benefit of the two miserable triflers who had made so light of my love and honour, was now completely altered and—*reversed*! Glorious Absinthe! What is it the poet sings?—

> "*Avec l'absinthe, avec ce feu*
> *On peut se divertir un peu*
> *Jouer son rôle en quelque drâme!*"[2]

True enough! "Jouer son rôle en quelque drâme!" Why not? All things are possible to Absinthe,—it can accomplish more marvellous deeds than its drinkers wot of! It can quench pity—freeze kindness,—kill all gentle emotions, and rouse in a man the spirit of a beast of prey! The furious passions of a savage, commingled with the ecstasies of a visionary wake together at its touch, and he who drains it deeply and often, becomes a brute-poet, a god-centaur,—a thing for angels to wonder at, and devils to rejoice in;—and such an one am I! Who is there living that can make

---

[1]   French word meaning "riff-raff."

[2]   "With absinthe, with this fire / One can amuse oneself a little / Play one's role in some drama." From the poem "Lendemain" in *Le Coffret de santal* by Charles Cros. For full poem see Appendix G.5.

me regret a single evil deed I have committed, or prove to me at all satisfactorily that my deeds *are* evil? No one! Whosoever has Absinthe for
his friend and boon companion has made an end of conscience, and for
this blessing at least, should thank the dreadful unseen gods! And, while
we are about it, let us not forget to thank the fine progressive science of
to-day! For we have learnt beyond a doubt,—have we not? that we are
merely physical organizations of being,—that we have nothing purely
spiritual or God-born in us,—and thus, this Conscience that is so much
talked about, is nothing after all but a particular balance or condition of
the grey pulpy brain-matter. Moreover, it is in our own power to *alter*
that balance!—to *reverse* that condition!—and this once done, shall we
not be more at peace? Knowing the times to be evil, why should we
weary ourselves with striving after imaginary good? The mind that
evolves high thought and plans of lofty action, is deemed more or less
crazed,—it is fevered,—exalted,—foolishly imaginative,—so say the
wise-acres of the world, who with bitter words and chill satire make a
jest of their best poets and martyrize their noblest men. Come, then, O
ye great dreamers of the better life!—come, sweet singers of divine things
in rhythm!—come, ye passionate musicians who strive to break open
the gates of heaven with purest sound!—come, teachers, thinkers, and
believers all!—re-set the wrong and silly balance of your brains,—*reverse*
the inner dial of your lives, as I have done!—steep your fine feelings in
the pale-green fire that enflames the soul,—and make of yourselves
absintheurs,—the languid yet ferocious brutes of Paris, whose ferocity
born of poison, yet leaves them slaves!

The night of wakeful vision past, I arose from my bed,—I reeled back
as it were out of a devil's shadow-land, and faced God's morning unafraid.
It was the day of my father's expected return from England,—and I
surveyed myself curiously in the mirror to see if there was anything
noticeably strange or unsettled in my looks. No!—my own reflection
showed me nothing but a rather pale countenance, and preternaturally
brilliant eyes. I dressed with more than usually punctilious care, and while
I took my early coffee, wrote the following lines to Silvion Guidèl:—

*"I know all! To your treachery there can be but one answer. I give you to-
day to make your preparations,—to-morrow, at whatever time and place I shall
choose, of which I will inform you through my seconds, you will meet me,—
unless, as is possible, you are coward as well as liar.*

"GASTON BEAUVAIS."

I sealed this, and with it in my hand, sallied forth to the house of the curé, M. Vaudron. The day was chill and cloudy, but the rain had entirely ceased, and the lately boisterous wind had sunk to a mere cold breeze. I walked leisurely;—my mind was so thoroughly made up as to my course of action, that I felt no more excitement about the matter. The only thing that amused me now and then, and forced a laugh from me as I went, was the remembrance of that absurd idea I had indulged in on the previous night,—namely, that of actually pardoning the vile injury done to me, and exerting myself to make the injuring parties happy. That *would* be playing Christianity with a vengeance! What a ridiculous notion it now seemed!—and yet I had felt so earnestly about it then, that I had even shed tears to think of Pauline's wretchedness!

Well!—it was a weakness,—and it was past!—and I arrived at M. Vaudron's abode in a perfectly placid and vindictively settled humour. The good curé owned one of those small houses with gardens which, in Paris or near it, are getting rarer every year,—a cottage-like habitation, with a moss-green paling set entirely round it, and two neatly-trimmed flower-beds adorning the grass-plat in front. I knocked at the door,—and old Margot opened it. Her sharp beady black eyes surveyed me with complete astonishment at first—she was evidently cross about something or other, for her smile was not encouraging.

"*Eh bien,*[1] M. Beauvais!" she observed, setting her arms akimbo. "What can one do for you at this early hour in the morning? Not eight o'clock yet, and M. Vaudron is at mass-service—and his breakfast is not yet prepared,—and what should he do with visitors before noon?"

All this breathlessly, and with much pettish impatience.

"Tut, Margot! You must not look upon me as a visitor," I said quietly. "My errand is soon done. This"—and I held out my sealed-up challenge—"is for M. Silvion Guidèl, *voilà tout!*"

"For M. Guidèl!" she exclaimed, with a toss of her head and a quivering of her nostrils, which always betokened rising temper. "*Hein!*[2] best send it after him, then! He is not here any longer—he is gone!"

"Gone!" I echoed stupidly. "Gone!"

"Gone! Yes!—and why should he not go, if you please?" she inquired testily. "*I* have had enough of him! He is as difficult to please as an English *milord*,—and he has no more heart than a bad onion! I have been as kind to him as his own mother could have been,—and yet, away

[1] French for "oh well."
[2] French expression meaning "hey!" or "what!"

he went last night without a thank-you for my trouble! He left ten francs on my table—bah!—what is ten francs when one wants a kind word! And M.Vaudron is grieving for the loss of his company like a cat for a drowned kitten!"

I was so confounded by this unexpected turn to affairs, that for a moment I knew not what to say.

"Where has he gone?" I asked presently, in a faint unsteady voice.

"Back to Brittany, of course!" shrilled Margot irritably. "Where else should such a pretty babe be wanted? His father has met with a dangerous accident,—a horse kicked him, I believe—anyhow, he is thought to be dying—and the precious Silvion was telegraphed for in haste. And, as I tell you, hè left last night, without a word or a look or a 'Dieu vous bénisse'[1] to *me*!—me,—who have worked for him and waited upon him like a *slave*!—ah! the wicked ingratitude of the young to the old!"

I looked at her in vague surprise,—she was always more or less touchy, but there was evidently something deeper than mere touchiness in her present humour.

"Margot, you are cross!" I said, endeavouring to smile.

"Yes, I *am* cross!"—and she stamped her foot viciously,—then all at once tears welled up in her hard old eyes,—"I am cross and sorry both together, *voilà!*[2] He was a *beau garçon;*[3]—it was pleasant to see him smile,—and he had pretty ways, both for his uncle and for me,—that is, when he remembered me, which truly was not often. But then it was enough, so long as he was in the house, *voyez-vous?*[4]—and though he would do strange things, such as taking those long walks in the Bois by himself, for no earthly reason that I could see,—still one could look at him now and then, and think of the days when one was young. Bah!"—and she stamped her foot again, and rubbed away her tears with her coarse apron—"I am an old fool, and he is, I dare say, a thriftless *vaurien*, in spite of all his prayers and fasting!"

I laughed rather bitterly.

"*Parbleu!*[5] Did *he* pray?—did *he* fast?" I inquired, with a touch of sarcastic amusement.

Margot flared round upon me quite indignantly.

"Did he pray?—did he fast?—Why, what else was he made for?" she

---

[1]   French expression meaning "God bless you."
[2]   French term meaning "so there!"
[3]   French for "handsome boy."
[4]   French for "you see?"
[5]   French expression meaning "By jove."

snapped out. "He was always praying—and he ate enough for a bird—no more! He would kneel before his crucifix so long that I used to fancy I heard the rustle of the Blessed Virgin's robes about the house,—for if *his* petitions would not bring her to take care of us all, then I wonder what *would*? And once—ah, truly! where would he have been if I had not looked after him!—I found him in a faint in the church itself—he had been walking in the Bois as usual, and had come back to pray without touching a morsel of food,—but what else could you expect? He was a great big innocent!—the holy saints were the same!"

I shrugged my shoulders disdainfully.

"Do you know, Margot, that there are several ways of fighting the devil out of a man?" I said; "and starvation is one! Yet even then, it sometimes happens that the devil still gets the upper hand! Can you tell me whether M. Guidèl is coming back to Paris?"

"No, I cannot!" she retorted snappishly. "It is certain that he is gone, and that I have work to do,—and that if you want more news of him, you had better speak to M. le Curé. I have no time to stand talking here any longer!"

"*Bien! Bon jour,*[1] Margot!" and I raised my hat to her playfully.

"*Bon jour,* M. Gaston!" she returned tartly; "and try not to be jealous of young men whom God has made better-looking than yourself!"

And, with a bang, she shut the door upon me. I laughed, and sauntered slowly away. Idiotic old woman! She too, withered and wan and uncomely, had also felt the influence of Silvion Guidèl's accursed beauty,—so much so, as to be actually fretting over his careless omission to say good-bye to her! And she became rude to me directly she saw that I was inclined to depreciate his value! What dolts women were, I thought! Caught by a charming smile,—a pair of fine eyes, and a graceful form,—caught and infatuated to folly, and worse than folly, all for a man's outward bearing! Positively, when one comes to think of it, with all our intellectual progress, we are little better than the beasts in love! Physical perfection generally enchains us far more than mental,—as the tiger paces round his mate, attracted by her sinuous form, her velvety skin and fiery eyes, so we court and ogle the woman whose body seems to us the fairest,—so women, in their turn, cast amorous eyes at him whose strength seems the best comparison to their weakness. Of course there are exceptions to the rule,—but so rarely do they occur, that they are chronicled among the world's "romances," not realities. And we want

---

[1] French for "Well, good day."

realities nowadays, do we not?—no foolish glozing over of true and ugly facts? Well!—one very true and very ugly fact is paramount in human history; namely, that this *merely* physical attraction between man and woman is of the briefest continuance, and nearly always turns to absolute loathing! We are punished when we admire one another's perishable beauty to the exclusion of all mental or intelligent considerations,— punished in a thousand frightful ways,—ways which have truly a savour of Hell! It is, perhaps, unjust that the punishment should fall so heavily,—but fall it does, without question—unless,—unless one is an *absintheur*! Then, neither crime nor punishment matter one iota to the soul that has thus been rendered brutishly impervious to both!

I had plenty of food for reflection as I walked away from the curé's house,—and to give myself time to think quietly, I entered the Bois which was close by, and roamed up and down there for more than an hour. Silvion Guidèl had left Paris;—did Pauline know of this, I wondered? I tore up the challenge I had written him, and flung the little bits of paper far and wide into the air,—should I follow him to his home in Brittany? I was not at all inclined for the trouble of the journey. Old Margot's allusion to those long walks he used to take had opened my eyes to the manner in which he and Pauline must have arranged their clandestine interviews;—the nervous presentiments of Héloïse St. Cyr had evidently been only too well founded! Pauline, under pretence of attending mass at M. Vaudron's church, had really gone to meet her lover;—while he, after assisting his uncle at the first celebration, had hastened off to keep the tryst at whatever part of the Bois they had secretly appointed,—and so the *amour*[1] had been cleverly carried on in the early morning hours, without awakening any suspicion of wrong in those whose simple belief in woman's virtue and man's honour had been thus deliberately outraged. Other meetings elsewhere too, might easily have been arranged,—liars have a thousand cunning ways of keeping up their lies! What dupes we had all been!—what unsuspecting, blind, good-natured, trusting fools!—for I felt certain that even Héloïse, though she might have had her private fears of Pauline's impulsiveness and Guidèl's attractiveness, never imagined her idolized cousin would have fallen so far as she had fallen now. I meditated on the whole position for awhile, and finally returned home,—the result of my solitary reverie framing itself into the following letter:—

---

[1]   French for "love affair."

"TO MADEMOISELLE PAULINE DE CHARMILLES."
"MADEMOISELLE,

"I hear this morning that M. Silvion Guidèl has left Paris. Has he made his departure known to you, or signified in any way his future intentions? If not, I presume that his return to Brittany will be for good, in which case I may *possibly* (I do not say *certainly*) endeavour to forget our painful interview of last night. To make the best of the terrible position you are in, and also for the sake of those to whom your honour is dear, you will do well, at any rate for the present, *to keep silence*—and allow the arrangements for our marriage to proceed uninterruptedly. As time progresses, some new course of action may suggest itself to me,—but, till either definite news is heard from M. Guidèl, or I can see my way to an alteration of the contract settled and agreed upon by our respective families, you will serve every one concerned best, by allowing things to remain as they are. Accept my respectful salutations!

"GASTON BEAUVAIS."

I wrote this,—but why? Did I really intend to "endeavour to forget" her crime? Certainly not! What then did I mean?—what did I propose to do? *I cannot tell you!* I had, or seemed to have, an ulterior motive lurking in the background of my thoughts,—but what that motive was, I could not explain even to myself! Some force outside of me apparently controlled my movements,—I was a passive slave to some unseen but imperative master of my will! There is such a thing as hypnotism, remember!—the influence of one mind acting upon and commanding the other even at a distance. But there is something stronger even than hypnotism—and that is Absinthe! The suggestions IT offers are resistless and implacable,—no opposing effort will break ITS bonds! And IT had placed an idea,—a diabolical conception of revenge somewhere in my brain,—but whatever the plan was it did not declare itself in bold form as yet, it was a fiery nebula of disconnected fancies from which I could obtain no settled fact. But I was satisfied that I meant *something*,—something that would, I supposed, evolve itself into action in due time,—and for that time I was languidly content to wait.

CHAPTER 14

About a couple of hours after I had written my letter, I called at the De Charmilles' house, and delivered it in person to Pauline's own maid. I bade this girl tell her mistress that I waited for an answer,—and presently the answer came,—a little blotted blurred note closely sealed.

"I cannot, will not, believe he has gone!"—it ran—"without a word to me!—it would be too cruel! What shall I do?—I am desolate and helpless. But *I trust you*, Gaston,—and, as you wish it, I will say nothing, though to keep silence breaks my heart,—nothing—until you give me leave to speak.

"PAULINE."

This was all, but it satisfied me. I read it, standing on the doorstep with the *femme-de-chambre*[1] watching me somewhat curiously. Smiling unconcernedly, I inquired—

"How is mademoiselle this morning?"

"Not very well, monsieur. She has a severe headache and has not slept."

I feigned a proper anxiety.

"I am exceedingly sorry! Pray convey to her the expression of my deep solicitude! By the way, have you any news of Mademoiselle Héloïse?"

"*Oh oui, monsieur!*[2] She returns to-morrow afternoon."

With this information I retired,—and straightway proceeded to the Gare du Nord[3] to meet my father. He arrived, punctual to time, and greeted me with the utmost affection.

"*Gloire à la France!*" he exclaimed, as he alighted on the platform and clasped me by both hands. "What a joy it is to be out of gloomy England! It is the month of May as we all know,—and yet I have only seen the sun three times since I left Paris! But thou art pale, *mon fils*? Thou hast worked too hard?"

"Not at all," I assured him.

"The little Pauline has been cruel?"

I laughed.

---

[1] French for "chambermaid."

[2] French for "Oh yes, sir."

[3] North Station. Paris rail station serving passengers travelling to England, Belgium, and Germany.

"Cruel! She is an angel of sweetness, *mon père!*—too kind, too virtuous and too true for such a worthless fellow as I!"

My father gave me a quick puzzled glance.

"You speak with a strange harshness in your voice, Gaston," he said anxiously. "Is there anything wrong?"

I tried to be as much like my old self as possible, and took his arm affectionately. "Nothing, *mon père!*—nothing! All is well. I have lost a friend, that is all;—the admirable Silvion Guidèl has gone back to Brittany."

"*Tiens!*[1] What a pity!" and my father looked quite concerned about it. "He had become thy favourite comrade too! When did be go?"

"Last night only, and quite suddenly;" and I detailed the news of the morning as received from Margot.

My father shook his head vexedly.

"Ah well! Then he will have to be a priest after all, I suppose! *Quel dommage!*[2] Such a brilliant young man should have chosen a different career. I had hoped Paris would have changed him."

"You are as fascinated with him as everybody else!" I said, laughing somewhat nervously. My father laughed too.

"Well! He *is* a fascinating boy!" he admitted; "I am already quite sorry for the ladies, old and young, who may need to have recourse to his spiritual counsels!"

"By my faith, so am I!" I rejoined emphatically, in a half *sotto-voce*, which my father, just then busy with his luggage, did not hear.

All that day was one of comparatively empty leisure; but, though I had both chance and opportunity, I did not venture to visit Pauline. Old Vaudron came disconsolately in at dinner-time, the forlorn expression of his countenance betokening how greatly he missed his nephew, though he brightened up a little in my father's company. I watched him,—thinking of the secret I held—yet saying nothing.

"Who would have thought," he dismally complained, "that the boy Silvion could have become so dear to me! And to Margot also!—she is inconsolable! What a warning it is against setting too much store by the ties of earthly affection! It is altogether very unfortunate; for now I suppose his parents will hardly bear him out of their sight for months! You see, *mon ami,*"—and his kind old eyes moistened as he spoke—"he is such a beautiful and gentle soul that one considers him more an angel than a human being,—he is unlike everybody else. Yet, all the same, I

---

[1] French interjection translating in this instance as "Indeed!"
[2] French expression meaning "What a pity."

think Paris scarcely agreed with him. There was an odd restlessness about his manner of late,—and a certain bitterness of speech that did not well become his nature; and once indeed we had together a very melancholy discussion which, if I had not handled it with the nicest care, might have led to his indulgence in a deadly sin!"

"Impossible!" I ejaculated with a slight smile, "Sin and Silvion Guidèl are leagues apart!"

"True, very true!" responded the gentle, unsuspecting old man. "And I thank God for it! Yet, without carnal errors, there are spiritual transgressions which must be avoided,—and one of these Silvion was inclined to fall a prey to,—namely, despair! Despair of God's mercy!—ah! this is terrible presumption, and we find it so designated in the Holy Roman Missal.[1] He put strange and awful questions to me at that time, such as this,—'Whether I believed God really cared how we lived or what good or evil we committed!' Such a frightful idea!—a positive tempting of Divine justice!—it quite alarmed me, I assure you!"

"And you answered—what?" I queried, vaguely interested.

"Why, *mon cher garçon*,[2] I answered as my faith and duty taught me," he replied with mild austerity. "I told him that God certainly *did* care,—or else He would not have placed in the inner consciousness of every human being such a distinct comprehension betwixt right and wrong."

"But—pardon me—it is not always distinct," I interposed; "it is frequently very doubtful and uncertain. If it were more plainly defined, right action would perhaps be easier."

"Not so, *mon p'tit*,"[3] declared Vaudron gently. "Because the unfortunate fact is that, though men *have* this distinct feeling of the difference between right and wrong, they invariably choose the wrong,—the reason being that Right is the hardest road,—Wrong the easiest."

"Then one would argue Wrong to be natural, and Right *un*natural," I said, "and also that it is useless to oppose Nature!"

The curé's eyes opened wide at this remark, and my father shook his head at me smilingly.

"Do not thou be a sophist, Gaston!" he said kindly. "One can argue any and every way,—but Right is God's compass to the end of all worlds!"

I made no reply;—I thought I had begun to know the meaning of this "God's compass,"—it was nothing but the small, delicately poised

---

[1] A book containing prayers and directions for the celebration of Mass in the Catholic Church.

[2] French for "my dear boy."

[3] French term of affection meaning "my little one."

balance of the brain which could, by man's own wish and will, be as easily set wrong as right!

After dinner I left the two elderly gentlemen over their wine and slipped out, for a sudden craving possessed me,—a craving, the unwholesome nature of which I perfectly understood, though I had neither strength nor desire to resist it. The action of Absinthe can no more be opposed than the action of morphia. Once absorbed into the blood, a clamorous and constant irritation is kept up throughout the system,—an irritation which can only be assuaged and pacified by fresh draughts of the ambrosial poison. This was the sort of nervous restlessness that shook me now,—and, as it was a fine night, I made my way down to the Boulevard Montmartre,[1] where I entered one of the best and most brilliant *cafés*, and at once ordered the elixir that my very soul seemed athirst for! What a sense of tingling expectation quivered in my veins as I prepared the greenish-opal mixture, whose magical influence pushed wide ajar the gates of dreamland!—with what a lingering ecstasy I sipped to the uttermost dregs two full glasses of it,—enough, let me tell you, to unsteady a far more slow and stolid brain than mine! The sensations which followed were both physically and mentally keener than on the previous evening,—and when I at last left the *café* and walked home at about midnight, my way was encompassed with the strangest enchantments. For example: there was no moon, and clouds were still hanging in the skies heavily enough to obscure all the stars,— yet, as I sauntered leisurely up the Champs Elysées, a bright green planet suddenly swung into dusky space, and showered its lustre full upon my path. Its dazzling beams completely surrounded me, and made the wet leaves of the trees overhead shine like jewels; and I tranquilly watched the burning halo spreading about me in the fashion of a wide watery rim, knowing all the time that it was but an image of my fancy. Elixir Vitae!—the secret so ardently sought for by philosophers and alchemists!—*I* had found it, even I!—I was as a god in the power I had obtained to create and enjoy the creations of my own fertile brain,— for, truly, this is all that even high Omnipotence can do,—namely, to command worlds to be born by the action of His thought,—and again, to bid them die by an effort of His will! The huge Creative Force of all time and all space can be no more than an endless and boundlessly immense Imagination. And one spark of this Imagination is perhaps the only divine thing we have in our mortal composition,—though, of

---

[1] Busy street on the Right Bank with many cafés, restaurants, and shops.

course, like Reason, it can easily be perverted to false and criminal ends. But we of Paris care nothing as to whether our thoughts run in wholesome or morbid channels so long as self-indulgence is satiated. *My thoughts, for instance, were poisoned,—but I was satisfied with their poisonous tendency!* And I was in no wise disconcerted or dismayed when, on reaching home and ascending the steps, I found the door draped with solemn black, as if for a funeral, and saw written across it in pale yet lustrous emerald scintillations—

"LA MORT HABITE ICI!"[1]

Quietly I put out my hand and made as though I would touch these seemingly substantial sable hangings,—they rolled away like rolling smoke,—the dismal inscription vanished, and all was clear again! Entering, I found my father sitting up for me.

"Thou art late, Gaston!" he said, as I came towards him, yet smiling good-naturedly as he spoke. "Thou hast been at the De Charmilles'?"

"Not to-night," I answered carelessly. "I have only walked to the Boulevards and back."

"*Vraiment!* A new sort of amusement for thee, is it not? Thou art not likely to become a *boulevardier*?" And he clapped me kindly on the shoulder as we ascended the stairs together to our respective bedrooms. "But, no! Thou hast worked too well and conscientiously to have such a suggestion made to thee even in jest. I am well pleased with thee, *mon fils*,—I know how difficult thy duties have been during my absence, and how admirably thou hast fulfilled them."

I received his praise passively without remark, and he continued—

"For the next week take holiday, Gaston, and for the week after that again! Then comes thy marriage,—and I will strive to do without thee for a full two months. Where wilt thou spend thy *lune-de miel*?"[2]

"Where? In Paradise, of course!" I answered, with a forced smile.

My father laughed,—brushed his bearded lips against my cheek, an old French custom of his whenever he felt particularly affectionate, and we parted for the night. What a sound sleep that good man would have, I thought, as I watched him turn into his room, and saluted him respectfully in response to his last cheerful nod and glance. He would not see what *I* saw when I entered my own chamber! Pauline was there,

---

[1]   French for "Death resides here!"
[2]   French for "honeymoon."

asleep!—she lay on my couch, her head resting on my pillows,—her lips parted in a sweet drowsy smile,—while over her whole fair form fell a shimmering veil of green, like mist hanging above the lakes and mountains in a halcyon midsummer noon! Ah, gentle soul!—image of childlike innocence and love!—there she was, reflected on the mirror of my brain as purely and faithfully as she had been cherished in my thoughts for many and many a day! I stood, silently looking on for a space at the beautiful phantom of my lost idol,—looking as gravely, as sadly and as regretfully as I would have looked at the dead. Then, extending my hands slowly as a wizard might do, I attempted to touch that delicate recumbent figure,—and lo!—it melted into naught—my bed was once more smooth, bare, and empty,—empty of even the spectre of delight! I threw myself down upon it, fatigued in body and mind, yet not unpleasantly so;—closing my aching eyes, I wandered away into a cloudy realm of confused phantasmal pageant and fantastic vision, and, dreaming, fancied that I slept!

CHAPTER 15

That same week, Héloïse St. Cyr returned from Normandy, and, two days after her arrival in Paris, my father and I were invited to dine with the De Charmilles, our good friend the *curé* being also of the party. I was vaguely amused at the whole affair,—it went off so well, and there were two such admirable actors at table, namely, myself and Pauline. Trust a woman to eclipse every one in the art of feigning! She, Pauline, was a mere brilliant scintillation of dazzling mirth and *coquetterie*[1] from the beginning of the dinner to its end. It was only pretence, I knew, but who would have thought she could have pretended so well! Now and then I was smitten with a sudden amaze at her,—but observing her narrowly, I noticed the feverish flush on her cheeks, the almost delirious brilliancy of her eyes, the unnatural scarlet of her lips,—and I realized that however unconcerned she might appear in outward bearing, she was inwardly enduring agonies of mental torture such as few could imagine. This conviction filled me with a certain morbid satisfaction, though I often

---

[1] French word for "flirtatiousness."

found my attention wandering from her to her cousin Héloïse, whose stay in Normandy certainly seemed to have freshened and intensified her beauty. For she *was* beautiful,—I who had formerly been loth to admit this, acknowledged it at last. There was more colour in her face,—and she possessed a tranquil, almost imperial stateliness of manner that was singularly attractive. My gaze dwelt upon her with a sort of fascination,—and occasionally I caught her pure serious eyes regarding *me* with an anxious wistfulness and wonder. The Comte and Comtesse de Charmilles were evidently delighted to have their fair niece once more under their roof,—and as for Pauline,—why, she very cleverly affected to be glad!—she could do no less and no more! Of course the conversation turned frequently upon Silvion Guidèl and his sudden departure; and M. Vaudron told us he had received a telegram announcing his nephew's safe arrival at his home in Brittany, but no further news than this.

"He will never come back to Paris again, I am sure!" said Pauline, laughing quite hilariously. "He has gone for good!"

"I am afraid he has, my child," returned the old curé regretfully. "But perhaps it is better so. Paris is not the place for men of serious purpose,—and he has seen it—he knows what it is like,—that is quite enough for him."

Pauline gave not the faintest sign of interest in these remarks,—she had been daintily dividing a large bunch of grapes with the grape-scissors, and she now held out a cluster of the fruit to me, smiling. As I accepted it, I looked her full and steadily in the eyes,—but she did not blush or tremble. What mummers we both were, I thought!—and what a part we had chosen to play! Why did we not blurt out the truth of the position like honest folk and take the consequences? Why?—Well, why does not every sinner make a clean breast of his secret evil thoughts and misdeeds, and, blazoning them to the world, abide calmly by the result? It would be noble,—it would be stern-principled,—but afterwards? When we had all frankly admitted ourselves to be more or less liars and knaves not worth a hand-shake or a thank-you, what then? Nothing but this,—society would be at an end, and we might as well pull down our cities and return in howling nudity to the forests of primeval barbarism. Besides, we in France always like to feign a little virtue, however much we may feel prone to vice,—we are fond of alluding melodramatically to "*nôtre mère*"[1] and "*le tombeau de nôtre père*"[2]—in fact, we generally

---

[1] French for "our mother."
[2] French for "our father's grave."

manage to draw in our dead ancestors to support us in our feverish hours of strong mental excitement or high-pressure morality. And, as regarded Pauline and her wretched secret, she was in *my* hands,—*I* had the ruling of the game,—I and my "green-eyed fairy" whose magical advice I now followed unhesitatingly; and I did not choose to speak,—*yet*. I waited, and the miserable child Pauline also waited—on *my* will.

There are some few uncomfortable people in the world, however, who cannot be altogether deceived, and Héloïse St. Cyr was one of these. She always took things very tranquilly and with a sort of even Socratic philosophy,—but she would probe to the bottom of them somehow. And she was very difficult to deal with, as I found, when, after dinner, I entered the drawing-room as usual with the other gentlemen. It was a warm and beautiful evening,—the windows stood wide open,—the garden was gay with flowers, and across the small lawn in front strolled Pauline, carolling softly to herself the refrain of a song. Héloïse, in one of those straight simple white gowns she was so fond of wearing, stood within the window-embrasure looking out, but turned quickly round as soon as she was aware of my entrance.

"M. Gaston," she said hurriedly, in a half whisper, "tell me!—what is wrong with Pauline?"

I met her eyes with a studied expression of complete amazement.

"Wrong with Pauline?" I echoed. "Why nothing! Hear how she sings!—like a lark in full sunshine!—See how merry she is!—how well she looks!"

"Her merriment is *forced*," declared Héloïse emphatically. "And she is *not* well. Oh, cannot you, who love her, see that she is unhappy? She is changed,—quite changed, even to me,—she turns every thing I say to a jest even when jesting is entirely out of place,—she is restless—irritable,—she will hardly remain quiet for an hour. She used to be so fond of me,—and now!—why she did not seem to be at all glad to see me come back, and she avoids my eyes so strangely! Oh, M. Gaston!—did you think of the warning I gave you before I left?—or did it slip your memory? Did I not ask you to see that the child was not left too much alone?"

What a strange hardness there was at my heart!—her anxious words, her eager looks excited no more emotion in me than this—that with each moment I grew increasingly conscious of her exceeding physical grace and beauty.

"I always remember everything *you* say, Héloïse," I answered, steadfastly regarding her with, as I know, a look of open admiration, and watching with a half smile, the rich blood mounting to her cheeks, while an amazed embarrassment gathered in her eyes. "But I never quite comprehended why you should so greatly concern yourself about the matter. Pauline can surely be trusted! Do you not think so?"

"I *do* think so!" she responded swiftly—brave girl!—true friend!—"But it is hardly fair to expect the discretion of age and experience from one who is almost a child,—and such a beautiful child too! Pauline is all impulse,—she is sensitive,—wayward sometimes,—she takes sudden fancies and sudden dislikes,—and, as I told you once before, she hardly understands herself——"

Here she broke off and caught her breath, while her large eyes dwelt on me in a vague fear. "Why do you look at me so strangely, M. Gaston?" she faltered nervously. "What is it?"

I laughed coldly. "What is it? Why—nothing, *ma chère*[1] Héloïse!—what should there be? It is you who seem to have vague ideas of something which you do not express—and it is I who should ask, 'What is it?'"

She still breathed quickly, and suddenly laid her hand on my arm.

"You too are changed!" she said. "Tell me truly!—do you still love Pauline?"

"Can you doubt it?" and I smiled. "I love her,—madly!"

And I spoke the truth. The passion I felt for the little frail thing whom I could see from where I stood, flitting about the garden among the flowers, was indeed *mad*,—no sane mind would have ever indulged in such a tumult of mingled desire and hatred, as burned in mine!

"I am going to her," I added more tranquilly, seeing that Héloïse seemed alarmed as well as uneasy. "I shall ask her for one of those roses she is gathering, as a *gage d'amour*."[2] I moved away,—then paused a moment. "Your trip to Normandy has done you good, Héloïse. You are looking adorable!"

What a lightning-glance she gave me!—it swept over me like the death-flash of a storm! I stopped, rooted to the ground, as it were, by the sudden spiritual dazzlement of her beauty,—why did my heart-throbs send such clamorous vibrations through my frame?—what force was there in the air that held us twain, man and woman, spell-bound for a moment, gazing at each other wildly as though on the brink of some strange destiny? In that one brief space of time all life seemed waiting in suspense,—and had I yielded to the fiery impulse that possessed me then, I should have clasped that fair angelic woman in my

---

[1] French for "my dear."
[2] French term for "pledge of love."

arms and called her love, salvation, hope, rescue!—I should have told her all,—given her my very soul to keep, and so I might have missed perdition! But it was a mere passing madness,—I could not account for it then, and can hardly account for it now,—but what ever shock it was that thus by magnetic impulse shook our nerves, it moved us both with strong and singular agitation, for Héloïse fled from my sight as though pursued by some avenging spirit,—and I, after a couple of minutes pause, recovered my composure, and stepping out into the garden there joined Pauline. She looked up at me as I approached—her face wore an expression of extreme weariness.

"How long is this to last, Gaston?" she murmured. "How long must I play this terrible part of seeming to be what I am not? I am so tired of it!—Oh God!—so tired!"

I walked silently by her side round among the shadows of some tall trees to a spot where we were out of the observation of any one who might be looking from the house-windows.

"Have you heard from your lover?" I then asked coldly.

Her head drooped. "No!"

"Do you think it likely that you *will* hear?"

She sighed. "I believe in him," she said. "If my belief is vain—then God help me!"

I studied her fair and delicate features scrutinizingly. She was lovely,—lovelier in her grief than in her joy, I thought—a broken angel in a ruined shrine. But her beauty left me cold as ice,—impervious as adamant,—Absinthe had numbed the tenderer fancies of my brain, and in obedience to its promptings I answered her.

"That is what all criminals say, when confronted with the disastrous consequences of crime—'God help me!' But God's assistance is not always to be relied upon,—it frequently fails us in cases of the direst necessity. The beggar says, 'God help me!' yet continues to beg on,— the suffering cry, 'God help us,' and still they starve and weep,—the dying man in his agony exclaims, 'God help me!' and his torments are not softened a whit,—and you, poor little thing, are like the rest of us, trusting to a divine rescue that is frequently too late in coming, if indeed it ever comes at all."

She gave a languid gesture of hopelessness.

"Then God is cruel," she said wearily. "And yet—He made these."

And she held out the roses she had lately plucked and made a posy of,—but as she did so, the fairest bud suddenly crumbled and fell in a shower of pale pink leaves upon the ground.

"Yes!—He made them,—made them to perish!—for which strange and unaccountable end He has seemingly made all things, even you and me," I responded, taking her cold passive hand in mine. "As the rose-leaves fall, so beauty dies,—so hope passes,—so fidelity proves naught! Silvion Guidèl has deserted you, Pauline!"

She shivered, but made no reply.

"What will you do?" I went on mercilessly. "What way is there left for you to escape dishonour? How will you avert shame from those parents whose pride is centred in you? Think! As yet they know nothing,—but when they *do* know, what then?"

Her blue eyes fixed themselves unseeingly upon the roses in her hands,—her lips moved, and she murmured faintly—

"I can die!"

I was silent.

She could die,—this little fair thing for whom life had scarcely begun,—certainly, she could die! We all have that universal remedy. And there was no power on earth that could prevent her, if she chose, from deliberately shutting out the world for ever from her sight, and finding peace in death's acceptable darkness. Yes—she could die—even she!

"Pauline, Pauline! what a fate!" I said at last. "How terrible to realize it!—to think that you—you for whom nothing seemed too good, too happy, or too bright, should be at this pass of dire misfortune,—and all through the black base treachery of a liar, a traitor,—a dishonourable cowardly villain——"

"Stop!" she exclaimed in a low fierce voice that startled me. "You shall not blame him in *my* hearing! I have told you I can die,—but I shall die loving him,—*adoring* him,—to the end!"

Oh the love of a desperately loving woman! Can anything under the sun equal its strength, its tamelessness, its marvellous tenacity! This fragile girl—wronged, deserted, ruined,—still clung to the memory of her betrayer with such constancy that she, not having yet seen full nineteen years of existence, could calmly contemplate death for his sake! Ah God!—why could she not have loved *me* thus tenderly! I looked at her, and she met my gaze with an almost queenly challenge of mingled sorrow and pride.

"You are brave, Pauline," I said quietly, "brave to recklessness,—brave to the extremest limits of unreasoning despair! But pray compose yourself and listen to me. I am more cautious—perhaps more practical in the foreseeing of events than you can be. Of course it is well-nigh impossible to calculate the social result of our unhappy position towards each other should we decide to make the whole affair public,—but, in the meanwhile, I want you to understand that your secret is safe in my hands,—the honour of the De Charmilles is not yet given over to the dogs of scandal!" I paused, and a tremor ran through her frame,—she knew, as I knew, that her sin was one that her father, proud of his lineage and ancestral glories, would never forgive and never forget. "You gave me credit once for generosity," I continued, "and the most generous thing I could do would be to still take you as my wife, and shield your name from blemish under cover of mine. For your parents' sake this would be best and kindest,—but for me, not so well! I doubt much whether I could ever reconcile myself to such a course of action! It is therefore, sincerely to be hoped that M. Silvion Guidèl will find it consistent with his *honour*"—and I laid a sarcastic emphasis on this word—"to write and inform you of his intentions before the day appointed for your marriage with me comes much closer at hand. As you must be aware, there is only a space of about ten days between then and now."

She looked up at me in anguished entreaty.

"And must I still keep silence?" she asked.

"Really, mademoiselle, that is entirely as you please!" I returned composedly. "I shall not speak—as yet;—but if *you* choose to make full confession to your parents, or to your cousin, that is a different matter. No doubt such frankness on your part would greatly simplify the whole disastrous affair,—but this must be left to your own discretion!"

And I smiled slightly. I knew she was of far too shrinking and nervous a temperament to brave her father's fierce wrath, her mother's despair, and the wondering horror and reproach of all her friends and relatives, so long as there remained the least chance of escape from such a terrible *exposé*.[1] If Silvion wrote to her,—if Silvion sent for her,—she would of course fly to join him and leave everything to be discovered when she had gone,—but if, on the contrary, he kept silence and made no sign, why, there was nothing to be done but to *wait*—to wait as I before said, on *my* will! I offered her my arm to escort her back to the house,—she accepted it mechanically, and together we returned to the drawing-room. Héloïse was there, reading aloud from a newspaper an account of the triumphs of a celebrated violinist whose name had recently become a sort of musical watchword to the ardent and aspiring,—and her eyes sparkled with animation as, looking up from the journal, she told us she had been invited to meet this same brilliant

---

[1] French for "exposure."

"star" at a neighbour's house the next evening. Her aunt smiled at her enthusiasm,—and the Comte de Charmilles remarked—

"Thou should'st ask him to try thy violin, Héloïse;—it is not every *demoiselle*[1] who possesses a real undoubted Stradivarius."[2]

"Is it a Strad?" I asked, with some interest, fixing my eyes on Héloïse, who for once avoided my direct gaze as she replied—

"Yes. It is an heirloom, and has been in my mother's family for more than a hundred years, but no one among us ever played it till I suddenly took a fancy to try my skill upon it. There is rather a sad legend attached to it too."

"Ah, now we shall have you at your best, Mademoiselle Héloïse!" said my father, smiling. "You will, of course, tell us this legend?"

"If you wish." And Héloïse, moving to the further end of the room, opened her violin-case and took out the instrument. "But you must look at it carefully first. Through the F holes you will see the sign-manual of Stradivarius, and also something else. There are several other words,—can you make them out?"

We gathered round her, and each in turn examined the interior of the violin, and finally managed to decipher the following—

> "*Je meurs parce que j'aime l'amour plus que ma vie—*
> *Parle, violon, quand je suis mort, de ma reine Marie.*"[3]

Beneath these lines was a monogram of two letters entwined in a wreath of laurel, and as we handed back the instrument to its fair owner, our eyes inquired the meaning of the motto.

"This Strad belonged, so the story goes," said Héloïse softly, "to one who in his time was considered the greatest violinist in the world. His name no one knows,—his monogram is there, but cannot, as you see, be distinctly deciphered. The legend however is, that he loved a great lady of the Court of France, and that she showed him many favours for a little while, till suddenly, out of some cruel and unaccountable caprice, she deserted him, and would never receive him or even look upon his face again. Maddened by despair he slew himself,—and these lines inscribed inside the violin are written in his own blood. It is supposed

---

[1] A young lady.

[2] Violin made by Antonio Stradivari of Cremona (1644?-1737) or one of his followers.

[3] "I die because I love love more than my life—/ Speak, violin, when I am dead, of my queen Marie."

that he took the instrument apart to write the device within it, as, according to one account, it is said to have been found seemingly broken by the side of his dead body. If this be true, then skilled hands must have put it together again, for here it is, as you see, intact, and with a strange pathos in its tone, or so I fancy,—a pathos that it would be difficult to equal. Listen!"

And she drew the bow across the G string slowly, while we involuntarily held our breath. It was such a weird, wild, full, and solemn sound,—something like the long grave organ-note drawn forth by the wind from the close-knit branches of old trees. "Parle, violon, quand je suis mort!" Such had been the last prayer of its long-ago dead master,—and truly its eloquence had not ceased to be convincing. The "reine Marie" had been careless of love and capricious, as beautiful women so often are, but still the passionate tones of her lover's instrument bore faithful witness to her beauty's conquering charm! We were all in expectation that Héloïse would play something; but in this we were doomed to disappointment, for she quietly put the violin back in its case and locked it, in spite of her aunt's affectionate entreaty that she would favour us with one little *morçeau*.[1]

"I am not in the humour, aunt," she said simply—and there was a weary look in her eyes—"and I should not play well. Besides"—and she smiled a little—"you must remember that there is a grand *maestro* just now in Paris,—and the very consciousness of his presence in this city seems actually to paralyze my efforts!"

A vague irritation stirred me that she should attach so much importance to the arrival of a mere professional "star" in the art of violin-playing.

"Do you know the man?" I asked abruptly.

"Not personally," she replied. "As I told you, I am to meet him tomorrow evening. But I have heard him play—that is enough!"

I shrugged my shoulders.

"You are enthusiastic, Héloïse!" I remarked satirically. "I thought you were a veritable Pallas Athene[2]—always calm, always cold!"

She looked at me with a strange deepening brilliancy in her eyes.

"Cold!" she faltered, "I?"

I was near her as she spoke and our glances met. Once more that curious magnetic thrill ran through me,—once more that inexplicable

---

[1]   French for "piece."
[2]   Greek goddess of war, patron of the arts and crafts, and the personification of wisdom.

shock seemed to agitate us both. But it passed as it had passed before,—and just then M. Vaudron came up to us with some ordinary remark that scattered our thoughts into all sorts of different and commonplace directions. The evening ended, to all appearances, as satisfactorily as it had begun,—our elders evidently had no shadow of suspicion that anything was wrong,—and when I parted from Pauline, it was with a carefully studied assumption of that lover-like reluctance to say farewell which once had been too real to need feigning. Héloïse, as she murmured "Good night!" gave me her hand,—I held it a moment in my own,—then kissed it with grave courtesy. What could have possessed me then, I wonder, that I should have felt such a keen sense of delight as I saw the colour rush over her fair pale cheeks like a sudden glow of sunset on alabaster! I suppose it must have been the consciousness of the growing devil within me,—the devil that had already begun to preach away conscience and make a gibe of principle, and that in a short time was destined to become so strong that whatever there was of true manhood in me would be utterly exterminated by its insidious power. The devil born of Absinthe!—the fair, brave fiend, whose fidelity to the soul it seizes upon, like that of its twin-sister Morphia, never releases till death! Every hour of every day its hold on my brain grew closer, firmer, and more absolute, till I ceased to feel even so much as a passing throb of compunction; and with my eyes open to the abyss of darkness before me, voluntarily drifted slowly yet steadily *down*!

CHAPTER 16

Time went on, and yet no sign from Silvion Guidèl. One letter only, from his mother to the curé, thanking him for all the care and kindness he had shown to "nôtre cher et bien-aimé *Saint* Silvion,"[1] and stating that this same "saint" was in excellent health and progressing admirably with his religious studies, was all the news we received. Now and then I thought I would go to Brittany, and seek him out and fight him to the death there,—but, after a little cogitation, I always dismissed the idea. It was better, I decided, to wait on. For Pauline had written to him twice,—and I naturally imagined that his answer to the desperate appeals of the girl he had betrayed, would be a swift and unexpected

---

[1] French expression meaning "our dear and beloved."

return to Paris,—unless, indeed, he should prove himself to be altogether a man beneath even a beggar's contempt. Meantime all the
arrangements for my marriage with Pauline went smoothly on, without any interference from either of the principal parties concerned. It
was settled that the civic registration should take place first, in the grand
drawing-room of the Comte de Charmilles, before a large and brilliant
assemblage of friends and guests,—the religious ceremony was to follow
afterwards in the pretty little church of which M. Vaudron was the
presiding genius. The invitations had all been sent out,—one going to
Silvion Guidèl in due course,—and I, languidly amused thereat,
wondered how he would take it! As for me, I was now quite resolved
on my own plan of action. My drugged brain had evolved it in the
wanderings of many dreamful nights,—and though the plot was devilish, to me, in my condition, it seemed just. Why should not the wicked
be punished for their wickedness? Holy Writ supports the theory,—for
did not David, "a man after God's own heart," pray that his enemies
might be consumed as with fire, and utterly destroyed?[1] Dear, good,
gentle, Christian friends!—you who love your Bibles and read them
with diligent attention, I beg you will study the inspired pages thereof
again and yet again, before you dare to utterly abhor me, who am your
fellow-mortal! Consider the pious joy with which you yourselves look
forward to seeing those particular persons whom you specially abhor,
roasting in Hell for all eternity, while you, sweet, clean souls, walk
placidly the golden pavement of serenest Heaven! It is possible, nay
more than probable, that you will be disappointed in these sublime
anticipations,—still, you can nurse the generous hope while here below,
only do not turn round and condemn *me*, because I also, in the spirit
of David, desired to see my enemies "confounded and put to shame"[2]
in *this* life! Had I no patience, you may piously ask, to wait till after
death? No! Because "after death" is a shadowy circumstance; one
cannot be certain what will happen, and the present wise age does well
to seize its opportunities for good or for evil while it can, *here* and *now*!

In the short interval that had yet to elapse before the day of my
intended nuptials, a curious change worked itself in me,—a change of
which I was palpably, physically conscious. I can only explain it by

---

[1]   David, the first king of the Judean dynasty, is described in this way in the Bible in the first
book of Samuel (13.14) and in the Acts of the Apostles (13.22-23). Though chosen by God,
David is a complex figure whose violent acts undermine his claims to piety and holiness.

[2]   From the Old Testament of the Bible, Psalms 35.4.

saying that my brain seemed dead. A stony weight lay behind my temples, cold and hard and heavy. I shall perhaps make myself understood better if I analyze my sensations thus:—namely, that when my brain was in its former normal condition before the *absinthe-furia* had penetrated to its every cell, it was like a group of sensitive fibres or cords which, when touched by memory, sentiment, affection, or any feeling whatsoever, would instantly respond in quick pulsations of eager and easy comprehension. Now, it seemed as if all those fibres had snapped in some strange way, leaving in their place a steel reflector of images,— a hard bright substance on which emotion simply flashed and passed without producing any actual responsive vibration. Yet certain plans of action seemed to be part of this steel pressure,—plans which, though they appeared in a manner precise, still lacked entire consecutiveness,— and not the least remarkable phase of my transformation was this,— that *good*, or what moralists call good, presented itself to me as not only distinctly unnatural, but wholly absurd. In brief, the best and clearest expression I can give to my condition of mind for the benefit of those medical experts who have perhaps not thoroughly comprehended the swift and marvellous influence of the green nectar of Paris on the human nerves and blood is, that my former ideas and habits of life were completely and absolutely *reversed*. We are told that the composition of the brain is a certain grey matter in which countless shifting molecules work the wheels of thought and sensation;—in the healthy subject they work harmoniously and in order,—but—and this is to be remembered—a touch will set them wrong,—a severe blow on the outside case or skull may, and often does, upset their delicate balance;—what think you then of a creeping fire, which, by insidious degrees, quickens them into hot confused masses, and almost changes their very nature? Aye!—this is so!—and neither gods nor angels can prevent it. Give me the fairest youth that ever gladdened a mother's heart,—let him be hero, saint, poet, whatever you will,—let me make of him an *absintheur!*— and from hero he shall change to coward, from saint to libertine, from poet to brute! You doubt me? Come then to Paris,—study our present absinthe-drinking generation,—*absintheurs*, and children of *absintheurs*,— and then,—why then give glory to the English Darwin![1] For he was a wise man in his time, though in his ability to look back, he perhaps lost the power to foresee. He traced, or thought he could trace man's *ascent*

---

[1] Charles Darwin (1809-82); English naturalist whose evolutionary theory based on natural selection was a subject of controversy in the Victorian period.

from the monkey,—but he could not calculate man's *descent* to the monkey again. He did not study the Parisians closely enough for that! If he had, he would most assuredly have added a volume of prophecies for the future to his famous pedigree of the past!

Curious and significant too, among my other sensations, was the dull aversion I had taken to the always fair, though now sorrowful, face of Pauline. The girl in her secret wretchedness annoyed me,—there were moments when I hated her,—and again, there were times when I loved her. Loved her?—yes!—but not in a way that good women would care to be loved. Moreover, Héloïse St. Cyr had come to possess an almost weird fascination for me. Yet I saw very little of her,—for a new interest had suddenly entered her life,—the great violinist whom she had been so eager to meet, had heard her play, and had been so enchanted, either with her, or the valuable Stradivarius she owned, that he had volunteered, for art's sake, to give her a lesson every day during the brief time he remained in Paris. After some little hesitation, and an anxious consultation with her aunt as to the propriety of this arrangement, the offer was accepted,—and she was straightway drawn into an artistic and musical circle which was considerably divided from ours. I never had a chance of either seeing or hearing the brilliant violin-*maestro* whose triumphs were in every one's mouth,—I only knew that he was not old,—that some people considered him handsome, and that he was entirely devoted to his art,—but no more personal news than this could I obtain concerning him. Héloïse too was singularly reticent on the subject,— only her wonderful grey-green eyes used to shine with a strange fire whenever he was mentioned, and this vaguely vexed me. However I was not given much opportunity to brood on the matter,—as the famous "star" very soon took his departure, and beyond the fact that Héloïse played more divinely than ever, I almost forgot, in the rush of more pressing events, that he had crossed the even tenor of her existence.

Three days before my intended marriage—only three days!—I received, to my utter amazement, a letter from Silvion Guidèl. It began abruptly, thus—

"I understand that you know everything,—therefore you will realize that no explanation can make me more of a villain than I acknowledge myself to be. *I cannot marry.* I was ordained a priest of Holy Church yesterday. Circumstances have moulded my fate in opposition to my will,—and I can only throw myself upon your mercy and ask you not to visit my crime on the head of the poor child I have wronged. I cannot write to her—I dare not; I am weak-natured and afraid of woman's grief. The only way left to me for the atonement of the evil I have done is through a life of hard penitence and prayer. This I have chosen, entreating you all to pardon me and to think of me as one dead.

"SILVION GUIDÈL."

A fierce oath broke from me as I crushed this epistle in my hand. Specious villain!—canting hypocrite! Ordained a priest!—sheltered in the pale of the Church—vowed to perpetual celibacy,—and what was worse still, exempt from the call of a duel! If I could have seen him at that moment before me, I would have sprung at him like a wild beast, thrown him on the ground, and trampled upon his fair false face till not a vestige of its beauty was left! For some minutes I gave way to this impotent mad fury,—then, gradually recollecting myself, smoothed out the crumpled letter and read it through again. The coils of fate round the unfortunate Pauline had grown more and more entangled, for now, supposing the whole truth were told, she would be in a worse predicament than ever,—since, unless her lover chose to leave the priesthood as rapidly as he had entered it, marriage was impossible. True enough, her only rescue lay with me!—true, that if I chose to accept Silvion Guidèl's cast-off light-o'-love as my wife, no one need be any the wiser save only myself and the unhappy girl whose miserable secret was in my hands. But I resented the position which appeared thus forced upon me, and in this I think I was no worse than any other man might have been under similar circumstances. Combined however with my natural resentment, there was another and more cruel feeling,—an insatiate longing to make Pauline understand thoroughly the heinous enormity of her sin. For at present, she seemed to me to have merely the stagey sentiment of the French melodramatic heroine, who, after disgracing herself, dishonouring her parents, and dealing wholesale misery all round, scruples not to boast of her "*amour*" as a wonderful virtue recommendable to the special intercession of Heaven. It was in this particular phase of her character that she had grown hateful to me,—while her physical beauty remained what it always had been in my eyes,—exquisitely captivating to the senses and resistlessly adorable. Yet with all my busy brooding on the one subject, I cannot say I ever came to any definitely settled plan. What I *did* do in the long run was the wild suggestion of a moment, worked out by one hot flash from the burning glance of the "green fairy" in whose intoxicating embrace I had drowsed my soul away for many nights and days. I considered deeply as to whether I should show the letter I had received from Silvion Guidèl to Pauline or not? Better wait, I thought, and see how the tide of events turned,—there was yet time,—let her cling to her false hope a little longer—that frail sheet-anchor would all too soon be torn from her feeble hold!

And so the dull minutes rounded into hours,—hours that passed in the usual uneven way, some slow, some rapidly, according to the mood in which they were severally met and disposed of, and the eve of my marriage came. All seemed well. I played my part,—Pauline played hers. I called at the De Charmilles', and found everything in the bustle of active preparation,—the dining-room was being decorated with flowers,—large garlands and bouquets occupied almost every available space in the entrance-hall, and on my inquiring for my *fiancée*, I was shown by the smiling excited maid-servant into the morning-room where, after a few minutes, Pauline entered. She looked very pale, but very calm,—and came straight up to me with a strange wistfulness in her deep blue eyes.

"*You* have not heard from Silvion?" she said at once, in a low but earnestly inquiring tone.

"I!" and I shrugged my shoulders as though in amazement at the absurdity of such a question.

"No,—I suppose he would not write to you," she murmured sadly. "Then, he must be ill, or dead."

Strange tenacity of woman's faith! She could not, would not, believe he had deserted her. She resumed, with a curious air of grave formality—

"It seems you really intend to marry me, Monsieur Beauvais?"

"It seems so, truly, mademoiselle!" I returned frigidly.

She looked at me steadfastly.

"Listen!" she said. "I know why you do it,—for my father's sake— and for the sake of good M. Vaudron,—to save honour and prevent scandal,—you do it for this,—and I—I do not know whether to thank you or curse you for your pity!" She paused, trembling with the excess of her emotion, then continued—"But—understand me, Gaston—I will never live with you! I will never owe to you so much as a crust of bread! I will go on with this ceremony of marriage, as you seem, for the sake of others, to think it best—but afterwards—afterwards I will go away to die somewhere by myself, where I shall trouble no one, and where not even dear good Héloïse will be able to find me. Disgraced, I will bear the solitude of disgrace,—ruined, I will abide by my ruin!"

I studied her features with a cold scrutiny that made her cheeks flush and her limbs tremble, though her eyes remained quietly fixed on mine.

"You have made your plans, I see," I said. "But I—I also have plans! You say you will go away to 'die'—not so!—you mean you will go in search of your lover! Has it ever struck you that he may not want you? Men are like children—when their women-toys are broken, they care for them no longer. So far, things have gone on smoothly in our two families, and by reticence we have fought off scandal,—but I must ask you to remember that *if* I once bestow my name upon you, you will owe me obedience,—*if* I make you my wife, the past must be blotted out for ever, and I shall expect from you a wife's duty."

I smiled as I spoke, for I saw her shrink and shiver away from me as though an icy wind had touched her with its breath.

"How can the past be blotted out for ever," she faltered, "when——" Here she paused suddenly and drew herself erect. "Gaston Beauvais, when I came to you and told you all that night, I placed my fate in your hands. I asked you to break your engagement with me—and you made excuse and delay—you would not. Nor would you let *me* speak. You told me you would act for the best, and I trusted everything to you,—I thought you would spare me,—I believed that you would be gener-ous and pitiful. But you have changed,—you have changed so greatly that I scarcely know you—except that I am sure you do not wish me well. There is something cruel in your eyes—something fatal in your smile! Tell me truly—*why* do you marry me?"

She regarded me with a touch of fear as she put the question.

"Pardon, mademoiselle; but you anticipate!" I replied calmly. "I have not married you—yet!"

"To-morrow——" she began.

Springing to her side I grasped her suddenly by the arm. I felt a strange fire pricking in my veins,—one of those accesses of heat and fury which were growing frequent with me of late.

"To-morrow has not come!" I said in low fierce accents. "Wait till it does! What do you take me for, silly child? Do you think you can play with a man's heart as you have played with mine, and meet with *no* punishment? Do you think you can wreck a whole life and not be scourged for such wanton cruelty? I have, it is true, screened your name from obloquy up till now,—with yourself alone and me rests the horri-ble secret of your shame. But wait—wait!—you are not married to me *yet*—and if you have enough courage for the task, you can still escape me! Proclaim your own infamy to your parents—to your pure and saintly cousin Héloïse, to-night,—break their hearts—shake down their high faith in you to the dust of dishonour,—but *before* doing so, mark you!—it would be as well to ask M. Vaudron for the latest news of his admirable nephew!"

Her eyes dilated with terror, and she repeated the words after me, like a dull child learning some difficult lesson.

"Ask M. Vaudron for the latest news of his nephew!"—and her very lips turned white as she spoke—"the latest news of Silvion! *You* know it then?"—and she turned upon me with a gesture of imperial authority—"Tell me what it is! How dare you withhold it? Tell me instantly!—for, if he is ill, I must go to him,—if he is dead, I must die!"

I laughed savagely.

"He is dead to *you*, mademoiselle!" I said. "But otherwise, he is alive and well, and at this very moment he is probably at his holy prayers! He has entered the priesthood!—and by that simple act, has escaped both my sword and your embraces!"

She gave a smothered cry—staggered and seemed about to fall,—I caught her on my arm, and she leaned against me struggling for breath.

"Silvion,—Silvion a priest!" she gasped. "Oh no!—not after all his promises!—it is not—it cannot be true!"

"Ask the curé," I said. "He no doubt has the news by this time. He is a good man,—not used, like his nephew, to the telling of lies."

She put away my supporting arm gently, yet decidedly, and pressing one hand against her heart, looked me full in the eyes.

"How do you know this?" she asked. "Why should *you*, of all people in the world, be the first to tell it to me?"

I read her suspicions,—and returned her glance with one of the utmost scorn. "You distrust my word?" I queried ironically. "Well, perhaps you will accept your lover's own voucher for the information. Here it is,—pray read it for yourself and be satisfied."

And drawing from my pocket the letter I had received, I unfolded it and spread it open on the table before her. With a sharp exclamation, she snatched it up and quickly perused its every word,—then—oh strange nature of woman!—she covered it with passionate kisses and tears.

"Good-bye, Silvion!" she sobbed softly. "Good-bye, my love!—my dearest one!—good-bye!"

Turning to me, she said, while the drops still rained through her lashes—

"May I keep this letter?"

I shrugged my shoulders disdainfully,—her melodramatic sentimentality filled me with abhorrence.

"Certainly, if you choose!"

"It is my death-warrant," she went on quietly, trying to steady her quivering lips, "and it is signed by the dearest hand in the world to me! Oh, I shall die quite bravely now!—there will be nothing to regret, even as there is nothing to hope. But, Gaston, you are very cruel to me!— you are not like your old kind self at all. I am so poor and slight and miserable a thing—I cannot understand how it can be worth your while to judge me so harshly. Never mind—it does not matter—I shall not trouble you long. I have been very wicked,—yes—I know that,—and you, Gaston, you wish me to be punished? Well then, does it not please you to know that my heart is broken? My heart—my heart—Silvion!"

And, covering her face with her hands, she suddenly turned and fled from the room. I heard the door close behind her,—and I thought myself alone. Every nerve in my body pulsated with the suppressed excitement of my mind, and, leaning one hand against my hot brows, I pressed my fingers over my eyes to try and shut out the pale green light that now and then flashed before them, when a touch on my shoulder startled me. I looked up,—Héloïse St. Cyr stood beside me, pale and grave as a sculptured nun, and I stared at her in vague amazement.

"What is the matter, M. Gaston?" she inquired.

I forced a laugh.

"Matter, Héloïse? Truly,—nothing!"

"Nothing!" she echoed incredulously. "Why, then, was Pauline in tears? She passed me just now without a word,—but I heard her sobbing."

I met her questioning gaze unconcernedly.

"A lover's quarrel, *chère* Pallas Athene!" I said lightly. "Have you never heard of such things?"

A frown darkened the fairness of her classic brows.

"A quarrel on the eve of marriage?" she queried coldly. "It seems unnatural and unlikely. You are deceiving me, M. Gaston."

I smiled.

"Possibly!" I answered. "But what would you? I fancy we were born into the world, all of us, for the singular purpose of deceiving each other!"

Her eyes filled with a vague fear and surprise.

"What do you mean?" she faltered nervously.

"Do not ask me, Héloïse!" And, advancing a step or two, I caught her shrinking hand, and held it prisoned in my fevered clasp. "I cannot tell you what I mean! I do not know, myself. There are certain phases of feeling and passion—are there not?—which storm the soul at times,—we are shaken, but we cannot explain the shock even to our innermost consciences! Do not speak to me—do not look at me!—

Your eyes would draw out the secret of a madman's misery! Ask your own heart if there are not strange and complex emotions within it, as in mine, which have never been uttered, and never *will* be uttered! If we could only speak frankly, we men and women, at certain moments when the better part of us is paramount,—my God!—if we could only dare to be ourselves, who knows the world might be happier!"

With this incoherent outburst, the drift of which I myself scarcely understood, I hurriedly kissed the hand I held, released it, and left her. How she looked, I know not,—something clamorous and wild in my blood warned me against another chance meeting of her eyes with mine. I should have caught her to my breast and frightened her with the passion of my embrace,—and yet—did I love her? I cannot tell,—I think not. It was only the indefinable attraction of her personality that over-powered my senses,—when I was once away from her and outside in the open air, my emotion passed, just as a faintness that has been brought on by the powerful perfume of tropical lilies will pass in the reviving breath of a cool wind. I walked rapidly homeward, thinking as I went of the morrow, and wondering what it would bring forth. Either Pauline de Charmilles would be mine, or she would not. It all seemed to rest on the mere turn of a hair. For in my condition of brain nothing in the whole world appeared decided, because the eventuality of death was always present. I calmly considered and balanced the probability that Pauline, now knowing the pusillanimous part her lover had chosen to play, might kill herself. It is the common way out of a love-difficulty with many Frenchwomen. Or—*I* might die! That would be droll! and unex-pected too,—for I felt life's blood beating very strong in me, and I had now something to live for. I considered with a good deal of self-congrat-ulation, the admirable cunning with which I had managed to keep the secret of my growing Absinthe-mania from my father and every one connected with me. True, some stray remarks had been made once or twice on a certain change in my looks, but this was chiefly set down to overwork. And my father had occasionally remonstrated with me against a quick, querulous impatience of temper which I frequently displayed, and which was new to my disposition,—but with his usual good-nature, he had found plenty of excuses for me in the contemplation of all the business I had successfully got through during his absence in England. The alteration in me was really almost imperceptible to unsuspecting outsiders; only I myself knew how complete and permanent it was.

That night,—the night before my wedding-day, I drank deeply and long of my favourite nectar,—glass after glass I prepared, and drained each one off with insatiable and ever-increasing appetite,—I drank till the solid walls of my own room, when at last I found myself there, appeared to me like transparent glass shot through with emerald flame. Surrounded on all sides by phantoms,—beautiful, hideous, angelic, devilish,—I reeled to my couch in a sort of waking swoon, conscious of strange sounds everywhere, like the clanging of brazen bells, and the silver fanfaronade of the trumpets of war,—conscious too of a singular *double* sensation,—namely, as though Myself were divided into two persons, who opposed each other in a deadly combat, in which neither could possibly obtain even the merest shadow-victory! It was a night of both horror and ecstasy,—the beginning of many more such nights,— and though I was hurried to and fro like a leaf on a storm-wind, among crowding ghosts, open tombs, smiling seraphs, and leering demons, I was perfectly content with the spectral march of my own brain-pageantry. And I quite forgot—as I always wish to forget—that there are fools in the world for whom heart-freezing Absinthe has no charms, and who therefore still prate like children and idiots, of God and Conscience!

CHAPTER 17

My marriage-morning!—it broke out of the east with the sweetest forget-me-not radiance of blue over all the tranquil sky. I rose early— I was aware of a violent throbbing in my temples,—and now and then I was seized with a remarkable sensation, as though some great force were, so to speak, being *hurled* through me, compelling me to do strange deeds without clearly recognizing their nature. I took a long walk before breakfast, but though the air and motion did me some amount of good, I nevertheless found myself totally unable to resist certain impulses that came over me,—as, for instance to laugh aloud when I thought of that white half-naked witch who had been my chief companion in the flying phantasmagoria of the past wild night. How swiftly she had led me into the forgotten abodes of the dead, and how her mere look and sign had sufficed to lift the covers of old coffins and expose to view the mouldering skeletons within!—the eyeless skulls that, for all their lack of vision, had yet seemed to stare upon us while we mocked their helpless desolation! Oh, she was a blithe brave phantom, that Absinthe-witch of mine!—and one thing she had done had pleased me right well. We had flown through the dark, she and I, on

green outspread wings, and finding on our way a church-door standing open, we had entered in. There we had seen silver lamps steadily
burning,—there we had heard the organ pealing forth strange
psalmody, and there we had discovered a priest kneeling on the altar-
steps with wondrous Raffaelle-like[1] face upturned to the shining Host
above him. "Silvion Guidèl!" we had shrieked loudly in his ears, my
elfin-comrade and I—"Die, Silvion Guidèl!" And "Die, Silvion
Guidèl!" was echoed back to us in a thunder of many voices,—while,
as the chorus smote the air, lo! the Host vanished from sight,—the altar
crumbled into dust,—there was no more sign of salvation, hope, or
rescue for that criminal there who dared to kneel and pray,—there was
nothing—nothing but the yawning blackness of an open grave! How
my fair witch laughed as she pointed to that dull deep hole in the
ground!—how I kissed her on the ripe red lips for the appropriateness
of her deathful suggestion!—how I toyed with her fiery-gold hair!—
and how we fled off again, more swiftly than the wind, through scenes
wilder, yet not so haunting to the memory! My glorious Absinthe-
fairy!—she was nearly always with me now,—in different shapes,
arrayed in different hues, but always recognizable as a part of *me*. Her
whispers buzzed continually in my brain and I never failed to listen;—
and on this particular morning—the morning of my intended
marriage,—she was as close to me as my very blood:—she clung to me,
and I made no effort, as I had no desire, to shake her off.

Ten o'clock was the hour fixed for the civic ceremony, in order that
ample time might be given to allow the religious one to take place
before noon. Just as we were about to start for the scene of the nuptials,
my father, who had been watching me attentively, suddenly said—

"Gaston, art thou well?"

I looked full at him and laughed.

"Perfectly well, *mon père*! Why ask such a question?"

"Your eyes look feverish," he answered, "and I have noticed that
your hand shakes. If you were not my son, I should say you had been
drinking!"

I bit my lips vexedly,—then forced a smile.

"*Merci!*[2] But cannot you allow for a little unusual excitement on
one's wedding-day?"

---

[1] The Italian painter Raphael (1483–1520) is noted for his ability to depict subjects who
exude humanity and holiness, as in his many representations of the Holy Family.

[2] French for "thank you."

His countenance cleared, and he laid one hand affectionately on my shoulder.

"Of course! Still—to be quite honest with you, Gaston, I must say I have lately observed an alteration in your looks and manner that does not bode well for your health. However, no doubt a change of air will do you good. A month in Switzerland is a cure for almost any ailing man."

Switzerland! I laughed again. It had been settled for us by our friends that we were to pass our honeymoon, my bride and I, by the shores of the blue romantic lakes that Byron loved and sang of.[1] I had never seen the splendour of the snow-mountains,—I have never yet seen them, and it is very certain now that I never shall!

I avoided any further converse with my father, and was glad that so little time was left us for the chance of a *tête-à-tête*.[2] Punctual to the hour appointed, we drove to the De Charmilles' residence and found the outside of the house lined and blocked with carriages;—the guests were arriving in shoals. We entered the grand drawing-room; it was exquisitely adorned with palms and flowers, and for one dazed moment I saw nothing but a whirl of bright faces, and magnificent bouquets tied with floating ends of white and coloured ribbon. People seized my hand and shook it warmly;—I heard myself congratulated, and managed to enunciate a few formal replies. Presently I came face to face with the bridesmaids,—all clad in palest pink,—all ready for the church ceremony, which to them, as women, was of course the most interesting part of the performance,—and in the centre of this group stood Héloïse St. Cyr, looking strangely pale and grave. Whether it was the pink colour of her robe, or the brilliant tint of the superb roses she carried, I could not then decide, but certain it was that I had never seen her so wan and wistful-eyed, and as I gravely saluted her, I wondered whether she knew anything,—whether Pauline, in a sudden fit of desperate courage, had told her all? An odd fierce merriment began to take hold of me,—I smiled as I pressed her extended gloved hand.

"You are looking lovely as usual, Héloïse," I said, in a low tone,—for, indeed, her fair and spiritual beauty exercised over me a spell of mingled fear and fascination,—"but are you not somewhat fatigued?"

Her eyes rested steadily on mine.

---

[1] George Gordon, Lord Byron (1788-1824), English Romantic poet. Byron spent time in Switzerland and lived for a time with Percy Bysshe Shelley and Mary Shelley at Lake Geneva.

[2] French expression for "a private conversation."

"No," she replied calmly; "I am only a little anxious about Pauline. To me, she seems very ill."

I feigned the deepest concern.

"Indeed! I trust——"

She swept out of the group of bridesmaids and beckoned me to follow her apart. I did so.

"Something terrible has happened,—I am sure of it!" she said, with passionate emphasis. "*You* spoke so strangely yesterday, and *she* has wept all night. Oh, why—why will you not tell me what it is? The child is afraid of you!"

"Pauline afraid of *me*!" I exclaimed, raising my eyebrows in simulated amazement. "Really, Héloïse, I cannot understand——"

She made a movement of impatience and laid her bouquet of flowers lightly against her lips.

"Hush! we cannot speak now,—it is too late! But—if you meditate any wrong or cruelty to Pauline—well!—God may forgive you, but *I* will not!"

Her eyes flashed a positive menace,—she looked empress-like in that moment of wrath, and my admiring glance must have told her as much, for the colour crimsoned her cheeks to a deeper hue than that of the red roses in her hand. But that she resented my look was evident,—for she turned from me with a gesture of dislike and disdain, and as I noted her proud step and mien, a sudden ferocity possessed me. A curse, I thought, on all such haughty, beautiful women who dare to wound with a glance, and slay with a smile! Let them learn to suffer as they make men suffer!—nothing less will bring down their wantonness or impress upon their arrogant natures the value of humility! I walked with a firm step up to the table where the civic authorities were already seated with their books and pens, and gaily shook hands with all I personally knew. M. Vaudron was of course not present,—his part of the business was to be transacted at the church, where no doubt he was even now waiting. The Comtesse de Charmilles stood near me,—there were tears in her eyes, and she, like her niece Héloïse, looked pale and anxious, while in her smile, as she saluted me affectionately, there was something almost appealing. The Count himself had left the room; naturally, all present knew his errand. There was a hush of expectation,—the bright eyes of the lovely and fashionable women assembled were turned eagerly towards the door,—it opened, and Pauline entered, in full bridal attire, leaning on her father's arm. White as a snowflake,—impassive as marble,—she seemed to be walking in her sleep, her eyes fixed on vacancy,—she looked neither to the right nor to the left,—she returned none of the gay greetings of her friends, who recoiled from her in evident amazement at her strange demeanour;—once or twice only a thin shadowy smile parted her lips, and she bowed mechanically as though the action were the result of a carefully learned lesson. On she came,—and I heard whispered observations on her deadly paleness; but I was too busy with my own rising frenzy to heed aught else. I was enraged!—what business had she, this fair, frail, helpless-looking girl, to come to me as though she were a white fawn being led up to have its tender throat slit!—how dared she *pose* before me like a statue of grief with that look of quenchless unutterable despair frozen on her face!— aye!—how dared she, knowing herself so vile, thus mutely invite compassion! One of those irresistible sudden rushes of demoniacal impulse stronger than myself seized me;—I felt the blood surging in my ears and burning at my finger-tips,—I was in the grasp of a force more potent than fire to destroy,—and without actually realizing quite what I meant to do or to say, I waited; waited, till the stately Comte de Charmilles,—proud parent!—reached me where I stood,—waited, till he, by a gracefully courteous gesture, appeared to dumbly present me with my bride! *Then* the clamorous devil in me broke loose and had its way,—*then*, yielding to its subtle suggestion, I tasted my revenge!—*then*, I had the satisfaction of seeing the haughty old aristocrat blench and tremble like a leaf in the wind, as he met my coldly scornful gaze and the mockery of my smile! Drawing myself stiffly erect just as he came within an arm's length of me, I made a distinct and decided movement of rejection—then, raising my voice so that it might be heard by all present, I said slowly and with studied politeness—

"M. le Comte de Charmilles, I am sincerely sorry to give you pain!—but truth is truth, and must sometimes be told, no matter how disagreeable! In the presence therefore of these our relatives, friends, and guests, permit me to return your daughter to your paternal care!— I, Gaston Beauvais, refuse to marry her!"

For one moment there was a horrified stillness,—the old Count turned a ghastly white and seemed paralyzed—Pauline moved not at all. Then my father's clear voice rang through the hushed room sharply.

"Gaston, art thou mad!"

I looked at him calmly.

"*Au contraire*, I am quite sane, I assure you, *mon père*! I repeat,—I utterly decline the honour of Mademoiselle Pauline de Charmilles' hand in marriage. That is all!"

Another dead silence. Not a person in the room stirred, and all eyes were fixed upon me. Every one seemed stricken with alarm and amazement, save Pauline herself, who, like a veiled image, might have been carved in stone for any sign of life she gave. Suddenly one of the civic authorities turned round from the table on which the books of registration lay prepared. He was an old man of punctilious and severe manner, and he regarded me sternly as he said—

"Upon what grounds does Monsieur Gaston Beauvais propose to break his plighted word to Mademoiselle De Charmilles? He should state his reasons as publicly as he has chosen to state his withdrawal!"

I looked at the Count. His face was flushed and he breathed heavily; I saw him nervously press his passive daughter's arm closer to his side.

"Yes! on what grounds?" he demanded thickly and hurriedly. "Truly it is a question that needs answering!—on what grounds?"

I *felt* rather than saw the instinctive movement of the whole brilliant assemblage of guests towards me,—every one was bending forward to listen,—I caught a glimpse of the pale horrified face of Héloïse St. Cyr, and just then, Pauline raised her sorrowful blue eyes and fixed them upon me with a world of silent reproach in their grief-darkened depths. But what cared I for her looks? I was mad, and I revelled in my madness! What mattered anything to me save the clutch of the fiend at my throat—the devil that compelled me to fling away every thought of gentleness, every merciful and chivalrous impulse to the winds of hell!

"On what grounds?" I echoed bitterly. "Simply—dishonour!— shame! Is this not enough? Must I speak still more plainly? Then take all the truth at once!—I cannot accept as my wife the cast-off mistress of Silvion Guidèl!"

CHAPTER 18

The blow had fallen at last, and with crushing effect.

"Oh vile accusation!" cried the Count, shaking his daughter from his arm. "Pauline!—Speak! Is this true?"

Unsupported she stood, and feebly raised her hands, clasping them together as though in prayer; a strange wild smile crossed her pale lips,— such a smile as is sometimes seen on the faces of the dying; but in her eyes,—beautiful passionate dark-blue eyes!—the fatal confession of her misery was written. No one looking upon her then could have doubted her guilt for an instant. In a single upward despairing glance she admitted everything,—her lips moved, but not a sound issued from them,—then, all silently, as snow slips in a feathery weight from the bending branch of a tree, she fell prone, like a broken flower. A tremulous murmur of compassion rippled through the room,—but nevertheless, every one hung back from that insensible form,—aye, every one!—for the Comtesse de Charmilles had swooned in her chair, and it was more *comme il faut*[1] to minister to her, the blameless wife and respectable matron, than to the wretched child whose disgrace had been thus publicly proclaimed! *Every one* hung back did I say? No,—not every one; for while I stood gazing at the scene, savagely satisfied at the havoc I had wrought, Héloïse St. Cyr sprung forward like an enraged pythoness, her whole form quivering with wrath and sorrow, and flinging herself on her knees beside her unconscious cousin, she lifted her partially from the ground, and held her to her breast with passionate tenderness.

"*Lâche!*"[2] she cried, flashing her indignant eyes full upon me, while the scornful word from her lips whipt me as with a scourge. "Coward! Cruel, vile coward! Shame upon you!—shame! Oh, what a fine boast of honour you can make now, to think you have cast down this poor little life in the dust and blighted it for ever! A *woman's* life too!—a life that is powerless to do more than suffer the wrongs inflicted upon it by the wanton wickedness of men! Pauline! Pauline! Look at me, darling! Look at Héloïse, who loves thee,—who will never forsake thee— *pauvre, pauvre petite!*[3] Leave her to me!" she exclaimed almost fiercely as one of the younger bridesmaids, trembling and tearful, timidly came forward to volunteer her assistance. "Leave her—desert her, as every one will, now she is broken-hearted; it is the way of the world! Why do *you* wait here, Gaston Beauvais?"—and her contemptuous glance fell so witheringly upon me, that for the moment I was awed, and the hot frenzy of my brain seemed to grow suddenly stilled—"You have done your pre-meditated work—go! You have had vengeance for your wrong—enjoy it! Had you been a true man you would have wreaked your wrath on the chief actor in this tragedy,—the murderer, not the victim!" She paused, white and breathless; then, seeming to summon all her forces together, she continued passionately, "May your wickedness recoil on your own head!—may the ruin you have brought on others

---

[1] French expression meaning "proper."
[2] French for "coward."
[3] French for "poor, poor little one."

come down with ten-fold violence upon yourself!—oh! may God punish you!—He must—He will—if Heaven holds any justice!" She paused again, panting excitedly, and one of the lady guests here touched her on the shoulder.

"Héloïse! Héloïse! Be calm—be calm!"

"Calm!" she echoed with a wild gesture. "How can I be calm when Pauline may be dead! Dead!—and he—he has killed her! Oh, Pauline, Pauline! my little darling!—my pretty one!—Pauline!" And, breaking into sobs and tears, she kissed her cousin's cold hands and death-like face again and again.

Now to *me*, all this disorder and excitement presented itself merely as a curious scene,—quite stagey in fact, like a "set" from a romantic opera,—I could have laughed aloud, after the fashion of the murderess Gabrielle Bompard, when she was shown the graphic police-illustrations of her own crime,[1]—and even as it was, I smiled. I noticed several people looking at me in amazed disgust,—but what did I care for that! The merest *soupçon*[2] of truth always disgusts society! Meanwhile, the assemblage had broken up in entire confusion,—every one was departing silently and almost as if by stealth. The civic authorities had taken solemn and sympathizing leave of the Comte de Charmilles, who sat rigidly erect in an arm-chair, making no response whatever to anything that was said to him,—some one had been despatched with a message to the curé, M. Vaudron, to inform him that the ceremony was broken off,—the Comtesse had been assisted to her apartment,—servants were now lifting the insensible figure of Pauline from the ground,—and amid it all, I stood quietly looking on, vaguely amused at the whole performance. It entertained me in a sort of dim fashion to observe that I was now generally avoided by those who had previously been eager to claim acquaintance with me,—the departing guests made me no salutation, and I appeared to be held in sudden and singular abhorrence. What a droll world, I thought! Always prating about morality,—and yet when a man makes a bold stand for morality and publicly declares he will not marry a woman who is the victim of an *esclandre*,[3] he is looked upon

---

[1] A murderess who, with the aid of her lover, murdered a bailiff named Gouffé in 1889. Accounts of the crime were much in the news at the time Corelli was writing the novel. The case did not go to trial until December 1890. Corelli's account of Bompard's cold-heartedness corresponds to contemporary accounts which described her as "morally colour-blind."

[2] French term for "a small amount."

[3] French for "scandal."

as a heartless wretch and cruel barbarian! Such a thing should be done quite quietly and privately, whispers society. Indeed! Why? How are the interests of "morality" to be served by hushing such matters up among the exalted few? I was still musing on this, and on human inconsistency generally, when my father touched me on the arm.

"Come away from this house of affliction," he said sternly. "Come away! Your presence here now is nothing but an insult!"

How fierce the fine old man looked, to be sure! It occurred to me as being rather odd that he should seem so indignant; but I followed him mechanically. We were just about to leave the house, when a servant ran after us with a card which she put into my hands, departing instantly again without a word. A challenge, I thought derisively!— who was there in all that fashionable crowd of men that would care to draw a sword in Pauline's honour? No one, truly; for the card simply bore the name of the Comte de Charmilles, with the following words written across it in pencil: "I request that Monsieur Gaston Beauvais will call upon me to-morrow before noon." I thrust it in my pocket, and walked after my father who had preceded me, and who was now waiting impatiently for me outside the great *porte-cochère*[1] of the Count's residence, keeping his head carefully turned away from the gaze of the various owners of the departing carriages, in order that he might not be compelled to recognize them or talk with them of what had just taken place. When I joined him, he marched on stiffly and in perfect silence till we were well out of sight of everybody,—then he turned round upon me and gave vent to a short sharp oath,—his eyes glittering and his lips trembling.

"Gaston, you have behaved like a villain! I would not have believed that *my* son could have been capable of such a coward's vengeance!"

I looked at him, and shrugged my shoulders.

"You are excited, *mon père!* What have I done save speak the truth, and, as the brave English say, shame the devil?"

"The truth—the truth!" said my father passionately. "*Is* it the truth? and if it is, could it not have been told in a less brutal fashion? You have acted like a fiend!—not like a man! If Silvion Guidèl be a vile seducer, and that poor child Pauline his credulous, ruined victim, could you not have dealt with *him* and have spared *her?* God! I would as soon wring the neck of a bird that trusted me, as add any extra weight to the sorrows of an already broken-hearted woman!"

---

[1] French term for "carriage gate."

Gallant old *preux-chevalier!*[1] He meant what he said, I knew,—and I—I had been wont to share his sentiments, not so very long ago! But I said nothing in response to his outburst; I merely hummed the fragment of a tune under my breath, my doing so causing him to stare at me in indignant surprise.

"I suppose it *is* true?" he broke forth again. "It is not a malicious trumped-up lie?"

"As I heard of it first from the lips of the lady concerned in it, I have no reason to doubt its accuracy!" I murmured coldly.

"Then you have known of it for some time?"

I bent my head assentingly.

"Then why not have spoken?" he cried wrathfully. "Why not have told *me*? Why not have done everything,—anything, rather than proclaim the fact of the poor miserable little girl's disgrace to all the world? Why, above all, did you not challenge Guidèl?"

"I was prepared to do so when he suddenly left for Brittany," I rejoined tranquilly; "and once there, he knew how to give my justice the slip; he has entered the priesthood!"

"By Heaven, so he has!" And my father struck his walking-stick heavily on the ground. "Miserable poltroon!—sanctimonious young hypocrite!"

"I am glad," I interrupted, smiling slightly, "that you at last send the current of your wrath in the right direction! It is rather unjust of you to blame *me* in the affair——"

"*Parbleu!* you are as much a villain as he!" exclaimed my father fiercely. "Both cowards!—both selfishly bent on the ruin of a pretty frail child too weak to resist your cruelty! Fine sport, truly! Bah! I do not know which is the worst *scélérat*[2] of the two!"

I stopped in my walk and faced him.

"Are we to quarrel, sir?" I demanded composedly.

"Yes!—we *are* to quarrel!" he retorted hotly. "There is something in my blood that rises at you!—that sickens at you, though you are my son! I do not excuse Guidèl,—I do not excuse Pauline,—I do not say you could have married one who by her own confession was dishonoured;—but I do say and swear that in spite of all, you could have comported yourself like an honest lad, and not like a devil incarnate. Who set you up as a judge of justice or morality? What man is there in

---

[1]   French term for "gallant knight."
[2]   French word for "scoundrel."

the world with such clean hands that he dare presume to condemn the meanest creature living! I tell you plainly that, after your conduct of today, the same house cannot hold you and me together in peace!—there is nothing for it but that we must part!"

"As you please!" I answered coldly. "But you will allow me to remark that it is very curious and unreasonable of you to find such fault with me for publicly refusing to marry one who was certainly not fit to be your daughter, or to inhabit the house where my mother died."

"Don't talk of your mother!" And such a sudden fury lighted his eyes that I involuntarily recoiled. "She would have been the first to condemn your behaviour as cruel and unnatural. She had pity, tenderness, and patience for every suffering thing! She was an angel of grace and charity! You cannot have much of *her* nature; and truly you seem now to have little of mine! Some strange demon seems to inhabit your frame,—and the generous, warm-hearted young fellow I knew as my son might be dead for aught I recognize of him in you! I do not condemn you for refusing to marry Pauline de Charmilles,—I condemn you for the *manner* of your refusal! Enough!—I repeat, we must part,—and the sooner the better! I could not bear to meet the friends we know in your company and think of the ruthless barbarity you have displayed towards a fallen and utterly defenceless girl. You had best leave Paris and take a twelve-month's sojourn in some other land than this,—I will place plenty of cash at your disposal. It is impossible that you should stay on here after what has occurred;—*mon Dieu!*—a madman,—a drunkard,—a delirious *absintheur* might be capable of such useless ferocity;—but a man with all his senses about him—pah! it is the action of a beast rather than of a rational, reasoning human being!"

I made no reply. The words "a delirious *absintheur* might be capable of such useless ferocity," reiterated themselves over and over again in my ears, and caused me to smile! Of course I might have gone on arguing the *pros* and *cons* of my case *ad infinitum*,[1] from the vantage-ground of that particular sort of moral justice I had chosen to take my stand upon,—but I was not in the humour for it,—besides which, my father was too indignant to be argued with.

Arrived at our own house, our man-servant Dunois greeted us with a surprised face, and the information that the curé M. Vaudron, "looking very ill," was waiting in the library.

"There is no marriage?" he questioned, gazing at us open-eyed.

---

[1] Latin phrase meaning "forever."

"None, Dunois!" returned my father sharply. "Mademoiselle is not well; it is postponed!"

Oh, famous old courtier! He would tell a lie thus to his own servant, just to shield a woman's reputation a moment longer! There are a good many men like him;—I used to be of a similar disposition till the "fairy with the green eyes" taught me more worldly wisdom!

"I will see poor Vaudron alone," he said, addressing me stiffly as Dunois retired. "His grief must be beyond expression,—and he can dispense with more than one witness of it."

I bowed,—and ascended the staircase leisurely to my own room. Once shut in there alone, I was seized with an uncontrollable fit of laughter! How absurd it all seemed! What a triumph of bathos! To think of all those fine birds of Parisian society flocking to see a grand wedding, and coming in for a great scandal instead! And the pride of the De Charmilles!—where was it now? Down in the dust!—down, down like the lilies of France, never to bloom white and untarnished again! What a terrified fool the old Count had looked when I made my formal rejection!—and as for Pauline—she was not Pauline!—she was a ghost!—a spectre without feeling, voice, or voluntary movement! All the life she had was in her eyes,—great reproachful blue eyes!—they haunted me like twin burning sapphires hung in a vault of darkness!

Sitting listlessly in an arm-chair at my window, I looked out, doing nothing, but simply thinking, and trying to disentangle the thronging images that rose one after the other with such confusing haste in my brain. I wondered what my father and old Vaudron were talking about below! Me? Yes!—no doubt they were shaking their grey heads mournfully over my strange waywardness! Smiling at the idea, I shut my eyes—and straightway saw a wealth of green and gold and amber flame—waves of colour that seemed to rise heavingly towards me, while faces, lovelier far than mortal ones, floated forth and smiled at me in wise approval of all that I had done! Opening my eyes again, I gazed into the street,—the people passed hither and thither,—jingling trams ran by with their human freight to and fro,—the soft young foliage of the trees shimmered in the bright sun,—it was the perfect ideal of a marriage-day! And in my heart of hearts a wondrous wedlock was consummated,—an indissoluble union with the fair wild Absinthe-witch of my dreams!—she and she alone should be part of my flesh and blood from henceforth, I swore!—why, even the words of the marriage-ritual could be made to serve our needs! "Those whom God hath joined let no man put asunder!" God—or Chance! They are both one and the same thing—to the *Absintheur!*

Watching the street with drowsy unintelligent eyes I presently saw my father and M. Vaudron come out of the house and cross the road together. The old curé's head was bent,—he appeared to walk with difficulty, and he was evidently more than half supported by my father's stalwart arm. Respectable old fellows both—with warm hearts and clear consciences!—wonderful! It seemed so absurd to me that any one should try to lead an uncorrupt life in such a corrupt world! What was the use of it? Was there any possible end but death to all this aggressive loving-kindness and charity towards one's fellow-men? Yet a faint sense of admiration stirred me, as I looked after the slowly retreating figures of the two old friends; and a lingering regret just touched my heart as with a pin's prick to think that my father's indignation should have made him resolve to send me from him so suddenly. Not only was I sorry to lose his always agreeable and intellectual companionship,—I felt instinctively that when I bade *him* farewell, I should also bid farewell to the last link that held me to the rapidly vanishing shadow of honour.

Tired of the whirling confusion of my thoughts, I shut my eyes once more, and allowed my senses to slip into the spectral land of visions,— and my brain-wanderings took me so far, that when I started back to common-place reality at last, I was in total darkness. I had not been asleep—that I knew well enough!—but I had been actively dream-ing,—and the afternoon was over. Night had descended upon me all unawares,—and suddenly seized with a nervous terror at the silence and obscurity of my room, I groped about for matches, trembling like a leaf, and afraid of I knew not what. Not finding what I sought, and unable to resist the fantastic horror of myself that had stolen over me, I flung open the door wildly, and to my intense relief, admitted a flood of light from the gas-lamps in the outer hall. Just as I did so, my father's voice cried suddenly—

"Gaston! Gaston!"

He had come back then, I mused hazily. What did he want *me* for,— me, the 'pariah' of Parisian society, rejected because I had dared to make a woman's vice public! My mouth was parched and dry—I could not answer him immediately.

"Gaston! Gaston!" he called for the second time, and there was a sharp ring of pain in his tone.

Without reply, I descended the stairs,—entered the library,—and there, to my amazement, came face to face with Héloïse St. Cyr! Pale, impassioned, wondrously beautiful in grief, she stood beside my father whose face was full of grave and pitying sympathy,—great tears were in her eyes,—and as soon as she saw me she gave me no time to speak, but sprang forward, extending her hands appealingly.

"Oh, M. Gaston, help me!" she cried sobbingly. "Help me—and I will forgive all your cruelty to poor Pauline! only help me to find her!—she has left us!—she has gone!—and we know not where!"

CHAPTER 19

I gazed at her a moment in blank silence;—then, remembering that she, even she, was the same fair woman, who had but lately *cursed* me,—I rallied my forces and smiled a little.

"Gone!" I echoed. "*Bien!* I fail to see what difficulty you can possibly have in tracing her, mademoiselle? She has only fled to her lover!"

As I said this with freezing tranquillity, Héloïse suddenly gave way, and, breaking into smothered sobbing, hid her face on my father's arm.

"Oh, I hope," she cried piteously. "I hope God is more merciful than man! Oh, what shall I do, what *shall* I do! My poor, poor Pauline!—alone at night in Paris!—such a little, soft, timid thing! Oh, cruel, cruel! She would never go to Silvion Guidèl, now he has become a priest—never!—and see—see, Monsieur Beauvais, what she has written here,"—and, addressing herself to my father, she drew from her bosom a little crumpled note and unfolded it. "I had left her," she sobbed, "lying on her own bed, after we had carried her upstairs in her swoon,—and when I came back after attending to my aunt, who is very, very ill, she had gone! Her bridal dress was thrown aside,—she had not taken one of her jewels,—and I do not think she had any money. Only a little black dress and cloak and hat were missing from her wardrobe,—and this letter I found on her table. In it she says"—here Héloïse tried to master her tears, and, steadying her voice, she read—"'Try to forgive me, darling Héloïse; you are so good that you will even pity those who are wicked. Never think of me again except when you say your prayers,—then ask God just once to be kind to your little Pauline.'"

My father's old eyes brimmed over;—*his* heart was touched, but not mine! I sat down leisurely, and looked on as unconcernedly as a cynical critic looks on at a new play.

"Poor child—poor child!" murmured my father huskily; then he turned towards me. "Have *you* nothing to say, Gaston?—no suggestion to make?"

I shrugged my shoulders.

"Absolutely I am powerless in the matter;" I said coldly. "I am in a very peculiar position myself,—a position which neither you nor Mademoiselle St. Cyr seem at all to recognize. I am a wronged man,— yet I receive not the slightest sympathy for my wrong,—all the compassion and anxiety being, oddly enough, bestowed on the perpetrators of the injury done to *me*. I confess, therefore, that I am not particularly interested in the present *dénouement!*"[1]

Héloïse looked straight at me, and then, suddenly approaching me, laid her hand on my arm.

"After all, did you never *love* Pauline?" she asked.

At this question my blood rose to fever-heat, and I spoke, scarcely knowing what I was saying.

"Love her!" I cried. "I loved her with such a passion as *she* never knew! I hallowed her with a worship such as *she* never dreamt of! She was everything to me—life, soul, hope, salvation!—and you ask me if I loved her! Oh, foolish woman! you cannot measure the love I had for her!—such love that once betrayed, must and ever will, turn to loathing for its betrayer!"

My father looked startled at this sudden outburst of feeling on my part,—but Héloïse did not flinch. Her grey eyes shone upon me through the mist of tears as steadfastly as stars.

"Such love is not love at all!" she said. "It is selfishness;—no more! The injury done to *you* appears all paramount,—you have no thought, no pity for the injury done to *her*. The world is still open to you; but on her it is shut for ever. *You* may sin as she has sinned, without even the plea of an overwhelming passion to excuse you,—and society will not turn its back on you! But it will scorn her for the evil it endures in you and in all men! Such is humanity's scant justice! If you had ever loved her truly, you would have forgotten your own wrong in her misery; you would have raised her up, not crushed her down lower than she already was; you would have saved her, not destroyed her! I warned you long ago that she was a creature of impulse, too young and too inexperienced to be certain of her own mind in the perplexities of love or marriage; but you paid no heed to my warning. And now, she is ruined,—desolate!—a mere child cast out on the cruel wilderness of Paris all alone;—think of it, Gaston Beauvais!—think of it!—and take comfort in the thought that you have had your miserable revenge to the uttermost end of man's cowardice!"

---

[1] French word for "outcome."

Every word fell from her lips with a quiet decisiveness that stung me in spite of my enforced calm; but I restrained myself, and when she had finished speaking, I simply bowed and smiled.

"Your brave and eloquent words, mademoiselle, make me regret that I was so unwise as to love your cousin instead of yourself! It was a serious mistake!—for both of us, perhaps!"

She drew back,—the colour flushing proudly to her cheeks,—and her look of indignation, surprise, reproach, and anguish dazzled and confounded me for an instant. What chance arrow had sped to its mark now? I wondered vaguely,—I had nigh insulted her by my remark,— and yet grief expressed itself in her eyes more than anger. Had she ever cared for me?—Not possible! she had always mistrusted me,—and now she hated me! With supreme disdain, she turned from me to my father.

"I must go home now, Monsieur Beauvais"—she said quietly and with dignity—"I have come here on a useless errand I see! Will you take me to the carriage?—it is in waiting. My uncle does not yet know of Pauline's flight; we are afraid to tell him;—and we thought—my aunt and I—that perhaps you might help us to some clue———" She hesitated, and nearly broke down again.

"My dear girl"—returned my father, hastily offering her his arm in obedience to her mute sign—"be certain that if I hear the slightest rumour that may lead you on the right track, you shall know it at once. I will make every possible private inquiry;—alas, alas! what an unfortunate day it was for everybody when that nephew of my poor old friend Vaudron came to Paris! Who would have thought it! Vaudron is broken-hearted; he would as soon have believed in an angel turning traitor, as that his favourite Silvion would have been guilty of such deception and cruelty. But whatever his grief, I know he will assist us in the search for Pauline; that you may be sure of. Try, try to take comfort my dear; you must not give way. There is always the hope that the poor child may be terrified at her sudden loneliness, and may write to you and tell you where she is."

Thus talking, he led her out of the room,—she passed me without acknowledging my presence by the slightest gesture of farewell; and I waited, sitting near the table and turning over the newspapers, till I heard the carriage drive away, and my father's returning steps echoed slowly along the hall. He entered the room, sat down, and was silent for many minutes. I felt that he was looking at me intently. Presently he said with some sharpness—

"Gaston!"

"Sir?"

"Are you satisfied with the evil you have done?"

I smiled.

"Really, *mon père*, you talk as if I were the only criminal in the matter! There are others——"

"And they are punished!" he declared passionately. "Punished more bitterly than most people are for their misdeeds; and the heaviest punishment has fallen on the weakest offender, thanks to you! As for Silvion Guidèl, you may depend upon it, he is a prey to the deepest remorse and misery!"

"You think so?" I queried languidly, without raising my eyes. "Now I should fancy he finds quite sufficient atonement for his sins in the muttering of an '*Ave*' or a '*Pater-noster*.'"[1]

"I tell you he *suffers*!" and my father struck his hand emphatically on the table,—"I have studied his nature, and I know he has the scholar's mind,—the subtle and self-tormenting disposition which is always a curse to its owner! He has behaved like a coward and a villain, and he knows it! But you,—you also have behaved like a coward and a villain, and you do not seem to know it!"

"No!—you are right;" I responded calmly. "I do not!"

"*Dieu!* Have you no heart?"

"None!" and I fixed my eyes quietly upon him. "How should you expect it? I gave what heart I had to my betrothed wife, and she has killed it. It is stone dead! I forget that it ever existed! Pray do not let us talk any more of the matter, *mon père*; I am perfectly content to leave Paris for a time as you suggest,—indeed I think the plan an admirable one. It will certainly be best that I should remove my presence from you, and from all to whom I have suddenly become obnoxious. But, before we part, I will ask you to remember, first,—that I have never wilfully, through all my life, given you a moment's cause for pain or reproach,—and secondly, that in this rupture of a marriage which was to have been the completion of life's happiness for me, I am guiltless of anything save a desire to wreak just punishment on the betrayers of my honour. Thirdly, that the only offence you can charge against me is, a want of sympathy with a dishonoured woman, who has not only confessed, but almost glories in her dishonour!"

With that, I saluted him profoundly and left him to his own reflections. I had shown no heat—I had displayed no temper—I had stated

---

[1] Prayers. 'Ave (Maria)' (Latin for "Hail Mary") is a devotional recitation and prayer to the Virgin Mary; 'Pater Noster' (Latin for "Our Father") is the Lord's prayer.

my case with the coolest logic,—the logic of an *absintheur*! But once up again in the solitude of my own room with the door shut fast, I laughed aloud and bitterly at the persistent and ridiculous wrong-sidedness with which everybody insisted on viewing the whole affair. All the pity was for Pauline! and yet people *would* go on prating about 'morality!' Judged strictly, Pauline de Charmilles had not a shadow of defence on her side; but because she was young, beautiful, and a woman, her fate excited sympathy. Had she been ugly and misshapen, she might have been scourged and driven from pillar to post till she died of sheer exhaustion for aught any one would have cared! We are most of us ruled by the flesh and the devil; and very few of us have any real conception of justice.

But do not imagine, good friends, that I, a confirmed drinker of Absinthe, want to be moral! Not I! I should win scanty attention from some of you, if I did! I only observe to you, *en passant*,[1] that, considering how the barriers between vice and virtue are being fast broken down in all great "civilized" countries; how, even in eminently virtuous and respectable "Albion,"[2] women of known disreputable character are allowed to enter and mix with the highest aristocratic circles,—and how it will most probably soon be necessary to establish in church-going London and under the very nose of good Mrs. Grundy,[3] a recognized *demi-monde* after the fashion of my dear Paris,— in the face of all these facts, I say, surely it is time to leave off sermonizing about dull household virtues!—an age of Realism and Zola[4] has no time for them! But whatever you may think of *my* opinions,—opinions born of blessed Absinthe;—sit in judgment on yourselves, my readers, before you venture to judge *me*! Believe me, I used, like many other young men, to have my ideals of greatness and goodness; the beautiful, the mystical, the impersonal and sublime had attractions for my spirit; but the wise "green fairy" has cured me of this unworldly foolishness. Formerly, I loved to read noble poetry; I could lose myself in inward communion with the divine spirit of Plato, and other thinkers grand and true as he,—but now!—now, I grin in company with the "educated" masses over the indecent wit of the cheap Paris press,— now, like "un vrai absintheur"[5] I enjoy a sneer at virtue,—now, like

---

1 French expression meaning "by the way."
2 Original Greek and Roman name for Great Britain.
3 A name personifying the tyranny of social opinion in matters of conventional propriety.
4 See note on realism, page 72, note 8. Émile Zola (1840-1902) was the writer most associated with the Realist (or Naturalist) school of writing.
5 French for "a true absinthe addict."

many of my class who wish to "go with the time," I fling a stone or a handful of mud at any one presuming to live a cleaner and greater life than his fellows. I am one of your "newer" generation, you poor old world!—the generation under which you groan as you roll silently on in your fate-appointed orbit; the generation of brute-selfishness, little-ness, and godlessness,—the generation of the finite Ego opposed to infi-nite Eternities! I please *myself* in the way I live; I am answerable to none other! And you, dear reader, whose languid eyes rest carelessly on this printed page,—*entre nous soit dit!*[1]—do not *you* follow the same wise rule? Is not your every thought, idea, and plan, however much it may at first seem for the benefit of others, really for your own ultimate inter-est and good? Of course! Excellent! Let us then metaphorically shake hands upon our declared brotherhood,—for though you may be, and no doubt are, highly respectable, while I am all together disreputable,—though you may be everything that society approves, while I am an absinthe-drinking outcast from polite life, a skulking pariah of the slums and back streets of Paris, we are both at one—yes, my dear friend, I assure you,—entirely at one!—in the worship of Self!

CHAPTER 20

Next day I remembered I had a visit to make. The Comte de Charmilles expected me to call upon him before noon. I meant to go, of course; I had no wish to disappoint him! I was prepared for a stormy scene with him; I could already picture the haughty old aristocrat's wounded pride and indignation at the dishonour brought on his name,—but I could not quite imagine what he would be likely to say. Certes, he could not excuse his daughter or her partner in iniquity; he might pour out his wrath upon me for making the affair public to all his friends and acquaintances, but that would be the utmost he could do. I determined to hear him out with the utmost patience and cour-tesy,—my quarrel was not with him,—he had never given me offence, save by his stupid Royalist tendencies and bigoted Catholicism,—and it was quite enough for me, a nineteenth century Republican, to have lowered his pride and broken it,—I wanted nothing more so far as *he* was concerned! Before starting on my ceremonious errand, I packed a

---

[1] French expression translating as "just between you and me, of course."

few clothes and other necessaries in my portmanteau ready for immediate departure from home, and this done, I went in search of my father. He was just preparing to leave the house for his usual duties at the Bank, and he looked fagged and wearied. He lifted his eyes and regarded me steadily as I approached him,—his lips quivered, and, suddenly laying his hand on my shoulder, he said—

"Gaston, it goes to my old heart to part with you!—for I love you! But something has embittered and crossed your once sweet and generous nature; and though I have thought about it anxiously all night, I have still come to the same conclusion,—namely, that it will be best for us both that we should separate for a time, especially under the unhappy circumstances that have just taken place. The whole position is too painful for everybody concerned! And I am quite ready to admit that the suffering you have personally undergone has been, and is, of a nature to chafe and exasperate your feelings. Change of scene and different surroundings will do much for you, *mon garçon*,—and, this miserable *esclandre* will possibly die out during your absence. Choose your own time for going——"

"I have chosen it"—I interrupted him quietly—"I shall leave you to-day."

An expression of sharp pain contracted his fine old features for a moment,—then apparently rallying his self-possession, he returned—

"*Soit!* It is perhaps best! You will find a note from me in your desk in the library; I have thought it wisest to give you at once a round sum sufficient for present needs. Your share in the Bank as my partner naturally continues,—and shall be religiously set aside for your use on your return. I do not know whether you have any idea of a destination,—I should suggest your visiting England for a time."

I smiled.

"Thanks! I am too truly French in my sympathies to care for the British climate. No!—if, like a new Cain,[1] I am to be a vagabond on the face of the earth, I will wander as far as my fancy takes me; Africa, *par exemple*, presents boundless forests, where, if one chose, one could almost lose one's very identity!"

My father's eyes flashed a keen and sorrowful reproach into mine.

"*Mon fils*, why speak so bitterly? Is it necessary to add an extra pang to my grief?"

---

[1] Son of Adam and Eve who murdered his brother Abel. Cain's punishment was to be made a vagabond roaming the earth.

A sudden impulse moved me to softer emotion,—taking his hand I kissed it respectfully.

"*Mon père*, I regret beyond all words that I am unhappily the cause of any distress to you! We part;—and it is no doubt advisable, as you say, that we should do so,—for a time; but in bidding you farewell I will ask you to think of me at my best,—and to believe that there is no man in all the world whom I admire and honour more than yourself! Sentiment between men is ridiculous I know, but——" I kissed his hand once more, and I felt his fingers tremble as they clung for a moment to mine.

"God bless thee, Gaston!" he murmured. "And, stay!—let me have time to think again! Do not leave Paris yet—wait till to-morrow!"

I made a half sign of assent—but uttered no promise; and watched him with a curious forsaken feeling, as with a kindly yet wistful last look at me, he left the house and walked rapidly along on his usual way to business. Should I ever dwell with him again in the old frank familiarity of intercourse that had made us more like comrades than father and son? I doubted it! *My* life was changed,—*my* road lay down a dark side-turning; *his* continued fair and open, with the full sunshine of honour lighting it to the end!

Entering the library, I looked in my desk for the packet my father had mentioned, and found it,—a bulky envelope containing French notes to the amount of what would be about five hundred pounds in English money. I took possession of these,—and then wrote a note to my father, thanking him for his generosity, and bidding him farewell, while, to satisfy him as to my destination, I added that it was my immediate intention to visit Italy. A lie of course!—I had no such intention; I never meant to leave Paris, but of this hereafter. I then finished my packing and other preparations, and went out of the dear old house at Neuilly with scarce a regret,—not realizing, as I afterwards realized, that I should never, never enter it again! Hailing a passing carriage I bade the driver take me to the *Gare de l'Est*.[1] Our man-servant Dunois, who put my portmanteau into the vehicle and watched my departure more or less curiously, heard me give this order, which was precisely what I wanted. I knew he would repeat it to my father, who by this means would receive the impression that I had carried out my written intention, and departed for Italy by the Lucerne and Chiasso route to Milan. Arrived at the *Gare*, I put my portmanteau in charge of the official to whom such baggage

---

[1] East Station. Paris railway station serving passengers travelling to Germany, Italy, and Switzerland.

is consigned for safe keeping—and then I leisurely proceeded to retrace my route on foot, till I reached the residence of the Comte de Charmilles. The very outside of the great house looked dreary; some of the blinds were down,—there was a deserted melancholy aspect about it that was doubly striking in comparison with the glitter and brilliancy that had surrounded it on the previous day. The maid who opened the door to me looked scared and miserable as though she had been up all night,—and, murmuring under her breath and with averted eyes that her master had been expecting me for some time, she showed me into the Count's private study and announced me by name. The Count himself was sitting in his arm-chair, his back turned towards me,—his figure rigidly erect,—and he gave no sign of having heard my entrance.

The servant departed noiselessly, closing the door behind her,—and I stood irresolute, waiting for him to speak. But he uttered not a word. All at once my eyes lighted on a case of pistols open on the table,—from the position and appearance of the weapons, I saw they were loaded and ready for use. The situation flashed upon me in an instant, and I smiled with some contempt as I realized it. This foolish old man—this withering stump of ancient French chivalry,—had actually resolved to fight out the question of his daughter's honour with me, face to face! Was ever such a mad scheme! What a Don Quixote[1] of a father to be sure! If he had taken up arms for a stage mistress now,—if he had risen in eager defence of some coarse painted dancing woman, whose nearly nude body was on view to the public for so many francs per night, one would not have blamed him, or thought him ridiculous,—no, not in Paris! But to think of fighting a duel for merely a *daughter's* reputation!—*Dieu!* it was a freak worthy of laughter! Yet there was a touch of the romantic and pathetic about it that moved me in spite of myself,—though of course I determined to refuse his challenge. I did not want to shed the blood of that old white-haired man! But suppose he still persisted? Well, then I must defend myself, and if I killed him, it would be unfortunate, but it could not be helped. The idea of *his* dispatching *me* never entered my head. There was something in *me*, or so I imagined, that could *not* be killed!—not yet!

Meanwhile the object of my musings remained immovably silent,—and I began rather to wonder at such obstinate taciturnity. His indomitable pride had met with a terrific fall, I reflected!—probably he found it difficult to begin the conversation. I advanced a little.

---

[1]   The hero of Cervantes' *Don Quixote*. A kind but simple-minded man who sets out as knight-errant to redress the wrongs of the world.

"M. de Charmilles! You bade me come to you, and I am here!"

He made no answer. His left hand, thin and wrinkled, rested on the carved oak arm of the chair, and I thought I saw it tremble ever so slightly. Was his rage so great that it had rendered him absolutely speechless? I moved a few steps nearer.

"M. de Charmilles!" I repeated, raising my voice a little—"I am here—Gaston Beauvais. Have you anything to say to me?"

No answer! A vague awe seized me, and instinctively hushing my footsteps, I approached and ventured to touch the fingers that were lightly closed round the arm of the chair,—they were warm, but they did not move,—only the diamond signet on the third finger glittered coldly like a wintry star.

"M. de Charmilles?" I said loudly once more; then, mastering the curious sensation of terror that held me momentarily inert and uncertain what to do I went resolutely forward and round, so that I could look him full in the face. As I did so I recoiled with an involuntary exclamation; the old man's features were rigid and bloodless,—the eyes were wide open, fixed and glassy, though they appeared to stare at me with an expression of calm and freezing disdain,—the lips were parted in a stern smile,—and the fine white hair was slightly roughened about the forehead as though a hand had been lately pressed there to still some throbbing ache. A frozen figure of old-world dignity he sate,[1] surveying me, or so it seemed, in speechless but majestic scorn; while I, for one amazed breathless moment stood confronting him, overpowered by the cold solemnity and grandeur of his aspect. Then—all suddenly— the set jaw dropped; the ghastly look of Death darkened the erstwhile tranquil countenance; and my awe gave way to the wildest nervous horror. Springing to the bell I rang it violently and incessantly; the servants flocked in, and in a few seconds the room was a scene of confusion and lamentation. As in a dream I saw the Comtesse de Charmilles feebly totter in and distractedly fall on her knees by her husband's passive form; I saw Héloïse busying herself in chafing her uncle's yet warm hands,—I heard the sound of convulsive sobbing;—and then I became dimly aware of a physician's presence, and of the sudden hush of suspense following his arrival. A brief examination sufficed;—the words "Il est mort!"[2] though uttered in the lowest whisper, reached the ears of the desolate Countess who, with a long shuddering wail of

---

[1]   Archaic form of the word "sat."
[2]   French for "He is dead."

agony, sank senseless at the dead man's feet. It was all over!—some little vessel in the heart had snapt,—some little subtle chord in the brain had given way under the pressure of strong indignation, grief, and excitement,—and the proud old aristocrat had gone to that equalizing dust where there is neither pride nor shame! He was dead,—and some narrow-minded fools may consider, if they like, that *I* killed him. But how? What crime had *I* committed? None! I had merely made a stand for moral law in social life! My career was stainless, save for the green trail of the Absinthe-slime which no one saw. And Society never blames vice that does not publicly offend. Pauline was the sinner,—little, child-like, blue-eyed Pauline!—and I took a sort of grim and awful pleasure in regarding her as a *parricide*! Why, because she had a sweet face, a slim form and a bright smile, should she escape from the results of her own treachery and crime? I could not see it then,—and I cannot see it even now! No one can make *me* responsible for the old Count's death,—no one I say!—though at times, his white, still, majestic face confronts me in the darkness with a speechless reproach and undying challenge. But I know it is only a phantasm!—and I quickly take refuge in the truth as declared by the fashionable world of Paris when his death became generally known,—namely, that his daughter's dishonour (not my proclamation of it, observe!) had broken his heart;—and that even so, broken-hearted for her sake, he died!

CHAPTER 21

From this period I may begin to date my rapid downward career,—a career that however disreputable and strange it may seem to those who elect to be virtuous and self-controlled, has brought to me, personally, the wildest and most unpurchasable varieties of pleasure. Pleasure, such as a forest-savage may know when the absolute freedom of air, woodland, and water, is his,—when no laws bind him,—and when he has no one to whom he is bound to account for his actions. I hate your smug, hypocritical civilization good world!—I would rather be what I am, than play the double part your rules of life enjoin! I am an alien from all respectability; what then? Respectability is generally dull! And I am never dull; my Absinthe-witch takes care of that! Her kaleidoscope of vision is exhaustless,—and though of late she has shown me the same sights somewhat too often, I am perchance, the most to blame for this,—the tenacity of my own brain holding fast to certain images that it would be best to forget. This is the fault of my constitution,—a tendency to remember,—I cannot forget, if I would, and whereas on some temperaments the emerald nectar bestows oblivion, on mine it sharpens and intensifies memory. Nevertheless the feverish excitation of pleasure never dies out, and my disposition is such that I am able to brood on things that would appal most men, with the keenest and most appreciative delight! It is not perhaps agreeable, is it, to peaceable and right-minded people to dwell gloatingly on the harrowing details of a murder, for instance? To me, however, it is not only agreeable, but absolutely fascinating!—and I have merely to shut my eyes to see— what? Water glimmering in the moonlight,—trees waving in the wind—and a face upturned to the quiet skies drifting steadily and help-lessly down stream,—but, stop! I must not brood too tenderly upon this picture yet;—though it is difficult to me sometimes to keep my thoughts in sequence. No "absintheur" can be always coherent; it is too much to expect of the green fairy's votaries!

Well! the Comte de Charmilles was dead,—and a whole fortnight had elapsed since his funeral had wound its solemn black length through the streets of Paris to *Père-la-Chaise*,[1] where the family vault had opened its stone jaws to receive the mortal remains of him who was the last male heir of his race. His great house was shut up as a house of mourning; the widowed Comtesse and her niece Héloïse dwelt there together, so I learned, in melancholy solitude, denying themselves to all visitors. Under any other circumstances they would most probably have left the city, and sought in change of scene a relaxation from grief, but *I* knew why they remained immured in their desolate town mansion,— simply in the hope that now, having nothing to fear from the wrath of her father, the lost Pauline might return to her home.

And I—I also was still in Paris. As I said before, I had never for a moment intended to leave it. I had formed certain plans of my own respecting the wild new mode of life I purposed to follow,—and these plans I was able to carry out with entire success. I took a small apartment in an obscure hotel, under an assumed name, and in my daily and nightly rambles, I carefully kept to the back streets, partly to avoid a chance meet-ing with any of my acquaintance, and partly under the impression that in one of these poorer quarters of Paris I should find Pauline. I had no idea

---

[1] A large cemetery in the northeast end of Paris for residents of this part of town but also for persons of distinction from other parts of Paris.

what I should do if I really did happen to discover her whereabouts,—part of the quality of one in my condition of *absinthism*, is that he cannot *absolutely* decide anything too long beforehand. When the time for decision comes, he acts as suddenly as a wild beast springs,—on impulse,—needless to add that the impulse is always more or less evil.

A fortnight is not a long time is it?—save to children and parted lovers,—yet it had sufficed me to make deadly progress in my self-chosen method of enjoying existence; so much so, in fact, that nothing in the world seemed to me of real importance provided Absinthe never failed. I think, at this particular juncture, that if any one possessing the power to deny me the full complement of the nectar which was now as necessary to me as the blood in my veins, *had* denied it, I should have killed him on the spot without a moment's compunction! But fortunately, Absinthe is obtainable everywhere in Paris,—it is not a costly luxury either,—and I soon became familiar with the different haunts where the most potent forms of it were obtainable. It must of course be understood by the inquisitive reader, that the effects of this divine cordial are different on different temperaments. On the densely stupid brain it can only render the stupefaction more complete. The habituated Chinese opium-eater, for example, gets no dreams out of his drug, his own mind being too slow and sluggish for the creation of any sort of vision. But, put a quick-witted Frenchman or Italian in an Oriental opium-den, and the poison-fumes will invoke for him a crowd of phantom images, horrible or beautiful, according to the tendency of his thoughts. So with Absinthe. Only that Absinthe differs from opium in this respect,—namely that it has not only one, but three distinct gradations of action. Imagine, for the sake of metaphor, the brain to be a musical instrument, well strung and in perfect tune,—Absinthe first *deadens* the vibrating power; then, one by one, *reverses* the harmonies; and finally, completely alters the very nature of the sounds. Music can still be drawn from it,—but it is a different music to what it erstwhile was capable of. On the active brain, its effect is to quicken the activity to feverishness, while hurling it through new and extraordinary channels of thought; on a slow brain it quenches whatever feeble glimmer of intelligence previously existed there, the result in such a case being frequently cureless idiotcy. But what does this matter? Its charm is irresistible for both wit and fool; and in this age, when to follow our own immediate desires is the only accepted gospel,—the gospel of Paris at least, if of no other city, Absinthe is to many, as to me, the chief necessity of life. Because, however uncertain in its other phases it may prove, it can be absolutely relied upon to kill Conscience!

I lived on from day to day in my hidden retirement, perfectly contented with my lot, and doing nothing whatever but dreamily wander about the byways of the city, looking for Pauline. Yet I could not have told any one *why* I looked for her. I did not want her. Nevertheless, reason or no reason, the impulse of search continued; and every woman of youthful and shrinking appearance I met, came in for my close and eager scrutiny. Once or twice in my lonely walks I saw Héloïse St. Cyr, robed in deepest black and closely veiled, and I guessed by the character of the places in which I encountered her, that she also was seeking for the lost one. She never saw me,—for I always slunk away in swift avoidance of any possible glance of recognition from her beautiful disdainful eyes. And, as I have stated, a fortnight had elapsed,—when, one evening, an irresistible yearning came over me to take a stroll in the direction of Neuilly—to pass the old house of my other days,—to look up at the windows, on the chance of seeing merely the shadow of my father's figure silhouetted by the lamp-light on the drawn blind. He thought me far away by this time, and was no doubt surprised and irritated at receiving no letters from me. I wondered if he were solitary?—if he regretted the loss of my companionship? Yielding to my fancy, I started on the well-known route which I had up till now carefully avoided. I stopped now and then to re-invigorate my forces with the Absinthe-fire that I fully believed was the only thing that kept me alive,—but when once I had passed all the *cafés* where the best form of that elixir was obtainable, I continued my road steadily and without interruption along the Champs Elysées.

It was a fine night; the trees were in full foliage; a few stray birds twittered sleepily among the branches; and under the light of the soft moon, many an amorous couple wandered to and fro, entranced in each other's society, and telling each other the same old lies of love and perpetual constancy that all wise men laugh at. I walked slowly,—following, as I always followed, the flickering rays of green that trembled on my path,—to-night they took the shape of thin arrows that pointed forward,—ever forward and straight on! Neuilly at last!—and a few minutes more brought me to the house I had so lately known as "home." All the windows were empty of light save that of the library,—and here the blind was only half down, so that I was able to see my father through it, busily writing. His table was strewn with papers; he looked fatigued and careworn,—and for one brief second my heart smote me. Troublesome conscience was not quite dead;—yonder old man's fine, placid, yet weary face roused in me a struggling passion of regret and remorse. It was a mere flash of pain!—it soon passed,—I pressed my hand heavily over my eyes to still their burning ache,—and turning from the house, I looked down on the dark asphalte pavement at my feet. There were those little flickering green shafts of light pointing ahead as before!—and, careless as to where I went I continued to follow in their spectral lead. So I walked on and on; surrounded as I went by strange sights and sounds to which I had now grown almost accustomed, and which, even at their worst brought me much weird and fantastic delight. To a great extent, my sensations, though purely imaginary, *seemed* real; nothing could have been more substantial in appearance than the faces and forms that hovered about me,—it was only when I strove to touch them that they vanished. But the odd part of it was that I could feel them touching *me*; kisses were pressed on my lips,—soft arms embraced me,—the very breath of these phantoms seemed at times to lift and fan my hair. And more real than the faces and forms, were the voices I heard;—these never left me alone,—they sang, they talked, they whispered, of things strange and terrible,—things that might have turned the blood cold in the veins of an honest man;—only that I was no longer honest. I knew that! I was neither honest to myself, nor in my feelings towards the world,—but this did not appear to me at all a matter for compunction. Because, after all, there was no one to care particularly what my principles were,—no one except my father,—and he was an old man,—his term of life would soon be ended. Self-respect is the root of honour; and with me self-respect was dead and buried! I had taken to self-indulgence instead. Most men do, if truth were told, though their favourite vice may not be the love of Absinthe. But that nearly every man has some evil propensity to which he secretly panders,—this is a fact of which we may be perfectly sure!

For my part, I was quite content to listen to the ghastly prattle of the suggestive air-voices about me; and my brain was wondrously quick to conjure up the scenes they told me of,—scenes in graves, where the pain-tranced man, thought to be dead, but living, is buried in the haste ordained by the iniquitous French law, and struggles choking in his coffin, while the sexton fully aware of, yet terrified by his moans, calmly throws the earth over him all the same and levels it down;[1]—of lazar-houses and dissecting-rooms, and all the realistic wonders of obscurity and crime, on which the "cultured" Paris public dwells with rapt and ecstatic interest,—such beauteous things as these were as vivid and

---

[1]   [Corelli's note] A case of this kind happened near Paris last year.

sweet to me now as they had once been repulsive. And so I strolled along under the moon-silvered sky, heedless of distance, careless of time, till the more brilliant clustering lights of Paris were left behind me, and I woke up with a start from my sinister musings, to find myself in the quiet little suburb of Suresnes.[1]

Do you know Suresnes? On a fine summer's afternoon it is worth while to journey thither, and walk over the bridge, stopping half-way across to look up and down at the quietly flowing river, that on the right-hand parts with a broad shining ribbon-breadth the Bois, and the opposite undulating hills. Down almost to the brink of the water slope a few exquisite lawns and gardens belonging to those white villas one sees glimmering among the rich foliage of the trees; and round by these in a semicircle sweeps the Seine, onward and out of sight like the silver robe of a queen vanishing into stately distance. To the left is Paris;—a vision of aerial bridge, building and tower,—and at times when the sunset is like fire and the wind is still,—when the bells chime musically forth the hour, and every turret and chimney is bathed in roseate light, one might almost imagine it a fairy city gleaming aloft mirage-like for one marvellous moment, only to disappear the next. Once past the bridge you enter the Bois, where the open road leads to Longchamps;[2] but there are many nooky paths and quiet corners down under the tall trees by the edge of the river itself, where one may bask whole hours in happy solitude,— solitude so complete that it is easy to believe oneself miles away from any city. Often and often I had wandered hither in my boyhood, reading some favourite book or giving myself up to pleasant day-dreaming and air-castle-building; yet to-night I gazed upon the familiar scene entirely bewildered and with all the puzzled uncertainty of a stranger ignorant of his whereabouts. Suresnes itself was quiet as a crypt; its principal *café* was shut up and not a single lamp glimmered in any window of any house that I could see,—the moon-beams alone silvered the roofs and doors and transformed the pretty bridge to a sparkling span of light. The tide was high,—it made a musical rushing and gurgling as it ran; I leaned upon the bridge-parapet and listened to its incessant murmur, half soothed, half pained. Then, sauntering slowly, and trying, as I went, to understand something of the hushed and spiritual beauty of the landscape,—for this sort of comprehension was daily becoming more difficult to me,—I moved on towards the Bois. The great leaf-covered trees rustled myste-

---

[1] Small town at the base of Mont Valérien. A bridge over the Seine leads from Longchamp in the Bois de Boulogne to Suresnes.

[2] Misspelling of Longchamp, a racecourse in the Bois de Boulogne.

riously, and mingled their sighs with the liquid warbling of the waters;—there was no living soul to be seen,—this hour of solemn quietude and rest seemed all for me, and for me alone.

Once across the bridge I paused, looking into the further stretches of the woodland. The air was so very still, that I could hear the distinct fall of the artificial cascade, that, with its adjacent *café*, is the scene of many a pleasant summer *rendezvous*; and, for a moment I thought I would walk thus far. Suddenly, with a loud silvern clang, a neighbouring church clock struck the hour—eleven. It sounded more like the Mass-bell than a clock chime,—and my thoughts, which were always in a scattered and desultory condition, began to swarm like bees round the various ideas of religion and worship it suggested. I reflected how many a canting hypocrite earned dishonest bread by playing a sanctimonious part before the so-called sacred altars,—altars polluted by such paid service; how, in every church, in every form of creed, men, preaching one thing and openly practising another, offered themselves as "Christian examples" forsooth!—to their less professing brethren;—how smug priests and comfortable clergymen, measuring Christianity solely as a means whereby to live, profaned the name of Christ by the mere utterance of it in their false and greedy mouths;—and how, in these days, religion was rendered such a ghastly mockery by its very teachers, that it was no wonder if some honest folk preferred to believe in no God at all, rather than accept a God in whom His servants could profess to find such inconsistency and absolute lack of principle!

All at once my thoughts took flight like a flock of scared birds, as they often did; a sick swimming sensation in my head made me clutch at the near branch of a tree for support,—the whole landscape went round in a green circle, and the stars looked pushed forth from the sky in jets of flame. All was red, green, and white dazzlement before me for a moment,—and to master this uncomfortable faintness which threatened to end in a swoon, I moved unsteadily, feeling my way as though I were blind, down towards the river's brink. I had an idea that I would rest there awhile on the cool grass till I recovered; and I went towards one of the most sequestered and lonely nooks I could just then confusedly remember;—a tiny plat of velvety greensward shaded about by huge umbrageous elms, where, from the encircling shadows, one could look out on the brighter waters, and inhale the freshness of whatever light wind there was. I went on very feebly, for my senses were in a whirl and seemed on the point of deserting me altogether; I bent aside the branches, and slipped between the closely-set and intertwisted trunks in order to gain as speedily as possible the spot I sought,—when, as though I had received a paralyzing electric shock, I stopped, staring ahead of me in doubt, wrath, and wonder;—a rush of strength was hurled into me—a superhuman force that strung up my every nerve and sinew to almost breaking tension,—and I sprang furiously forward, uttering an oath that was half a cry. A man stood near the river's edge,— a man in the close black garments of a priest; and he turned his face, fair, cold, and pale, fearlessly towards me as I came.

"You—you!" I whispered hoarsely, for rage choked my voice,— "You here! *You*,—Silvion Guidèl!"

CHAPTER 22

His eyes rested on me quietly, almost indifferently; dense, dark, weary eyes they were that night!—and he sighed.

"Yes, I am here," he said slowly. "I have tried to keep away, but in the end I could not. Is she well?"

I stared at him,—too maddened by wrath and amazement for the moment to speak. He, never removing his gaze from me, repeated his question anxiously—

"Tell me, is she well? I have no right to know, perhaps,—you are her husband,—but I—I was her lover, God forgive me!—and again I ask,— is she well?"

He was ignorant then of all that had happened! As this fact forced itself on my comprehension, my fury froze into sinister calm.

"She is dead!" I answered curtly and with a chill smile.

He gave a slight disdainful gesture, still keeping his eyes upon me.

"I do not believe you," he said. "She could not die,—not yet; she is too young,—too beautiful! Would she *were* dead!—but I know she is not."

"You know she is not!" I retorted. "*How* do you know? I tell you she is dead!—dead to every one that honoured or loved her! What!— has she not sought *you* out before this?—she has had ample time!"

His face grew very white—his look expressed sudden fear and bewilderment.

"Sought *me* out!" he stammered hurriedly. "What do you mean? Is she not your wife?—have you not married her?"

My hands clenched themselves involuntarily till the nails dug into my flesh.

"*Lâche!*" I cried furiously: "*Dare* you suppose that I would wed your cast-off mistress?"

With a sudden supple movement he turned upon me, and seizing me by both shoulders held me as in a vice.

"Do not say that, Gaston Beauvais!" he muttered fiercely, his rich voice trembling with passion. "Do not fling one word of opprobrium at the child whose very innocence was her ruin! Here, as we two stand face to face alone with the night and God as witnesses, do we not know the truth, you and I, as men, that it is *we* who take dastardly advantage of the passionate impulse of a young girl's tenderness, and that often her very sin of love looks white virtue compared to our black vice! I— I alone am to blame for my darling's misery;—you have not married her, you say,—then where is she? As mine was the fault, so shall mine be the reparation,—God knows the bitterness now of my remorse! But do not you presume to judge her, Gaston Beauvais!—you are no more than man, and as such, the condemnation of a woman ill becomes you!"

He loosened his grasp of me so swiftly that I reeled slightly back from him,—the old magnetic charm of his voice restrained my rage for an instant, and I gazed at him half stupefied. The wonderful spiritual beauty of his face was intensified by the moon's mellow lustre; his proud, almost defiant attitude would have suggested to any ordinary observer that it was he who was the offended, and I the offender! Had we been playing our life-parts on the theatrical stage, the sympathy of the audience would have assuredly gone with him and away from me, all because he looked handsome, and spoke fearlessly! Such is the world's villainous inconsistency! He waited, as though to rally his forces;—I waited too, considering how best I could pierce that saintly exterior down to the satyr heart within! A curious nervous trembling seized me; my pulses began to gallop and the blood hummed tumul-tuously in my ears, but nevertheless I managed still to keep up the outward appearance of perfect composure.

"Where is she?" he again demanded.

"On the streets of Paris!" I answered sneeringly.

"My God!" and he sprang towards me. "Her father——"

"Is dead and buried! What next? Ask!—I shall not scruple to tell you the result of your work, Silvion Guidèl! It is well that when you perform Mass, you should know for whom to pray!"

And I laughed bitterly. His head drooped on his breast,—his features grew wan and rigid, and a deep sigh shuddered through his frame.

"Pauline! Pauline!"—I heard him mutter under his breath. "Poor little child!—what can I do for thee?"

At this, the venomous passion of my soul seemed to urge itself into full-voiced utterance.

"What can you do?" I exclaimed. "Nothing! You are too late! You talk of reparation,—what reparation is possible, *now*? You had it in your power to make amends,—you could at least have married the girl whose mind you contaminated and whose life you wronged! But no!—you slunk into the refuge of the priesthood like a beaten cur!—you proved yourself a betrayer, deserter, and coward!—and like a sanctimonious fool and hypocrite as you were, trusted to my generosity to cover your crime! As well trust a tiger not to tear! What! Did you take *me* for a church saint? Have I ever played that part?—have I ever pretended to be more than man? I told you once that I would never forgive even the closest friend who dared to deceive me,—do you think my words were mere feigning? Listen! Pauline de Charmilles confessed her shame to me in secret,—*I* proclaimed it in public! I do not love dishonour,—I set no value on flawed jewels! I rejected her!—mark you that, Silvion Guidèl, holy servant of the church as you are!—I rejected her on the very day appointed for our marriage, in presence of all those fine birds of fashion that came to see us wedded!—ah, it was a rare vengeance, and sweeter to me than any fortune or fame! What now? Is there something unusual in my aspect to so arouse your pious wonder? You stare at me as if you saw a dead man mouldering in his grave!"

His eyes flashed forth a fierce and unutterable scorn.

"I see worse than that!" he answered passionately. "I see—oh God!— I see what I never imagined I *should* see!—a baser villain than myself!"

He paused, his breath coming and going rapidly,—then, with a wild gesture he cried out as though suddenly oblivious of my presence—

"Oh Pauline, Pauline! My little love!—my angel! Lost, ruined, and deserted!—oh Pauline!—Pauline!"

The yearning tenderness in his voice set astir a strange new throbbing in my blood, and drawing a stealthy step or two nearer I studied his agonized face as I would have studied some rare or curious picture. He glanced at me where I stood, and a strange smile curved his lips.

"Why do you not kill me?" he said, with an inviting gesture. "I should be glad to die!"

I made no immediate answer. *Why did I not kill him!* It was a foolish question, and it hummed in my ears with foolish persistency! To escape from it I forced myself into a side-issue of the argument.

"Why did you become a priest?" I asked.

He sighed.

"Because I was compelled," he answered wearily. "Of course you will not believe me. But you do not understand,—and it would take too long to explain. I could not help myself; circumstance is often stronger than will. I strove against it,—all in vain!—you are right enough when you speak of church tyranny. The Church *is* a tyrant,—none crueller, more absolute, or more lacking in Christian charity—its velvet glove covers a merciless hand of iron. Once made a priest, I was sent on to Rome; and there, under pretence of special favour and protection I was kept in close attendance on cardinals and *monsignori*;[1]—I prayed for news from home,—none ever reached me,—till tired of waiting, I came away by stealth and travelled straight to Paris;—I only arrived to-day."

"And why are you *here*?" I demanded, indicating by a gesture the surrounding woodland and rippling water.

"Why?"—he sighed again, and looked upward to the peaceful sky above him—"Because here the heavens smiled upon the only happiness I ever knew! Love, the natural claim and heritage of man,—this was bestowed upon me *here*;—here I won the tender birthright of my blood,—a birthright which priestly usage would have defrauded me of! I came here too, because I dared not go elsewhere;—for, though I was ignorant of all you have told me, I avoided my uncle's house—I know not why—save that I felt I could not bear to enter it,—now!"

I remained silent, watching him.

"Here was our secret trysting-place!" he went on dreamily. "Here under these trees, beloved for her sake, Pauline has wandered with me, her sweet eyes speaking what her lips were afraid to utter—her little hand in mine—her head resting on my heart! Here we two have tasted the divinest joy that life can ever give, or death take away,—joy that you have never known, Gaston Beauvais!—no! for my darling never loved you! Your touch never wakened in her one responsive throb of passion;—she loved me, and me alone! Ay!—even if you had married her, and if my faults were ten thousand times greater than they are, she would still love me faithfully to the end!"

Here was specious 'French' reasoning with a vengeance! I thought I must have gone mad with fury as I saw the expression of serene

---

[1] The title of Roman Catholic prelates, officers of papal court, and others.

triumph on that pale poet-face, fair as an angel's in the radiance of the moon.

"You boast of that?" I said hoarsely. "You dare to boast of that?"

He smiled victoriously.

"Even so! I boast of that! It is something to be proud of, to have been loved truly, once!"

My hands clenched.

"Will you seek her out?" I asked breathlessly.

"I will!"

"When?"

"To-morrow!"

"To-night is not ended!" I muttered, edging a little nearer to him still, and trying to keep my thoughts steady in the surging tumult of hissing and whispering noises that buzzed in my brain. "And,—if you find her,—what then?"

"What then?"—and with a reckless gesture of mingled defiance and passion, he lifted his eyes once more to the observant stars—

"Why, then it may be that I shall condemn my soul to hell for her sake! I shall, if the Church is the Voice of God! But, should it chance, as I have thought,—that God is something infinitely more supreme than any Church,—more great, more loving, more tenderly wise and pitiful than can be imagined by His subject-creature Man,—I doubt not, if this be true, that when I rescue and comfort the woman I have wronged as only love can comfort her,—when I kneel at her feet and ask her pardon for the evil I have wrought,—even thus shall I make my surest peace with Heaven!"

Canting hypocrite!—vile traducer!—worse in my sight than ever for his braggart pretence of piety! Quick as a lightning flash the suppressed ferocity of my soul broke forth,—and without warning or premeditation I threw myself savagely upon him.

"Best make peace with it now!" I cried. "For, by God! it is your last chance!"

For one panting second we stared into each other's eyes,—our faces almost touching, our very breaths commingling; then, yielding to the natural impulse of self-defence, he closed with me and fought strenuously for life. He was light, agile and muscular, and would have proved a powerful opponent to most men,—but his strength was as nothing to the super-human force that possessed *me*—the force of twenty devils as it were, brought into opposition against this one struggling existence! Wild voices sang, shouted, and yelled in my ears "Kill! Kill! Kill him!"—circles of fire swam before me,—and once as he swerved back from my grasp and nearly fell, I laughed aloud,—laughed, as I sprang at him anew, and shook him furiously to and fro as a wild beast shakes its prey! Closing with me again, he managed to seize my arms in such wise that for the moment I was rendered powerless; and once more his great dark eyes flamed into mine.

"Are you mad, Gaston Beauvais?" he gasped. "Do you want to murder me?" As he spoke, my rapid glance travelled upward to his neck which showed itself bare and white just above the close-set priestly band of his black habit,—I saw where I could win my fearful victory! I made a pretence of falling beneath his hold,—and involuntarily his grasp relaxed;—in one breath of time I had wrenched myself free,—in another, my two hands were closed fast on that smooth, full, tempting throat, gripping it hard as a vice of steel!... Tighter!—tighter!—and the fair face above me grew dark and convulsed,—the flashing grey-black eyes started horribly from their sockets!—tighter still!—one desperate choking struggle more, and he fell prone on the sward, I falling upon him, so that the deadly clutch of my fingers never relaxed for a second! Once down, my murderous task was easier,—my wrists had more power,—and I pressed all my weight upon the swelled and throbbing arteries beneath my relentless hands. Those eyes!—how they glared at me!—wide open and awfully protruding!—would the cursèd life in them never be quenched?

"Die!—die!" I muttered fiercely under my breath. "God!—That it should take so long to kill a man!"

Suddenly a great shudder shook the limbs over which I crouched brute-like and watchful,—those pulsing veins beneath my fingers stopped,—the head fell further back,—the lips parted, showing a glimmer of pearly teeth within, in the ghastly semblance of a smile,—and then,—then came silence! Silence!—horror! What now? What did it all mean? What was this cold awfulness?—this dumb, rigid, staring thing?—was this Death? Seized by a swift frenzied fear, I sprang up,— I looked about me everywhere. Everywhere solitude!—only the whispering of trees and shining of stars! Only Nature, and *that*,—that strange still figure on the grass with arms outspread on either side, like a Christ without the cross. What had I done? I considered doubtfully; looking vaguely at my own hands the while. No stain of blood was on them! Had I then killed him? No,—no!—not possible! He had swooned!

I stepped close up to him,—I took his hand,—it was warm.

"Guidèl!" I said,—and the sound of my own voice startled my sense of hearing—"Come, get up!—do not lie there as if I had murdered you! Get up, I tell you!—Our quarrel is over,—we will fight no more!"

Silence! The wide open eyes regarded me fixedly,—they were glazing over with a strange film! A bird darted from one of the branches overhead, and flew rustlingly through the air,—the sound of its wings threw me into a cold perspiration, and I fell on my knees shuddering through and through. I crawled reluctantly up to that dark recumbent mass, ... if he were dead, ... if he were dead, I thought, quaking in every limb,—why then—I would shut those eyes! My previous mad fury had given place to weak, half delirious terror;—I could scarcely summon up the courage to reach out my hands and let them hover above those pallid features, that in all the contorted agony of their last expression were already freezing under my very gaze, into a marble-like rigidity! I touched the eyelids,—I pressed them firmly down over the glassy balls beneath, ... So!—they could look at me no longer!

With a sigh of relief I crawled away again, and once at arm's length from the corpse, stood upright, wondering what next I should do. I had killed Silvion Guidèl;—this seemed evident;—and yet I strove to represent to myself that it was not, could not be so. Some inherent weakness of the heart's action might have done the deed;—it could not have been the mere grasp of my hands! But, after all,—had I not *meant* to kill him? Had not the idea slept in my brain for weeks without declaring itself?— and had it not become actively paramount with me from the moment I saw him that night? Yes!—it was a murder—and a premeditated one if truth were told! I had violently taken a man's life!—I! I looked awfully round at my victim,—and looking, shrieked aloud! The eyes—the eyes that I had shut so fast, were *open*,—wide open and protruding more than ever! How they stared at me!—with what fixed and pertinacious solemnity! In a delirium of haste I rushed back to the horrible figure lying prone, and pressed my fingers hard and heavily once more upon the cold yet rebellious lids. But in vain!—they curled upwards again from under my very touch, and again left the eyeballs glassy and bare! I moaned and shivered, while the sweat poured from my forehead in the extremity of fear that possessed me;—and then all at once a ghastly thought flashed across my brain. I had heard scientists say that the eyes of a murdered man took in their last look the portrait of his murderer, and that this so terribly painted miniature could be reproduced faithfully, line for line! Was such a thing possible?... Oh why, why could I not shut those eyes! I could stamp them out with my heel if I dared,—but, I did not dare!

Again I looked up at the stars,—then down at the river, whereof the tide, now risen higher, made a roaring-rush of music,—and while I waited thus, the church clock, the same I had heard before, struck midnight. Only an hour had passed since I stood on the bridge, an evil-brooding man, but not—not a *murderer*! Only an hour!—it seemed an eternity,—and truly it had wrought an eternal change in my destiny. I had shed no blood,—and yet the air was red about me,—the very stars seemed to dart at me fiery tongues of flame,—but the worst thing of all was the horrible passiveness, the dreadful inertness of my strangled foe,—for oddly enough though I knew I had killed him, at the same time I could not comprehend why he should be dead!

I had turned my back upon the corpse,—but now I forced myself to confront it once more,—though I strove my utmost to avoid its terrible eyes. Silvion Guidèl's eyes they were,—imagine it!—those strained, glazed, anguished, crystalline-looking things,—the eyes that had darkened with thought and lightened with love,—the eyes that had flashed their passionate prayer into the eyes of Pauline!—ha! what would *she* say if she could see them now? Pauline's lover!—Pauline's seducer!—The libertine,—the Priest!—there he lay, the holy chosen servant of Mother Church,—*dead*! Dead, and I had killed him! Good! For the millionth time or more, the world's Cain had proved himself stronger than God's favoured Abel![1] And yet, you say, some of you, that God is "omnipotent." Tell this to children if it please you,—but spare me, an *absintheur*, from so unnecessary a Lie!

For a time my brain reeled under its pressure of sickening thought; but at last the idea came to me that I must somehow or other get rid of the body. I could not bury it;—I could perhaps drag it or carry it to that shelving bank which jutted slopingly into the river at a little distance from where I stood, and from thence I could fling it into the Seine. And the Seine would wash it to and fro and disfigure it with mud and weedy slime, and carry it perchance down like a log, past cities, towns, and villages, to the sea,—the wide merciful, blank sea, where so many things are sunk and forgotten. Unless—unless it should be found and dragged ashore!—but I would not suffer myself to think of this probability; and stringing up every nerve and sinew to the labour, I began my task. I lifted the corpse from the ground, always appalled by the never-closing eyes, and by dint of the strongest effort, managed to support its chill and awful weight across my shoulder, while I staggered to the river's brink. There stopping and panting for breath, I laid it down, struck once more by the tremulous sense that life after all might still be fluttering within this

---

[1] Sons of Adam and Eve. Cain killed Abel because he was jealous that God had accepted Abel's sacrifice and not his own.

stiffening mass of clay. Keeping my courage firm, I bent down and felt the heart;—it was stone-still; but some small thing like a packet lay pressed above it. An *Agnus Dei*?[1] Oh no!—priests do not always wear purely sacred symbols! I took it out,—it was a folded paper which I opened, and found inside a thick curl of soft dark hair. Pauline's hair!— I knew it well!—the touch of it, the delicate scent of it, made me tremble as with an ague-fit—and I hastily thrust it into my own breast. Then I stared again down at my work,—and smiled! There was no beauty in this lifeless lump before me,—death by strangulation had so blackened and distorted the features that their classic regularity and fairness was no longer perceivable,—the very parting of the lips, which had at first seemed like a faint serene smile, had now stiffened into a hideous grin. Death is not always beautiful, *mes amis*![2] The pretty sentimentalists may imagine it so if they choose, but it is far more often repulsive in its effects than admirable, believe me! And if it chance that you are doomed to die by the close pull of the hangman's cord about your throat, or the grip of a madman's fingers close on your windpipe, you may be sure your countenance will not be a model for sculptors afterwards!

Now, as I stood regarding my victim steadfastly, a certain grim pleasure began to stir throbbingly in my veins. I—I, alone and unassisted, had destroyed all that subtle mechanism of manhood called God's handiwork; I had defaced all that comeliness on which Nature seemed to have set her fairest seal! Why should I have been so terrified at those open eyes, I thought, self-scorningly?—they were dead things and lustreless;—their reproachful expression was mere *seeming*! Quick!— Into the quiet waters with such useless carrion!—let it first sink like a stone, and then float, a disfigured blubber mass, on the destroying tide! For water, like earth, breeds hungry corpse-devouring creatures, who will make short work of even such sacred goods as a priest's dead body!—besides,—there is no blood—no sign of violence anywhere,— no proof of—of—*murder*! Stay, though!—there are marks on the throat,—the marks of my throttling fingers—but what of that? Surely the river's quiet working will efface these in an hour!

Raising myself stiffly erect, I peered round about me on all sides, and scanned the opposite bank of the Seine scrutinizingly, lest haply some lonely musing soul should be walking there and watching the water ripple caressingly beneath the moon,—but there was no one visible. I

---

[1] Cake of wax blessed by the pope and stamped with an emblem of a lamb bearing a cross or flag (representing Christ).

[2] French for "my friends."

might have been alone in a desert, so profoundly still and solitary was the night;—all nature seemed gravely occupied in watching *me,* or so I fancied; the heavens leaned towards me with all their whirling stars, as though I had drawn them down to stare wonderingly at my slain man! Once more I lifted the body;—this time the head fell back over my arm with sickening suddenness, and a light wind fanned the clustering hair backwards from the brow. Looking,—for some resistless instinctive force compelled me to look,—I saw a slight but deep scar running just across the left temple,—whereupon a new fear assailed me. If found, would the corpse be recognized by that scar?—was there anything else that might give a clue to its identity, and so start long and circumstantial inquiries and researches which in the end might track *me* out as the murderer? I laid my horrid burden down again, and hastily ransacked the pockets of the priestly garments,—there was not a letter or paper by which anything could be traced,—only a return ticket to Rome, which I tore up,—an old breviary and a purse containing about four hundred francs. There was no name in the breviary, and I put it back together with the purse, in the place where I had found it. In leaving the money thus untouched, I calculated that if discovered at all, the body would probably be taken for that of a suicide,—as a murdered man is generally, especially in France, deprived of valuables. That sort of suspicion,—that idea of *murder*—how the word chilled me!—would in this case be averted;—for I attached no importance to the circumstance of the priest's garb. Priests are as apt to kill themselves as other people, are they not? They have more reason, I should say,—knowing themselves to be such false pretenders!

Satisfied with my examination,—though I could not do away with that scar on the temples,—I raised the rigid weight, now grown heavier, once more,—the arms hung downwards, stiff and inert,—one of the hands swinging round as I moved, touched me, and I nearly shrieked aloud, it was so clammy cold! I reached the edge of the shelving bank, and then, staggering slowly, inch by inch, along the natural pier of stones that ran out into the river, I flung the corpse from me, far forward, with all my might! It fell crashingly through the water, the sonorous echo of its fall resounding on both banks of the stream to such an extent that it seemed to me as if all the world must instantly awaken from sleep and rush upon me in crowds to demand a knowledge of my crime! I waited—my heart almost standing still with sheer terror,—waited till the close circles in the water widened and widened and melted in smooth width away. No sound followed,—no cry of "Murder!" startled the night,—all was quiet as before,—all as watchfully observant of me as if each separate leaf on the branches of the trees had eyes!

I hurried back to the spot where the struggle had taken place, and there with eager hands and feet, I scraped and smoothed the torn and trampled earth, and walked and re-walked upon it till it looked neatly flat as a board in the clear light of the moon; aye!—I even overcame my shuddering reluctance so far that I coaxed and pulled and brushed up the crushed grass on which Silvion Guidèl had fallen down to die!

So!—all was done!—and, pausing, I surveyed the scene. Oh scene of perfect peace!—Oh quiet nook for love indeed!—such love as brought Pauline here in the dewy hush of early mornings when instead of praying at Mass as she so prettily feigned, she listened to a pleading more passionate than the cold white angels know! For love—the love we crave and thirst for,—is not methinks of holy origin!—it was germinated in hell,—born of fire, tears, and restless breathing;—the bright chill realms of heaven hold no such burning flame! I cursed the fairness of the place, and Nature mocked my curses with her smile! The tranquil moon gazed downwards pensively, thinking her own thoughts doubtless as she swept through the sky—the trees quivered softly in their dreams, touched perchance by some tender rush of memory; and the river lapped whisperingly against the shore as though delivering kisses from the blossoms on one side to the blossoms on the other. The sleepy enchantment of the mingling midnight and morning seemed to hang like an opaline mist in the air,—and as I looked, I suddenly felt that I, standing where I did, had all at once become a mere outcast and alien from the beautiful confidence of Nature,—that the dead body I had just thrown in the murmuring waters was far more gathered into the heart of things than I!

Slowly and with an inexplicable reluctance I crept away,—slinking through the trees like a terrified beast that shuns some fierce pursuer, afraid of both moonbeams and shadows, and still more afraid of the deep calm about me—a calm that could almost be felt. I stole out of the Bois, and set foot on the Suresnes bridge—a loose plank creaked beneath my tread, and the sound sent the blood up to my brow in a hot rush of pain,—and then—then some impulse made me pause. Some deadly fascination seized me to lean my arms upon the bridge-parapet and look over, and down, into the river below. The water heaved under me in a silvery white glitter,—and while I yet gazed downwards,—a dark mass drifted into view—a heavy floating blackness, out of which two glistening awful eyes stared at me and at the moon!... Clutching at the edge of the parapet, I hung over it, with beating heart and strain-ing sight—anon, I broke into a fit of delirious laughter!

"Silvion!" I whispered. "Silvion Guidèl! What!—are you there again? Not at rest yet? Sleep, man!—sleep!—Be satisfied with God now you have found Him!—Good night, Guidèl; good night!"

Here my laughter suddenly spent itself in a fierce sobbing groan,—I shrank back from the parapet trembling in every limb,—and like a sick man waking out of a morphia-sleep I suddenly realized that the tide seemed turning towards Paris,—not down to the sea! Well!—what then?

I dared not stop to think! With a savage cry I covered my face and fled,—fled in furious panting haste and fear, rushing along the silent road to the city with the reckless speed of an escaped madman, and followed as it seemed by the sound of a whispered "*Murder! Murder!*" hissed after me by the vindictive, upward-flowing Seine, that pursued me closely as I ran, bearing with it its awful witness to the black deed I had done!

CHAPTER 23

For the next three or four days I lived in a sort of feverish delirium, hovering betwixt hope and terror, satisfaction and despair. But by degrees I began to make scorn of my own cowardice,—for though I searched all the newspapers with avidity, I never saw the one thing I dreaded,—namely an account of the discovery of a priest's body in the Seine, and a suggestion as to his having come to his death by foul means. Another murder had been committed in Paris just the day after I had killed Silvion Guidèl,—and it was a particularly brilliant one—quite dramatic in fact. The mistress of a famous opera-tenor had been found in her bed with her throat cut, and the tenor,—a ladies' favourite,—had been arrested for the crime in spite of his gracefully stagey protestations of sorrow and innocence. This event was the talk of Paris,—so that one corpse more or less found floating in the river would at such a time of superior excitement, awaken very little if any interest. For though the natural stupidity of the unofficial man is great, that of the strictly offi-cial personage is even greater. I allude to the chiefs of the police. They are a very excellent class of blockheads, and their intentions are no doubt admirably just and severe,—but they have too much routine,—too many little absurd minutae of rule and etiquette out of which they can seldom be persuaded to move. It follows therefore that the perpetrators of crime having *no* specially designed routine, and being generally totally lacking in etiquette, very often get the best of it, and that nine out of every ten murders remain undiscovered. It was so in my case;—it is so, you may be sure, in many another. Mere formal rule must be done away with in the task of discovering a murderer,—there must be less writing of documents, and tying of tape and docketing of accounts, and more instant and decisive action. When, for example, a policeman on duty finds the body of a murdered and mutilated woman in a pool of blood on a doorstep, and after much cogitation and reflection, decides that bloodhounds might be useful in tracking the murderer, he would do well to get those bloodhounds at once, and not wait till the next day when the scent will be more than difficult to pursue. But *I* have no wish to complain of the respectable muddlers who sit in their offices carefully writing descriptive reports and compiling evidence, while the criminal they are in search of probably passes under their very windows with a triumphant grin and scornful snap of his gory fingers,—not at all! On the contrary, I am very much obliged to them for never taking any trouble about me, and allowing me to roam through Paris at perfect liberty. For at the time I strangled my priestly victim, I had no wish to be even known as a murderer. 'Extenuating circumstances' would no doubt have been found sufficiently strong to save me from the guillotine,—but I really should not have cared particularly for the renown thus attained! Yes, *renown!*—why not? A notorious Paris murderer gains more renown in a day than a great genius in ten years! There is a difference in the quality of renown, you say? I fail to see it! There is a difference, if you like, in the character of the *person* renowned,—but the renown itself,—the dirty hand-clapping of the many-tongued mob,—is almost the same. Because, they, the mob, never praise a great man without at the same time calumniating him for some trifling fault of character,—likewise, they never cast their opprobrium at a criminal without discovering in him some faint speck of virtue of which they frequently make such a hullabaloo, that it sometimes looks as if they thought him a martyred saint after all! "Not this man but Barrabas!"[1] is shouted all over the world to this day,—the crucifixion of great natures and the setting free of known robbers is the common and incessant custom of the crowd. We are told by the teachers of the present age, that Christianity is a myth,—its Founder a legendary personage,—but by all the creeds of this world

---

[1] Misspelling of Barabbas, the robber and insurrectionary leader whom Pilate released from prison instead of Christ.

and the next, the story remains, and I fancy will continue to remain, a curiously true and significant symbol of Humanity!

I suppose nearly a week must have passed since I had sent Silvion Guidèl to his account with that Deity he professed to serve, when one day, straying down a back-street which was a short cut to the obscure hotel I inhabited, I saw Pauline! It was dusk, and she was hurrying along rapidly; but for one instant I caught sight of the young childish face, the soft blue eyes, the dark curling clusters of hair. She did not perceive me, and I followed her at a distance, wondering whither she was bound and how she lived. She was miserably clad,—her figure looked thin and shadowy;—but she walked with a light swift step,—a step which to my idea seemed to imply that some interest, or hope, or ambition still kept her capable of living on, though lonely and abandoned in the wild and wicked world of Paris. Suddenly at a corner she turned and disappeared,—and though I pursued her almost at a run I could not discover in what direction she had gone. Provoked at my own stupidity, I rambled aimlessly up and down the place I found myself in, which was a mere slum, and was on the point of asking some questions at one of the filthy-looking hovels close by, when a hand grasped me from behind, a loud laugh broke on my ears, and I turned to confront André Gessonex.

"Have you come to pay me a visit, *mon cher*?" he asked, with a half mock, half ceremonious salutation. "By my faith, you do me an inestimable honour! I live here"—and he pointed to a miserable tenement house, the roof of which was half off and the three upper windows broken. "Behold!—'*Appartements Meublés!*'"[1] And true enough, this grandiose announcement was distinctly to be read on a wooden placard dangling from one of the aforesaid broken windows. "I have the best floor," he continued, "the 'salon' let us call it!—the other apartments I have not examined, but I should imagine they must be airy! No doubt they also command an open view from the roof, which would probably be an attraction. But enter, *cher* Beauvais!—enter!—I am delighted to welcome you!—the best I have of everything is at your service!"

And with the oddest gestures of fantastic courtesy, he invited me to follow him.

I hesitated a moment,—he looked so wild about the eyes, so gaunt and ghastly, that for the moment I wondered whether I was not perhaps entrusting myself to the tender mercies of a madman. Then I quickly remembered my own condition,—what if he *were* mad, I thought, his

---

[1]   French for "furnished apartments."

madness had not led him to commit Murder,—not yet! I had a certain dull curiosity to see what sort of a place he dwelt in,—I therefore complied with his request, and stumbled after him up a crooked flight of stairs, nearly falling over a small child on the way,—a towzled half-naked creature who sat crouched in one of the darkest corners, biting a crust of bread and snarling over it in very much the fashion of an angry tiger-cat. Gessonex, hearing my smothered exclamation, turned round, spied this object, and laughed delightedly.

"*Ah voilà!*"[1] he cried. "That is one of my models of the Stone Period! If you have kicked that charming boy by accident, Beauvais, do not trouble to ask his pardon! He will not appreciate the courtesy! Two sentiments alone inspire him—fear and ferocity!" And seizing the mass of hair and rags by its neck, he shook it to and fro violently, exclaiming, "*Viens ici, bête! Montre tes dents et tes ongles! Viens!*"[2]

The creature uttered some unintelligible sound, and got on its feet, still biting the crust and snarling,—and presently we all three stood in a low wide room, littered about with painter's materials and various sorts of tawdry rubbish, where the first thing that riveted the eye was an enormous canvas stretched across the wall, on which the body of a nude Venus was displayed in all its rotundity,—the head, not yet being painted in, was left to the imagination of the spectator. Gessonex, still grasping the bundle he called his "*bête,*"[3] threw himself down in a chair, after signing to me to take whatever seat I found convenient,—and, with the handle of a long paint-brush, began by degrees to lift the matted locks of hair from off the face of the mysterious object he held, who bit and growled on continuously, regardless of his patron's attentions. Presently, a countenance became visible—the countenance of a mingled monkey and savage,—brutish, repulsive, terrible in all respects save for the eyes, which were magnificent,—jewel-like, clear and cruel as the eyes of a wolf or a snake.

"There!" said Gessonex triumphantly, turning the strange physiognomy round towards me,—"There's a boy for you! He would do credit to the antediluvian age, when Man was still in process of formation. The chin, you see, is not developed,—the forehead recedes like that of the baboon ancestor,—the nose has not yet received its intellectual prominence,—but the eyes are perfectly formed. Now about these

---

[1] French for "Ah, there!"
[2] French for "Come here, beast! Show your teeth and your nails! Come!"
[3] French for "beast."

eyes,—you have in them the most complete disprovers of the poetical sentiment about 'eyes being the windows of the soul,'[1] because this child has simply *no* soul. He is an animal, made merely, if we quote Scripture, to 'arise, kill and eat.'[2] He has no idea of anything else,—his thoughts are as the thoughts of beasts, and the only sentences of intelligible speech he knows are my teaching. Hear him!—he will give you an excellent homily on the duty of life. Now tell me, *mon singe,*"[3] he went on, addressing the boy, and artistically lifting up another of his matted curls with the paint-brush handle,—"What *is* life! It is a mystery to us! Will you explain it?"

The savage little creature glared from one to the other of us in sullen curiosity and fear,—his breath came quickly, and he clenched his small grimy hands. He was evidently trying to remember something and found the effort exhausting. Presently between his set teeth came the words—

"*J'ai faim!*"[4]

"Bravo!" said Gessonex approvingly, still arranging the hair of his *protégé*. "Very well said! You see, Beauvais, he understands life thoroughly, this child! '*J'ai faim!*' All is said! It is the universal cry of existence— hunger! And the remarkable part of the whole affair is, that the complaint is incessant; even *Monsieur Gros-Jean,*[5] conscious of the well-rounded paunch he has acquired through over-feeding, has never had enough, and at morning, noon, and evening, propounds the hunger problem afresh, and curses his *chef* for not providing more novelties in the *cuisine.*[6] Humanity is never satisfied,—it ransacks earth, air, ocean,— it gathers together gold, jewels, palaces, ships, wine—and woman,—and then, when all is gotten that can be gained out of the labouring universe, it turns its savage face towards Heaven and apostrophizes Deity with a defiance. 'This world is not enough for my needs!' it cries. 'I will put Orion in my pocket and wear the Pleiades in my button-hole![7]—I will have Eternity for my heritage and Thyself for my comrade!—*j'ai faim!*'"

He laughed wildly, and opening a drawer near him, took out a small apple and threw it playfully aloft.

---

[1]   Proverbial.

[2]   From the New Testament of the Bible, Acts 10.13.

[3]   French for "my monkey."

[4]   French for "I'm hungry."

[5]   French term for "bumpkin," "countryman," or "coarse person."

[6]   French word for "kitchen."

[7]   Orion is a constellation of stars which form the shape of a hunter; the Pleiades is a cluster of stars in the constellation Taurus, especially the seven larger ones.

"Catch!" he cried, and the boy, tossing up his head caught it between his teeth with extraordinary precision as it fell. "Well done! Now let us see you munch as Adam[1] munched before you—ah! what a juicy flavour!—if it were only a stolen morsel, it would be ever so much sweeter! Sit there!"—and he pointed to an old bench in the opposite corner, whereon the strange child squatted obediently enough, his wonderful eyes sparkling with avidity as he plunged his sharp teeth in the fruit which was to him an evident rare delicacy. "He is the most admirable rat-hunter in Paris, I should say," went on Gessonex, eyeing him encouragingly. "Sharp as a ferret and agile as a cat, he kills the vermin by scores, and what is very human, eats them with infinite relish afterwards!"

I shuddered.

"Horrible!" I exclaimed involuntarily. "Does he starve, then?"

Gessonex regarded me with a rather pathetic smile.

"My friend, we all starve here," he answered placidly. "It is the fashion of this particular *quartier*.[2] Some of us,—myself for instance,—consider food a vulgar superfluity; and we take a certain honest pride in occasionally being able to dispense with it altogether. It is more *à la mode* in this neighbourhood, which, however, is quite aristocratic compared to some others close by! All the same I am really rather curious to know what has brought *you* here, *mon cher*! May I, without rudeness, ask the question?"

"I saw a woman I thought I knew," I answered evasively. "And I followed her."

"Ah!—And the result?"

"No result at all. I lost sight of her suddenly, and do not know how or where she disappeared."

"Ah!" said Gessonex again meditatively. "Women are very plentiful in these parts,—that is, a certain sort of women,—the flotsam and jetsam of the *demi-monde*. From warm palaces, and carriages drawn by high-fed prancing horses they come to this,—and then,—to that!"

He pointed through the window and my eyes followed his gesture,—a glittering strip of water was just pallidly visible in the deepening twilight,—a curving gleam of the Seine. A faint tremor shook me, and to change the subject, I reverted once more to the 'brute' child, who had now finished his apple and sat glowering at us like a young owl from under his tangled bush of hair.

---

[1] The first man in traditional theology. The Fall of man occurred when Adam and Eve disobeyed God's prohibition against eating from the tree of knowledge.

[2] Paris is divided into neighbourhoods called "quartiers," meaning "quarters."

"What is he?" I asked abruptly.

"My dear Beauvais, I thought I had explained!" said Gessonex affably. "He is a type of the Age of Stone! But if you want a more explicit definition, I will be strictly accurate and call him a production of Absinthe!"

I started,—then controlled myself as I saw that Gessonex regarded me intently. I forced a smile.

"A production of Absinthe?" I echoed incredulously.

"Precisely? Of Absinthe and Mania together. That is why I find him so intensely interesting. I know his pedigree, just as one knows the pedigree of a valuable dog or remarkable horse,—and it is full of significance. His grandfather was a man of science."

I burst out laughing at the incongruity of this statement, whereupon Gessonex shook his head at me in mock-solemn reproach.

"Never laugh, *mon ami*, at a joke you do not entirely understand. You cannot understand, and you never *will* understand the awful witticisms of Mother Nature,—and it is a phase of her enormous jesting that I am about to relate to you. I repeat,—this boy's grandfather was a man of science;—with a pair of spectacles fixed on his nose and a score or so of reference volumes at hand, he set about prying into the innermost recesses of creation. Through his *lunettes*[1] he peered dubiously at the Shadow-Brightness called God, and declared Him to be *non est*.[2] He weighed Man's heart and mind in his small brazen scales, and fossilized both by his freezing analysis. He talked of Matter and of Force,—of Evolution and of Atoms. Love went on, Faith went on, Grief went on, Death went on,—he had little or nothing to do with any of these,— his main object was to prove away the flesh and blood of Life, and leave it a mere bleached skeleton. He succeeded admirably,—and at the age of sixty, found himself *alone with that skeleton*! He dined with it, supped with it, slept with it. It confronted him at all hours and seasons, rattling its bones, and terrifying him with its empty eye-sockets and dangling jaws. At last,—one stormy night,—its hand roused him from sleep, and showed him the exact spot where his razor lay. He took the hint immediately,—made the long artistic slit across his throat which the skeleton so urgently recommended,—and died—or, to put it more delicately, departed to that mysterious region where *lunettes* are not worn, and knowledge is imparted without the aid of printer's ink. He was a very

---

[1] French for "eyeglasses."
[2] Latin for "non-existent."

interesting individual,—great when he was alive, according to the *savants*,[1]—forgotten in the usual way, now he is dead."

He paused, and I looked at him enquiringly.

"Well?"

"Well! He left one son, a charmingly dissolute individual, whose sole delight in life was to drink and dance the hours away. A remarkable contrast to his father, as you may imagine!—and herein Dame Nature began her little psychological game of cross-purposes. This fellow, born in Paris, and a worshipper of all things Parisian, took to Absinthe in very early manhood,—not that I blame him for that in the least,—because it is really a fascinating hobby!—and afterwards, through some extraordinary freak of the gods, became an actor. Night after night, he painted his face, padded his legs, and strutted the boards, feigning the various common phases of love and villainy in that lowest of all professions, the ape-like art of Mimicry. He, unlike his revered parent, never troubled himself concerning the deeper questions of life at all; Chaos was his faith, and Nonentity his principle! His stage-appearance, particularly his leg-padding, captivated a dancer, who went by the *sobriquet*[2] of 'Fatima'; — she passed for an Odalisque,[3] but was really the daughter of a Paris washerwoman,—and *he* was likewise smitten by *her* abundant charms,— wild eyes, flowing hair and shapely limbs,—and after a bit the two made up their minds to live together. Marriage of course was not considered a necessity to people of their reputable standing,—it seldom is, in these cases! Love however, or the passion they called by that name, proved much too weak and inadequate a rival to cope with Absinthe,—the 'green fairy' had taken a firm hold of our friend the actor's mind,—and whether his *amour* had turned his head, or whether the emerald elixir had played him an ill turn I cannot tell you, but for some months after he had taken up his residence with the charming 'Fatima' he was the victim of a singular and exceedingly troublesome frenzy. This was neither more nor less than the idea that his '*chère amie*'[4] was a scaly serpent whose basilisk eyes attracted him in spite of his will, and whose sinuous embraces suffocated him and drove him mad. His behaviour under these curious mental circumstances was excessively irritating,—and finally, after enduring his preposterous eccentricities till her patience (of which she had a very slight

---

[1] French term for "scholars" or "learned persons."
[2] French word for "nickname."
[3] Beautiful female slave or concubine in an Eastern harem.
[4] French for "dear friend."

stock) was entirely exhausted, *la belle*[1] Fatima bundled him off to a lunatic asylum, where, finding no sharp instrument convenient to his hand as his father had done before him, he throttled himself with his own desperate fingers. Imagine it!—such a determined method of strangulation must have been a most unpleasant exit!"

A tremor ran through me as he spoke, and I averted my gaze from his.

"It was a most unfortunate affair altogether," continued Gessonex reflectively—"and I'm afraid it must be set down chiefly to the fault of Absinthe, which though a most delightful and admirable slave, is an exceedingly bad master! Yes!"—and he mused over this a little to himself—"an exceedingly bad master! If people would only imitate *my* example, and take all its pleasures without its tyranny, how much wiser and better that would be!"

I forced myself to speak,—to smile.

"The '*passion verte*'[2] never subdues you, then? You subdue *it*?"

Our eyes met. A yellowish-red flush crept through the sickly pallor of his skin, but he laughed and gave a careless gesture of indifference.

"Of course! Fancy a man being mastered and controlled by a mere *liqueur*! The idea is sublimely ridiculous! To complete my story;—this boy here,—this exponent of the Stone Age,—is the child of the *absintheur* and his 'serpent,'—begotten of mania and born of apathy,—the result is sufficiently remarkable! I knew the parents,—also the *savant* grand-papa,—and I have always taken a scientific interest in this their only descendant. I think I know now how we can physiologically resolve ourselves back to the primary Brute-period, if we choose,—by living entirely on Absinthe!"

"But are you not a lover of Absinthe?" I queried half playfully. "A positive epicure in the flavour of the green nectar?—Why then, do you judge so ill of its effects?"

He looked at me in the most naïve wonderment.

"My friend, I do *not* judge ill of its effects!—there you quite mistake me! I say it will help us to recover our brute-natures,—and that is precisely what I most desire! Civilization is a curse,—Morality an enormous hindrance to freedom. Man was born a savage, and he is still happiest in a state of savagery. He has been civilized over and over again, believe me, through innumerable cycles of time,—but the savage cannot be gotten out of him, and if allowed to do so, he returns to his pristine

---

[1]   French expression meaning "the beautiful."

[2]   The "green passion" or, the passion for absinthe.

condition of lawless liberty with the most astonishing ease! Civilized, we are shackled and bound in a thousand ways when we wish to give the rein to our natural impulses; we should be much more contented in our original state of brutishness and nudity. And contentment is what we want,—and what in our present modes of constrained culture we never get. For example, *I* am not half as civilized as the slain unit once known as Me, whom I buried,—I told you about that remarkable funeral, did I not?—and as a natural consequence I am much happier! The Me who died was a painfully conscious creature, always striving to do good,—to attain the impossible perfection,—to teach, and love, to help and comfort his fellow-men;—now, *there* was a frightful absurd-ity! Yes! that Me was an utter fool!—he painted angels, poetic ideals and visions of ethereal ecstasy—and all the art-critics dubbed him an ass for his pains! And, *apropos* of art,—as you are here, Beauvais, I want you to see my last work—it's not a bit of use now,—but it may be worth some-thing a hundred years hence."

"Is that it?" I inquired, with a movement of my hand towards the headless undraped Venus.

"That!—oh no! That is a mere study of flesh-tints *à la* Rubens.[1] *This* is what I call my '*chef-d'oeuvre!*'"[2]

And springing up from his chair excitedly, he went towards the further end of the room, where the entire wall was covered with a dark curtain which I had not perceived before,—while, in a sort of auto-matic imitation of his patron's movements, the boy with the wild eyes followed him and crouched beside him on the floor, watching him. Slowly, and with a fastidious lingering tenderness, he drew the drapery aside, and at the same time pushed back the blind from an upper window, thus allowing the light to fall fully on the canvas displayed. I stared at it fascinated, yet appalled,—it was so sombrely grounded, that for a moment I could not grasp the meaning of the weird and awful thing. Then it grew upon me by degrees, and I understood the story it told. It was the interior of a vast church or cathedral, gloomy and unil-lumined save by one or two lamps which were burning low. In front of the altar knelt a priest, his countenance distorted with mingled rage and grief, wrenching open, by the sheer force of his hands, a coffin. Part of the lid, split asunder, showed a woman's face, still beautiful with a

---

[1] "In the style of" Peter Paul Rubens, Flemish Baroque painter (1577-1640) renowned for his paintings of voluptuous nudes.

[2] French expression meaning "masterpiece."

strangely seductive, sensuous beauty, though the artist's touch had marked the blue disfiguring shadow of death and decay beginning to set in about the eyes, nostrils, and corners of the mouth. Underneath the picture was written in distinct letters, painted blood-red—"*O Dieu que j'abjure! Rends-moi cette femme!*"[1]

A whole life's torture was expressed in the dark and dreadful scene,—and on me it had a harrowing nervous effect. I thought of Silvion Guidèl,—and my limbs shook under me as I approached to look at it more nearly. The savage child curled up on the floor, fixed its eyes upon me as I came, and pointing to the picture, muttered—

"*Joli! Joli! Il meurt!—n'est-ce pas qu'il meurt?*"[2]

Gessonex heard him and laughed.

"*Oui chère brute, il meurt!*[3] He dies of disappointed passion, as we all die of disappointed something or other, if it only be of a disappointment in one's powers of breathing. What do you think of it, Beauvais?"

"It is a magnificent work!" I said, and spoke truly.

"It is!—I know it is!" he responded proudly. "But all the same I will starve like a rat in a hole rather than sell it!"

I looked at him in surprise.

"Why?"

"Why? Because I want my name properly advertised when I am dead,—and the only way to get that done royally is to bequeath the picture to France! France, having nothing to pay for it, will be liberal of praise,—and the art-critics knowing my bones cannot profit by what they say, will storm the world with loud eulogium!"

He dropped the curtain over the painting and turned upon me abruptly.

"Tell me, Beauvais, have you tasted *absinthe* again since that night we met?"

"Of course! Frequently!"

His eyes flashed into mine with a singularly bright and piercing regard. Then he seized my hand and shook it with great fervour.

"That is right! I am glad! Only don't let the charming fairy master you, Beauvais!—always remember to keep the upper hand, *as I do!*"

He laughed boisterously and pushed his long matted locks from his temples; of course I knew he was as infatuated a prey to the fatal passion

---

[1]   French for "Oh God whom I abjure! Restore this woman to me!"
[2]   French for "Pretty! Pretty! He's dying—he's dying, isn't he?"
[3]   French for "Yes, dear beast, he's dying!"

as myself. No one loves Absinthe lukewarmly, but always entirely and absorbingly.

"Come!" he cried presently. "Let us do something amusing! Let us go to the Morgue!"[1]

"To the Morgue!" I echoed, recoiling a little,—I had seen the place once long ago and the sight had sickened me—"Why to the Morgue just now?"

"Because it is dusk, *mon ami*,—and because the charm of the electric light will give grace to the dead! If you have never been there at this hour, it will be a new experience for you,—really it is a most interesting study to any one of an artistic temperament! I prefer it to the theatre!—pray do not refuse me your company!"

I thought a moment, and then decided I would go with him. He, putting on his hat, turned to the "brute" child.

"Wait till I come back, *mon singe!*" he said, patting its towzled mane,—"Kill rats and eat them if thou wilt,—I have at present nothing else for thee."

Hearing these words I took out a couple of francs from my pocket and offered them to the boy. For a second he stared as if he could not believe his eyes,—then uttered such an eldritch screech of rapture as made the rafters ring. He kissed the money—then crawled along the floor and kissed my feet,—and finally sprang up and dashed away down the rickety stairs with the speed of a hunted antelope, while Gessonex looking after him, laughed.

"He is a droll little creature!" he said. "Now he will buy no end of things with those two silver coins,—he knows how to bargain so well that he will get double what I should get with the same amount,— moreover the people about here are afraid of his looks and his savage jabbering, and will give him anything to be rid of him. Yet the nature of the animal is such that he will put all his purchases on this table, and sit and glare at the whole *menu* without touching a morsel till I come back! He is like a dog, fond of me because I feed him,—and in this, though a barbarian, he resembles the rich man's civilized poor relations!"

---

[1] The morgue housed the bodies of unknown persons who had committed suicide or died under other mysterious circumstances. They were displayed here for identification purposes, but the morgue also became a popular attraction for the general public and for tourists.

CHAPTER 24 *paper*

We left the house together and walked through the wretched slum in which it was situated, I looking sharply from right to left to see whether, among the miserable women who were gathered gossiping drearily at different doorways, there was any one like Pauline. But no,— they were all ugly, old, disfigured by illness or wasted by starvation,— and they scarcely glanced at us, though the fantastic Gessonex took the trouble to raise his battered hat to them as he passed, caring nothing for the fact that not one of them, even by way of a jest, returned his salutation. We soon traversed the streets that lay between the quarter we had left and the Morgue, and arrived at the long, low gruesome-looking building just as a covered stretcher was being carried into it. Gessonex touched the stretcher in a pleasantly familiar style.

"*Qui va là?*"[1] he inquired playfully.

One of the bearers glanced up and grinned.

"Only a boy, m'sieu!—Crushed on the railway."

"Is that all!" and Gessonex shrugged his shoulders—"*Dieu!* How uninteresting!"

We entered the dismal dead-house arm-in-arm,—the light was not turned full on, and only a pale flicker showed us the awful slab, on which it is the custom for unknown corpses to be laid side by side, with ice cold water dripping and trickling over them from the roof above. There were only two there at the immediate moment,—the crushed boy had to be carried away "*pour faire sa toilette*"[2] before he could be exposed to public view. And not more than five or six morbid persons besides ourselves were looking with a fascinated inquisitiveness at that couple of rigid forms on the slab,—the emptied receptacles of that mysterious life-principle which comes we know not whence, and goes we know not where. As I have said, the light was very dim, and it was difficult to discern even the outlines of these two corpses,—and Gessonex loudly complained of this inconvenience.

"*Sacre bleu!*[3] We are not in the catacombs!" he exclaimed. "And when a great artist like myself visits the dead, he expects to *see* them,— not to be put to the trouble of guessing at their lineaments!"

---

[1] French phrase meaning "Who goes there?"
[2] French expression meaning "to be washed and dressed."
[3] French term for "Damn" or "Confound it!"

Those who were present stared, then smiled and seemed to silently agree with this sentiment,—and just then a sedate official-looking personage made his sudden appearance from a side-door, and recognizing Gessonex, bowed politely.

"*Pardon m'sieu!*" said this individual—"The light shall be turned on instantly. The spectators are not many!" This apologetically.

Gessonex laughed and clapped him on the shoulder.

"Ha! Thou art the man of little economies, *mon ami!*" he said. "Thou dost grudge even the dead their last lantern on the road to Styx![1] Did'st never hear of the Styx?—no matter! Come, come, light up! It may be we shall recognize acquaintances in yonder agreeably speechless personages,—one of them looks, in this dim twilight, amazingly massive,—a positively herculean monster!"

The official smiled.

"A monster truly! That body was found in the river two days ago, and m'sieu is perhaps aware that the water distends a corpse somewhat unpleasantly."

With these words and an affable nod he disappeared,—and something—I know not what, caused me to carelessly hum a tune, as I pressed my face against the glass screen, and peered in at the death-slab before me. Suddenly the light flashed up with a white glare,—hot, brilliant, and dazzling,—and for a moment I saw nothing. But I heard Gessonex saying—

"The old lady is prettier than the young man in this case, Beauvais! Death by poison is evidently more soothing to the muscles than death by drowning!"

I looked,—and gradually my aching sense of vision took in the scene. The first corpse, the one nearest to me, was that of the woman of whom Gessonex spoke;—some one standing close by began detailing her wretched history,—how she had, in a fit of madness, killed herself by eating rat-poison. Her features were quite placid—the poor old withered body was decently composed and rigid, and the little drops of trickling water rolled off her parched skin like pearls. But that other thing that lay there a little apart,—that other dark, livid, twisted mass,—was it, could it be all that was mortal of a man?

"What is that?" I asked, pointing at it, a little vaguely no doubt, for my head throbbed, and I was conscious of a peculiar straining, choking

---

[1] Mythological river of the Underworld over which the souls of the dead are ferried by Charon.

sensation in my throat that rendered speech difficult.

"'That' *was* a man, but is so no longer!" returned Gessonex lightly. "He is now an It,—and as an It is remarkably hideous!—so hideous that I am quite fascinated! I really must have a closer look at death's handiwork this time,—come, Beauvais!—M. Jéteaux knows me very well, and will let us pass inside."

M. Jéteaux turned out to be the official personage who had previously spoken to us,—and on Gessonex stating that he wanted to make a sketch of that drowned man, but that from outside the glass screen he could not see the features properly, we were very readily allowed to enter.

"Only that the face is hardly a face at all," said M. Jéteaux with affable indifference. "One can scarcely make out its right lineaments. The oddest thing about this particular corpse is that the eyes have not been destroyed. It must have been floating to and fro in the water three days if not more, and it has been here two,—but the eyes are like stone and remain almost uninjured."

Thus speaking, he accompanied us close up to the marble slab, and the full view of the dead creature loomed darkly upon us. The sight was so ghastly that for a moment the careless Gessonex himself was startled,—while I,—I staggered backward slightly, overcome by a reeling sense of nausea. Ugh!—those blue, swollen, contorted limbs!—It had been impossible to straighten them, so said the imperturbable M. Jéteaux,—in fact a "toilette" for this twisted personage had been completely beyond the skill of the valets of the Morgue. I mastered the sick fear and abhorrence that threatened to unsteady my nerves,—and came up, out of sheer bravado, as closely as I could to the detestable thing,—I saw its face, all horribly distended,—its blue lips which were parted widely in a sort of ferocious smile,—its great protruding eyes— God!—I could hardly save myself from uttering a shriek as the man Jéteaux, desirous of being civil to Gessonex, lifted the unnaturally swollen head into an upright position, and those stony yet wet-glistening eyes stared vacantly at me out of their purple sockets! *I knew them!*— truth to tell I had known this repulsive corpse all the time if I had only dared to admit as much to myself! And if I had had any doubts as to its identity, those doubts would have been dispelled by that straight scar on the left temple, which, as the drenched hair was completely thrown back from the forehead, was distinctly visible. Yes!—all that was mortal of *Silvion Guidèl* lay there before me, within touch of my hand,—I the murderer stood by the side of the murdered!—and as far as I could control myself, I showed no sign of guilt or horror. But there was a loud singing and roaring about me like the noise of an angry river rising into flood,—my brain was giddy,—and I kept my gaze pertinaciously fixed on the body out of sheer inability to move a muscle or to utter a word. The cool business-like voice of M. Jéteaux close at my ear, startled me horribly though, and nearly threw me off my guard.

"He was a priest,"—said the official with a slight accent of contempt—"the clothes prove that,"—and he indicated by a gesture a set of garments (*I* recognized them well enough!) hanging up, as is the Morgue custom, immediately above the corpse they once covered,—"but of what Order, and where he came from no one can tell. We found a purse full of money upon him, and a breviary with no name inside,—he has not been identified and he will not keep any longer,—so to-morrow he will be removed."

"Where to?" I inquired,—my voice sounding thick and far away, and I coughed violently, as a sort of excuse for huskiness.

Gessonex laughed. He was busy making a rapid pencil sketch of the corpse.

"Where to? My dear friend, to the comfortable '*fosse*,'[1]—the ditch of death wherein we all drown in the end. Of course we can have our own private patches of ditch if we choose to pay for such a luxury,—but we shall fertilize the earth better if we allow ourselves to be thrown all together in one furrow,—it is more convenient to our survivors, and we may as well be obliging. The public '*fosse*' is really the most sensible sort of grave, and the most truly religious because it is the most equalizing. This man"—and he gave a few artistic finishing touches to his sketch—"was evidently good-looking once."

Jéteaux smiled incredulously.

"*M'sieu* is an artist, and can imagine good looks where none have ever existed," he observed politely.

"Not at all,"—returned Gessonex still working rapidly with his pencil. "This body is certainly very much swollen by the water, but one can guess the original natural outlines. The limbs were finely moulded,—the shoulders and chest were strong and nobly formed,—the face—yes!—it is probable the face was an ideal one—there are faint marks upon it that still indicate beauty,—the eyes were evidently remarkable,—why Beauvais!—what pleasant jest amuses you?"

For I had broken out into an uproarious fit of laughter,—laughter

---

[1] French for "grave." Those who could not afford cemetery burial (which was about two-thirds of the population in the 1880s and 1890s) were placed in the "fosses communes," large pits, each containing forty to fifty coffins.

that I could no more restrain than an hysterical woman can restrain her causeless tears. And when Gessonex and his friend Jéteaux stared at me in surprise I became fairly convulsed and laughed more than ever! Presently, struggling for utterance—

"*Mon Dieu!*" I said. "Would you have me play tragedian over such a spectacle as this? M. Jéteaux says he was a priest!—well, look at him now, how well he represents his vocation! Is not his mouth most piously open and ready to say an 'Ave!'—and his eyes—those admirable eyes!—have they not quite the expression of sanctimonious holiness so ingeniously practised by all of his crafty calling?—A priest, you say!—a worshipper of God,—and see what God has done for him! Defaced his beauty, if beauty he ever had, and brought him to the Morgue!—what a droll way this GOD has of rewarding His sworn servants!"

M. Jéteaux appeared vaguely troubled by my words.

"Perhaps he was a bad priest,"—he suggested. "There are many,—and this one may have committed so flagrant an error of discipline that he probably imagined the only way out of it was suicide."

I laughed again.

"Oh! you think him a suicide?"

"Assuredly! There are no marks of violence,—and besides, he was not robbed of his money."

These foolish officials! Always the same ideas and the same routine! Inwardly I congratulated myself on my own cunning,—and turning to Gessonex, asked him if he had finished his sketch.

"Though what you want it for I cannot imagine!" I added irritably.

Gessonex shrugged his shoulders.

"Only for the sake of study," he returned. "Just to see what Death can do for a man's anatomy! See!"—and he touched the throat of *that* which had been Guidèl,—"the arteries here are swollen, and in such a way, that one could almost fancy he had been strangled! Again, observe the ribs,—they start through the flesh,—not from meagreness, but from having made a powerful effort,—a struggle for life. Here the sinews of the leg are strained as though they had used all their resisting power against some opposing body. I am not an artist for nothing,"—he continued, affably turning to Jéteaux—"and I assure you, life did not go easily or willingly out of this priest,—he was probably murdered."

Curse him and his knowledge of anatomy, I thought!—why the devil could he not hold his tongue! M. Jéteaux however only smiled, shrugged his shoulders as Gessonex had done, and spread out his hands with a deprecatory gesture.

"*Mais*[1]—m'sieu, there are no proofs of such a crime," he said. "And besides—a priest!"

"True!" I interposed, the passion of ribald laughter once more threatening me,—"a dead priest is a ridiculous object! A dead dog or a dead cat is more worthy of pity in these times! France—our France—has nobly declared herself sick of priests, *mon ami*"—and I clapped him familiarly on the shoulder—"and one less in the world is a relief to us all!"

Jéteaux was quite delighted with this remark.

"M'sieu is a thinker?" he queried pleasantly, as we left the Morgue death-chamber, and turned our backs on the livid mass of perishing clay once called "*le beau*"[2] Silvion Guidèl.

"In a way—yes!" I responded swiftly. "I think as Paris thinks—that life is a *bagatelle*, and death a satisfactory finish to the game! And to invent a God and pay priests to keep up the imposture is a disgrace to humanity and civilization! But we are progressing quickly!—we shall soon sweep away the old legends and foolish nursery superstitions—and bury them,—bury them,—as—as yonder lump of dead priestcraft is to be buried to-morrow,—in the common 'fosse,' the receptacle for all decayed and useless lumber which obstructs or is offensive to the world!" I paused,—then on a sudden impulse added—"He *is* to be buried to-morrow—positively?"

Jéteaux looked surprised.

"The body in there?—*Mais, certainement!*[3]—it could not be kept another day!"

This idea diverted me extremely. "It" could not be kept another day! Here was this brave Silvion Guidèl,—once beautiful as Antinous, brilliant, witty, amorous,—he was no more than so much tainted flesh that could not be kept above ground another day! And I had brought about this pleasant end for him—even I! I had murdered him,—I could have identified him,—and yet—no one guessed—no one imagined the secret that there was between that quiet corpse and me! Despite my efforts I laughed wildly again, when we went out of the Morgue, though I did not venture to give another backward glance through the glass screen,—laughed so loudly and long that Gessonex, always easily moved, began to laugh also, and soon agreed with me that the sight of a dead priest was after all a very amusing entertainment.

---

[1] French for "but."
[2] French for "the handsome."
[3] French for "but certainly."

"Let me see your sketch"—I said to him presently, when we stopped a moment to light our cigarettes,—then, as he handed it to me—"It's not badly done!—but you have made the eyes like saucers! '*Bon Dieu!*' they seem to say—'*Rends-moi la grace d'être amoureux pour une fois, quoique je suis prêtre! Qu'est-ce-que la vie sans aimer une femme!*'"[1]

I broke into another laugh, and with an air of complete unconsciousness, tore the sketch into minute fragments, and sent the bits floating on the breeze. Gessonex uttered a quick exclamation.

"*Sacre-bleu!* Do you know what you have done, Beauvais?"

I looked at him blankly.

"No! What?"

"You have torn up my sketch!"

"Have I? Positively I was not aware of it! I thought it was a bit of waste paper! Forgive me!—I often get frightfully abstracted every now and then,—*ever since I took to drinking Absinthe!*"

He turned upon me with nervous suddenness.

"*Dieu!* Have you taken to drinking it then, as a matter of course?"

"As a matter of life!—and death!" I replied curtly.

He stared at me, and seemed to tremble,—then he smiled.

"Good! Then—you must also take the consequences!"

"I find the consequences fairly agreeable,—at present."

"Yes—so you may,—so you will,—until——" He broke off, then looked sharply behind him,—he had an unpleasant trick of doing that, I noticed,—and he had frequently startled and annoyed me by those quick glances backward over his own shoulder;—"Can you see him?" he whispered abruptly, a peculiar expression coming into his eyes as they met mine.

"See him? See whom?" I queried amazed.

He laughed lightly.

"A friend,—or rather I should say, a creditor! He wants his bill paid,—and I am not disposed to settle with him—not just yet!"

We were standing at the quiet corner of a quiet street,—I looked from right to left, and round and about everywhere, but not a soul could I perceive but our two selves.

I shrugged my shoulders.

"Pshaw! You are dreaming, Gessonex!"

He smiled,—very strangely, I thought.

---

[1] French for "Good God ... Take mercy on me and let me love just once, even though I am a priest! What is life without loving a woman!"

"*So are you!*" he responded calmly. "Dreaming heavily,—a fiery, drunken dream! I know!—I know all the pleasure of it—the madness of it! But Absinthe has its waking hours as well as its sleep,—and your time for waking has not come. But it will come—you may be sure of that!" He paused,—then added slowly—"I am sorry you tore up my sketch!"

"I also regret it, *mon cher*!" I declared, puffing away at my cigarette— "But it was an ugly memory,—why did you want to keep such a thing?"

"To remind me of death"—he replied,—"to teach me how hideous and repulsive and loathsome the fairest of us may become when the soul has been snatched out of us and lost in the elemental vortex. God!—to think of it!—and yet, while the soul still remains in us we are loved,—actually *loved*!"

"While the *life* is in us, you mean!" I said, with a cold smile. "There is no soul, so say the Positivists."[1]

"The soul—the life;"—murmured Gessonex dreamily—"are they not one and the same? I think so. The vital principle,—the strange etherial essence that colours the blood, strings the nerves, lights the eyes, and works the brain,—we call it Life,—but it is something more than life—it is Spirit. And imagine it, Beauvais!—we have it in our own power to release that subtle thing, whatever it is,—we can kill a man and lo!—there is a lump of clay, and that strange essence has gone!— or, we can kill ourselves,—with the same result. Only, one wonders,— what becomes of us?"

"*Nirvana*![2]—Nothingness!" I responded airily. "That is the Buddhist idea of eternal bliss—an idea that is very fashionable in Paris just now!"

Gessonex turned his great wild eyes upon me with a look of vague reproach.

"Fashionable in Paris!" he echoed bitterly—"even so may one talk of being fashionable in Hell! The city that permits the works of a Victor Hugo[3] to drop gradually into oblivion, and sings the praises of a Zola who with a sort of pitchfork pen turns up under men's nostrils such literary garbage as loads the very air with stench and mind-malaria!—faugh! Religion of any sort for Paris in its present condition is absurd,—it is like offering the devil a crucifix! Do not accept Paris opinions, Beauvais!— there is something more than 'nothingness' even in apparently clear

---

[1] Those who believe only in positive facts and observable phenomena and reject metaphysics and theism. Positivism was a philosophy ascribed to by Republicans.

[2] Buddhist and Hindu concept of beatitude achieved through the extinction of individuality and desires.

[3] French Romantic novelist, dramatist, and poet (1802–85).

space"—and he glanced about him with an odd touch of dread in his manner—"Believe me, there is *no* nothingness!" He paused,—laughed a little, and passed his hand across his brows as though he swept away some unpleasing thought. "Good night!" he said then,—"I must return to my *enfant terrible*,[1] who will starve till I come. Again I wish you had not torn up that sketch!"

"So do I, as you harp upon the subject so persistently"—I said, with mingled irritation and contrition,—the latter feeling I feigned as best I could—"I am really very sorry! Shall we go back to the Morgue and ask permission to take another view?"

"No, no!"—and Gessonex shuddered slightly—"I could not look at that dead priest again!—There was something clamorous in his eyes,—they were alive with some ghastly accusation!"

I forced a smile.

"How unpleasantly grim you are this evening Gessonex!" I said carelessly. "I think I will leave you to your own reflections. *Au revoir!*"

"Wait!" he exclaimed eagerly; and catching my hand in his own he pressed it hard. "I *am* 'grim,' as you say—I know it! I am at times more gloomy than a monk whose midnight duty it is to dig his own grave to the sound of a muffled bell. But it is not always so!—my natural humour is gay,—mirthful enough to please the wildest *bon viveur*,[2] I assure you! You shall see me again soon, and we will have sport enough!—tell me where I can meet you now and then?"

I named a *café* on the Boulevard Montmartre,—a favourite resort for many a sworn *absintheur*.

"Ah!" he said laughingly. "I know the place,—it is too grand for me as a rule,—I hate the light, the gilding, the painted flowers, the ugly fat *dame de comptoir*,[3]—but no matter!—I will join you there some evening. Expect me!"

"When?" I asked.

"Soon! When my creditors will allow me to appear in public! *Bon soir!*"[4]

He lifted his hat with his usual fantastic flourish,—smiled, and was gone. I drew a deep breath of relief. For some moments the strain on my nerves had been terrific,—I could scarcely have endured his companionship a moment longer. I looked about me. I was in a very

---

[1] French expression for a person who causes embarrassment by unruliness.
[2] French for "pleasure seeker."
[3] French for "barmaid."
[4] French phrase meaning "Good evening."

quiet thoroughfare,—there were trees, and seats under the trees,—but I was near the river,—too near! I turned resolutely away from it, and walked onward,—walked till I found myself in the lively and brilliant Avenue de l'Opéra. Here I presently saw a man pacing slowly ahead of me, clad in a priest's close black garments. He annoyed me terribly,—I had no desire to be reminded of priestcraft just then. Could I not get in front of this leisurely strolling fool? I hurried my steps,—and with an effort came up with him,—passed him—looked round—and recognized *Silvion Guidèl!*... Silvion Guidèl,—pale-faced, dreamy-eyed, serene as usual,—only, ... as I stared wildly at him, his lips fell apart in the horrible leering smile I had seen on the face of the corpse in the Morgue! Heedless of what I did, I struck at him fiercely,—my clenched fist passed *through* his seeming substance!—he vanished into impalpable nothingness before my eyes! I stamped and swore,—a hand seized and swung me to one side.

"*Va-t'en, bête!*" said a rough voice. "*Tu te grises trop fort!*"[1]

Drunk! I! I reeled back from the push this insolent passer-by had given me, and rallying my forces, took to walking again as rapidly as possible, concentrating all my energies on speed of movement; and refusing to allow myself to *think*.

I soon reached a *café* whereof I was a known frequenter, and called for the one, the only elixir of my life, the blessed anodyne of conscience, the confuser of thought; and drank and drank till the very sense of being was almost lost, and all ideas were blurred and set awry in my brain,—drank, till with every vein burning and every drop of blood coursing through my body like hissing fire, I rushed out into the calm and chilly night, maddened with a sort of furious, evil ecstasy that was perfectly indescribable! The spirit of a mocking devil possessed me,—a devil proud as Milton's Satan,[2] insidious as Byron's Lucifer,[3] and malevolently cunning as Goethe's Mephistopheles,[4]—the world seemed to me a mere child's ball to kick and spurn at,—the creatures crawling on it, stupid emmets born out of a cloud of dust and a shower of rain! Yes—

---

[1] French for "Get going, beast!...You're getting too drunk."

[2] John Milton, English poet (1608-74) whose representation of Satan appears in *Paradise Lost* (1667), an epic poem detailing the fall of man.

[3] George Gordon, Lord Byron, English Romantic poet (1788-1824) who represents the devil as Lucifer in *Cain* (1821), a story of the first family of Genesis told from the perspective of Cain who is influenced by Lucifer to reject God.

[4] Johann Wolfgang von Goethe (1749-1832), German poet, playwright, and novelist whose devil, Mephistopheles, appears in *Faust* (1808), offering to use his supernatural powers in the service of Faust in exchange for Faust's soul.

I was maddened—gloriously maddened!—maddened into a temporary forgetfulness of my crime of Murder!—and bent on some method of forgetting it still more and more utterly! Where should I go?—what should I do? In what resort of fiends and apes could I hide myself for a while, so as to be sure, quite sure that I should not again meet that pale yet leering shadow of Silvion Guidèl?

END OF VOLUME 2

CHAPTER 25

Pausing for a moment, while the pavement rocked unsteadily beneath me, I tried to shape some course of immediate action, but found that impossible. To return to my own rooms and endeavour to rest was an idea that never occurred to me; rest and I were strangers to each other. I could not grasp at any distinct fact or thought,—I had become for the time being, a mere beast, with every animal instinct in me awake and rampant. Intelligence, culture, scholarship,—these seemed lost to me,—they occupied no place in my drugged memory. Nothing is easier than for a man to forget such things. A brute by origin, he returns to his brute nature willingly. And I,—I did not stand long considering, or striving to consider my own condition there where I was, close by the Avenue de l'Opéra, with the stream of passers-by coming and going like grinning ghosts in a dream,—I hurled myself, as it were, full into the throng and let myself drift with it, careless of whither I went. There were odd noises in my ears,—ringing of bells, beating and crashing of hammers,—it seemed to my fancy that there, spread out before me was a clear green piece of water with a great ship upon it;—the ship was in process of building, and I heard the finishing blows on her iron keel,— the throbbing sound of her panting engines;—I saw her launched, when lo!—her giant bulk split apart like a sundered orange—and there, down among her sinking timbers lay a laughing naked thing with pale amber hair, and white arms entwined round a livid corpse that crumbled into a skeleton as I looked, and anon, from a skeleton into dust! All the work of my Absinthe-witch!—her magic lantern of strange pictures was never exhausted! I rambled on and on—heedless of the people about me,—eager for some distraction and almost unconscious that I moved,—but burning with a sort of rapturous rage to the finger-tips,—a sensation that would easily have prompted and persuaded me to any deed of outrage or violence. Mark me here, good reader, whoso-ever you are!—do not imagine for a moment that my character is an uncommon one in Paris! Not by any means! The streets are full of such as I am,—men, who, reeling home in the *furia*[1] of Absinthe, will not stop to consider the enormity of any crime,—human wolves who would kill you as soon as look at you, or kill themselves just as the fancy takes them,—men who would ensnare the merest child in woman's

---

[1] Latin for "frenzy" or "madness."

shape, and not only outrage her, but murder and mutilate her afterwards,—and then, when all is done, and they are by some happy accident, caught and condemned for the crime, will smoke a cigar on the way to the guillotine and cut a joke with the executioner as the knife descends! You would rather not know all this perhaps?—you would rather shut your eyes to the terrific tragedy of modern life and only see that orderly commonplace surface part of it which does not alarm you or shock your nerves? I dare say!—just as you would rather not remember that you must die! But why all this pretence?—why keep up such a game of Sham? Paris is described as a brilliant centre of civilization,—but it is the civilization of the organ-grinder's monkey, who is trained to wear coat and hat, do a few agile tricks, grab at money, crack nuts, and fastidiously examine the insect-parasites of his own skin. It is not a shade near the civilization of old Rome or Athens,—nor does it even distantly resemble that of Nineveh or Babylon. In those age-buried cities,—if we may credit historical records,—men believed in the dignity of manhood, and did their best to still further ennoble it;—but we in our day are so thoroughly alive to our own ridiculousness generally, that we spare neither time nor trouble in impressing ourselves with the fact. And so our most successful books are those which make sport of, and find excuse for, our vices,—our most paying dramas those which expose our criminalities in such a manner as to just sheer off by a hair's breadth positive indecency,—our most popular preachers and orators those which have most rant and most hypocrisy. And so we whirl along from hour to hour,—and the heavens do not crack, and no divine thunderbolt slays us for our misdeeds—if they *are* misdeeds! Assuredly the Greek Zeus[1] was a far more interesting Deity than the present strange Immensity of Eternal Silence, in which some people perchance feel the thought-throbbings of a vast Force which broods and broods and waits,—waits maybe for a fixed appointed time when the whole universe as it now is, shall disperse like a fleece of film, and leave space clear and clean for the working out of another Creation!

As I tell you, if I had wanted money that night, I would have murdered even an aged and feeble man to obtain it! If I had wanted love,—or what is *called* love in Paris, I would have won it, either by flattery or force. But I needed neither gold nor woman's kisses,—of the first I still had sufficient,—of the second, why!—in Paris they can always be secured at the cost of a few napoleons and a champagne supper. No!—I wanted

---

[1]   Supreme deity of Greek mythology.

something that gold could not buy nor woman's lips persuade,—Forgetfulness!—and it enraged me to think that this was the one, the only thing that my Absinthe-witch would not give me in all its completeness. Some drinkers of the Green Elixir there are who can win this boon,—they sink into an apathy that approaches idiotism, as the famous Dr. Charcot[1] will tell you,—they almost forget that they live. Why could not *I* do this? Why could I not strike into fragments at one blow, as it were, this burning, reflecting, quivering dial-plate of memory that seared and scorched my brain? Aimlessly hurrying on as though bound on some swift errand, yet without any definite object in view, I arrived all at once in front of a gateway over which a garish arch of electric light flashed its wavering red, blue, and green,—a sort of turnstile wicket marked the side-entrance, with an inscription above it in large letters—"BAL MASQUÉ! ENTRÉE LIBRE!!"[2] There are plenty of such places in Paris of course, though I had never set foot in one of them,—dancing-saloons of the lowest type where the "Entrée Libre" is merely held out as a bait to attract a large and mixed attendance. Once inside, everything has to be paid for,—that is always understood. It is the same rule with all the *cafés-chantants*—one enters *gratis*,[3]—but one pays for *having* entered. The sound of music reached me where I stood,—wild, harsh music such as devils might dance to,—and without taking a second's thought about it,—for I could not think,—I twisted the bars of the turnstile violently and rushed in,—into the midst of a hurly-burly such as no painter's brush has ever dared devise,—a scene that could not be witnessed anywhere save in "civilized" Paris. In a long *salle*, tawdry with bright paint and common gilding, whirled a crowd of men and women fantastically attired in all sorts of motley costumes,—some as clowns, others as sheeted corpses,—others as laundresses, fishermen, sailors, soldiers, *vivandières*,[4]—here was a strutting caricature of Boulanger,[5]—there an exaggerated double of the President of the Republic;[6]—altogether a wild and furious crew, shrieking, howl-

---

[1] French physician (1825-93) who specialized in neurological disorders and hysteria.
[2] French, meaning "Masked ball. Free admission."
[3] Latin word meaning "free."
[4] French for a woman who follows the army or lives in a garrison town and sells provisions to soldiers.
[5] George Ernest Jean Marie Boulanger (1837-91). French General and member of the Radical party whose popularity with the people made him a menace to the parliamentary Republican government. At the height of his power in 1889 he was tried and condemned for treason.
[6] Marie François Sadi Carnot (1837-94). Fourth president of the third French Republic.

ing, and dancing like lunatics just escaped from detention. Some few wore masks and dominos,—but the greater part of the assemblage were unmasked,—and my entrance, clad merely as a plain civilian, excited no sort of notice. I was to the full as *de rigueur*[1] for such an entertainment as any one else present. I flung myself into the midst of the gesticulating, gabbling vortex of people with a sense of pleasure at being surrounded by so much noise and movement,—here not a soul could know me,—here no unpleasant thought or fanciful impression would have time to write itself across my brain,—here it was better than being in a wilderness,— one could yell and scream and caper with the rest of one's fellow-apes and be as merry as one chose! I elbowed my way along, and promised an offi- cious but very dirty waiter my custom presently,—and while I tried to urge my muddled intelligence into a clearer comprehension of all that was going on, the crowd suddenly parted asunder with laughter and shouts of applause, and standing back in closely pressed ranks made an open space in their centre for the approach of two women discreetly masked,—one arrayed in very short black gauze skirts, the other in blood-red. Attitudinizing for a moment in that theatrical *pose* which all dancers assume before commencing their evolutions, they uttered a peculiar shout, half savage, half mirthful,—a noisy burst of music answered them,—and then, with an indescribable slide forward and an impudent bracing of the arms akimbo, they started the "*can-can*,"—which though immodest, vile, vulgar, and licentious, has perhaps more power to inflame the passions of a Paris mob than the chanting of the 'Marseillaise.'[2] It can be danced in various ways, this curious fandango of threatening gesture and amorous invitation,—and if the dancers be a couple of heavy Paris laundresses or *pétroleuses*,[3] it will probably be rendered so ridiculously as to be harmless. But, danced by women with lithe, strong, sinuous limbs,—with arms that twist like the bodies of snakes,—with bosoms that seem to heave with suppressed rage and ferocity,—with eyes that flash hell-fire through the black eye-holes of a conspirator-like mask,—and with utter, reckless, auda- cious disregard of all pretence at modesty,—its effect is terrible, enrag- ing!—inciting to deeds of rapine, pillage, and slaughter! And why? Why, in Heaven's name, should a mere dance make men mad? Why?—Mild

---

[1] French expression meaning "required by custom or etiquette."

[2] National anthem of France, written in 1792 by Claude Joseph Rouget de Lisle. It was offi- cially adopted in 1795, but was then shunned by Napoleon I, the restored Kings, and Napoleon III. It was permanently adopted in 1879 during the French Republic.

[3] French term for a female miscreant who commits arson by means of petroleum, an act which was practised frequently, by both men and women, during the Paris Commune.

questioner, whoever you are, I cannot answer you! Why are men made as they are?—will you tell me that? Why does an English Earl marry a music-hall singer? He has seen her in tights,—he has heard her roar forth vulgar ditties to the lowest classes of the public,—and yet he has been known to marry her, and make her "my lady"—and a peeress of the realm! Explain to me this incongruity,—and I will explain to you then why it is that the sight of the "*can-can*" danced in all its frankness, turns Parisian men for the time being, into screeching, stamping maniacs, whom to see, to hear, to realize the existence of, is to feel that with all our 'culture,' we are removed only half a step away from absolute barbarism! On me, the spectacle of those two strong women, the one wearing the colour of the grave, the other the colour of blood, acted as a sort of exhilarating charm,—and I howled, stamped, shrieked, and applauded as furiously as the rest of the onlookers. More than this, when the dance was over, I approached the black siren and besought her to honour me with her hand in a waltz,—an invitation which I accompanied by a whisper in her ear—a whisper that had in it the chink of base coin rather than the silvery ring of courtly homage,—she had her price of course, like all the women there, and that price I paid. I whirled her several times round the room—for she waltzed well,—and finally, sitting down by her side, asked her, or rather I should say commanded her, as I was paymaster for the evening, to remove her mask. She did so,—and displayed a handsome coarse visage,—badly rouged, and whitened with pearl powder,—her way of life had rendered her old before her time,—but the youth and wickedness in her magnificent eyes made amends for her premature wrinkles.

"*Tiens Madame! Comme tu es laide!*" I said with brusque candour. "*Mais c'est une jolie laideur!*"[1]

She laughed harshly.

"*Oui! je suis laide —je le sais!*"[2] she responded indifferently. "*Que veux-tu, mon jeune farouche? J'ai vécu!*"[3]

It was my turn to laugh now, and I did so uproariously. She had *lived*—she! She thought so, in all good faith,—she believed she knew life inside and out, and all through. She, who had probably never opened a noble book or looked at a fine picture,—she, who would certainly have no eyes for scenery or the wonder and science of Nature,—she, whose experience had been limited to the knowledge of the most despicable

---

[1] French for "How ugly you are madame!... But it's a pretty ugliness!"
[2] French for "Yes, I am ugly—I know!"
[3] French for "What do you expect, my young wild one? I've lived!"

side of despicable men's characters;—she had *lived*, which was tanta-
mount to saying that she comprehended the object and intention of
living! What a fool she was!—what a shallow-brained fool!—and yet, it
is for such women as she was, that men occasionally ruin themselves and
their families. The painted successful wanton of the stage never lacks
diamonds or flowers,—the honest wife and mother often lacks bread!
Such is the world and the life of the world, and God does nothing to
improve it. What an impassively dumb spectator of things He is in His
vast, clear empyrean! Why does He not "rend the heavens and come
down"—as the old Psalmist implored Him to do,[1]—then we should
understand,—we should not have to wait for death to teach us. And the
question is, *will* death teach us? Is death a silence, or an overpoweringly
precise explanation? Ah!—At present, not knowing, we laugh at the
idea,—but—it is a laugh with a shudder in it!

Well! I danced again and yet again with the female fiend who had
"lived," as she said,—I gave her champagne, ices, *bon-bons*,—all that her
greedy appetite demanded, and I watched her with a certain vague amusement, as she ate and drank and laughed and jested, while the wine flushed
her cheeks and lent an extra devilish sparkle to her eyes. Between the
dances, we sat together in a sort of retired alcove adorned with soiled
hangings of faded crimson, and at the next table to us, in a similar kind of
compartment, were a clown and a harlequin,—the clown a man, the harlequin a woman. These two were noisily drunk—and they sang scraps of
song, whistled and screeched alternately, the female harlequin sometimes
beating her sword of lath against her knees, and anon laying it with a resonant "crack!" across her grinning companion's shoulders. Half stupefied
myself, and too confused in mind to understand even my own actions, I
stared at this pair of fools disporting themselves much as I might have
stared at a couple of dancing bears in a menagerie—and then growing
suddenly tired of their rough antics, my eyes wandered from them down
and across the length and breadth of the *salle*, where the vari-coloured
crowd still twirled and flitted and swung to and fro, like a merry-go-round
of puppets at a fair. And then I perceived a new figure in the throng,—a
stranger in black, who looked curiously out of place and incongruous, so
I fancied,—and I turned to my siren of the "can-can," who with both her
muscular white arms folded on the table, was staring hard at me with, as
I thought, an expression of intense inquisitiveness, not unmixed with fear.

---

[1] From the Old Testament of the Bible, Isaiah 64.1. The Book of Isaiah is an invective
against arrogance, corruption, and hypocrisy, and a plea for justice and salvation.

"*Voilà!*"[1] I said laughing. "A priest at a *bal masqué*! Does he not look droll? See what temptations these gentlemen of the Church yield to!"

She turned her black eyes in the direction I indicated.

"What priest?" she asked. "Where?"

"There!"

And I pointed straight before me into the *salle*, where I plainly saw the individual I meant,—a man, wearing the closely buttoned-up clerical black garment I had learned to abominate so heartily.

"I do not see him!" she said. "No real priest would dare to come here, I fancy! Some one in priest's clothes perhaps—dressed up for fun—yes!—that is very, likely. A priest is always ridiculous! Find him, and I will dance with him!"

I laughed again, and flipped her on the bare arm that lay nearest to me.

"You will be a fool if you do!" I told her carelessly. "He will have no money for you, and you have had enough champagne. *There* he is!— there, with his back turned to us! Don't you see him now?"

She stared and stared,—then shrugged her shoulders.

"No!"

A sudden horrible fear froze my blood. I sprang up from my seat.

"Come!" I said hoarsely. "Come!—Quick!—Give me another dance and dance your best!"

I snatched her round the waist, and whirled her into the throng with so much celerity and violence that she nearly lost her footing and fell— but I cared little for that,—I plunged madly with her through the room and straight up to the spot where that priest was standing—standing quite still.

"Look,—look!" I whispered. "You can see him plainly enough!—I told you he was a priest, and I was right! Look!—he does not move!"

Under her rouge her face grew very pale.

"*Où donc?*" she murmured nervously. "*Je ne vois rien!*"[2]

Closer and closer we waltzed towards that motionless shape of man, and I saw the dark outlines of his figure more and more distinctly.

"You can touch him now!" I said, my voice shaking as I spoke. "Your dress brushes against him!—what!—have you no eyes!—Ah, *diable!*"[3]—and I uttered a furious cry as the figure turned its face upon me. Silvion Guidèl again, by all the Furies of fact or fiction!—Silvion

---

1   French exclamatory term meaning "There!"
2   French for "Where then?... I don't see anything!"
3   French for "devil."

Guidèl!... And this time, as I looked, he moved away rapidly, and began to slip stealthily through the crowd;—roughly flinging my partner from me I followed fast, striking out right and left with my two hands to force a passage between the foolish flocks of dancing masqueraders,—I heard shrieks of terror and amazement,—loud shouts of "*Il est fou!—il est fou!*"[1]—but I heeded nothing—nothing, save that black figure gliding swiftly on before me,—nothing until in my wild headlong rush I was stopped by the sudden consciousness of being in the fresh air. The wind blew coldly on my face,—I saw the moonlight falling in wide patterns around me,—but—was I alone? No!—for Silvion Guidèl stood there also, by the side of a great tree that spread its huge boughs downwards to the ground,—he gazed straight at me with wistful, beautiful, impassioned eyes,—but no smile crossed the quiet pallor of his countenance. He looked—yes!—exactly as he had looked before I murdered him!... Perhaps—perhaps, I thought vaguely—there was some mistake?—perhaps I had not killed him after all!—he *seemed* still to be alive!

"Silvion!" I whispered. "What now?—Silvion!"

A light breeze rustled the branches overhead,—the moonbeams appeared to gather and melt into a silvery sea—and I sprang forward, resolvedly intent on grasping that substantial-looking form in such a manner as to establish for myself the fact of its actual existence,—it rose upward from my touch like a cloud of ascending smoke and vanished utterly!... while I, striking my forehead sharply against the rough trunk of the tree where the accursëd phantom of my own brain had confronted me, fell heavily forward on the ground, stunned and insensible!

CHAPTER 26

I lay there in a dead stupor for some hours,—but I was roused to my senses at last by the ungentle attentions of a *gendarme*[2] who grasped and shook me to and fro as if I were a bag of wheat.

"*Lève-toi!*[3] Get up, beast!" he growled, his rough provincial accent making the smooth French tongue sound like the ugly snarl of a savage

---

[1] French phrase meaning "He is crazy."
[2] French word for a "policeman."
[3] French for "get up."

bull-dog. "Drunk at nine in the morning! A pretty way of earning the right to live!"

I struggled to my feet and stared haughtily at him.

"I am a gentleman!" I said. "Leave me alone!"

The fellow burst out laughing.

"A gentleman! Truly, that is easily seen! One of the old aristocracy doubtless!"

And he picked up my hat,—it was entirely battered in on one side,—and handed it to me with a derisive bow.

I looked at him as steadily as I could,—everything seemed to flicker and dance to and fro before my eyes,—but I remembered I had some money left in my pockets. I searched,—and drew out a piece of twenty francs.

"What do you know about gentlemen or aristocrats?" I said. "Do you not measure them all by this?"—and I held up the gold coin— "You called me a beast,—what a mistake that was! A drunken beggar is a beast if you like, but a *grand seigneur*[1] who amuses himself!" here I dropped the piece into his quickly outstretched palm—"*C'est autre chose, n'est-ce pas, mon ami?*"[2]

He touched his hat,—and the laughter was all on my side now! He looked such a ridiculous puppet of officialism!

"*Mais oui, monsieur!—mais oui!*"[3] he murmured confusedly, pocketing his gold. "*Mille pardons!... c'est le devoir,—vous le savez!... Enfin— monsieur, j'ai l'honneur de vous saluer!*"[4]

And he edged himself away with as much dignity as was possible in the very undignified position he occupied,—namely that of taking money to prove a beast a gentleman! His first exclamation at sight of me was honest, and *true*,—my condition was worse than bestial, for beasts never fall so low as men,—and *he* knew it and *I* knew it! But for twenty francs he could be made to say,—"*Monsieur, j'ai l'honneur de vous saluer!*" Poor devil!—Only one out of thousands like him in this droll world where there is so much bombastic prating about Duty and Honour!

Nine o'clock in the morning! So late as that!—I looked about me, and realized that I was close to the Champs Elysées; I could not imagine how I had come there, nor could I remember precisely where I had been during the past night. I was aware of a deadly sense of sickness, and

---

[1] French term for "great lord."

[2] French for "That's another thing altogether, isn't it my friend?"

[3] French for "Why yes, sir!—yes!"

[4] French for "A thousand pardons!... it's my duty, you understand! Anyway—sir, I have the honour of greeting you."

I was very unsteady on my feet, so that I was obliged to walk slowly. My hat was damaged beyond repair,—I put it on as it was, all crushed and beaten in,—and what with my soiled linen, disordered garments and unkempt hair, I felt that my appearance was not, on this fine bright morning in Paris, altogether prepossessing. But what did I care for that?—Who was to see me?—who was to know me? Humming the scrap of a tune under my breath I sauntered giddily along,—but the horrible sickness upon me increased with every step I took, and finally I determined to sit down for a while, and try to recover a firmer hold of my physical faculties. I staggered blindly towards a bench under the trees, and almost fell upon it, thereby knocking heavily against an upright dignified-looking old gentleman who just then happened to cross my path, and to whom I feebly muttered a word or two by way of apology. But the loud cry he gave startled me into a wide-awake condition more successfully than any cold *douche*[1] of water could have done.

"Gaston!—My God! *Gaston!*"

I stared stupidly at him with eyes that blinked painfully in the spring sunshine,—who was he, this tidy, respectable, elderly personage who, pale as death, regarded me with the terror-stricken air of one who sees some sudden spectral prodigy?

"Gaston!" he cried again.

Ah!—Of course! I knew him now! My father! Actually my father!—who would have thought it! I felt in a dim sort of way that I had no further claim to relationship with this worthy piece of honesty,—and I laughed drowsily as I made a feeble clutch at my battered hat and pulled it off to salute him.

"*Pardieu!*" I murmured. "This is an unexpected meeting, *mon père*? I rejoice to see you looking so well!"

White to the lips, he still stood, staring at me, one hand grasping his gold-headed cane,—the other nervously clenching and unclenching itself. Had I had any sense of filial compassion or decency left, which I had not, I should have understood that the old man was suffering acutely from such a severe shock as needed all his physical courage and endurance to battle against, and I should have been as sorry for him as I ought; but in the condition I was, I only felt a kind of grim amusement to think what a horrible disappointment I must be to him! His son! *I!* I laughed again in a stupid sort of fashion, and surveying my ill-used hat I remarked airily—

---

[1] French word for "shower."

"My presence in Paris must be a surprise to you, sir? I suppose you thought I was in Italy?"

He paid no attention to my words. He seemed quite stunned. Suddenly, rousing his faculties, as it were by a supreme effort, he made a stride towards me.

"Gaston!" he exclaimed sharply, "What does this mean? Why are you here? What has happened to you? Why have you never written to me?—what is the reason of this disgraceful plight in which I find you? *Mon Dieu!*—what have I done to deserve this shame!"

His voice shook,—and his wrath seemed close upon the verge of tears.

"What have you done, *mon père?*—why nothing!" I responded tranquilly. "Nothing, I assure you! And why talk of shame? No shame attaches to you in the very least! Pray do not distress yourself! You ask me a great many questions,—and as I am not particularly well this morning——"

His face softened and changed in an instant, and he advanced another step or two hurriedly.

"Ah!—you are ill!—you have been suffering and have never told me of it," he said, with a sort of eager relief and solicitude. "Is it indeed so, my poor Gaston?—why then, forgive my hastiness!—here,—lean on my arm and let me take you home!"

A great lump rose in my throat,—what a good simple old fellow he was,—this far away half-forgotten individual to whom I dimly understood I owed my being! He was ready to offer me his arm,—he, the cleanly respectable honourable banker whose methodical regularity of habits and almost fastidious punctilio were known to all his friends and acquaintance,—he would,—if I had made illness my sole excuse,—he would have actually escorted my draggled, dirty, slouching figure through the streets with more than the tenderness of the Good Samaritan! I!—a *murderer!*—I smiled,—his simplicity was too sincere to merit any further deception from me.

"You mistake!" I said, speaking harshly and with difficulty. "I am not ill,—not with the sort of illness that you or any one else could cure. I've been up all night,—dancing all night,—drunk all night,—going to the devil all night!—ah! that surprises you, does it? *Enfin!*[1]—I do not see why you should be surprised!—*On va avec son siècle?*"[2]

---

[1] French for "anyhow."
[2] French for "We go with the times."

He retreated from me, and a frown of deepening indignation and scorn darkened his fine features.

"If this is a jest," he said sternly, "it is a poor one and in very bad taste! Perhaps you will condescend to explain——"

"Oh, certainly!" and I passed my hand in and out my rough uncombed hair—"*Voyons!* where shall I begin? Let me consider your questions. *Imprimis,*[1]—what does this mean? Well, it means that the majority of men are beasts and the minority respectable;—needless to add that I belong to the majority. It is the strongest side, you know!—it always wins! Next,—why am I here? I really can't tell you—I forget what I did last night, and as a natural consequence, my wits have gone wool-gathering this morning. As for being still in Paris itself instead of running away to other less interesting parts of Europe, I really, on consideration, saw no reason why I should leave it—so in Paris I stayed. One can lose one's self in Paris quite as easily as in a wilderness. I have kept out of your way, and I have not intruded my objectionable presence upon any one of our mutual friends. I did not write to you, because—well!—because I imagined it was better for you to try and forget me. To finish—you ask what has happened to me,—and what the reason is of this my present condition. I have taken to a new profession—that is all!"

"A new profession!" echoed my father blankly. "What profession?"

I looked at him steadfastly, dimly pitying him, yet feeling no inclination to spare him the final blow.

"Oh, a common one among men in Paris!" I responded with forced lightness—"Well known, well appreciated,—well paid too, albeit in strange coin. And perhaps the best part of it is, that once you adopt it you can never leave it,—it does not allow for any caprice or change of humour. You enter it,—and there you are!—an *idée fixe*[2] in its brain!"

The old man drew himself up a little more stiffly erect and eyed me with an indignant yet sorrowful wonder.

"I do not understand you," he said curtly. "To me you seem foolish,—drunk,—disgraced! I cannot believe you are my son!"

"I am not!" I replied calmly. "Do not recognize me as such any longer! In the way I have chosen to live, one cuts all the ties of mere relationship. I should be of no use to you,—nor would you—pardon me for saying so!—be of any use to me! What should I do with a home or home associations?—I,—an *absintheur!*"

---

[1]   Latin for "in the first place."

[2]   French expression meaning "fixed idea."

As the word left my lips, he seemed to stagger and sway forward a little,—I thought he would have fallen, and involuntarily I made a hasty movement to assist him;—but he waved me back with a feeble yet eloquent gesture,—his eyes flashed,—his whole form seemed to dilate with the passion of his wrath and pain.

"Back! Do not touch me!" he said in low fierce accents. "How dare you face me with such an hideous avowal! An *absintheur*? You? What! You, my son, a confessed slave to that abominable vice that not only makes of its votaries cowards but madmen? My God! Would you had died as a child,—would I had laid you in the grave, a little innocent lad as I remember you, than have lived to see you come to this! An *absintheur*! In that one word is comprised all the worst possibilities of crime! Why—why in Heaven's name have you fallen so low?"

"Low?" I repeated. "You think it low? Well,—that is droll! Is it more low for example than a woman's infidelity?—a man's treachery? Have I not suffered, and shall I not be comforted? Some people solace themselves by doing their duty, and sacrifice their lives for a cause—for an idea;—and sorry recompense they win for it in the end! Now, I prefer to please myself in my own fashion—the fashion of *absinthe*. I am perfectly happy,—why trouble about me?"

His eyes met mine,—the brave honest eyes that had never known how to play at treachery,—and the look of unspeakable reproach in them went to my very heart. But I gave no outward sign of feeling.

"Is this all you have to say?" he asked at last.

"All!" I echoed carelessly. "Is it not enough?"

He waited as if to gather force for his next utterance,—and when he spoke again, his voice was sharp and resonant, almost metallic in its measured distinctness.

"Enough, certainly!" he said. "And more than enough! Enough to convince me without further argument, that I have no longer a son. My son,—the son I loved and knew as both child and man, is dead,— and I do not recognize the fiend that has arisen to confront me in his disfigured likeness! You—you were once Gaston Beauvais,—a gentleman in name and position,—you, who now avow yourself an *absintheur*, and take pride in the disgraceful confession! My God!—I think I could have pardoned you anything but this,—any crime would have seemed light in comparison with this wilful debauchery of both intelligence and conscience, without which no man has manhood worthy of the name!"

I peered lazily at him from between my half-closed eyelids. He had really a very distinguished air!—he was altogether such a noble-looking old man!

"Good!" I murmured affably. "Very good! Very well said! Platitudes of course,—yet admirably expressed!"

His face flushed,—he grasped his stick convulsively.

"By Heaven!" he muttered, "I am tempted to strike you!"

"Do not!" I answered, smiling a little —"you would soil that handsome cane of yours, and possibly hurt your hand. I really am not worth the risk of these two contingencies!"

He gazed at me in blank amazement.

"Are you mad?" he cried.

"I don't think so," I responded quietly. "I don't feel so! On the contrary, I feel perfectly sane, tranquil, and comfortable! It seems to me that you are the madman in this case, *mon père*!—forgive me for the *brusquerie*[1] of the observation!"

"I!" he echoed with a stupefied stare.

"Yes—you! You, who expect of men what is not in them,—you, who would have us all virtuous and respectable in order to win the world's good opinion. The world's good opinion! Pshaw! Who, knowing how the world forms its opinion, cares a jot, for that opinion when it is formed? Not I! I have created a world of my own, where I am sole law-giver,—and the code of morality I practise is *au fond*[2] precisely the same as is followed under different auspices throughout society;—namely; *I please myself!*—which, after all, is the chief object of each man's existence."

Thus I rambled on half incoherently, indifferent as to whether my father stayed to listen to me or went away in disgust. He had however now regained all his ordinary composure, and he held up his hand with an authoritative gesture.

"Silence!" he said. "You shame the very air you breathe! Listen to me,—understand well what I say,—and answer plainly if you can. You tell me you have become an *absintheur*,—do you know what that means?"

"I believe I do," I replied indifferently. "It means, in the end,—death."

"Oh, if it meant only death!" he exclaimed passionately. "If it meant only the common fate that in due time comes to us all! But it means more than this—it means crime of the most revolting character,—it means brutality, cruelty, apathy, sensuality, and mania! Have you realized

---

[1] French for "abruptness."
[2] French for "fundamentally."

the doom you create for yourself, or have you never thought thus far?"

I gave a gesture of weariness.

"*Mon père*, you excite yourself quite unnecessarily! I have thought, till I am tired of thinking,—I have conned over all the problems of life till I am sick of the useless study! What is the good of it all? For example,—you are a banker,—I was your partner in business (you see I use the past tense though you have not formally dismissed me); now what a trouble and worry it is to consume one's days in looking after other people's money! To consider another profession,—the hackneyed one of fighting for 'La Patrie.'[1] What does 'La Patrie' care for all the blood shed on her battle-fields? She is such a droll 'Patrie!'—one week, she shrieks out '*Alsace-Lorraine! En revanche!*'[2]—the next, she talks calmly through her printing-presses of making friends with Germany, and even condescends to flatter the new German Emperor! In such a state of things, who would endure the toil and moil of military service, when one could sit idle all day in a *café*, drinking *absinthe* comfortably instead! Ah, bah! Do not look so indignant,—the days of romance are over, sir!—we want to do as we like with our lives,—not to be coerced into wasting them on vain dreams of either virtue or glory!"

My father heard me in perfect silence. When I had finished speaking—

"That is your answer?" he demanded.

"Answer to what? Oh, as to whether I understand the meaning of being an *absintheur*. Yes!—that is my answer,—I am quite happy!—and even suppose I do become a maniac as you so amiably suggest, I have heard that maniacs are really very enviable sort of people. They imagine themselves to be kings, emperors, popes, and what not,—it is just as agreeable an existence as any other, I should imagine!"

"Enough!" and my father fixed his eyes upon me with such a coldness of unutterable scorn in them, as for the moment gave me a dim sense of shame,—"I want to hear no more special pleadings for the most degrading and loathsome vice of this our city and age. No more, I tell you!—not a word! What I have to say you will do well to remember, and think of as often as your besotted brain can think! First, then, in the life you have elected to lead, you will cease to bear my name."

I bowed, smiling serenely.

"*Ça va sans dire!*[3] I have already ceased to bear it," I answered him.

---

[1]   French for "the homeland."

[2]   *En revanche*: see page 78, note 1.

[3]   French expressions meaning "That goes without saying."

"Your honour is safe with me, sir, I assure you, though I care nothing for my own!"

He went on as though he had not heard me.

"You will no longer have any connection with the Bank,—nor any share in its concerns. I shall take in your place as my partner your cousin Emil Versoix."

I bowed again. Emil Versoix was my father's sister's son,—a bright young fellow of about my own age;—what an opening for him, I thought!—and how proud he would be to get the position I had voluntarily resigned!

"I shall send you," continued my father "whatever sums are belonging to you on account of your past work and share with me in business. That, and no more. When that is spent, live as you can, but do not come to me,—our relationship must be now a thing dissolved and broken for ever. From this day henceforth I disown you,—for I know that the hideous vice you pander to, allows for no future repentance or redemption. I *had* a son!"—and his voice quivered a little,—"a son of whom I was too fondly, foolishly proud,—but he is lost to me,—lost as utterly as the unhappy Pauline, or her no less unhappy lover, Silvion Guidèl."

I started, and a tremor ran through me.

"Lost!—Silvion Guidèl!" I stammered—"How?—lost, did you say?"

"Aye, lost!" repeated my father in melancholy accents—"If you have not heard, hear now,—for it is you who caused the mischief done to be simply irreparable! Your quondam friend, made priest, was sent to Rome,—and from Rome he has disappeared,—gone, no one knows where. All possible search has been made,—all possible inquiry,—but in vain,—and his parents are mad with grief and desolation. Like the poor child Pauline, he has vanished, leaving no trace,—and though pity and forgiveness would await them both were they to return to their homes, as yet no sign has been obtained of either."

"They are probably together!" I said, with a sudden fierce laugh. "In some sequestered nook of the world, loving as lovers should, and mocking the grief of those they wronged!"

With an impetuous movement my father raised his cane,—and I certainly thought that this time he would have struck me,—but he restrained himself.

"Oh callous devil!" he cried wrathfully—"Is it possible——"

"Is what possible?" I demanded, my rage also rising in a tumult. "Nay, is it possible you can speak of 'pity and forgiveness' for those two guilty fools? Pity and forgiveness!—the prodigal son with the prodigal daughter welcomed back, and the fatted calf killed to do them honour! Bah! What fine false sentiment! I—I"—and I struck my breast angrily—"I was and am the principal sufferer!—but see you!—because I win consolation in a way that harms no one but myself,—*I* am disinherited—*I* am disowned—*I* am cast out and spurned at,—while she, Pauline the wanton, and he, Guidèl, the seducer, are being searched for tenderly, high and low, to be brought back when found, to peace and pardon! Oh, the strange justice of the world! Enough of all this,—go!—go, you who were my father!—go! why should we exchange more words? You have chosen your path,—I mine! and you may depend upon it, the much admired and regretted Silvion Guidèl has chosen his! Go!—why do you stand there staring at me?"

For I had risen, and confronted him boldly,—he seemed nothing more to me now than a man grown foolish in his old age and unable to distinguish wrong from right. No one was near us,—we stood in a sequestered corner of the Champs Elysées, and from the broader avenues came ringing between-whiles the laughter and chatter of children at play. He,—my father—looked at me with the strained startled gaze of a brave man wounded to the death.

"Can sorrow change you thus?" he said slowly. "Are you so much of a moral coward that you will allow a mere love-disappointment in youth, to blight and wither to nothingness your whole career? Are you not man enough to live it down?"

"I *am* living it down," I responded harshly. "But, in my own way! I am forgetting the world and its smug hypocrisies and canting mockery of virtue! I am ceasing to care whether women are faithful or men honourable,—I know they are neither, and I no longer expect it. I am killing my illusions one by one! When a noble thought, or a fine idea presents itself to me (which is but seldom!) I spring at its throat and strangle it, before it has time to breathe! For I am aware that noble thoughts and fine ideas are the laughing-stock of this century, and that the stupid dreamers who indulge in them are made the dupes of the age! You look startled!—well you may!—to you, *mon père*, I am dangerous,—for—I loved you! And what I once loved is now become a mere reproach to me,—a blackness on my horizon—an obstruction in my path—so, keep out of my way, if you are wise! I promise to keep out of yours. The money you offer me I will not have,—I will beg, steal, starve,—anything, rather than take one *centime* from you, even though it be my right to claim the residue of what I earned. You shall see my face no more,—I will die and make no sign,—to you I am dead already—let me be forgotten then as the dead always are forgotten,—in spite of the monuments raised to their memory!"

He gave a despairing gesture.

"Gaston!" he cried. "You kill me!"

I surveyed him tranquilly.

"Not so, *mon père*—I kill myself,—not you! You will live many years yet, in peace and safety and good repute among men,—and you will easily console yourself for the son you have lost in new ties and new surroundings. For you are not a coward,—I am! I am afraid of the very life that throbs within me,—it is too keen and devilish—it is like a sharp sword-blade that eats through its scabard,—I do my best to blunt its edge! Blame me no more,—think of me no more,—I am not worth a single regret, and I do not seek to be regretted. I loved you once, *mon père*, as I told you,—but now, if I saw much of you,—of your independent air, your proud step, your sincere eyes—I dare say I should hate you!—for I hate all things honest! It is part of my new profession to do so"—and I laughed wildly—"Honesty is a mortal affront to an *absintheur*!—did you not know that? However, though the offence is great, I will not fight you for it—we will part friends! Adieu!"

I held out my hand. He looked at it,—did not touch it,—but deliberately put his cane behind his back, and folded his own two hands across it. His face was paler than before and his lips were set. His glance swept over me with unutterable reproach and scorn,—I smiled at his expression of dignified disgust,—and as I smiled, he turned away.

"*Adieu, mon père!*" [1] I said again.

He gave no word or sign in answer, but with a slow, quiet, composed step paced onward,—his head erect,—his shoulders squared,—his whole manner as irreproachable as ever. No one could have thought he carried worse than a bullet-wound in his heart! *I* knew it—but I did not care. I watched his tall figure disappear through the arching foliage of the trees without regret,—without remorse—indeed with rather a sense of relief than otherwise. He was the best friend I ever had or should have in the world—this I realized plainly enough,—but the very remembrance of his virtues bored me! It was tiresome to think of him,—and it was better to lose him, for the infinitely more precious sake of—*Absinthe.*

---

[1]   French for "Farewell, my father."

CHAPTER 27

I passed the rest of that day in a strange sort of semi-somnolence,—a state of stupid dull indifferentism as to what next should happen to me. I cannot say that I even thought,—for the powers of thinking in me were curiously inert, almost paralyzed. The interview I had had with my father faded away into a sort of pale and blurred remembrance,—it seemed to have taken place years ago instead of hours. That is one of the special charms of the *Absinthe-furia*; it makes a confused chaos of all impressions, so that it is frequently impossible to distinguish between one event occurring long ago and one that has happened quite recently. True, there are times when certain faces and certain scenes dart out vividly from this semi-obscure neutrality of colour, and take such startling shape and movement as to almost distract the brain they haunt and intimidate,—but these alarms to the seat of reason are not frequent,—at least, not at first. Afterwards——But why should I offer you too close an explanation of these subtle problems of mind-attack and overwhelment? I tell you my own experience;—you can, and I dare say you will pooh-pooh it as an impossible one,—the mere distraught fancy of an excited imagination,—but,—if you would find out and prove how truly I am dissecting my own heart and soul for your benefit, why take to *Absinthe* yourself and see!—and describe the result thereafter more coherently than I—if you can!

All day long, as I have said, I roamed about Paris in a dream,—a dream wherein hazy reflections, dubious wonderments, vague speculations, hovered to and fro without my clearly perceiving their drift or meaning. I laughed a little as I tried to imagine what my father would have said, had he known what had truly become of Silvion Guidèl! If he could have guessed that I had murdered him! What would he have done, I wondered? Probably he would have given me up to the police;—he had a frightfully strained idea of honour, and he would never have been brought to see the justice of my crime as I did! It amused me to think of those stupid Breton folk searching everywhere for their "*bien-aimé*[1] *Silvion*"; and making every sort of inquiry about him, when all the while he was lying in the common *fosse*, festering away to nothingness! Yes!—he was nothing now,—he was dead—quite dead,—and yet, I could not disabuse myself of the impression that he was still alive! My nerves were

---

[1] French meaning "beloved."

in that sort of condition that at any moment I expected to see him,—it seemed quite likely that he might meet me at any corner of any street. This circumstance and others similar to it, make me at times doubtful as to whether Death is really the conclusion of things the Positivists tell us it is. True, the body dies—but there is something in us more than body. And how is it that when we look at the corpse of one whom we knew and loved, we always feel that the actual being who held our affections is no longer *there*? If not there, then—*where*? Silvion Guidèl for instance was everywhere,—or so I felt,—instead of being got rid of as I had hoped, he seemed to follow me about in a strange and very persistent way,—so that when he was not actually visible in spectral shape, he was almost palpable in invisibility. This impression was so pronounced with me, that it is possible, had I been taken unawares and asked some sudden question as to Guidèl's whereabouts, I should have answered; "He was with me here, just a minute ago!"

And yet—I had killed him! I knew this,—knew it positively,—and knowing, still vaguely refused to believe it! Everything was misty and indefinite with me,—and the interview I had just had with my father soon became a part of the shadowy chiaroscuro of events uncertain and nameless, of which I had no absolutely distinct memory.

I stared into many shops that afternoon, and went into some of them, asking the prices of things I had no intention of buying. I took a sort of fantastic pleasure in turning over various costly trifles of feminine adornment, such as bracelets, necklets, dangling *châtelaines*,[1] and useless fripperies of all possible design,—things that catch the eye and charm the soul of almost every simpering daughter of Eve that clicks her high Louis Quinze heels along the asphalte of our Lutetian pavements and avenues. Why was it, I mused, that Pauline de Charmilles had not been quite like the rest of her sex in such matters? I had given her costly gifts in abundance,—but she had preferred the fire of Silvion's passionate glance,—and his kiss had outweighed in her mind any trinket of lawless pearl or glistening diamond! Strange!—Yet she was the child who had laughed up in my eyes the first night I met her, and had talked in foolish school-girl fashion of her favourite "*marrons glacés*"! Heavens!—what odd material women are made of! Then, one would have thought a box of *bon-bons* sufficient to give her supremest delight,—a string of gems would surely have sent her into an ecstasy!— and yet this dimpling, babyish, frivolous, prattling feminine thing had

---

[1] Set of short chains attached to a woman's belt for carrying keys, watch, etc.

dared the fatal plunge into the ocean of passion,—and there,—sinking, struggling, dying, lost,—with fevered pulses and parched lips, still clung to the frail spar of her own self-centred hope and drifted,—content to perish so, thirsting, starving, under the cruel stars of human destiny that make too much love a curse to lovers,—yes!—actually content to perish so,—proud, thankful, even boastful to perish so, because such death was for Love's sweet-bitter sake! It was remarkable to find such a phase of character in a creature as young as Pauline; or so I thought,—and I wondered dimly whether I had loved her as much as she had loved Guidèl. No sooner did I begin to meditate on this subject than I felt that cold and creeping thrill of brain-horror which I know now,—(for it comes often and I fight as well as I can against it) to be the hint,— the far fore-warning of madness,—wild, shrieking, untameable madness such as makes the strongest keepers of maniac-men recoil and cower! I tell you, doubt it as you will, that my love for Pauline de Charmilles— the silly child who tortured and betrayed me,—was immeasurably greater than I myself had deemed it,—and I dare not even now dwell too long on its remembrance! I loved her as men love who are not ashamed of loving,—every soft curl of hair on her head was precious to me,—once!—and as I thought upon it, it drove me into a paroxysm of impotent ferocity to recall what I had lost,—how I had been tricked and fooled and mocked and robbed of all life's dearest joys! At one time, as I wandered aimlessly about the streets, I had a vague idea of setting myself steadily to track out the lost girl by some practical detective method,—of finding her, probably in a state of dire poverty and need,—and of forcing her still to be mine,—but this like all other plans or suggestions of plans, lacked clearness or certainty in my brain, and I merely played with it in my fancy as a thing that possibly might, and still more possibly might not, be done ere long.

I ate very little food all that day, and when the evening came I was conscious of a heavy depression and sense of great loneliness. This feeling was of course getting more and more common with me,—it is the deadly stupor of the *absintheur* which frequently precedes some startling phase of nightmare fantasy. I had a craving, similar to that of the previous night for the rush of crowds, for light and noise,—so I made my way to the Boulevard Montmartre. Here throngs of people swept forward and backward like the ebb and flow of an ocean-tide,—it was fine weather, and the little tables in front of the *cafés* were pushed far out, some almost to the edge of the curbstone,—while the perpetual shriek and chatter of the Boulevard monkeys, male and female, surged through the quiet air with incessant reverberations of shrill discord. Here and there one chanced on the provincial British *pater-familias*[1] new to Paris, with his coffee in front of him, his meek fat-faced partner beside him, and his olive-branches spreading around,—and it is always to a certain extent amusing to watch the various expressions of wonder, offence, severity, and general superiority which pass over the good stupid features of such men when they first find themselves in a crowd of Parisian idlers,—men who are so aggressively respectable in their own estimation that they imagine all the rest of the world, especially the Continental world, must be scoundrels. Once, however, by chance I saw a British "papa," the happy father of ten, coming out of a place of amusement in Paris where *certes*[2] he had no business to be,—but I afterwards heard that he was a very good man, and always went regularly to church o' Sundays *when he was at home*! I suppose he made it all right with his conscience in that way. It is a droll circumstance, by the bye,—that steady going-to-church of the English folk in order to keep up appearances in their respective neighbourhoods. They know they can learn nothing there,—they know that their vicars or curates will only tell them the old platitudes of religion such as all the world has grown weary of hearing—they know that nothing new, nothing large, nothing grand can be expected from these narrow-minded expounders of a doctrine which is not of God nor of Christ, nor of anything save convenience and self-interest, and yet they attend their dull services and sermons regularly and soberly without any more unbecoming behaviour than an occasional yawn or brief nap in the corner of their pews. Droll and inexplicable are the ways of England!—and yet withal, they are better than the ways of France when everything is said and done. I used to hate England in common with all Frenchmen worthy the name,—but now I am not so sure. I saw an English woman the other day,—young and fair, with serious sweet eyes,—she walked in the Champs Elysées by the side of an elderly man, her father doubtless,— and she seemed gravely, not frivolously, pleased with what she saw. But she had that exquisite composure, that serene quietude and grace,— that fine untouchable delicacy about her air and manner which our women of France have little or nothing of,—an air which made *me*, the *absintheur*, slink back as she passed,—slink and crouch in hiding till she, the breathing incarnation of sweet and stainless womanhood, had

---

[1]   Latin for "head of the family or household."
[2]   Latin for "assuredly."

taken her beauty out of sight,—beauty which was to me a stinging silent reproach, reminding me of the dignity of life,—a dignity which I had trampled in the dust and lost for ever!

Yes!—it was merry enough on the bright Boulevards that evening,—there were many people,—numbers of strangers and visitors to Paris among them. I strolled leisurely to the *café* I knew best, where my absinthe-witch brewed her emerald potion with more than common strength and flavour,—and I had not sat there so very long, meditatively stirring round and round the pale-green liquor in my glass when I saw André Gessonex approaching. I remembered then that I had told him to meet me some evening at this very place on the Boulevard Montmartre, though I had scarcely expected to see him quite so soon. He looked tidier than usual,—he had evidently made an attempt to appear more gentlemanly than ever,—even his disordered hair had been somewhat arranged with a view to neatness. He saw me at once, and came jauntily up,—lifting his hat with the usual flourish. He glanced at my tumbler.

"The old cordial!" he said with a laugh. "What a blessëd remedy for all the ills of life it is, to be sure! Almost as excellent as death,—only not quite so certain in its effects. Have you been here long?"

"Not long," I responded, setting a chair for him beside my own. "Shall I order your portion of the nectar?"

"Ah!—do so!"—and he stroked his pointed beard absently, while he stared at me with an unseeing, vague yet smiling regard—"I am going to purchase a '*Journal pour Rire*';[1]—it has a cartoon that—but perhaps you have seen it?"

I had seen it—a pictured political skit,—but its obscenity had disgusted even me. I say 'even' me,—because now I was not easily shocked or repelled. But this particular thing was so gratuitously indecent that, though I was accustomed to see Parisians enjoy both pictorial and literary garbage with the zest of vultures tearing carrion, I was somewhat surprised at their tolerating so marked an instance of absolute grossness without wit. It astonished me too to hear Gessonex speak of it,—I should not have thought it in his line. However I assented briefly to his query.

"It is clever"—he went on, still thoughtfully stroking his beard—"and it is a reflex of the age we live in. Its sale to-day will bring in much more money than I ask for one of my pictures. And that is another reflex of the age! I admire the cartoon,—and I envy the artist who designed it!"

I burst out laughing.

---

[1]   An illustrated humour magazine of the period.

"*You!* You envy the foul-minded wretch who polluted his pencil with such a thing as that?"

"Assuredly!" and Gessonex smiled,—a peculiar far-away sort of smile. "He dines, and I do not—he sleeps, and I do not,—he has a full purse,—mine is empty!—and strangest anomaly of all, because he pays his way he is considered respectable,—while I, not being able to pay my way, am judged as quite the reverse! Foul-minded? Polluted? Tut, *mon cher*! there is no foul-mindedness nowadays except lack of cash,—and the only pollution possible to the modern artist's pencil is to use it on work that does not pay!"

With these words he turned from me and went towards the little *kiosque* at the corner close by, where the journals of the day were sold by the usual sort of painted and betrinketed female whom one generally sees presiding over these street-stalls of the cheap press,—and I watched him curiously, not knowing why I did so. He was always affected in his walk,—but on this particular evening his swaggering gait seemed to be intensified. I saw him take the "*Journal pour Rire*" in his hand,—and I heard him give a loud harsh guffaw of laughter at the wretched cartoon it contained,—laughter in which the woman, who sold it to him, joined heartily with that ready appreciation which nearly all low-class Frenchwomen exhibit for the questionable and indelicate,—and I turned away my eyes from him, vaguely vexed at his manner,—I had always deemed him above mere brute coarseness. It was to me a new phase of his character, and ill became him,—moreover it seemed put on, like a mask or other disfiguring disguise. I looked away from him, as I say,—when, all at once,—the sharp report of a pistol-shot hissed through the air,—there was a flash of flame—a puff of smoke,—then came a fearful scream from the woman at the *kiosque*, followed by a sudden rush of people,—and I sprang up just in time to see Gessonex reel forward and fall heavily to the ground! In less than a minute a crowd had gathered round him, but I forced my way through the pressing throng till I reached his side,—and then,—then I very quickly realized what had happened! *Absinthe* had done its work well this time!—and no divine intervention had stopped the suicide of the body any more than it had stopped the suicide of the soul! The powers of heaven are always very indifferent about these matters,—and Gessonex had taken all laws both human and superhuman into his own hands for the nonce,—he had shot himself! He had coolly and deliberately sent a bullet whizzing through his brain,—his fingers still convulsively grasped the weapon with which he had done the deed—his mouth was streaming with blood,—and the "*Journal pour Rire*," with its detestable cartoon, lay near him, spotted and stained with the same deadly crimson hue. A ghastly sight!—a horrible end!—and yet—there was something indescribably beautiful in the expression of the wide-open, fast-glazing eyes! Mastering my sick fear and trembling I bent over him,—a young surgeon who had happened to be passing by at the time, was bending over him too and gently wiping away the blood from his lips,—and to this man I addressed a hurried word.

"Is he dead?"

"No. He still breathes. But, a couple of minutes,—*et c'est fini!*"[1]

Gessonex heard, and made a slight movement to and fro with one hand on his breast "*Oui, c'est fini!*" he muttered thickly. "*Le dernier mot du Christ!—le dernier mot de tout le monde!—c'est fini! Enfin—j'ai payé ... tout!*"[2]

And stretching out his limbs with a long and terrible shudder he expired. The features whitened slowly and grew rigid—the jaw fell,—all was over! I rose from my kneeling attitude on the pavement like one in a dream,—scarcely noting the awed and pitying faces of the crowd of bystanders,—and found myself face to face with a couple of gendarmes. They were civil enough, but they had their duty to perform.

"You knew him?" they asked me, pointing to the corpse.

"Only slightly,"—I responded,—"a mere acquaintance."

"Ah! But you can give us his name?"

"Assuredly! André Gessonex."

"What? The artist?" exclaimed some one near me.

"Yes. The artist."

"*Mon Dieu!* What a calamity! André Gessonex! A genius!—and we have so few geniuses! *Messieurs, c'est André Gessonex qui est mort! grand peintre, voyez-vous!—grand homme de France!*"[3]

I listened, stupefied. It was like one of the scenes of a wild nightmare! "Grand homme de France!" What!—so soon great, now that he was dead? Utterly bewildered I heard the name run from mouth to mouth,—people who had never known it before, caught it up like a watch-word, and in a moment the fever of French enthusiasm had

---

[1] French for "and it's over!"

[2] French for "Yes, it's over. The last word of Christ!—The last word of the whole world!—It's over! Finally—I've paid ... all."

[3] French for "Sirs, it's André Gessonex who is dead! A great painter, you see!—Great man of France!"

spread all along the Boulevards. The man who had first started it, talked louder and louder, growing more and more eloquent with every bombastic shower of words he flung to his eager and attentive audience,—the excitement increased,—the virtues of the dead man were proclaimed and exalted, and his worth found out suddenly, and as suddenly acknowledged with the wildest public acclaim! A stretcher was brought,—the body of Gessonex was laid upon it and covered reverently with a cloth,—I was asked for, and gave the address of the miserable room where the poor forlorn wretch had struggled for bare existence,—and in a very few minutes a procession was formed, which added to its numbers with every step of the way. Women wept,—men chattered volubly in true Parisian fashion concerning the great gifts of one whom they had scarcely ever heard of till now,—and I watched it all, listened to it all in a vague incredulous stupor which utterly darkened all my capability of reasoning out the mingled comedy and tragedy of the situation. But when the silly, hypocritical mourning-train had wound itself out of sight, I went away in my turn,—away from everything and everybody into a dusky, cool, old and unfrequented church, and there in full view of the sculptured Christ on the cross, I gave way to reckless laughter! Yes!—laughter that bordered on weeping, on frenzy, on madness, if you will!—for who would not laugh at the woeful yet ridiculous comedy of the world's ways and the world's justice! André Gessonex, alive, might starve for all Paris cared,—but André Gessonex dead, hurried out of existence by his own act, was in a trice of time discovered to be "grand homme de France!" Ah, ye cruel beasts that call yourselves men and women!—cruel and wanton defacers of God's impress on the human mind, if any impress of God there be,—is there no punishment lurking behind the veil of the Universe for you that shall in some degree atone to all the great who have suffered at your hands? To be nobler than common is a sufficient reason for contempt and misprisal by the vulgar majority,—and never yet was there a grand spirit shut in human form, whether Socrates or Christ, that has not been laid on the rack of torture and wrenched piecemeal by the red-hot flaying-irons of public spite, derision, or neglect. Surely there shall be an atonement? If not, then there is a figure set wrong in the mathematical balance of Creation,—a line awry,—a flaw in the round jewel,—and God Himself cannot be Perfect! But why do I talk of God? I do not believe in Him,—and yet,—one is always perplexed and baffled by the Inexplicable Cause of things. And,—somehow,—my laughter died away in a sob, as I sat in the quiet gloom of the lonely old church and watched the dim lamps twinkle above the altar; while all that was mortal of André Gessonex was being carried mournfully back to his miserable attic by the capricious, weeping, laughing, frivolous crowds of Paris that had let him die, self slain!

CHAPTER 28

A few days elapsed, and the rest of the little miserable farce of Fame was played out with all the pomp and circumstance of a great tragedy. The wretched hole which had served poor Gessonex for both studio and sleeping-room was piled so high with wreaths of roses and laurel that one could scarcely enter its low door for the abundance of flowers,—all his debts were paid by voluntary contributions from suddenly discovered admirers, and the merest unfinished sketch he had left behind him fetched fabulous sums. The great picture of the priest in the cathedral was found uncurtained, with a paper pinned across it bearing these words—

"Bequeathed to France
In exchange for a Grave!"

And the fame of it went through all the land,—everybody spoke of "Le Prêtre"[1]—as it was called,—all the newspapers were full of it,—it was borne reverently to the Musée du Luxembourg,[2] and there hung in a grand room by itself, framed with befitting splendour and festooned about with folds of royal purple;—and people came softly in to look at it and to wonder at the terror and pathos of its story,—and whispering pity for the painter's fate was on the lips of all the fair and fashionable dames of Paris, who visited it in crowds and sent garlands of rare value to deck its dead creator's coffin. And I,—I looked on, sarcastically amused at everything,—and all I did, was to visit the blossom-scented garret from time to time to see the "*brute*,"—the strange, uncouth little boy, whom Gessonex had designated as his "model for the Stone Period,"—and "a production of Absinthe." This elvish creature would not believe his patron was dead,—he could not be brought to understand it in any sort of way,—neither could he be persuaded to touch a

---

[1]   French for "the priest."
[2]   A gallery in Paris housing the works of contemporary artists.

morsel of food. Night after night, day after day, he kept watch by the mortal remains of his only friend, like a faithful hound,—his whole soul concentrated as it seemed in his large bright eyes, which rested on the set waxen features of the dead man with a tenderness and patience that was almost awful. At last the final hour came,—the time for the funeral, which was to be a public one, carried out with all the honours due to departed greatness,—and it was then that the poor "*brute*" began to be troublesome. He clung to the coffin with more than human strength and tenacity,—and when they tried to drag him away, he snarled and bit like a wild cat. No one knew what to do with him,—and finally a suggestion was made that he should be gagged, tied with cords, and dragged away by force from the chamber of death, in which the poor child had learned all he knew of life. This course was decided upon, and early in the afternoon of the day on which it was to be carried out, I went into the room and looked at him, conscious of a certain vague pity stirring at my heart for his wretched fate. The sunlight streamed in, making a wide pattern on the floor,—wreaths and cushions of *immortelles*,[1] and garlands of laurel were piled about everywhere,—and in the centre of these heaped-up floral offerings, the coffin stood,—the lid partly off, for the little savage guardian of it would never allow it to be actually shut. The face of Gessonex was just visible,—it had changed from meagreness to beauty,—a great peace was settled and engraved upon it,—and fragrant lilies lay all about his throat and brow, hiding the wound in his temple and covering up all disfigurement. The boy sat beside the coffin immovable,—watchfully intent as usual,—apparently waiting for his friend to awake. On an impulse I spoke to him,—

"*Tu as faim, mon enfant?*"[2]

He looked up.

"*Non!*" The reply was faint and sullen,—and he kept his head turned away as he spoke.

I waited a moment, and then went up and laid my hand gently on his shoulder.

"Listen!" I said slowly, separating my words with careful distinctness, for I knew his comprehension of language was limited,—"You wait for what will not happen. He is not asleep—so he cannot wake. Try to understand me,—he is not here."

The great jewel-like eyes of the child rested on me earnestly.

---

[1] Flower of papery texture that retains its shape and colour after being dried.

[2] French phrase meaning "Are you hungry, my child?"

"Not here?" he repeated dully. "Not here?"

"No," I said firmly. "He has gone! Where? Ah,—that is difficult!—but—we believe, not so very far away. See!"—and I moved the flowers a little that covered the breast of the corpse,—"This man is pale—he is made of marble,—he does not move, he does not speak—he does not look at you,—how then can it be your friend? Surely you can observe for yourself that he cares nothing for you,—if it were your friend he would smile and speak to you. He is not here,—this white, quiet personage is not he!—he is gone!"

Some glimmer of my meaning seemed to enter the boy's brain, for he suddenly stood up, and an anxious look clouded his face.

"Gone?" he echoed. "Gone?—but why should he go?"

"He was tired!" I replied, smiling a little. "He needed peace and rest. You will find him, I am sure, if you look, among the green trees where the bird's sing—where there are running brooks and flowers, and fresh winds to shake the boughs,—where all artists love to dwell when they can escape from cities. He has gone, I tell you!—and Paris is making one of its huge mistakes as usual. This is not Gessonex,—why do you not go after him and find him?"

An eager light sparkled in his eyes,—he clenched his hands and set his teeth.

"Oui,—oui!" he murmured rapidly. "*Je vais le chercher—mon Dieu!—mais ... où donc?*"[1]

Now was my opportunity, if he would only suffer himself to be persuaded away!

"Come with me," I said. "I will take you to him."

He fixed his gaze upon me,—the half-timorous, half-trusting gaze of a wild animal,—a look that somehow shamed me by its strange steadfastness, so that it was as much as I could do to meet it without embarrassment. He was a little savage at heart,—and he had the savage's instinctive perception of treachery.

"Non!" he muttered resolutely—"*Je vais le chercher, seul!... Il n'est pas ici?*"[2]

And with this query addressed more to himself than to me, he sprang again to the side of the coffin and looked in;—and then for the first time as it seemed, the consciousness of the different aspect of his friend, appeared to strike him.

---

[1] French for "Yes,—yes!... I will look for him—my God!—but ... where?"

[2] French for "No!... I will look for him myself!... He is not here?"

"*C'est vrai!*" he said amazedly. "*Il n'est pas ici! ce n'est pas lui! J'ai perdu le temps;—je vais le chercher!—mais, seul!—seul!*"[1]

And without another moment's delay he crept past me like the strange, stealthy creature he was, and running swiftly down the stairs, disappeared. I sat still in the room for some time expecting he would return, but he did not,—he was gone, heaven only could tell where. A little later in the day the men came who were prepared to take him captive,—and glad enough they were to find him no longer in their way, for no one had much relished the idea of a tussle with the wild, devilish-looking little creature whose natural ferocity was so declared and so untameable; and all the arrangements for the last obsequies of André Gessonex were now completed without any further delay or interruption. As for me, I knew I had sent the child into a wilderness of perplexities that would never be cleared up,—he would search and search for his patron probably till he died of sheer fatigue and disappointment,—but what then? As well die that way as any other,—I could not befriend him,—besides, even had I wished to do so, the chances were that he would not have trusted me. Anyway I saw him no more,—whatever his fate I never knew it.

And so it came about that the funeral of the starved, unhappy, half mad painter of "Le Prêtre" was the finest thing that had been seen in Paris for many a long day! Such pomp and solemnity,—such prancing of black steeds—such glare of blessëd candles—such odorous cars of flowers! Once upon a time a suicide was not entitled to any religious rites of burial,—but we, with our glorious Republic which keeps such a strong coercing hand on the priests, and will hear as little of God as may be,—we have changed all that! We do as seemeth good unto ourselves,—and we do not despise a man for having sent himself out of the world,—on the contrary we rather admire his spirit. It is a sort of defiance of the Divine,—and as such, meets with our ready sympathy! And I smiled as I saw the mortal remains of my absinthe-drinking friend carried to the last long rest;—I thought of his own fantastic dreams as to what his final end should be. "The Raphael of France!"—so he had imagined he would be called, when he had, in his incoherent, yet picturesque style, described to me his own fancied funeral. Well!—so far he had been a fairly accurate seer;—and in leaping the boundary-line of life he had caught Fame like a shooting-star and turned it into a torch to shed strange brilliancy on

---

[1] French for "It's true!... He is not here! That is not him! I've wasted time;—I will look for him!—but alone!—alone!"

his grave. All was well with him,—he had not missed glory in death though he had lacked food in life! All was well with him!—he had received the best possible transformation of his being,—his genius was everything, and *he* was nothing! I watched his solemn obsequies to their end,—I heard one of the most famous orators of France proclaim his praise over the yawning tomb in which they laid him down,—and when all was done, I, with every one else, departed from the scene. But some hours later,—after the earth had been piled above him,—I returned to Père-la-Chaise and sat by the just-covered grave alone. I remembered he had said he liked white violets,—and I had yielded to a foolish sentiment and had bought a small garland of them. I laid them on the cold and fresh-turned soil,—their scent sweetened the air—and I rested quietly for a few moments, thinking. My mind had been clearer since the last one or two days,—my faculties, instead of being dulled, were more than usually acute,—painfully so at times,—for every nerve in my body would throb and quiver at the mere passage of an idea through my brain. I looked up at the sky,—it was a dappled grey colour, flecked here and there with gold,—for the setting of the sun was nigh,—then I looked again at the white violets that lay, fragrant and pure, on the top of all the other wreaths of laurel and myrtle that covered Gessonex's grave. There was to be a fair monument raised above it, so the people said,—but I doubted it! Doré's[1] last resting-place remains unmarked to this day! My countrymen promise much more than they perform,—it is charming "politesse" on their part, so we do not call it lying!

Presently my eyes began to wander round and about the cemetery, which is beautiful in its way,—a veritable City of the Dead, where no rough rumours stir the air,—and by-and-bye I caught sight of the name "De Charmilles" carved on the marble portal of a tomb not very far distant. I realised that I was close to the funeral-vault of the once proud family Pauline (not I!) had disgraced and ruined,—and acting on a sudden instinct which I could not explain to myself, I rose and went towards it. It was built in the shape of a small chapel, as many of these tombs are,—it had stained glass windows and armorial bearings, and a pair of sculptured angels guarded it with uplifted crosses and drooping wings. But there was a figure in front of it kneeling at the closed door that was no angel,—but merely a woman. She was slight, and clad in poorest garments,—the evening wind blew her thin shawl about her like a gossamer sail,—but the glimmer of the late sunlight glistened on

---

[1]   Gustave Doré (1832–82). French illustrator and graphic artist.

a tress of nut-brown hair that had escaped from its coils and fell loosely over her shoulders,—and my heart beat thickly as I looked,—I knew—I felt that woman was Pauline! Now, should I speak to her, or should I wait,—wait till those open-air devotions of hers were done, and then follow her stealthily and track her out to whatever home she had found in the wilderness of the city? I pondered a moment and decided on the latter course,—then, crouching behind one of the gravestones hard by, I watched her and kept still. How long she knelt there!—and what patience women have! They never seem to tire of asking favours of the God who never hears,—or if He does hear, never answers! It must be dull work,—and yet they do it! The sun went down—the breeze blew more coldly,—and at last, with a long sigh that was half a moan, a sound that came shuddering forlornly to me where I was in hiding, she rose, and with slow, rather faltering tread went on her way out of the cemetery. I followed, walking on the grass that my footsteps might not be heard. Once she turned round,—I saw her face, and seeing it, recoiled. For it was still so wondrously fair and child-like, though ravaged by grief and made pallid by want and anxiety,—it was still the face that had captivated my soul and made me mad!—though I had now discarded that form of madness for another more lasting! Out into the public thoroughfare we passed, she and I, one following the other,—and for more than half an hour I kept her in sight, closely tracking the movement of her slender figure as it glided through the throng of street-passengers,—then,—all suddenly I lost her! With a muttered curse, I stood still, searching about me eagerly on all sides,—but vainly,—she was gone! Was she a phantom too, like Silvion Guidèl? What a fool I had been not to at once attack her with a rough speech while she was kneeling at her father's grave! It was no sentiment of pity that had held me back from so doing,—why had I let her go? Heartily enraged at my own stupidity, I sauntered discontentedly homeward. I had changed residence of late,—for my money was not inexhaustible,—and as I had refused the additional funds I might have had by right at my father's hands, it was well I had already decided to exercise economy. I had taken a couple of small rooms, decent and tidy enough in their way, in a clean and fairly respectable house,—that is, respectable for the poorer quarters of Paris,—it is only recently that I have come to the den where I live now. But that is the humour of Absinthe!—it leads one down in the social scale so gently, step by step,—so insidiously,—so carefully—that one cannot see the end. And even for me, the end is not yet!

CHAPTER 29

In the thickest part of the woods of Boulogne it is easy to fancy one's self miles away from Paris,—the landscape is gently pleasing and pastoral, and to the eyes that are unsatiated with grander scenery, it will assuredly seem beautiful. I found myself there one morning about an hour before noon,—I had taken a sudden fancy to see the green trees, to inhale the odour of the pines, and to watch the light breath of the wind sweep over the grass, ruffling it softly, just as water is ruffled, into varying ripples of delicate greys and greens. I avoided those avenues where the pretty young girls of Paris may be seen with their *gouvernantes*,[1] walking demurely along with downcast eyes and that affectation of perfect innocence which does so charm and subdue the spirits of men until,—well!—until they find it is all put on for show, to ensnare them into the marriage-market! I strolled into bosky dells, rendered sweeter by the luxury of solitude,—I, though I had the stain of murder on my soul, for once felt almost at peace! I wandered about dreamily and listlessly,—the *absintheur* has his occasional phases of tranquillity like other people,—tranquillity that is as strange and as overpowering as a sudden swoon,—in which the tired senses rest, and the brain is for the nonce empty of all images and impressions. And so I was scarcely startled when, pushing aside the boughs that screened a mossy turn in the pathway, I came upon what at first seemed like the picture of a woman reading,—till at last it resolved itself into substantial fact and form, and I recognized Héloïse St. Cyr. She sat alone on a little rustic bench,— her face and figure were slightly turned away from me,—she was dressed in black, but she had taken off her hat and placed it beside her, and the sunlight flickering through the boughs above her, played fully on her glorious gold hair. Her head was bent attentively over the book she held,—her attitude was full of graceful ease and unstudied repose,— and as I watched her from a little distance, a sense of sudden awe and fear stole over me,—I trembled in every limb. A good girl, mark you!— a brave, sweet, pure-minded woman, is the most terrific reproach that exists on earth to the evil-doer and wicked man. It is as though the deaf blind God suddenly made Himself manifest,—as though He not only heard and saw, but with His voice thundered loud accusation! Many of us,—I speak of men,—cling to bad women, and give them our

---

[1] French word for "governesses."

ungrudging admiration—and why? Because they help us to be vile!—because they laugh at our vices and foster them,—and we love them for that! But *good* women!—I tell you that such are often left loveless and alone, because they will not degrade themselves to our brute-level. We want toys,—not angels!—puppets, not queens! But all the same, when the angel or the queen passes us by with the serene scorn of our base passions written in her clear calm eyes, we shrink and are ashamed,—aye! if only for a moment's space!

And she,—Héloïse,—sat there before me, unconscious of my presence—unconscious that the pure air about her was tainted by the unquiet breathing of a murderer and coward! For I knew myself to be both these things,—Absinthe had given me the spirit of braggardism, but had deprived me of all true courage. Boastfulness is not valour,—yet it often passes for such in France. Poor France,—fair France,—dear France!—there are some of her sons still left who would give their life blood to see her rise up in her old glory, and be again what she once was—a queen of nations. But alas!—it is not because of the German conquest,—nor because she has had foolish rulers, that she has fallen and is still falling,—it is because the new morals and opinions of the age, propounded and accepted by narrow-minded, superficial, and materialistic thinkers, breed in her a nest of vipers and scorpions instead of men; and your ordinary modern Frenchman has too low an estimate of all high ideals to risk his life in fighting for any one of them. There are exceptions to the rule certainly,—there are always exceptions;—but they are rare;—so rare, that we have let all Europe know there is no really strong, wise ruling brain in France, any more than there is in England. One would no more accept M. Carnot as a representative of the French national intellect, than one would accept Mr. Gladstone[1] and his contradictions as a representative of English stability.

The wind rustled the boughs,—a bird sang softly among the upper cool bunches of leaves,—and I stood, screened by the foliage, nervously hesitating, and looking at Héloïse, the sweetest and best woman I had ever known. Always fond of reading she was!—and my restless mind flew off to a hazy consideration of what her book might possibly be. One might safely conclude it was not by Zola,—the literary scavenger of Paris would have no charm for that high-souled, proudly-delicate

---

[1]   William Ewart Gladstone (1809-98); four-time Prime Minister of Great Britain (1868-74, 1880-85, 1886, and 1892-94).

Normandy-bred maiden. Probably it was one of her favourite classics,—or a volume of poems,—she was a great lover of poesy. I heard
her sigh,—a deep fluttering sigh that mingled itself with the low-
whispering wind,—she suddenly closed her book,—and raising her
eyes, looked out on the quiet landscape,—away from me. My heart beat
fast,—but I resolved to speak to her,—and with a hasty movement I
thrust aside the intervening boughs.

"Héloïse!"

She started,—what a pale, amazed, scared face she turned upon me!
Did she not know me?

"Héloïse!" I said again.

She rose nervously from her seat, and glanced about her from right
to left, apparently searching for some way of escape,—it was evident
she took me for some drunken or impertinent stranger. I had forgotten how changed I was,—I had forgotten that I looked more like a
tramp than a gentleman! I laughed a little confusedly, and lifted my hat.

"You do not seem to recognize me, Héloïse!" I said carelessly. "Yet
Gaston Beauvais was once no stranger to you!"

Oh, what a wondering, piteous look she gave me!—what a speechless sorrow swam suddenly into the large, lovely grey eyes!

"Gaston Beauvais!" she faltered—"oh no;—not possible! You,—
you—Gaston? Oh no!—no!"

And, covering her face with her two fair white hands, she broke into
sudden weeping!... My God!—it would have been well if I could have
killed myself then! For my heart was touched;—my hard, hard heart
that I thought had turned to stone! Her tears, the sincere outflow of a
pure woman's womanly grief, fell like dew on my burnt and callous
soul, and for a moment I was stricken dumb with an aching remorse,—
remorse that I should have voluntarily placed such a chasm of eternal
separation between all good things and the accursëd Me that now
seemed to usurp Creation rather than belong to it. I felt a choking
sensation in my throat,—my lips grew parched;—I strove to speak once
or twice but failed,—and she,—she, poor child, wept on. Presently,
making an effort to conquer myself, I ventured to approach her a step
or two more nearly.

"Héloïse! Mademoiselle St. Cyr!"—I said unsteadily—"Pray—
pray do not distress yourself like this! I was foolish to have spoken to
you—you were not prepared to see me;—I have startled,—alarmed
you!—I am much altered in my looks, I know,—but I forgot,—pray
forgive me!"

She checked her sobs,—and uncovering her tear-wet eyes, turned their humid lustre full upon me. I shrank a little backward,—but she stretched out her trembling hands.

"It is really you, M. Gaston?" she murmured nervously. "Oh, have you been very ill? You look so strange and pale!—you have greatly changed!"

"Yes, for the worse!—I know that!" I interrupted her quietly. "You could scarcely expect me to improve, could you, Héloïse? Nay, did you not yourself curse me, not so very long ago?—and are you surprised to find the curse fulfilled?" .

She sank on the rustic bench she had just quitted, and regarded me with an affrighted look.

"I cursed you?" she echoed—"I?—oh yes, yes! I remember—I was wicked—on that dreadful day of Pauline's disgrace and ruin, I said hard things to you—I know!—I was full of pain and anger,—but, believe me, that very night I prayed for you!—indeed I have prayed for you always—for you and my lost Pauline!"

The tenderness her presence had aroused in me, froze suddenly into chill cynicism.

"*Pardieu!* Women are curious creatures!" I said, with a bitter laugh. "They curse a man at noon-day,—and pray for him at midnight! That is droll! But beware how you couple perjured lovers' names together, even in prayer, mademoiselle—your God, if He be consistent can scarcely care to attend to such a petition,—as an instance, you see how He has taken care of *me!*"

Her head drooped;—a shudder ran through her frame, but she was silent.

"Look at me!" I went on recklessly. "Look! Why, you would not have known me if I had not declared myself! You remember Gaston Beauvais?—what a dandy he was,—how spruce and smart and even fastidious in dress?—a silly young fool for his pains!—you remember how he never took much thought about anything, except to make sure that he did his work conscientiously, ran into no debts, acted honourably to all men and stood well with the world. He was the stupidest creature extant,—he believed in the possibility of happiness!—he loved, and fancied himself beloved! He was duped and deceived,—all such trusting noodles are!—and he took his whipping and scourging at the hands of Fate rather badly. But he learnt wisdom at last,—the wisdom of the wisest!—he found out that men were sots and knaves, and women coquettes and wantons, and he resolved to make the best of an eternally bad business and please himself since he could please nobody else. And he has succeeded!—here he is!—here *I* am to answer for the truth of his success! I am very happy!—one does not want a new coat to be contented. I have heard say that a woman always judges a man by his clothes,—but if you judge me by mine you will do wrongly. They are shabby, I admit—but I am at ease in them, and they serve me better than a court suit serves a lacquey. I look ill, you tell me,—but I am not ill;—the face is always a tell-tale in matters of dissipation,—and I do not deny that I am dissipated,"—here I laughed harshly as I met her grieved and wondering gaze,—"I live a fast life,—I consort with evil men and evil women,—that is, people who do not, like the hypocritical higher classes of society, waste valuable time in pretending to be good. I am a gamester,—an idler—a *fainéant*[1] of the Paris *cafés*,—I have taken my life in my own hands and torn it up piecemeal for any dog to devour,—and to conclude, I am an *absintheur*, by which term, if you understand it at all, you will obtain the whole clue to the mystery of my present existence. Absinthe-drinking is a sort of profession as well as amusement in Paris,—it is followed by a great many men both small and great,—men of distinction, as well as nobodies,—I am in excellent company, I assure you!—and, upon my word, when I think of my past silly efforts to keep in a straight line of law with our jaded system of morals and behaviour, and compare it with my present freedom from all restraint and responsibility, I have nothing—positively nothing to regret!"

During this tirade, the fair woman's face beside me had grown paler and paler,—her lips were firmly pressed together,—her eyes cast down. When I had finished, I waited, expecting to hear some passionate burst of reproach from her, but none came. She took up her book, methodically marked the place in it where she had left off reading,—put on her hat, (though I noticed her hands trembled) and then rising, she said simply—

"Adieu!"

I stared at her amazed.

"Adieu!" I echoed—"What do you mean? Do you think I can let you go without more words than these after so many weeks of separation? It was in June I last saw you,—and it is now close upon the end of September,—and what a host of tragedies, have been enacted since then! Tragedies!—aye!—murders and suicides!"—and with an involuntary

---

[1]   French word for "idler" or "loafer."

gesture of appeal I stretched out my hand,—"Do not go Héloïse!—not yet! I want to speak to you!—I want to ask you a thousand things!"

"Why?" she queried in a mechanical sort of way—"You say you have nothing to regret!"

I stood mute. Her eyes now rested on me steadfastly enough, yet with a strained piteousness in them that disturbed me greatly.

"You have nothing to regret,"—she repeated listlessly—"Old days are over for you—as they are for me! In the space of a few months the best, the happiest part of our lives has ended. Only"—and she caught her breath hard—"before I go—I will say one thing—it is that I am sorry I cursed you or seemed to curse you. It was wrong,—though indeed it is not I that would have driven you to spoil your life as you yourself have spoiled *it*. I know you suffered bitterly—but I had hoped you were man enough to overcome that suffering and make yourself master of it. I knew you were deceived—but I had thought you generous enough to have pardoned deceit. You seemed to me a brave and gallant gentleman,—I was not prepared to find your nature weak and—and cowardly!"

She hesitated before the last word,—but, as she uttered it, I smiled.

"True, quite true, Héloïse!" I said quietly—"I am a coward! I glory in it! The brave are those that run all sorts of dangerous risks for the sake of others,—or for a cause, the successful results of which they personally will not be permitted to share. I avoid all this trouble! I am 'coward' enough to wish comfort and safety for myself,—I leave the question of Honour to the arguing tongues and clashing swords of those who care about it,—I do not!"

She looked at me indignantly, and her large eyes flashed.

"Oh God!" she cried. "Is it possible you can have fallen so low!—was not your cruel vengeance sufficient? You drove Pauline from her home,— her disgrace, which you so publicly proclaimed, killed, as you know, my uncle her father,—evil and misfortune have been sown broadcast by that one malicious act of yours,—even the wretched Silvion Guidèl has disappeared mysteriously—no trace of him can be found,—and not content with this havoc, you ruin yourself! And all for what? For a child's broken troth-plight!—a child who, as I told you at first, was too young to know her own mind, and who simply accepted you as her affianced husband, because she thought it would please her parents,—no more! She had then no idea, no conception of love;—and when it came, she fell a victim to it—it was too strong for her slight resistance. I warned you as well as I could,—I foresaw it all,—I dreaded it—for no woman as young and impressionable as Pauline could have been long in Silvion Guidèl's company without being powerfully attracted. I warned you,—but you would see nothing—men are so blind! They cannot—they will not understand that in every woman's heart there is the hunger of love—a hunger which must be appeased. When you first met Pauline she had never known this feeling,—and you never roused it in her,—but it woke at the mere glance, the mere voice of Silvion Guidèl! These things will happen—they are always happening,—one is powerless to prevent them. If one could always love where love is advisable!—but one cannot do so! Pauline's sin was no more than that of hundreds of other women who not only win the world's pardon, but also the exoneration of the sternest judges,—and yet I am sure she has suffered with a sharper intensity than many less innocent! But you—you have nothing to regret, you say—no!—not though two homes lie wasted and deserted by your pitilessness?—and, now you have ravaged your own life too!—you might have spared that!—yes, you might have spared that,—you might have left that—to God!"

Her breast heaved, and a wave of colour rushed to her cheeks and as quickly receded,—she pressed one hand on her heart.

"You need not"—she went on pathetically—"have given me cause to-day to even imagine that perhaps my foolish curse did harm to you. It is a vague reproach that I shall think of often! And yet I know I spoke in haste only—and without any malicious intent,—I could not,"—here her voice sank lower and lower—"I could not have truly cursed what I once loved!"

My heart gave a fierce bound,—and then almost stood still. Loved! What she once loved! Had she, then, loved me? Certes, a glimmering guess,—a sort of instinctive feeling that she might have loved me, had stolen over me now and then during my courtship of her cousin Pauline,—but that she had really bestowed any of her affection on me unasked, was an idea that had never positively occurred to my mind. And now?... We looked at each other,—she with a strange pale light on her face such as I had never seen there,—I amazed, yet conscious of immense, irreparable loss,—loss which those words of hers—"what I once loved"—made absolute and eternal! Both vaguely conscience-smitten, we gazed into one another's eyes,—even so might two spirits, one on the gold edge of Heaven, the other on the red brink of Hell, and all Chaos between them, gaze wistfully and wonder at their own froward fate,—aye!—and such, if such there be, may lean far out from either sphere, stretch hands, waft kisses, smile, weep, cry aloud each other's names,—and yet no bridge shall ever span the dark division,—no ray of light connect those self-severed souls!

"Héloïse!" I stammered,—and then, my voice failing me, I was silent.

She, moving restlessly where she sat on the rustic seat with the shadows of the green leaves flickering over her, entwined her white hands one within the other, and lifted her large solemn eyes towards the deep blue sky.

"There is no shame in it now"—she said, in hushed serious accents. "There is never any shame in what is dead. The darkest sin,—the worst crime—is expiated by death,—and so my love, being perished, is no longer blameable. I have not seen you for a long time—and perhaps I shall never see you again,—one tells many lies in life, and one seldom has the chance of speaking the truth,—but I feel that I must speak it now. I loved you!—you see how calmly I can say it—how dispassionately—because it is past. The old heart-ache troubles me no longer,—and I am not afraid of you any more. But before,—I used to be afraid,—I used to think you must be able to guess my secret, and that you despised me for it. You loved Pauline,—she was much worthier love than I,—and I should have been quite contented and at rest had I felt certain that she loved you in return. But I never was certain; I felt that her affection was merely that of a playful child for an elder brother,—I felt sure that she knew nothing of love,—love such as you had for her—or—as I had for you. But you—you saw nothing——"

She stopped abruptly, for I suddenly flung myself down on the seat beside her, and now caught her hands in mine.

"Nothing—nothing!" I muttered wildly. "We men never do see anything! We are bats,—moths!—flying desperately into all sorts of light and fire and getting burnt and withered up for our pains! Héloïse! Héloïse!—You loved me, you say—*you*?—Why, just for the merest hair's-breadth of mercy extended to us, I might have loved you!—we might have been happy! Why do you pray to God, Héloïse?—how can you pray to Him? Seeing you, knowing you, hearing you, why did He not save me by your grace as by an angel's intervention? He could have done so had He willed it!—and I should have believed in Him then! And you—why did you not give me one look—one word!—why did you not employ all the thousand charms of your loveliness to attract me?—why were you always so silent and cold?—was that your mode of defence against yourself and me, child? Oh, my God!—what a waste and havoc of life there is in the world! Listen!—there are plenty of women who by a thousand coquetteries[1] and unmistakable signs, give

---

[1] Flirtatious acts.

us men plainly to understand what they mean,—and we are only too ready to obey their signals—but you—you, because you are good and innocent, must needs shut up your soul in a prison of ice for the sake of—what? Conventionality,—social usage! A curse on conventionality! Héloïse—Héloïse!—if I had only known!—if I could have guessed that I might have sought your love and found it!—but now!—why have told me now, you beautiful, fond, foolish woman, when it is too late!"

I was breathless with the strange excitement that had seized me,— though I held myself as much as I could in strong restraint, fearing to alarm her by my vehemence,—but my whole soul was so suddenly overpowered by the extent of the desolation I myself had wrought, that I could not check the torrent of words that broke from my lips. It maddened me to realize, as I did, that we two had always been on the verge of love unknowingly,—and yet, by reason of something in ourselves that refused to yield to the attraction of each other's presence, and something in the whim of chance and circumstance, we had wilfully let love go beyond all possible recall! And she,—oh, she was cold and calm,—or if she were not, she had the nerve to seem so,—all your delicately-strung student-women are like that; so full of fine philosophies that they are scarcely conscious of a heart! Her face was quite colourless,—she looked like an exquisitely wrought figure of marble,—her hand lay passively in mine, chill as a frozen snowflake.

"Why"—I repeated half savagely—"why have you told me all this now, when it is too late?"

Her lips trembled apart,—but for a moment no sound issued from them. Then with a slight effort she answered me.

"It is just because it is too late that I have told you,—it is because my love is dead, that I have chosen you should know that it once lived. If there were the smallest pulse of life stirring in it now—you should never have known."

And she withdrew her hand from my clasp as she spoke.

"You are a strange woman Héloïse!" I said involuntarily.

"Possibly I may be," she replied, with a sudden quiver of passion in her voice that added richness to its liquid thrill. "And yet again, perhaps not as strange as you imagine. There are many women who can love without blazoning their love to the world,—there are many too who will die for love and give no sign of suffering. But we need speak no more of this. I only wished to prove to you how impossible it was that I could ever seriously and maliciously have wished you ill,—and to ask you, for the sake of the past, to refrain from perpetrating fresh injuries on your life and soul. Surely, however much a man has been wronged by others, he need not wrong himself!"

"If his life were of any value to any one in the world he need not and he would not," I responded. "But when it is a complete matter of indifference to everybody whether he lives or dies—*que voulez-vous?*[1] I tell you, Héloïse, I have gone too far for remedy,—even if you loved me now, which you do not, you could not raise me from the depths into which I have fallen, and where I am perfectly contented to remain."

Her eyes flashed with mingled indignation and sorrow.

"I thank God my love for you has perished then!" she exclaimed passionately. "For had I still loved you, it would have killed me to see you degraded as you are to-day!"

I smiled a little contemptuously.

"*Chère* Héloïse, do not talk of degradation!" I murmured. "Or if we must talk of it,—let us consider the fate of—Pauline!"

She started, as though I had stabbed her with a dagger's point.

"Have you seen her? Do you know where she is?" she demanded eagerly.

"Yes—and no," I replied. "I have seen her twice,—but I have not spoken to her, nor do I know where she lives. I saw her, the first time, wandering shabbily clad, in the back streets of Paris"—Héloïse uttered a faint cry and tears sprang into her eyes,—"and when I beheld her for the second time, she was kneeling outside her father's grave at Père-la-Chaise. But I intend to track her out;—I will find her, wherever she is!"

Oh, what a happy hopeful light swept over the fair pale face beside me.

"You will?" she cried. "You will find her?—you will restore her to her mother?—to me?—the poor poor unhappy child! Ah, Gaston!—if you do this, you will surely make your peace with God!"

I shrugged my shoulders.

"*Ma chère*, there is time enough for that! *Monsieur le bon Dieu*[2] and I have not quarrelled that I am aware of,—and if we had, we should perhaps not be very anxious to renew our friendship! I would rather make my peace with you. If I find Pauline, will you love me again?"

She gave a faint exclamation and recoiled from me as though afraid.

"Oh no!—never—never!" she said shudderingly. "Never! What power can revive a perished passion, Gaston Beauvais? Once dead—it is dead for ever! You are to me the merest phantom of the man I once

---

[1] French expression meaning "what can you expect?"
[2] French for "the good God."

adored in secret,—I could no more love you now than I could love a corpse long buried!"

She spoke with vehemence and fervour,—and every pulse in my body seemed to rebound with a smarting sense of anger against her. I felt that though she had as she said, once loved me, she now regarded me with something near positive aversion, though that aversion was mingled with a pity which I scorned. She was unjust,—all women are! The subtle nerves of her feminine organization had been wrenched and twisted awry by disappointed passion quite as much as mine had,—and I could read and analyze her emotion—I saw she instinctively despised herself for ever having bestowed a single tender thought on such a piece of unworthiness as I! No matter!—I would meet her on her own ground!—if she could not love me, she should fear me!

"*Merci, chère et belle amie!*"[1] I said satirically. "We have—for no reason that I can see—played a veritable game of cat and mouse together. You have caught me in your pearly claws—and you have purred prettily concerning your past affection for me,—and now you settle on me tooth and nail, and tear me into shreds of hopelessness and despair. *Soit!* It is the way of women,—I do not complain. I shall, as I told you, seek out Pauline,—but if I find her, do not imagine I shall restore her to your arms! *Pas si bête!*[2] I shall keep her for myself. I would not have her for my wife—no!—but there is no earthly objection to my taking her as my mistress! The idea will not shock or shame her—now!"

With one swift movement Héloïse sprang up and faced me—her whole figure trembling with suppressed emotion.

"Oh God! You would not be so base!" she cried. "You could not— you dare not!"

I rose in my turn and confronted her calmly.

"How inconsistent you are, Héloïse!" I said indolently. "Base! I see nothing base in such a proposal to such a woman as your too-much-loved young cousin! She has of her own free-will descended several steps of the ladder of perdition—no force will be needed to persuade her down to the end! You overrate the case——"

"I tell you you shall not harm her!" exclaimed Héloïse, with a sudden fierceness of grief and passion. "I too have searched for her and I will search for her still,—more ardently now that I know she must be defended from *you*! Oh, I will be near you when you least think it!—I

---

[1] French for "thank you, dear and beautiful friend."
[2] French expression meaning "I'm not such a fool."

will track you, I will follow you,—I will do anything to save her from the additional vileness of your touch!—your——"

She paused, breathless.

I smiled.

"Do not be melodramatic, *ma chère!*" I murmured coldly. "It suits you,—you look admirably lovely in anger—but still,—we are in the Bois,—and there may be listeners. I shall be charmed if you will follow me and track me out, as you say—but,—you will find it difficult! You cannot save what is hopelessly lost,—and as for 'daring'!—*Dieu!* how little you know me!—there is nothing I dare not do,—nothing, save one thing!"

She stood still,—her eyes dilated,—her breath coming and going quickly, her hands clenched,—but she said not a word.

"You do not ask what that one thing is," I went on, keeping my gaze upon her. "But I will tell you. The limit of my courage—such as it is,—stops with you. I dare not,—mark me well!—I dare not affront you,—so that, however much my heart may ache and hunger for love, I dare not love you! You are the one sacred thing on earth to me, and so you will remain—for I have voluntarily resigned home and kindred—my father has disowned me, as completely as I have disowned him!—and only the memory of your beauty will cling to me henceforth, as something just a little less valuable and sweet than—*Absinthe!*"

I laughed, and she surveyed me amazedly.

"Than Absinthe!" she repeated mechanically. "I do not understand——"

"No, I suppose you do not," I went on quietly, "you will probably never understand how *absinthe* can become dearer to a man than his own life! It is very strange!—but in Paris, very true. You have been in dangerous company, Héloïse, to-day!—be thankful you have escaped all harm! You have talked of past love and passion to a man who has fire in his veins instead of blood,—and who, had he once let slip the leash of difficult self-control, might have thought little of taking his fill of kisses from your lips, and killing you afterwards! Do not look so frightened,—I dare not touch you,—I dare not even kiss your hand! You are free as angels are,—free to depart from me in peace and safety,—with what poor blessing a self-ruined man may presume to invoke upon you. But do not ask me to consider Pauline as I consider you,—you might as easily expect me to pardon Silvion Guidèl!

She was silent,—I think from sheer terror this time,—and a restless inquisitiveness stirred in me,—an anxiety to find out how much she knew concerning the mysterious disappearance of that once holy saint of the Church whom I had sent to find out in other worlds the causes of his Creed!

"What has become of him, do you think?" I said suddenly. "Perhaps he is dead?"

How pale she looked!—how scared and strange!

"Perhaps!" she murmured half inaudibly.

"Perhaps"—I went on recklessly,—and laughing as I spoke,—"Perhaps he is *murdered*! Have you ever thought of that? It is quite possible!"

And at that instant our eyes met! What!—was my crime blazoned in my face? I could not tell,—I only know that she uttered a smothered cry,—an exclamation of fear or horror, or both,—and with a movement of her hands, as though she thrust some hideous object away from her, she turned and fled! I saw the sunlight flash on her hair like the heavenly halo above the forehead of an angel,—I heard the rustle of her dress sweep with a swift shuddering hiss over the long grass that bent beneath her tread,—she was gone! In her haste she had left behind her the book she had been reading, and I took it up mechanically. It was a translation of Plato,—it opened of its own accord at a passage she had marked.

"*When one is attempting noble things, it is surely noble also to suffer whatever it may befall us to suffer.*"[1]

Aye!—for the grand old Greeks this was truth,—but for modern men what does it avail? Who attempts "noble things" nowadays without being deemed half mad for his or her effort? And as for suffering there is surely enough of that without going out of one's way in search of it! Good Plato!—you are not in favour at this period of time,—your philosophies are as unacceptable to our "advanced" condition as Christ's christianity! So I thought;—but I took the volume with me all the same,—it had the signature of "Héloïse St. Cyr"—written on its fly-leaf in a firm characteristic woman's hand,—and I had a superstitious idea that it might act like a talisman to shield me from evil. Folly of course!—for there is no talisman in earth or in heaven that can defend a man from the baser part of himself. And to that baser part I had succumbed,—and I had no repentance—no!—not though I should have sacrificed the love of a thousand women as fair and pure-souled as this strange girl Héloïse, who had loved me once, and whose love I myself had turned into hatred.

---

[1] From Plato's Seventh Letter.

And yet,—yet—I was more awake to the knowledge of my own utter vileness than I had ever been before, as with the Plato in my hand, and my hat pulled low down over my brows I went slinkingly by side-paths and byeways out of the Bois like the accursëd thing I was,—accursëd, and for once, fully conscious of my curse!

CHAPTER 30

Weeks went past; with me their progress was scarcely noticed, for I lived in a sort of wild nightmare of delirium that could no more be called life than fever is called health. I was beginning to learn a few of the heavier penalties attached to the passion that absorbed me,—and the mere premonitory symptoms of those penalties were terrifying enough to shake the nerves of many a bolder man than I. I drank more and more Absinthe to drown my sensations,—sometimes I obtained a stupefying result with the required relief, but that relief was only temporary. The visions that now haunted me were more varied and unnatural in character,—yet it was not so much of visions I had to complain as *impressions*. These were forcible, singular, and alarmingly realistic. For example, I would be all at once seized by the notion that everything about me was of absurdly abnormal proportions, or the reverse; men and women would, as I looked at them, suddenly assume the appearance of monsters both in height and breadth, and again, would reduce themselves in the twinkling of an eye to the merest pigmies. This happened frequently,—I knew it was only an *impression*, or distortion of the brain-images, but it was nevertheless troublesome and confusing. Then there were the crowds of persons I saw who were *not* real,—and whom I classed under the head of "visions,"—but, whereas once there was a certain order and method in the manner of their appearance, there was now none,—they rushed before me in disorderly masses, with faces and gestures that were indescribably hideous and revolting. Therefore my chief aim now was to try and deaden my brain utterly,—I was tired of the torture and perplexity its subtle mechanism caused me to suffer. Meanwhile I gained some little distraction by searching everywhere for Pauline,—this was the only object apart from Absinthe that interested me in the least. The rest of the world was the most tiresome pageantry-show,—sometimes dim and indistinct—sometimes luridly brilliant,—but always spectral,—always like a thing set apart from me with which I had no connection whatsoever.

So, imperceptibly to my consciousness, the summer faded and died,—and autumn also came to its sumptuously coloured end in a glory of gold and crimson foliage, which fell to the ground almost before one had time to realize its rich beauty. A chill November began, attended with pale fog and drizzling rain,—the leaves lately so gay of tint, dropped in dead heaps, or drifted mournfully on the sweeping wings of the gusty blast,—the little tables outside all the *cafés* were moved within, and the sombreness of approaching winter began to loom darkly over Paris, not that Paris ever cares particularly for threatening skies or inclement weather, its bright interior life bidding defiance to the dullest day. If you have even a very moderate income, just sufficient to rent the tiniest *maisonette*[1] in Paris, you can live more agreeably there perhaps than in any other city in the world. You are certain to have lively colouring about you—for no little "appartement"[2] in Paris but is cheerful with painted floral designs, gilding, and mirrors,—if you be a woman your admirers will bring you white lilac and orchids in the middle of December, arranged with that perfectly fine French taste which is unequalled throughout the globe,—and on a frosty day your *cuisinière*[3] will make you a "*bouillon*"[4] such as no English cook has any idea of,—while, no matter whether you be on the topmost floor of the tallest house, you need only look out of window to see some piece of merriment or other afoot,—for we Parisians, whatever our faults, are merry enough,—and even when, monkey-like, we tear some grand ideal to bits and throw it in the gutter, we always grin over it! We dance on graves,—we snap our fingers in the face of the criminal who is just going to be guillotined—why not? "*Tout casse, tout passe!*"[5]—we may as well laugh at the whole Human Comedy while we can! Now I, for example, have never been in England,—but I have read much about it, and I have met many English people, and on the whole I am inclined to admire "*perfide Albion*." Her people are so wise in their generation! When your English lord is conscious of having more vices in his composition than there are days in the year, he builds a church and endows a hospital!—can anything be more excellent? He becomes virtuous at once in the eyes of the world at large, and yet he need never resign one of his favourite little peccadilloes! We do not manage things

---

[1]   French for "small house."
[2]   French for "apartment."
[3]   French for "cook."
[4]   French for "soup."
[5]   French for "everything breaks, everything passes away." Proverbial.

quite so well in France,—we are *blagueurs*[1]—even if we are vicious, *nous blaguons le chose!*[2] How much better it is to be secretive *à l'Anglaise!*[3]— to appear good no matter how bad we are,—and to seem as though all the Ten Commandments[4] were written on our brows even while we are coveting our neighbour's wife! But I digress. I ought to keep to the thread of my story, ought I not, dear critics on the press?—you who treat every narrative, true or imaginative that goes into print, as a *gourmet* treats a quail, leaving nothing on the plate but a fragment of picked bone which you present to the public and call it a "review!" *Ah mes garçons!*[5]—take care! Do not indulge your small private spites and jealousies too openly, or you may lose your occupation, which, though it only pay you at the rate of half-a-guinea a column, and sometimes less, is still an occupation. The Public itself is the Supreme Critic now,—its "review" does not appear in print, but nevertheless its unwritten verdict declares itself with such an amazing weight of influence, that the ephemeral opinions of a few ill-paid journalists are the merest straws beating against the strong force of a whirlwind. Digression again? Yes!— what else do you expect of an *absintheur*? I do not think I am more discursive than Gladstone of Hawarden,[6] or more flighty than Boulanger of Jersey![7] *Allons,*[8]—I will try to be explicit and tell you how pretty schoolgirl Pauline de Charmilles ended her troubles,—but I confess I have dallied with the subject purposely. Why? Why, because I hate yet rejoice to think of it,—because I dwell on it with loving and with loathing,—because it makes me laugh with ecstasy—and anon, weep and tremble and implore!—though what I implore, and to whom I address any sort of appeal, I cannot explain to you. Sometimes cowering on the ground I wail aloud—"Oh God—God!" half credulous, half despairing,—and then when the weak paroxysm is past, and the pitiless

---

[1] French for "jokers."

[2] French expression meaning "we joke about the thing."

[3] French meaning "in the English way."

[4] Precepts of Christian faith divinely revealed to Moses and engraved on stone tablets.

[5] French for "Oh, my boys."

[6] William Gladstone (1809-98), four-time Prime Minister of Great Britain. Hawarden Castle in Wales was Gladstone's home until his death.

[7] George Ernest Jean Marie Boulanger (1837-91); French General and member of the Radical party whose popularity with the people made him a menace to the parliamentary Republican government. When a warrant was issued for his arrest for treason in 1889, Boulanger fled Paris, eventually settling in Jersey. At the time Corelli was writing *Wormwood*, Boulanger's "flightiness" would have been much in the news.

[8] French for "let's go," but in this context, "Come, now."

blank Silence of things hurls itself down on my soul as the crushing answer to my cry, I rise to my feet, calm, tearless, and myself again—knowing that there is *no* God!—none at least that ever replies to the shriek of torture or the groan of misery. How strange it is that there are some folks who still continue to pray!

One cold dark evening,—how minutely I remember every small incident connected with it!—I was wandering home in my usual desultory fashion, a little more heavily drugged than usual, and in a state of sublime indifference to the weather, which was wet and gusty, when I heard a woman's voice singing in one of the bye-streets down which I generally took my way. There was something sweet and liquid in the thrill of the notes as they rose upward softly through the mist and rain,—and I could hear the words of the song distinctly, it was a well-known convent chant to the "Guardian Angel;" —these heavenly messengers seem rather idle in the world nowadays!

> "Viens sur ton aile, Ange fidèle
> Prendre mon coeur!
> C'est le plus ardent de mes voeux;—
> Près de Marie
> Place-moi bientôt dans les cieux!
> O guide aimable, sois favorable
> A mon désir
> Et viens finir
> Ma triste vie
> Avec Marie!"[1]

A wavering child-like pathos in the enunciation of the last lines struck me with a sense of familiarity;—involuntarily I thought of Héloïse and of the way she used to play the violin, and of the pleasant musical evenings we used to pass all together at the house of the De Charmilles. I sauntered into the street and down it lazily—the woman who sang was standing at the side of the curbstone, and there were a few people about her listening;—one or two dropped coins in her timidly outstretched hand. As I came close within view of her I stopped and stared, doubtful for a moment as to her identity,—then, in doubt no longer, I sprang to her side.

---

[1] "Come on your wing, faithful Angel / Take my heart! / This is the most ardent of my wishes;— / Near to Mary / In the skies place me soon! / O amiable guide, favour / My desire / And end / My sad life / With Marie!"

"Pauline!" I exclaimed.

She started, and shuddered back from me, her face growing paler than ever, her eyes opening wide in wistful wonder and fear. The little group that had listened to her song broke up and dispersed,—they had no particular interest in her more than in any other wandering street-vocalist, and in less than a minute we were almost alone.

"Pauline!" I said again,—then, breaking into a derisive laugh, I went on—"What!—has it come to this?—you, the sole daughter of a proud and ancient house, singing in the highways and the byeways for bread! *Dieu!*—one would have thought there were more comfortable ways of earning a living—for you at any rate!—you, with your fair face and knowledge of evil could surely have done better than this!"

She looked at me steadfastly but made no answer,—she was apparently as amazed and stricken at the sight of me as her cousin Héloïse had been. Meanwhile I surveyed her with a swift yet intent scrutiny—I noticed her shabby, almost threadbare clothes,—the thin starved look of her figure,—the lines of suffering about her mouth and eyes,—and yet with all this she was still beautiful,—beautiful as an angel or fairy over whom the cloud of sorrow hangs like blight on a flower.

"Well!" I resumed roughly, after waiting in vain for her to speak,—"we have met at last, it seems! I have searched for you everywhere—so have your relatives and friends. You have kept the secret of your hiding-place very well all these months—no doubt for some good reason! Who is your lover?"

Still the same steadfast look,—the same plaintive, patient uplifting of the eyes!

"My lover?" she echoed after me softly and with surprise. "If you are, as I suppose you must be, Gaston Beauvais, then you know—you have always known his name. Whom can I love—who can love me,—if not Silvion?"

I laughed again.

"*Bien!* You can love the dead then? Nay!—you are too fair to waste your beauty thus! A corpse can give no caresses,—and *le beau* Silvion by this time is something less even than a corpse! How you stare! Did you not know that he was dead?"

Her face grew grey as ashes,—and rigid in the extremity of her fear.

"Dead!" she gasped. "No—no! That could not be! Dead? Silvion? No, no!—you are cruel—you always were cruel—you are Gaston Beauvais, the cruellest of all cruel men, and you tell me lies to torture me! You were always glad to torture me!—yes, even after you had loved me! I never could understand that—for if one loves at all, one always forgives. And so I do not believe you,—Silvion is not dead,—he could not die—he is too young———".

"Oh, little fool!"—I interrupted her fiercely—"do not the young die? The young, the strong, and the beautiful, like your Silvion, are generally the first to go;—they are too good, say the old women, for this wicked world! Too good!—ha ha!—the axiom is excellent in the case of Silvion Guidèl, who was so perfect a saint! Come here, Pauline!"—and I seized her hand. "Do not try to resist me, or it will be the worse for you! One look at my face will tell you what I have become,—as vile a man as you are a woman!—scum, both of us, on the streets of Paris! Come with me, I tell you! Scream or struggle, and as sure as these clouds drop rain from heaven I will kill you! I never had much mercy in my disposition—I dare say you remember that!—I have less than ever now. There are many things I must say to you,—things which you must hear,—which you *shall* hear!—come to some remoter place than this, where we shall not be noticed,—where no one will interrupt us, or think that we are more than two beggars discoursing of the day's gains."

And clutching her arm I half dragged, half led her with me,—I myself full of a strange rising fury that savoured of madness,—she almost paralyzed, I think, with sheer terror. Out of the street we hurried,—and passed into a small obscure side-alley or court, from the corner of which could be perceived the shimmer of the Seine and the lights on the Pont Neuf.

"Now!" I said hoarsely, drawing her by force up so near to me that our faces were close together, and our eyes, peering into each other's, seemed to ravage out as by fire the secrets hidden in our hearts—"now let us speak the truth, you and I,—and since you were always the most graceful liar of the two, perhaps you had best begin! Fling off the mask, Pauline de Charmilles!—make open confession, and so in part mend the wounds of your soul!—tell me how you have lived all this while and what you have been doing? I know your past,—I can imagine your present!—but—speak out! Tell me how Paris has treated you,—what you *were* I can remember,—and all I want to know now, is what you *are*!"

How strangely quiet she had become!—this once playful, childish, coquettish creature I had loved! She never flinched beneath my gaze,—she never tried to draw her hands away from mine—her features were colourless, but her lips were firmly set, and no tears dimmed the feverish lustre of her eyes.

"What I am?" she murmured in faint yet clear accents. "I am what I have always been,—a poor, broken-hearted woman who is faithful!"

Faithful! I flung her hands from me in derision,—I stared at her, amazed at her effrontery.

"Faithful" I echoed. "You! You, who sported with a man's heart as though it were a toy,—you, who ruined an honest man's life to gratify a selfish, guilty passion,—you!—you dare to speak of faithfulness—you——"

"Stop!" she said softly and with perfect composure. "I think you do not understand,—it is seldom men can understand women. In selfishness, if we speak of that, you are surely more to blame than I,—for you think of nothing but your own wrong—a wrong for which, God knows, I would have made any possible reparation. And I repeat it, I am faithful! You cannot, you dare not call the woman false who is true to the memory of the only love she ever yielded herself to, body and soul! She who surrenders her life to many lovers—she it is who is unfaithful—she it is who is base,—but not such an one as I! For I have had but one passion,—one thought—one hope—one thread to bind me to existence,—Silvion! You know, for I told you all the truth, that my love was never centred upon you,—you know that I had never wakened to the least comprehension of love till he, Silvion, made me see all its glory, all its misery!—and neither he nor I are to blame for our unhappy destiny! Blame Nature, blame Fate, blame God, blame Love itself,—the joy, the despair of it all was to be! But faithfulness! Ah, Gaston Beauvais!—if ever any woman in the world was faithful, *I* am that woman! I can keep that one poor pride to comfort me when I die! If, in these weary months any other man's hand had touched mine with a gesture of affection,—if another man's lips had touched mine with the lightest caress—then,—then you might have spurned me as a vile and fallen thing—then you would have had the right to loathe me as I should have loathed myself! But I am as one vowed and consecrated—yes! consecrated to love, and to love's companion, sorrow,—and though I have, against my wish and will, brought grief to you and many who once were dear to me, I am faithful!—faithful to the one passion of my life, and I shall be faithful still until the end!"

Oh, quixotic fool! I thought, as I heard her impassioned words fall one by one, musically on the careless air. Why she might have been a saint for her fearless and holy look!—she of the corrupt heart and wayward will—even she,—it was laughable!—she might have been a saint! My God!—for one wild fleeting moment I thought her so,—for a comparison between her life and mine passed over me, and caused me to recoil from her as one unworthy to be near so pure a thing! Pure?—what? Because she had been true to her betrayer? Fine purity, indeed!—what was I dreaming of? The rain and mist were dark about us,—no heavenly aureole shone above her brows—she was a mere bedraggled wretch with a worn face, feigning a wondrous honesty! Faithful? Faithful to—that bruised and battered thing I had flung out into the river with such infinite trouble!—faithful,—to that forbidding lump of clay thrown long ago into the common grave of nameless suicides! What a jest!—what a mockery! I looked at her as she stood before me—as frail and slight a woman as ever was born to misery.

"So! And with all this famous fidelity you boast of, how have you lived?" I asked her derisively.

"I have worked," she replied simply—"and when I could get no work, I have sung, as you saw me to-night, in the poorer streets,—for the poor are more generous than the rich,—and many people have been very good to me. And sometimes I have starved,—but I have always hoped and waited——"

"For what?" I cried. "Oh, most foolish of all foolish women,— waited and hoped for what?"

"For one glimpse of Silvion!" and she raised her eyes with a trustful light in their dark blue depths to the murky and discontented heavens. "I have always felt that some day he would come to Paris,—and that I should see his face once more! I would ask him for nothing but a word of blessing,—I would not call him from the life he has been compelled to choose, and I would not reproach him for choosing it,—I should be quite, quite happy just to kiss his hand and let him go!—but—I should have seen him! Then I would go into some quiet convent of the poor and end my days,—I would pray for him——"

"Aye!—as though he were another Abelard!"[1] I interrupted her harshly. "Your prayers will probably take the form of Colardeau's poesy——"

"'*Un Dieu parle a mon coeur,*
De ce Dieu, ton rival, sois encore le vainqueur!'[2]

---

[1] Pierre Abelard (1079-1142); French scholastic philosopher and theologian famous for his tragic love affair with Héloïse.

[2] Charles-Pierre Colardeau (1732-76); French poet and playwright. His 1758 translation of Alexander Pope's "Héloïse to Abelard" was a popular success. These lines are a rough translation of Pope's lines "Fill my fond heart with God alone, for he / Alone can rival, can succeed to thee" (lines 205-206).

We all understand the ulterior meaning of such pretty sentiment! What!—will you actually swear to me that you have lived hidden apart like this to work and starve on the mere hope of seeing your lover again, when you know that by his own act he separated himself from you for ever?"

She did not speak; but she made a sign of patient assent.

I burst into laughter, loud, long and irresistible.

"And they say that God exists!" I cried—"A God of justice,—who allows His creatures to torment themselves with shadows! Oh, sublime justice! Listen, listen, you, child, who hold fast to a fidelity which nowadays is counted as a mere dog's virtue,—listen, and learn from me what a spendthrift you have been of your time, and how you have wasted your prayers! Listen!—listen!" and again I caught her hands in mine and bent my face downwards to hers—"Listen, for I am in the humour to tell you everything,—everything! You have spoken,—it is my turn to speak now. The truth, the whole truth, and nothing but the truth, so help me God! Do you hear that? That is a proper legal oath,—it suffices for a court of justice where not a man believes in the God adjured,—it must suffice for you who do believe—or so you say! Well then, by that oath, and by everything holy and blasphemous in this sacred and profane world of ours I swear to you Silvion Guidèl is dead! You can think his soul is in heaven if you like,—if it console you so to think,—but wherever his soul is, his body is dead,—and it was his fine, fair body you knew,—his body you loved,—you surely will not be such a hypocrite as to deny that! Well, that body is dead,—dead and turned to hideous corruption!—Ha!—you shudder?—you struggle?"—for she was striving to tear her hands from my grip. "Perhaps you can guess how he died? Not willingly, I assure you!—he was not by any means glad to go to the paradise whose perfect joys he proclaimed! No!—he was a rebellious priest,—he fought for every breath of the strong, rich, throbbing life that made mere manhood glorious to him,—but he was conquered!—he gave in at last—— Silence!—do not scream, or I shall kill you! He is dead, I say!—stone dead!—who should know it better than I, seeing that I—*murdered* him!"

CHAPTER 31

What fools women are! To break their hearts is sometimes as easy as to break fine glass,—a word will do *it*. A mere word!—one uttered at random out of the thousands in the dictionary! "*Murder*," for example,—a word of six letters,—it has a ludicrously appalling effect on human nerves! On the silly Pauline it fell like a thunderbolt sped suddenly from the hand of God;—and down she dropped at my feet, white as snow, inert as stone. I might have struck her across the brows with a heavy hammer, or pierced her body with some sharp weapon, she lay so stunned and helpless. The sight of her figure there, huddled in a motion-less heap, made me angry,—she looked as though she were dead. I was not sorry for her; no!—I was sorry for nothing now;—but I lifted her up from the wet pavement in my arms, and held her close against my breast in a mechanical endeavour to warm her back to consciousness.

"Poor, pretty little toy!" I thought, as I chafed one of her limp cold hands,—and then—hardly knowing what I did, I kissed her. Some subtle honey or poison, or both, was surely on her lips, for as I touched them I grew mad! What!—only one kiss for me who had been deprived of them so long? No!—ten, twenty, a hundred! I rained them down on cheeks, eyes, brow and hair,—though I might as well have kissed a corpse, she was so still and cold. But she breathed,—her heart beat against mine,—I could feel its faint pulsations; and I renewed my kisses with the ardour, not of love, but of hatred! You do not think it possible to kiss a woman you hate? Fair lady!—(for it cannot be one of my sex that suggests the doubt!) you know little of men! We are, when roused, tigers in our loves and hatreds,—and we are quite capable of embracing a woman whom we mentally loathe, so long as she has phys-ical attraction,—aye!—the very fact of our loathing will oftentimes redouble the fascination we have for her company! Oh, we are not all lath-and-plaster men, with a stereotyped smile and company manners! The most seeming-cold of us have strange depths of passion in our natures which, if once stirred, leap into flame and destroy all that is within our reach! Such fire was within me now as my lips almost breathlessly caressed the fair face that lay against my heart like a white flower,—and when at last the dark blue eyes opened and regarded me, first with vague doubt and questioning, then with affright and abhor-rence, a sense of the fiercest triumph was in me,—a triumph which grew hotter with every instant, as I reflected that now—now at any rate Pauline was in my power—I could make her mine if I choose!—she had been faithful to Silvion living, but she should not remain faithful to him dead! I held her fast in my arms with all my strength,—with all my strength?—my strength was as a reed in the wind before the sudden access of superhuman power that rushed upon her as she recovered from her swoon! She broke from my clasp,—she pushed me violently from her, and then stood irresolute, feebly pressing her hand against her eyes as though in an effort to recall her thoughts.

"Silvion—dead!" she muttered,—"dead!—and I never knew! No warning given—no message—no spirit-voice in the night to tell me— Oh no!—God would not be so cruel! Dead!—and—*murdered*! Ah no!" and her accents rose to a shrill wail—"it cannot be true!—it cannot! Gaston Beauvais, it was not you who spoke—it was some horrid fancy of my own!—you did not say it—you could not say it———"

She stopped, panting for breath. My blood burned as I looked at her,—in her agony and terror she was so beautiful! How wild and brilliant were those lovely eyes!—I took a fierce delight in pricking her on to such adorable frenzy!

"I said, Pauline, what I will say again, that your lover Silvion Guidèl is dead, and that it was I who killed him! Without a weapon, too,— with these hands alone!—and yet see!—there is no blood upon them!"

I held them out to her,—she craned her neck forward and looked at them strangely, with a peering horror in her eyes that seemed to make them fixed and glassy. Then a light flashed over her face—her lips parted in a shrill scream.

"Murderer!" she cried, clapping her hands wildly,—"Murderer! You have confessed—you shall atone! You shall die for your crime—I will have justice! *Au secours! au secours!*"[1]

I sprang upon her swiftly—I covered her mouth—I grasped her slim throat and stifled her shrieks.

"Silence, fool!" I whispered hoarsely. "I told you I would kill you if you screamed. Another sound, another movement, and I will keep my word. What are you shouting for?—what do you want with justice? There is no such thing, either in earth or heaven! Silvion Guidèl is dead and buried, but who can prove that he was murdered? He was buried as a suicide. If I tell you I killed him, I can tell others a different story, and your denunciation of me will seem mere hysterical raving! Be still!" Here, as I felt her swaying unsteadily beneath my touch, I took my hands from her mouth and throat and let her go. She tottered and sank down on the pavement, shuddering in every limb, and crouching there, moaned to herself like a sick and suffering child. I waited a minute or two, listening. Had any one heard her scream? I half expected some officious gendarme to appear, and inquire what was the matter,—but no!—

---

[1] French for "help."

nothing disturbed the dark stillness but the roar of passing traffic and the plash of the slow rain. Satisfied at last that all was safe, I turned to her once more, this time with something of derision.

"Why do you lie there?" I asked her—"you were warmer in my arms a few moments ago! I have stolen the kisses your Silvion left on those pretty lips of yours,—you did well to keep them from the touch of other men,—they were reserved for me! Fragrant as roses I found them, but somewhat cold! But you must wish to hear news of Silvion,—let me tell you of him. You were right,—he did come to Paris."

She made no reply, but rocked herself to and fro, still shivering and moaning.

"There is a pretty nook near Suresnes"—I went on. "The trees there have sheltered and hidden the shame of your love many and many a time. There are grassy nooks, and the birds build their nests to the sound of their own singing,—the river flows softly, and in the early morning when the bells are ringing for mass, the scene is fair enough to tempt even a prude to wantonness. Are you weeping? Ah!—we always grow sentimental over the scene of our pleasantest sins! We love the spot,— we are drawn to it by some fatal yet potent fascination, and after an interval of absence, we return to it with a lingering fond desire to see it once again. Yes, I know!—Silvion Guidèl knew,—and even so, he, in good time returned."

Still no answer! Still the same shuddering movement and restless moaning.

"I met him there"—I pursued,—I was beginning to take a fantastic pleasure in my own narrative. "It was night, and the moon was shining. It must have looked different when you kept your secret trysts,—for you chose the freshest hours of the day, when all your friends and relatives believed you were praying for them at mass like the young saint you seemed to be—it was all sunshine and soft wind for you,—but for me— well! the stars are but sad cold worlds in the sky, and the moon has a solemn face in spite of her associations with lovers,—and so I found there was something suggestive of death in the air when I chanced upon le beau Silvion! We spoke together; he had strange ideas of the possibility of mingling his love with his sworn duty to the Church,—indeed, he seemed to think that God would be on his side if he gave up his vocation altogether and returned to you.—Are you in pain that you keep up such a constant moaning?—But I soon convinced him that he was wrong, and that the Divine aid was always to be had for the right, providing the right was strong enough to hold its own! And for the nonce, this strong right found its impersonation in *me*. We did not quarrel,—there was no time for that. We said what we had to say and there an end. Life,—the life of a sensual priest—presented itself to me as a citadel to be stormed;—I attacked, he defended it. I had no weapon—neither had he,—my hands alone did the work of justice. For it must have been justice, according to the highest religious tenets, else God would not have permitted it, and my strength would have been rendered useless by Divine interposition! Now in France they guillotine criminals,—in England they hang them,—in the East they strangle them—it is all one, so long as the business of breathing is stopped. I remembered this and adopted the Eastern method—it was hard work I can assure you, to strangle a man without rope or bowstring!—it took me time to do it, and it was difficult,—also, it was very difficult for him to die!"

"Oh *God*!" The cry was like the last exclamation wrung from a creature dying on the inquisitional rack of torture,—it was terrible, even to me,—and for a moment I paused, my blood chilled by that awful, despairing groan. But the demon within me urged on my speech again, and I resumed with an air of affected indifference.

"All difficulties come to an end, of course, like everything else—and his were soon terminated. He died at last. I flung his body in the Seine,—well, what now?" for she suddenly sprang erect, and stared at me with a curiously vague yet hunted look, like some trapped wild animal meditating an escape. "You must not leave me yet,—you have not heard all. So!—stand still as you are,—you look like a young tragic Muse!—you are beautiful,—quite inspired!—I almost believe you are glad to know your betrayer is dead! I threw his body in the Seine, I tell you; and a little while afterwards I saw it in the Morgue"—here I began to laugh involuntarily. "I swear I should scarcely have known the Raffaelle-like[1] Silvion again! Imagine those curved red lips that used to smile at shadows like another Narcissus,[2] all twisted and blue!—think of the supple, straight limbs, livid and swollen to twice their natural size!—by Heaven, it was astonishing—amusing!—the grossest caricature of manhood,—all save the eyes. *They* remained true to the departed covetous soul that had expressed its base desires through them,—they still uttered the last craving of the wrenched-out life that had gone,— 'Love!—Love and Pauline!'"

---

[1] Raphael was famous for his depiction of the Holy family and for his ability to depict humanity and serene holiness in his subjects.

[2] Beautiful youth of Greek mythology. He renounced the adoring nymph Echo who took revenge upon him by making him fall in love with his own reflection.

As I said this I smiled. She stood before me like a stone image—so still that I wondered whether she had heard. Her hair had come unbound, and she fingered a tress of it mechanically.

"Love and Pauline!" I repeated, with a sort of satisfaction in the enunciation of the two words—"that is what those dead eyes said,—that is what my heart says now!—love, and Pauline! Silvion desired, and for a time possessed both,—at present it is my turn! For he is lost in the common *fosse*, among crowds of other self-slayers,—and you cannot find even his grave to weep over! Yet—strange to say—I have seen him many times since then——"

The passive form before me stirred and swayed like a slender sapling in a gust of wind—and a voice spoke hoarsely and feebly.

"Seen what?—seen whom?"

"Silvion!" I answered,—my brain suddenly darkening with phantasmal recollections as I spoke,—and, yielding to an involuntary sensation, I turned sharply round, just in time to perceive the figure of a priest outline itself dimly as though in pale phosphorescence against the dark corner of the narrow-built court where we stood. "*There!*" I cried furiously. "See you, Pauline?—There he is!—creeping along like a coward on some base errand! I have not killed him after all! There!—there! Look! He is beckoning you!"

She sprang forward,—her eyes blazing, her arms outstretched, her lips apart.

"Where? where?" she wailed. "Silvion! Silvion! Oh no, no! You torture me!—all is silence—blackness—death! Oh God—God!—is there no mercy?"

And suddenly flinging up her hands above her head, she broke into a loud peal of discordant delirious laughter and rushed violently past me out of the court. Horror or madness lent speed to her flight, for though I followed her close I could not get within touch of her. The rain and mist seemed to enfold her as she fled, till she looked like a phantom blown before me by the wind;—once in the open thoroughfare, one or two passengers stopped and stared after her as she ran, and after me too, doubtless;—but otherwise gave no heed to our headlong progress. Straight on she rushed,—straight to the Pont Neuf, which on this wet and dreary night was vacant and solitary. I accelerated my steps,—I strained every nerve and sinew to overtake her, but in vain. She was like a leaf in a storm,—hurled onwards by temporary insanity, she seemed literally to have wings—to fly instead of to run—but half-way across the bridge, she paused. One flitting second—and she sprang on the parapet!

"Pauline!" I cried. "Wait! Pauline!"

She never turned her head,—she raised her hands to heaven and clasped them as though in supplication,—then—she threw herself forward as swiftly as a bird pinioning its way into space! One small, dull splash echoed on the silence,—she was gone! I reached the spot a moment after she had vanished,—I leaned over the parapet,—I peered down into the gloomy water;—nothing there! Nothing but blank stillness —blank obscurity!

"Pauline!" I muttered. "Little Pauline!"

Then, as I strained my sight over the monotonous width of the river, I saw a something lift itself into view,—a woman's robe blew upwards and outwards like a dark, wet sail—it swirled round once—twice—thrice,—and then it sank again!... My teeth chattered,—I clung to the stone parapet to prevent myself from falling. And yet a horrible sense of amusement stirred within me,—the satirical amusement of a fiend!—it seemed such a ludicrous thing to consider that, after all, this weak, fragile child had escaped me,—had actually gone quietly away where I could not, *dared* not follow!

"Pauline!" I whispered. "Tell me,—what is death like? Is it easy? Do you know anything about love down there in the cold? Remember my kisses were the last on your lips,—mine, not Silvion's! God Himself can not undo that!—all Eternity cannot alter that! They will burn you in hell, they will taint you in heaven, those kisses of mine, Pauline! They will part you from Silvion!—ah!—there is their chiefest sting! You shall not be with him,—I say you shall not!"—and I almost shrieked, as the idea flashed across my perverted brain that perhaps after all the poets were right, and that lovers who loved and were faithful, met in the sight of a God who forgave them their love, and were happy together for ever. "May the whole space of heaven keep you asunder!—may the fire of God's breath sow the whirlwind between you!—may you wander apart and alone, finding paradise empty, and all immortality worthless and wearisome!—every kiss of mine on your lips be a curse, Pauline!—a curse by which I shall claim your spirit hereafter!"

Gasping for articulate speech, the wild imprecation left my lips without my realizing my own utterance; I was giddy and faint,—my temples throbbed heavily—the blood rushed to my brain,—the sky, the trees, the houses, the bridge rushed round and round me in dark whirling rings. All at once my throat filled with a cold sense of suffocation,—tears flooded my eyes, and I broke into a loud sob of fiercest agony.

"Pauline! Pauline!" I cried to the hushed and dreary waters,—"I loved you! You broke my heart! You ruined my life! You made me what I am! Pauline! Pauline! I loved you!"

The wind filled my ears with a dull roaring noise,—something black and cloudy seemed to rise palpably out of the river and sway towards me,—the pale, stern face of Silvion Guidèl came between me and the murky skies,—and with a faint groan, and a savour as of blood in my mouth, I lost my hold on thought and action, and reeled down into utter darkness, insensible.

CHAPTER 32

Dull grey lines with flecks of fire between them,—fire that radiated into all sorts of tints,—blue, green, red, and amber,—these were the first glimmerings of light on my sense of vision that roused me anew to consciousness. Vaguely, and without unclosing my eyes I studied these little points of flame as they danced to and fro on their neutral grey background;—then, a violent shivering fit seized me, and I stirred languidly into my wretched life once more. It was morning,—very early morning—and I was still on the Pont Neuf, lying crouched close to the parapet like any hunted, suffering animal. The mists of dawn hung heavily over the river, and a few bells were ringing lazily here and there for early mass. I struggled to my feet,—pushed my tangled hair from my eyes, and strove hard to realize what had happened. Little by little, I unravelled my knotted thoughts, and grasped at the central solution of their perplexity,—namely, this: Pauline was drowned! Pauline,—even she!—the little fairy thing that had danced and sung and flirted and prattled of her school at Vevey[1] and her love of 'marrons glacés'—even she had become a tragic heroine, wild as any Juliet[2] or Francesca![3] How strange it seemed!—as the critics would say—how *melodramatic!*

---

[1] Small town in the Swiss canton of Vaud and near the eastern extremity of the Lake of Geneva.

[2] Juliet Capulet, heroine of Shakespeare's *Romeo and Juliet*, a tragic story of star-crossed lovers who must keep their love secret because of a feud between their families.

[3] Given Corelli's love for Byron, this is probably a reference to Francesca, a Venetian maiden and daughter of the governor of Corinth who features in Byron's "Siege of Corinth." Francesca was in love with Alp, a man whom her father had exiled and sentenced to death. Bitter at his fate, Alp joins the Muslim Turkish army and fights against his homeland in the Siege of Corinth. He is killed in battle and Francesca dies of a broken heart. It might also refer to Francesca di Rimini who was forced into marriage with a deformed man but secretly loved his brother with whom she committed adultery.

For we are supposed to be living in very common-place days, though truly this is one of the greatest errors the modern wise-acres ever indulged in. Never was there a period in which there was so much fatal complexity of thought and discussion; never was there a time in which men and women were so prone to analyze themselves and the world they inhabit with more pitiless precision and fastidious doubt and argument; and this tendency creates such strange new desires, such subtle comparisons, such marvellous accuracy of perception, such discontent, such keen yet careless valuation of life at its best, that more romances and tragedies are enacted now than Sophocles[1] ever dreamed of. They are performed without any very great *éclat*[2] or stage-effects,—for we latter-day philosophers hate to give grand names to anything, our chief object of study being to destroy all ideals,—hence, we put down a suicide to temporary insanity, a murder to some hereditary disposition or wrong balance of molecules in the brain of the murderer, and love and all the rest of the passions to a little passing heat of the blood. All disposed of quite quietly! Yet suicides are on the increase,—so are murders; and love and revenge and hatred and jealousy run on in their old predestined human course, caring nothing for the names we give them, and making as much havoc as ever they did in the days of Caesar Borgia.[3] To modern casuists, however, Pauline would but seem "temporarily insane"—and during that fit of temporary insanity, she had drowned herself,—*voilà tout!*

Any way she was dead;—that was the chief thing I had to realize and to remember,—but with its usual obstinacy my brain refused to credit it! The mists rose slowly up from the river,—the church bells ceased ringing; a chill wind blew. I shuddered at the pure cold air—it seemed to freeze my blood. I looked abstractedly at the river, and my eyes lighted by chance on a long low flat building not far distant—the Morgue. Ah! Pauline,—if it were indeed she who had been "melodramatic" enough to drown—Pauline would be taken to the Morgue—and I should see her there. A little patience,—a day, perhaps two days,—and I should see her there!

Meanwhile, I was cold and tired and starved; I would go home,—home if I could walk there,—if my limbs were not too weak and stiff to support me. Oh, for a draught of Absinthe!—that would soon put

---

[1]   Greek tragic dramatist (496-406 BC).

[2]   A brilliant display.

[3]   Cesare Borgia (1476-1507); member of the infamous Borgia family who prospered during the Italian Renaissance. The Borgias are associated with unbridled power, lust, and greed.

fire into my veins and warm the numbness of my heart! I paused a moment, still gazing at the dull water and the dull mists; then all at once a curious sick fear began to creep through me,—an awful premonition that something terrible was about to happen, though what it was I could not imagine. My heart began to beat heavily;—I kept my eyes riveted on the scene immediately opposite, for while the sensation I speak of mastered me, I dared not look behind. Presently I distinctly heard a low panting near me like the breathing of some heavy creature,—and my nervous dread grew stronger. For a moment I felt that I would rather fling myself into the Seine than turn my head! It was an absurd sensation,—a cowardly sensation; one that I knew I ought to control and subdue, and after a brief but painful contest with myself I gathered together a slight stock, not of actual courage but physical bravado,—and slowly, irresolutely looked back over my own shoulder,—then, unspeakably startled and amazed at what I saw, I turned my whole body round involuntarily and confronted the formidable beast that lay crouched there on the Pont Neuf, watching me with its sly green eyes and apparently waiting on my movements. A leopard of the forest at large in the heart of Paris!—could anything be more strange and hideously terrifying? I stared at it,—it stared at me! I could almost count the brown velvet spots on its tawny hide,—I saw its lithe body quiver with the pulsations of its quick breath,—and for some minutes I was perfectly paralyzed with fear and horror;—afraid to stir an inch! Presently, as I stood inert and terror-stricken, I heard steps approaching, and a labourer appeared carrying some tin cans which clinked together merrily,—he whistled as he came along, and seemed to be in cheerful humour. I watched him anxiously. What would he do,—what would he say when he caught sight of that leopard lying on the bridge, obstructing his progress? Onward he marched indifferently,—and my heart almost ceased to beat for a second as I saw him coming nearer and nearer to the horrible creature.... What!—was he blind?—Could he not see the danger before him? I strove to cry out,—but my tongue was like stiff leather in my mouth,—I could not utter a syllable;—and lo!—while my fascinated gaze still rested on him he had passed me!— passed apparently *over* or *through* the animal I saw and dreaded!

The truth flashed upon me in an instant,—I was the dupe of my own frenzy—and the leopard was nothing but a brain-phantasm! I laughed aloud, buttoned my coat close over me and drew myself erect,—as I did this, the leopard rose with slow and stealthy grace, and when I moved prepared to follow me. Again I looked at it—again it looked at me,—again I counted the spots on its sleek skin,—the thing was absolutely real and distinct to my vision,—was it possible that a diseased brain could produce such seemingly tangible shapes? I began to walk rapidly,—and another peculiarity of my hallucination discovered itself,—namely, that *before* me as I looked I saw nothing but the usual surroundings of the streets and the passing people,—but *behind* me, I knew, I felt the horrible monster at my heels,—the monster created by my own poisoned thought,—a creature from whom there was no possible escape. The enemies of the body we can physically attack, and often physically repel,—but the enemies of the mind,—the frightful phantoms of a disordered imagination—these no medicine can cure, no subtle touch disperse!

And yet I could not quite accept the fact of the nervous havoc wrought upon me. I saw a boy carrying a parcel of '*Figaros*'[1] to a neighbouring *kiosque*—and stopping him, I purchased one of his papers.

"Tell me," I then said, lightly and with a feigned indifference. "Do you see a—a great dog following me? I chanced upon a stray one on the Pont Neuf just now, but I don't want it at my lodgings. Can you see it?"

The boy looked up and down and smiled.

"*Je ne vois rien, monsieur!*"[2]

"*Merci!*" and nodding to him I strolled away, resolved not to look back again till I reached my own abode.

Once there, I turned round at the door. The leopard was within two inches of me. I kept a backward watch on it, as it followed me in, and up the stairs to my room. I shut the door violently in a frantic impulse of hope that I might thus shut it out,—of course that was useless,—and when I threw myself into a chair, it lay down on the floor opposite me. Then I realized that my case was one in which there could be no appeal,—it was no use fighting against *spectra*.[3] The only thing to be done was to try and control the frenzy of fear that every now and then threatened to shake down all reason and coherency for ever, and make of me a mere howling maniac. I tried to read,—but found I could not understand the printed page,—I found more distraction in thinking of Pauline and her death,—if indeed she were dead. Then, all unbidden, the memory of the fair and innocent Héloïse came across my mind. Should I go and tell her that I had had a strange dream in which it seemed as

---

[1]   A French daily newspaper.
[2]   French for "I don't see anything, sir."
[3]   Apparitions or phantoms.

though I had frightened Pauline into drowning herself? No!—I would wait;—I would wait and watch the Morgue,—for till I saw her *there* I could not be sure she was dead. Anon, a fragment of that old Breton song Héloïse used to recite, repeated itself monotonously in my ears—

"Mon étoile est fatale,
Mon état est contre nature,
Je n'ai eu dans ce monde
Que des peines à endurer;
Nul chrétien sur la terre
Me veuille du bien!"[1]

I hummed this over and over again to myself till I began to shed maudlin tears over my own wretched condition; I had brought myself to it,—but what of that?——the knowledge did not ameliorate matters. If you *know* you have done ill, say the moralists, you have gained the greatest possible advantage, because knowing your evil you can amend it. Very wise in theory no doubt!—but no use in practice. I could not eliminate the poisonous wormwood from my blood,—I was powerless to obliterate from my sight that repulsive spectral animal that lay before me in such seemingly substantial breathing guise. And so I wept weakly and foolishly as a driveling drunkard weeps over his emptied flagon,—and thought vaguely of all sorts of things. I even wondered whether, notwithstanding my having gone so far, there might not yet be a remedy for me—why not?—there was a Charcot in Paris—no man wiser,—no man kinder. But suppose I went to him, what would be the result. He would tell me to give up Absinthe. Give up Absinthe?—why then, I should give up my life!—I should die!—I should be taken away to that terrible unknown country whither I had sent Silvion Guidèl,—where Pauline had followed him,—and I had no wish to go there;—I might meet them, so I stupidly fancied, and it was too soon for such a meeting—yet! No!—I could not give up Absinthe, my fairy with the green eyes, my love, my soul, my heart's core, the very centre and pivot of my being!—anything but that I would do gladly!—but not that,—never, never that! Pah!—how that leopard stared at me as I sat glowering and thinking, and pulling at the ends of my moustache, in a sort of dull stupor,—the stupor of mingled illness and starvation. For I had eaten nothing since the previous day, and

---

[1] Fifth verse of "Le Pauvre Clerc," cited in full on pages 117–18. See Appendix A.2 for translation.

though I was faint, it was not the faintness of natural hunger. That is another peculiarity of my favourite cordial,—taken in small doses it will provoke appetite,—but taken in large and frequent draughts, it invariably kills it. The thought of food attracted yet nauseated me, and so I remained huddled up in my chair engrossed in my own reflections, the nervous tears still now and then trickling from my eyes and dropping like slow hot rain on my closely clenched hands.

The sound of a bugle-note startled me for a moment, and sent my thoughts flying off among fragmentary suggestions of national pride and military glory. France! France!—oh, fair and radiant France!—how canst thou smile on in the faces of such degenerate children as are clambering at thy knees to-day! Oh, France!—what glories were thine in old time!—what noble souls were born of thee!—what white flags of honour waved above thy glittering hosts!—what truth and chivalry beat in the hearts of thy sons, what purity and sweetness ruled the minds of thy daughters! The brilliancy of native wit, of inborn courtesy, of polished grace, were then the natural outcome of naturally fine feelings;—but now,—now!—what shall be said of thee O France, who hast suffered thyself to be despoiled by conquerors and art almost forgetting thy vows of vengeance! Paris, steeped in vice and drowned in luxury, feeds her brain on such loathsome literature as might make even coarse-mouthed Rabelais and Swift[1] recoil,—day after day, night after night, the absinthe-drinkers crowd the *cafés*, and swill the pernicious drug that of all accursed spirits ever brewed to make of man a beast, does most swiftly fly to the seat of reason to there attack and dethrone it;—and yet, the rulers do nothing to check the spreading evil,—the world looks on, purblind as ever and selfishly indifferent,—and the hateful cancer eats on into the breast of France, bringing death closer every day. France!—my France! degraded, lost, and cowardly as I am,—too degraded, too lost, too cowardly to even fight in the lowest ranks for thee,—there are moments when I am not blind to thy glories, when I am not wholly callous as to thy fate! I love thee France!—love thee with the foolish, powerless love that chained and beaten slaves may feel for their native land when exiled from it,—a love that cannot prove its strength by any great or noble act,—that can do nothing,— nothing but look on and watch thee slipping like a loosened jewel out of the blazing tiara of proud nations,—and watching, know most surely that I and such as I, have

---

[1] François Rabelais (1494?-1553) and Jonathan Swift (1667-1745), writers known for their savage satires and coarse language.

shaken thee from what thou wert, and what thou still shouldst be! "*Aux armes, citoyens!*" I cry stupidly, as my patriotic reverie breaks in my brain like a soap-bubble in air,—"*Formez vos bataillons!*"[1]

Ah God!—I start from my chair, staggering to and fro, my head clasped between my hands;—I am dreaming again, like a fool!—dreaming,—and here I am, an *absintheur* in the City of Absinthe, and glory is neither for me, nor for thee, Paris, thou frivolous, lovely, godless, lascivious dominion of Sin! Godless!—and why not?—sinful!—and why not? God did not answer *us* when we prayed,—He was on the side of the Teutons![2] And we have found out that when we try to be good, life is hard and disagreeable; when we are wicked, or what moralists consider wicked, then we find everything pleasant and easy. Some people find the reverse of this, or so they say,—well!—they are quite welcome to be virtuous if they choose. I tried to be virtuous once, and with me it failed to prove its advantages. I loved a woman honestly, and was betrayed; another man loved the same woman *dis*honestly and—kept her faith! This was God's doing (because everything is done by the will of God) therefore you see it was no use my striving to be honest! False arguments? specious reasoning?—not at all! I have the logic of an *absintheur*! *voilà tout!*

That leopard again!—By-and-bye I began to find a certain wretched amusement in watching the sunlight play on the smooth skin of this undesired spectral attendant, and I endeavoured to accept its presence with resignation. After a while I discovered that when I remained passive in one place for some time, the hallucination was brought forward in front of my eyes,—whereas when I walked or was otherwise in rapid motion it was only to be seen behind me. Let scientists explain this if they can, by learned dissertations on the nerve-connections between the spine and brain-cells, the fact remains that the impression created upon me of the actual palpable presence of the animal was distinct and terribly real,— and though later on I found I could pass my hand through its seeming substance, *the conviction of its reality never left me.* Nor is there much chance of its ever leaving me,—it is with me now, and will probably continue to haunt me to my dying day. I walk through Paris apparently alone, but the huge, panting, stealthy thing is always close behind me,—my ears as well as my eyes testify to its presence,—I sit in *cafés* and it lies down in front of me, and we—the spectre and I—stare at each other for hours! People

---

[1] French for "To arms, citizens!... Form your battalions!" Lines from the chorus of "*La Marseillaise,*" the French national anthem.

[2] Germans.

say I have a downward look,—sometimes they ask why
rapid glance behind me as though in fear or anxiety;—y
I always have a vague hope that this phantasmal ᵤ.
suddenly as it came—but it never does—it never will! Andre ⌣
used to peer behind him in just the same fashion,—I remembered it now,
and understood it. And I idly wondered what sort of creature the
Absinthe-fairy had sent to him so persistently that he should have seen
no way out of it but suicide. Now *I* had the courage of endurance,—or
let us say, the cowardice; for I could not bear the thought of death,—it
was the one thing that appalled me. For I so grasped the truth of the
amazing fecundity of life everywhere, that I knew and felt death could
not be a conclusion,—but only the silence and time needed for the
embryo-working of another existence. And on that other existence I
dared not ponder. Oh, if there is one thing I rate at in the Universe more
than another, it is the uncertainty of Creation's meaning. Nature is a great
mathematician, so the scientists declare—then why is the chief number
in the calculation always missing? Why is it that no matter how we count
and weigh and plan, we can never make up the sum total? There is surely
a fault somewhere in the design,—and perchance the great unseen, silent,
indifferent Force we call God, has, in a dull moment, propounded a vast
Problem to which He Himself may have forgotten the Answer!

CHAPTER 33 put in paper

During the next two days I lived for the Morgue, and the Morgue only.
I could not believe Pauline was dead till I saw her there,—there on the
wet cold marble where her lover had lain before her! I haunted the
place,—I skulked about it at all hours like a thief meditating plunder.
And at last my patience was rewarded. An afternoon came when I saw
the stretcher carried in from the river's bank with more than usual pity
and reverence,—and I, pressing in with the rest of the morbid spectators, saw the fair, soft, white body of the woman I had loved and hated
and maddened and driven to her death, laid out on the dull hard slab
of stone like a beautiful figure of frozen snow. The river had used her
tenderly—poor little Pauline!—it had caressed her gently and had not
disfigured her delicate limbs or spoilt her pretty face,—she looked so
wise, so sweet and calm, that I fancied the cold and muddy Seine must
have warmed and brightened to the touch of her drowned beauty!

Yes!—the river had fondled her!—had stroked her cheeks and left them pale and pure,—had kissed her lips and closed them in a child-like happy smile,—had swept all her dark hair back from the smooth white brow just to show how prettily the blue veins were pencilled under the soft transparent skin,—had closed the gentle eyes and deftly pointed the long dark lashes in a downward sleepy fringe—and had made of one little dead girl so wondrous and piteous a picture, that otherwise hard-hearted women sobbed at sight of it, and strong men turned away with hushed footsteps and moistened eyes. The very offi-cials at the Morgue were reverent,—they stood apart and looked on solemnly,—one of them raised the tiny white hand and examined a ring on the finger, a small enamelled forget-me-not in gold, and seemed about to draw it off, but on second thoughts left it where it was. *I* knew that ring well,—Héloïse had given it to her—it was a trinket for which she had always had a sentimental fondness such as girls often indulge in for perfectly worthless souvenirs. I stared and stared,—I gloated on every detail of that delicate, half-nude form,—and my brain was steady enough to remind me that now—now it was my duty to identify the poor little corpse without a moment's delay, so that it might be borne reverently to the care of the widowed Comtesse de Charmilles and Héloïse St. Cyr. Then it would receive proper and honourable inter-ment,—and Pauline, like Shakespeare's Ophelia, would have

"Her maiden strewments, and the bringing home
Of bell and burial."[1]

But no!—I put away the suggestion as soon as it occurred to me. I took a peculiar delight in thinking that if her body were not identified within the proper interval, she too, like her lover, Silvion Guidèl, would be cast into the general ditch of death, without a name, without a right to memory! My deformed and warped intelligence found a vivid pleasure in the contemplation of such petty and unnecessary cruelty,—it seemed good

---

[1] Ophelia in Shakespeare's *Hamlet* is the innocent daughter of Polonius and sister of Laertes. She is in love with Hamlet but goes mad after Hamlet spurns her and kills herself after her father is murdered by Hamlet. Corelli quotes from the speech of the first priest in Act 5, scene 1, a passage in which Hamlet comments on the suspicious nature of Ophelia's death. Having committed suicide, she should not, he insists, have received a Christian burial. But, because of the wishes of people in high places, Ophelia is "allow'd her virgin crants, / Her maiden strewments, and the bringing home / Of bell and burial," and there-fore receives a proper burial.

to me to wreak spite upon the dead,—and as I have already told you, the brain of a confirmed *absintheur* accepts the most fiendish ideas as both beautiful and just. If you doubt what I say, make inquiries at any of the large lunatic asylums in France,—ask to be told some of the aberrations of absinthe-maniacs, who form the largest percentage of brains gone incurably wrong,—and you will hear enough to form material for a hundred worse histories than mine! What can you expect from a man, who has poisoned his blood and killed his conscience? You may talk of the Soul as you will—but the Soul can only make itself manifest in this life through the Senses,—and if the Senses are diseased and perverted, how can the messages of the spirit be otherwise than diseased and perverted also?

And so, yielding to the devilish humours working within me, I held my peace and gave no sign as to the identity of Pauline;—but I went to the Morgue so frequently, nearly every hour in fact, and stared so long and persistently at her dead body that my conduct at last attracted some attention from the authorities in charge. One evening, the third, I think, after she had been laid there, an official tapped me on the arm.

"*Pardon!* Monsieur seems to know the corpse?"

I looked at him angrily, and though there were a few people standing about us, I gave him the lie direct.

"You mistake. I know nothing!"

He eyed me with suspicion and disfavour.

"You seem to take a strange interest in the sight of the poor creature, all the same!"

"Well, what of that?" I retorted. "The girl, though dead, is beautiful! I am an artist!—I have the soul of a poet!" and I laughed ironically. "I love beauty—and I study it wherever I find it, dead or living,—is that so strange?"

"But certainly no, not at all!" said the official, shrugging his shoulders and still looking at me askance. "Only there is just this one little thing that I would say. If we could obtain any idea, however slight,—any small clue which we might follow up as to the proper identification of this so unfortunate *demoiselle*, we should be glad. She was a lady of gentle birth and breeding we have no doubt of that,—but the linen she wore was unmarked,—we can find no name anywhere except one contained in a locket she wore——"

My nerves shook, and I controlled myself with difficulty.

"What sort of locket?" I asked.

"Oh, a mere trifle,—of no value whatever. We opened it, of course,—it had nothing inside but a withered rose leaf and a small slip of paper, on which was written one word, 'Silvion.' That may be the name of a place or a person—we do not know. It does not help us."

No!—it did not help them—but it helped *me*!—helped me to keep my puny rage more firmly fixed upon that helpless, smiling, waxen-looking thing that lay before me in such solemn and chilly fairness. A withered rose leaf, and the name of that accursed priest!—these were her sole treasures, were they?—all she cared to save from the wreckage of her brief summer time! Well, well! women are strange fools at best and the wisest man that ever lived cannot unravel the mystery of their complex mechanism. Half puppets, half angels!—and one never knows to which side of their natures to appeal!

"We have given a very precise and particular description of the corpse in our *annonces*"[1]—went on the official meditatively—"but at present it has led to nothing. We should be really glad of identification,—though it is only a question of sentiment——"

"A question of sentiment! What do you mean?" I asked roughly.

He gave a deprecatory gesture.

"Monsieur, we Frenchmen have hearts! *La pauvre petite*[2] there is too delicate and pretty to lie in the common *fosse*!"

Good God! What an absurd influence the loveliness of a woman can exert on the weak minds of men! Here was a girl dead and incapable of knowing whether she was lying in the common *fosse* or any other place of interment, and yet this stern officer of the Morgue, touched by her looks, regretted the necessity of burying her thus harshly and without reverence.

I laughed carelessly.

"You are very gallant, Monsieur! I wish I could assist you! This girl-suicide is beautiful as you say,—I have contemplated her face and figure with much pleasure——"

"Will you look at her more closely, Monsieur?" he asked, suddenly turning a keen glance upon me.

I perceived his drift. He suspected me of knowing something, and wanted to startle me into confessing it! Cunning rogue!—But I was a match for him!

"I shall be charmed to do so!" I responded with easy indifference. "It will be a privilege!—a lesson in art!"

---

[1] French for "announcement" or "notice." In this instance, the official is referring to the notices put out to elicit responses from the public to help identify corpses in the possession of the morgue.

[2] French for "The poor little one."

He said nothing, but simply led the way within. One minute more, and the electric light flashed in a dazzling white effulgence over the drowned girl,—I felt the official's eyes upon me, and I kept firm. But in very truth I was sick—sick at heart!—and a chill crept through all my blood,—for I was near enough to touch the woman I had so loved!—I could have kissed her!—her little white stiff hand lay within a few inches of mine! I breathed with difficulty,—do what I would, I could not prevent a slight shiver visibly shaking my limbs. And she!—she was like a little marble goddess asleep—poor little Pauline!

Then—all suddenly—the official bent over her corpse and raised it up forcibly by the head and shoulders, ... I thought I should have shrieked aloud!

"Do not touch her!" I exclaimed in a hoarse whisper. "It is a—sacrilege!"

He looked at me steadily, quite unmoved by my words.

"You are sure you cannot identify the body?—you have no idea who she was when living?" he demanded, in measured accents.

I shrank backward. As he held the dead girl in that upright attitude I was afraid she might open her eyes!

"I tell you, no!" I answered with a sort of sullen ferocity. "No, no, no! Lay her down! Why the devil can you not let her be?"

He gave me another searching, distrustful look. Then he slowly and with a certain tenderness laid the body back in its former recumbent position, and beckoned me to follow him out of the mortuary. I did so.

"*Voyons,*[1] Monsieur"—he said confidentially—"this is not a case of murder,—there is no ground for any suspicion of that kind. It is simply a suicide,—we have many such,—and surely from your manner and words, you could, if you choose, give us some information. Why not speak frankly? *Par exemple*, will you *swear* that you know absolutely nothing of the woman's identity?"

Persistent fool! I returned his glance defiantly,—we were in the outer chamber now, and the glass screen was once more between us and the corpse, so I felt more at ease.

"Why, oaths are not of much value nowadays in France!" I answered carelessly. "Our teachers have left us no God, so what am I to swear by? By your head or my own?"

He was patient, this man of the Morgue, and though I spoke loudly, and there were people standing about, he took no offence at my levity.

---

[1] French expression meaning "Now then!"

"Swear by your honour, Monsieur!—that is enough."

My honour! Ha!—that was excellent!—I, who had no more sense of honour than a carrion crow!

"By my honour, then!" I said, laughing—I swear I know nothing of your pretty dead Magdalen[1] in there! A *fille de joie*,[2] no doubt! Strange that so many men have pity for such; even the amiable Christ had a good word to say on behalf of these naughty ones! What was it?—Yes—I remember;—'*Her sins, which are many, are forgiven her, for she loved much!*'[3] True!—love excuses many follies. And she,—the little drowned one,—is charming!—I admire her with all my heart!—but I cannot tell you who she is, or—to speak more correctly—who she was!"

As I uttered the deliberate lie, a sort of electric shock ran through me—my heart leaped violently and the blood rushed to my brows,—a pair of steadfast, sorrowful, lustrous eyes flashed wondering reproach at me over the heads of the little throng of spectators,—they were the eyes of Héloïse St. Cyr!

Yes!—it was she!—she had kept her word!—she had come to rescue Pauline,—to defraud me of my vengeance on the dead! Stately, angelic, pitiful, and pure, she stood in that cold and narrow chamber, her face pale as the face of her drowned cousin,—her hands tremblingly outstretched! As in a dream I saw the press of people make way for her,—I saw men take off their hats and remain uncovered as though a prayer were being spoken,—I saw the official in charge approach her and murmur some respectful inquiry,—and then—then I heard her voice, sweet though shaken with tears,—a voice that sent its penetrating music straight to the very core of my wretched and worthless being!

"I come to claim her!" she said simply, addressing herself to the official. "She is my cousin, Pauline de Charmilles,—only daughter of the late Count de Charmilles. We have lost her—long!"—and a half sob escaped her lips—"Give her to me now, —and I will take her—oh, poor Pauline!—I will take her ... home!"

Her strength gave way—she hid her face in her hands—and some women near her began crying for sympathy. It was what cynical people would call a "scene"—and yet—somehow, I could not mock at it as I would fain have done. The spirit of Humanity was here—even here

---

[1] Mary Magdalene was one of Jesus' followers. Jesus rescued her from her life as a prostitute.

[2] French term for "a prostitute."

[3] New Testament, Luke 7.47. Said of the woman who anointed Jesus' feet, a woman often identified as Mary Magdalene.

among the morbid frequenters of the Morgue, the "touch of nature which makes the whole world kin"[1] was not lacking anywhere—save in me!—and more than all, Héloïse was here,—and in her presence one could not jest. One believed in God;—one always believes in God, by the side of a good woman!

I raised my eyes,—I was resolved to look at her straight,—and I did so—but only for one second! For her glance swept over me with such unutterable horror, loathing, and agony, that I cowered like a slave under the lash! I crept out of her sight!—I slunk away, followed by the phantom beast of my own hideous degradation,—away—away—out into the chill darkness of the winter night, defeated! Defeated!—defrauded of the last drop in my delirious draught of hatred!—Alone under the cold and starless sky, I heaped wild curses on myself, on God,—on the world!—on life and time and space!—while she—the angel Héloïse, whose love I had once possessed unknowingly, bore home her sacred dead,—home to a maiden funeral-couch of flowers, sanctified by tears and hallowed by prayers,—home,—to receive the last solemn honours due to Innocence and—Frailty!

CHAPTER 34

What was there to do now? Nothing,—but to drink Absinthe! With the death of Pauline every other definite object in living had ended. I cared for nobody;—while as far as my former place in society was concerned I had apparently left no blank. You cannot imagine what little account the world takes of a man when he ceases to set any value on himself. He might as well never have been born,—or he might be dead,—he is as equally forgotten, and as utterly dismissed.

I attended Pauline's funeral of course. I found out when it was to take place,—and I watched it from a distance. It was a pretty scene,— a sort of white, fairy burial. For we had a fall of snow in Paris that day,— and the small coffin was covered with a white pall, and all the flowers upon it were white;—and when the big vault was unbarred to admit this dainty burden of death hidden in blossoms, its damp and gloomy walls were all covered with wreaths and garlands, as though it were a bridal chamber. This was the work of Héloïse, no doubt!—sweet saint

---

[1] From Shakespeare's *Troilus and Cressida* 3.3.175.

Héloïse! She looked pale as a ghost and thin as a shadow that after-noon;—she walked by the side of the widowed Comtesse de Charmilles, who appeared very feeble of tread, and was draped in black from head to foot. I gazed at the solemn cortège from an obscure corner in the cemetery,—and smiled as I thought that I—I only had wrought all the misery on this once proud and now broken-down, bereaved family!—I, and—Absinthe! *If* I had remained the same Gaston Beauvais that I once had been,—if on the night Pauline had made her wild confession of shame to me, I had listened to the voice of mercy in my heart,—if I had never met André Gessonex ... imagine!—so much hangs on an "if"! Now and then a kind of remorse stung me,—but it was a mere passing emotion,—and it only troubled me when I thought of or saw Héloïse. She was, as she now is, the one reproach of my life,—the only glimpse of God I have ever known! When Pauline was laid to rest,—when the iron grating of the cold tomb shut grimly down on all that was mortal of the bright foolish child I had first met fresh from her school at Vevey,—this same sweet, pale Héloïse lost all her self-control for a moment, and with a long sobbing cry fell forward in a swoon among the little frightened attendant acolytes and their flaring candles,—but she recovered speedily. And when she could once more stand upright, she tottered to the door of the mausoleum, and kissed it,—and hung a wreath of white roses upon it, on which the word "Amour!" was written in silver letters. Then she went away weeping, with all the rest of the funeral train—but I—I remained behind! Hidden among the trees I lay quiet, in undiscovered safety, so that when the night came I was still there. The guardians of Père-la-Chaise, patrolled the place as usual and locked the gates—but I was left a prisoner within, which was precisely what I desired. Once alone—all all alone in the darkness of the night, I flung up my arms in delirious ecstacy—this City of the Dead was mine for the time!—mine, all these moulding corpses in the clay! I was sole ruler of this wide domain of graves! I rushed to the shut-up marble prison of Pauline—I threw myself on the ground before it,—I wept and raved and swore, and called her by every endear-ing name I could think of!—the awful silence maddened me! I beat at the iron grating with my fists till they bled;—"Pauline!" I cried—"Pauline!" No answer!—oh God!—she would never answer—any call again! Grovelling in the dust I looked up despairingly—the word "Amour!" with its silvery glisten on Héloïse's rose-garland, flashed on my eyes like a flame. "Amour!" Love! God or the Devil! It is one or the other; it is the thing that rules the universe,—it is the only Deity we can never abjure! Love!—oh madness! Tell me, women and men, tell me whether love rules your lives most for good, or most for evil? Can we not get at the truth of this? If we can, then we shall know the secret of life's riddle. For if Love lead us most to evil, then the hidden Force of Creation is a Fiend,—if it lead us most to good, then—then we have a God to deal with! And I fear me much it is a God after all!—I shudder to think it,—but I am afraid—afraid! For if God exists, then they—all the dead creatures I know, whose spirits haunt me,—they are happy, wise, victorious and immortal,—while I—I am lower than the veriest insect that breeds in the mould and is blind to the sun! I must not dwell on this;—I must not look back to those hours passed outside Pauline's tomb. For they were horrible! Once, as the night waned, I saw Silvion Guidèl,—he leaned against the pillars of the vault and barred my way with one uplifted hand. I could not fight him—a creature of the mist and air!—but his face was as the face of an angel, and its serene triumph filled me with impotent fury! He had won the day, I felt!—Pauline was his—not mine! God had been on his side, and Death, instead of conquering him, had given him the victory!

One day, weeks after Pauline's burial, I was very ill. I could not move at all—the power of my limbs was gone. Such a strange weakness and sick fever beset me that I did nothing but weep for sheer helplessness. It was a sort of temporary paralysis—it passed away after a while, but it left me terrified and unstrung. When I got better, a droll idea entered my brain. I would go to confession! I, who hated priests, would see what they could tell me for once,—I would find out whether Religion, or what was called religion, had any mystical saving grace for an *absintheur*! I was abjectly miserable at the time,—a fit of the most intolerable depression had laid hold upon me. Moreover, I had been foolishly hurt by chancing to see my father walking along with his new partner,—the man he had adopted in my place,—a fine, handsome, pleasant, dashing-looking fellow,—and he,—my father,—had seemed perfectly happy!—Yes, perfectly happy! He had not seen me,—probably he would not have known me if he had,—he leaned upon the arm of his new "son"—and laughed with him at some jest or other;—he had forgotten me!—or if he had not actually forgotten, he was determined to appear as though he had. I thought him cruel,—callous;—I blamed fate, and everything and everybody except myself who had wrought my own undoing. That is the way with many of us,—we get wilfully and deliberately into mischief,—then we look about to see on which one of our fellow-creatures we can lay the fault!

"Open confession is good for the soul!"[1] says some moralist or other. I determined to try it—for a change! And my confessor should be good old Père Vaudron!—I wondered I had never thought of him before. He might perhaps be some comfort to me,—for he was an honest Christian, and therefore he would not be likely to turn away from any penitent, however fallen and degraded.

But was I penitent? Of course not! I was miserable I tell you; and I wanted the relief of unburdening myself to some one who would not repeat what I said. I was not sorry for anything—I was only tired, and made nervous by the spectral beast that followed me, as well as by other curious and frightful hallucinations. Fiery wheels in the air,—great, glittering birds of prey swooping down with talons outstretched to clutch at me,—whirlpools of green in the ground into which it seemed I must fall headlong as I walked—these were common delusions;—but I began to dread madness as I had never dreaded it before,—and the more I considered the matter, the more determined I became to speak to Père Vaudron, who had known me from boyhood;—it might do me good,—there were miracles in the Church,—who could tell!

And so one evening I made my way up to the little well-remembered chapel,—the place where, if all had gone smoothly, I should have been married to Pauline,—the altar where "*le beau* Silvion" had "assisted" his too-confiding uncle at early mass. Everything was very quiet,—there were flowers about,—and the sacred lamps of vigil were burning clearly. A woman was sweeping out the chancel,—I recognized her at once,—it was old Margot. She did not know me; she looked up as I entered, but finding (no doubt) my appearance the reverse of prepossessing, she resumed her task with increased vigour. Save for her and myself, the church was empty. After waiting a little I went up and spoke to her.

"Does M. the Curé hear confessions this evening?"

She stared at me and crossed herself,—then pointed to the sacristy bell. "*Sonnez, s'il vous plaît!*"[2]

She was always curt and cross, this old Margot!—I tried her again.

"It is not the usual hour, perhaps?"

She made no reply;—so, smiling a little at her acerbity I did as she bade me and rang the bell she indicated. A small boy appeared,—an acolyte.

"Does the reverend father attend the confessional this evening?"

"Yes. He will be in the church almost immediately."

---

[1] Proverbial.

[2] French phrase meaning "Ring, if you please."

I retired and sat down to wait. I was beginning to feel very much amused. This was the finest jest I had ever played with myself,—I was actually pretending to have a conscience! Meanwhile old Margot took her departure with her broom and all her cleansing paraphernalia—and left me alone in the church. She banged the big door behind her noisily,—and the deep silence that followed its hollow reverberation oppressed me uncomfortably. There was a large crucifix near me, and the figure of Christ upon it looked tortured and gruesome; what a foolish fond enthusiast He was, I thought, to perish for such a delusive idea as the higher spiritualization of Man! We shall never become spiritual; we are of the earth earthy—our desires are base,—our passions contemptible; but as we have been created so we shall remain, *selon moi*;[1]—others may hold a different opinion if they choose.

A slow step sounded on the marble floor, and I hastily bent my head as penitents do, looking between my clasped fingers at good old Vaudron as he came through the sacristy and paced gently towards the confessional. Heavens! how changed he was!—how he stooped!—and his hair was snow-white,—his face too, once so florid and merry, was wrinkled, careworn, and pale. He had suffered, even he, this poor old man,—and his suffering was also my work! God! what a fiendish power one human being has to ruin many others! I waited till he was seated in the usual niche—then I made my way to the penitent's corner. As I knelt I heard him mutter the usual Latin formula,—he deemed me also at my prayers, but I said nothing. I kept silence so long, that at last he sighed impatiently, and putting his lips close to the curtained grating said mildly—

"I am waiting, my son! Take courage!"

My sense of amusement increased. I could have laughed aloud, it was such a comedy.

"*Mon père*," I murmured, controlling myself by an effort, "my confession will be strange and terrible,—are you prepared for something quite unusual?"

I felt that he was startled,—but in his quiet accents there was only just the faintest touch of sternness as he replied—

"I am prepared. Commend yourself to God—to Him you speak as well as to me,—therefore be truthful and conceal nothing, as only by true confession can you hope for mercy."

"The jargon of the Church as usual!" I said contemptuously. "Spare me unnecessary platitudes, good father! My sins are not those of every

---

[1] French for "in my opinion."

day,—and everyday comfort will not do for me. And so to begin at once,—*I have murdered a man*! This and no less is my crime!—can you give me absolution?"

I heard a sudden agitated movement inside the confessional. Through the small holes of the grating I could see him clasp his hands as though in terror or prayer. Then he spoke.

"Absolution? Wretched soul, there is none—none! Unless you at once confess yourself to the authorities and give yourself up to justice, there is no forgiveness either in earth or heaven for such an evil deed. Who was the man?"

"My enemy!"

"You should have pardoned him!"

"Good father, you are not consistent! According to your own account, God Himself does not pardon till justice is done. I—like Deity—wanted justice! I killed a deceiver, a liar, a seducer,—a priest who robbed me of the woman I loved!"

A shuddering sigh—half a groan escaped him.

"A priest!—oh God!"

"Yes, a priest!" I went on recklessly. "What then? Priests are worse than laymen. Their vocation deprives them of love,—they crave for it because it is forbidden; they will have it at all risks. And he, the man I killed—had it,—he won it by a mere look, a mere smile; he had fine eyes and a graceful trick of manner. He was happy for a time at any rate. He was as beautiful as an angel—as gifted as a Marcus Aurelius![1]—Did you never know any one like him? He had the best of all the world could give him in the love of a woman as fair as the morning. She is dead too now. She drowned herself as soon as she knew he was gone— and that I had killed him! So he keeps her love to the end you see,— and I am baffled of it all. That is why I have come to you—just because I am baffled,—I want you to comfort me—I want a victory some- where! I want you to tell me that the man I murdered is damned to all eternity, because he had no time to repent of his sins before he died! I want you to tell me that she—the woman,—is damned also, because, she killed herself without God's permission! Tell me any lies the Church will allow you to tell! Tell me that I am safe because I endure!—because though loaded with sin and vice, I still *live on*, waiting for God to kill me rather than myself! Tell me this and I will read all the Penitential Psalms in the *café* this evening instead of the '*Petit Journal*!'" I paused for

---

[1]   Roman Emperor (AD 121-180) renowned for his high moral view of life.

lack of breath,—I could see Vaudron start up from his seat in horror as I uttered my reckless tirade—and now, when I gave him time to speak, his voice trembled with righteous indignation.

"Blasphemer, be silent!" he said—"Wretched, unhappy man!—how dare you presume to enter God's house in such a condition? You are mad or drunk!—you affront the Sacrament of Confession by ribald language!—you insult the Church! Pray for true contrition if you can pray—and go!—I will hear no more!"

"But you *shall* hear!" I said wildly. "You *must* hear! I have murdered a man, I tell you!—and the accursëd memory of his dying eyes, his dying face, clings to me like a disease in the air! You do not ask me who he was—yet you know him!—you loved him! He was your nephew—Silvion Guidèl!"

Hardly had the words left my lips when the confessional doors flew open, and Vaudron rushed upon me,—he clutched me by the arm, his fine old face burning with wrath.

"You murdered him!—you—you!" he gasped, his eyes glittering, his hand uplifted as though he would have struck me down before him.

I smiled.

"Even so, good father! I,—simply I! And here I am,—at your mercy—only remember this,—what I have said to you is *under the seal of confession!*"

His upraised arm dropped nerveless at his side—he stared fixedly at me, his breath coming and going rapidly as though he had been running a race. Then, still holding me in a fast grip, he dragged me to the front of the altar where the light shed by the swinging lamps could fall directly upon my features. There, like one in some feverish dream, he scanned me up and down, doubtfully at first, then with gradually dawning, horrified recognition.

"God have mercy upon me!" he ejaculated tremulously; "It is Gaston Beauvais!"

"Precisely so, *mon cher* Vaudron!" I replied composedly. "It is Gaston Beauvais! It is the Gaston Beauvais who was duped and betrayed,—and who has avenged his wrong in the good old Biblical fashion, by killing his betrayer! More than this—it is the Gaston Beauvais who drove Pauline de Charmilles to her self-sought death, by telling her the fate of her lover,—what could you expect!—she was a silly girl always! And now I unburden myself to you that you may know me; and that I also may know if there is any truth in the religion you profess. I think not,—for you, an ordained servant of the Church, have already shown something of unseemly violence! Your grip on my arm is not of the lightest, I assure you!—you have given way to anger,—fie, *père* Vaudron! Wrath in the sanctuary is not becoming to your order! What!—did you fancy you were a man for once,—instead of a priest?"

I did not mean to offer him this insult,—the bitter jest escaped my lips before I was aware of it. But it made no visible effect on him,—he merely loosened his hold of me and stood a step or two apart, looking at me with strained anguished eyes.

"You can break your vows, if you like," I went on carelessly. "Vows of every kind are brittle ware nowadays. You can tell my father I am a murderer,—the murderer of Silvion Guidèl—and so give him fresh cause to congratulate his foresight in having disowned me,—you can tell Héloïse St. Cyr that I goaded her cousin to madness,—you can betray me to the guillotine. All this is in your power, and by doing it you will only prove, like many another of your craft, how lightly a Creed weighs in the balance against personal passion, ... you will be wise in your generation like the Pharisees[1] of old——"

"Stop—stop!" he cried hoarsely, flinging up his hands and clasping them above his head. "I cannot bear it—oh God! I cannot bear it! Wretched man, what have *I* done to you that you should so torture me!"

I was silent. What had he done? Why—nothing! I watched him coldly,—his countenance was a strange study! He was fighting a mental battle,—a conflict of sworn duty against all the claims and instincts of manhood,—it seemed surprising to me that he should deem it worth his while to engage in such a struggle. A few minutes passed thus,—no one entered the church,—we were alone with all the familiar things of religion about us, the lamps above us shedding a blood-like hue on the figure of the Christ crucified. Presently, as though drawn by some compelling instinct he turned towards this Image of his Faith,—a great sigh broke from his lips,—and, tottering feebly forward, he fell upon his knees and hid his face,—I saw tears trickling slowly between his wrinkled fingers. Foolish old man! His simplicity vexed me—he looked like the picture of a praying apostle, with the faint glow from the light above the cross falling in the shape of a halo round his silvery hair!

And I—I stood irresolute,—half abashed, wholly embarrassed,—inclined to laugh or weep, I knew not which;—when all at once a

---

[1] An ancient Jewish sect distinguished by strict observance of traditional and written law, held to have pretensions to superior sanctity. Also used to denote a self-righteous person or hypocrite.

horrible sensation overwhelmed me,—something snapt asunder in my temples like a suddenly cut wire,—the whole nave of the church grew black as pitch, and I threw out my hands to keep myself from falling. Then came masses of pale green vapour that twisted and twirled, and sent shafts of lambent fire, or lightning as it seemed into the very centre of my brain!—but through it all, though I seemed caught up and devoured by flame, I saw Vaudron's devout figure kneeling at the crucifix; and I rushed to it as to some certain rescue.

"Save me!" I cried desperately. "Have you no pity?" and I clutched at his garment. "Do you not see?—I am going mad!—mad!"

And I burst into a peal of delirious laughter that woke loud echoes from the vaulted roof and startled my own ears with a sense of horror. But with that laughter, the paroxysm passed,—my brain cleared, and I regained my self-control as by an electric shock that only left my limbs trembling. Père Vaudron meanwhile had risen from his knees and now confronted me, his features pallid with woe and wonder.

"Pardon me!" I said, and forced a smile. "I am not well! I have nervous delusions,—I suffer from too much dissipation—I am a victim to pleasure! Self-indulgence is an agreeable thing,—but it has its consequences which are *not* always agreeable. It is nothing—a mere passing ailment! But now, good father,—as you have said your prayers—(and I hope gained much benefit thereby!) may I ask if you have no word for me? It is the duty of a priest, I believe, if he cannot give absolution, to at least enjoin penance!"

He met my satirical glance with a stern sorrow in his own eyes— the tears were still wet on his cheeks.

"The secret of your crime is safe with me!" was all he said,—and turned away.

I hastened after him.

"Is that all?" I asked, half banteringly. He stopped, and looked fixedly at me once more;—the agony depicted in his face would have touched me had my heart not been harder than adamant.

"All!" he exclaimed passionately. "Is it not the 'all' you need? You tell me you murdered the unhappy Silvion,—you,—Gaston Beauvais, of all men in the world!—and why have you told me? Simply to weigh me down to the grave with the awful burden of that hidden knowledge! You have no regret or remorse,—you speak of what you have done with the most horrible cynicism,—and to talk of penance to you would be to outrage its very name! For God's sake leave me!—leave me to the wretchedness of my lonely old age,—leave me, while I have strength to let you go unharmed—I am but human!—your presence sickens me—I have no force to bear—more——"

His voice failed him,—he made a slight gesture of dismissal.

"And I—do you not think *I* am miserable?" I said angrily. "What a set of egotists you are—you and my father, and the whole *baraque*![1] Fine Christians truly!—always pitying yourselves! Have you no pity for Me?"

The old curé drew himself up, the dignity and pathos of his grief making his homely figure for the moment majestic.

"I pity you, God knows!" he said solemnly. "I pity you more than the lowest pitiable thing that breathes! A man with the curse of Cain[2] upon his soul,—a man without a heart, without a conscience, without peace in this world or hope in the next;—as Christ lives, I pity you! But do not expect more of me than pity! I am a poor frail old man,— lacking in all the virtues of the saints—and I cannot—Heaven help me! I cannot forgive you!"—and his voice shook as, waving me back with one hand he walked feebly to the door of the sacristy—"I cannot!— Christ have mercy upon me!—I cannot! I have no strength for that,— the poor child Pauline—the wretched Silvion!—no, no! I cannot forgive!—not yet! God must teach me to do that—God must help me,—of my own accord I cannot!"

On a sudden impulse I flung myself on my knees before him.

"Père Vaudron!" I cried. "Remember!—You knew me as a child— you loved me as a boy,—you are my father's friend! Think—I am a wreck—a lost soul!—will you let me go without a word of comfort?"

He stood inert—his face pale as death, his lips quivering. The struggle within him was very bitter—his breath came hard and fast,—he too had loved that accursedly beautiful Silvion! After a pause, he raised his shaking hand and pointed to the crucifix.

"There—*there!*" he muttered brokenly—"Go there—and—pray! As a man I dare say nothing to you—as a priest I say, God help you!"

Poor old man! His Christian heroism was sorely tried! He drew his garment from my touch,—the sacristy-door opened and shut,—he was gone.

I sprang to my feet and looked about me. I was alone in the church,— alone and face to face with the crucifix,—the great, gaunt, bleeding Figure with the down-dropped Head and thorny Crown. "Go there—and pray!"

---

[1] French term used, in this instance, to denote "lot" as in "the whole lot."

[2] Cain's curse for having killed his brother Abel was to be made to wander the earth as a fugitive and vagabond.

What—I?—I, an *absintheur*? Kneel at a crucifix? Never? It could do *me* no good, I knew,—whatever miracle it might work on others!

Poor old Vaudron! I had made him miserable—poor, simple, silly, feeble soul! "God help you!" he had said—not "God pardon you!" He knew the Eternal Code of Justice better than to use the word "pardon." I should scarcely have thought he had so much firmness in him—so much stanch manhood. It was not in human nature to easily forgive such a criminal as I,—and he, in spite of his vocation, had been true to human nature. I honoured him for it. Human Nature is a grand thing! Sometimes noble, sometimes mean,—sometimes dignified, sometimes abject,—what an amazing phase of Creation it is!—and though so human, how full (at odd intervals) of the Divine! The crucifix is its Symbol,—for Man at his best is an Ideal,—and when he reaches this point of perfection, the rest of his race hang him up on a cross like a criminal in the sight of the centuries, to mock at, to worship now and then, and to sneer at still more frequently; for, says the world—"Look at this fool! He professed to be able to live a nobler life than we, and see where we have nailed him!"

And I passed the dead Christ with an indifferent shrug and smile as I stumbled out of the quiet church into the chill air of the night, and thought how little the Christian creed had done for me. It had (perhaps) persuaded Vaudron to "pity" me, and to say, "God help" me,—but what cared I for pity or a vaguely divine assistance? I had better material wherewith to deal!—and, humming the fragment of a tune, I sauntered drowsily down to the Boulevards, and there, as a suitable wind-up to my "religious" evening, got dead drunk,—on Absinthe!

CHAPTER 35

The time that immediately followed that night is a blur to me;—I have no recollection at all of anything that happened. For I was very ill. During the space of a whole month I lay in my bed, a prey to violent fever and delirium. So I was told afterwards;—I knew nothing. The people at my lodgings got alarmed and sent for a doctor,—he was a good fellow in his way, and took an amiably scientific interest in me. When I recovered my senses he told me what I knew very well before,—namely that all my sufferings were due to excessive indulgence in Absinthe.

"You must give it up," he said decisively, "at once,—and for ever. It is a detestable habit,—a horrible craze of the Parisians, who are positively deteriorating in blood and brain by reason of their passion for this poison. What the next generation will be, I dread to think! I know it is a difficult business to break off anything to which the system has grown accustomed,—but you are still a young man, and you cannot be too strongly warned against the danger of continuing in your present course of life. Moral force is necessary,—and you must exert it. I have a large medical practice, and cases like yours are alarmingly common, and as much on the increase as morphinomania amongst women,—but I tell you frankly no medicine can do good, where the patient refuses to employ his own power of resistance. I must ask you therefore, for your own sake, to bring all your will to bear on the effort to overcome this fatal habit of yours, as a matter of duty and conscience."

Duty and conscience! I smiled,—and, turning on my pillows, stared at him curiously. He was a quiet, self-possessed man of middle age, rather good-looking, with a calm voice and a reserved manner.

"Duty and conscience!" I murmured languidly. "How well they sound—those good little words! And so, doctor, you consider me in a bad condition?"

He surveyed me with a cold, professional air.

"I certainly do," he answered. "If it were not for the fact that you have the recuperative forces of youth in you, I should be inclined to pronounce you as incurable. Were I to analyze your state——"

"Do so, I beg of you!" I interrupted him eagerly. "Analyze me by all means!—I am fond of science!"

He looked at me dubiously and felt my pulse, watch in hand.

"Science is in its infancy," he said meditatively, "especially medical science. But some few facts it has entirely mastered. And so, speaking without any reserve, I must inform you that if you persist in drinking *absinthe* you will become a hopeless maniac. Your illness has been a sort of God-send,—it has forced you to live a month under my care without tasting a drop of that infernal liquid. And a certain benefit has been the result, so that, in a way, you are prepared to be cured. But your brain-cells are still heavily charged with the poison, and a violent irritation has been set up in the nerve-tissues. Your blood is contaminated—and its flow from the heart to the brain is irregular,—sometimes violently interrupted;—a state of things which naturally produces giddiness, swooning, and fits of delirium which resemble strong epilepsy. Such a condition might make you subject to hallucinations of an unpleasant kind——"

"Just so!" I interposed lazily. "And with all your skill, doctor, you have not got rid of that brute down there!"

He started,—and gazed inquiringly in the direction to which I pointed, where plain and tangible to my eyes, the tawny spectral leopard lay *on* my bed, not below it,—its great yellow forepaws resting close to my feet.

"What brute?" he demanded, bringing his calm glance to bear upon me once more, and again pressing his cool, firm fingers on my throbbing pulse.

I explained in a few words, the hateful delusion that had troubled me so long. His brows knitted, and he seemed perplexed.

"No cure for me?" I asked indifferently, noting the expression of his face.

"I do not know—I cannot tell," he answered hurriedly. "Such persistently marked *spectra* is generally the symptom of existing disease,—I had hoped otherwise—but——"

"You had hoped it was merely temporary," I said. "Ah, I understand! But if disease has actually begun, what is the remedy?"

He hesitated.

"Come—speak!" And I raised myself on my pillows impatiently. "You need not be afraid to give an opinion!"

"There is no remedy," he replied reluctantly. "Disease of the brain is incurable,—it can only be retarded. Care, good food, quiet, and total abstinence from any sort of spirituous poison,—this *régime*, can avert, and probably check any fresh symptoms,—in some cases a normal condition can be attained which very nearly approaches complete cure. More than this would be impossible to human skill ..."

"Thanks!" I murmured, lying back on my bed again. "You are very good! I will think over what you say; though to tell you the truth, it seems to me quite as agreeable to be mad as sane in this monotonous world!"

He moved away from me to the table, where he sat down and wrote a prescription. I noted his appearance drowsily,—his sleek head, his well-fitting clothes,—the clean, pale, business-looking hand that guided the pen.

"*Voyons!*" I said, with a laugh,—"In all the range of your experience, did you ever know an *absintheur* give up Absinthe?—even for the sake of 'duty and conscience'?"

He made no answer—he merely took up his hat, looked into the crown of it, bowed slightly, and took his departure.

A couple of weeks later on I was able to rise from my bed and crawl about again, and then it was that I found I was getting very short of money. My illness had cost me dear;—and I soon recognized that I should have to vacate my already poor apartment for one in some still cheaper and lower quarter. And I should have to do something for a living,—

something, if it were but to beg for pence,—something even to obtain the necessary coins wherewith to purchase Absinthe. And one day, the weather being warm and sunny, I wandered into the *Tuileries gardens*[1] and sat there, drowsily pondering on my own fate,—turning over the *pros* and *cons* of my miserable existence, and wondering what I should do to enable myself to live on. For worthless as my life was,—worthless as I knew it to be,—I did not want to die,—I had not the necessary courage for that.

All at once like a rainbow of hope in a dark sky, there came to me the thought of Héloïse St. Cyr. Her fair and saintly presence seemed to pass, like a holy vision, before my sight,—and in my weak and debilitated state, the tears rushed to my eyes at the mere remembrance of her womanly truth and sweetness. Her voice, with its soft musical cadence seemed to float invitingly towards me,—nay,—I even fancied I heard the melodies of the violin she played so well, echoing faintly through the quiet air. I would go to her, I thought;—would go, while I was crushed and broken down by the effects of my illness; I would tell her all and plead for pity— for pardon;—I would ask her to help me,—to save me from myself as only a good woman, God's angel on earth, ever can save a wretched man. And if she wished—if she commanded it—I would,—yes!—I would actually give up *absinthe* for her sake,—she should do with me what she would,—my wrecked life should be hers to dominate as she chose!

I rose up hastily, the tears still in my eyes,—and, leaning on a stick, for I was unable to walk without this support, I made my way with painfully slow steps towards the house of the De Charmilles. For all I knew the Countess and her niece might not be there,—they might have gone south for the winter. Still I felt that I must make an attempt, however futile, to see the only creature in the world who could, just at this juncture in my life, possibly even now be my saviour!

There were a great many people in the streets; everything looked bright and suggestive of pleasure,—the sunshine was brilliant, and the Champs Elysées were crowded with happy children sporting in the merry-go-rounds, and driving in the pretty goat-carriages, while their nurses and governesses mounted tender guard over their innocent pastimes. I thought I had never seen Paris wear such a beautiful aspect;—a gentle mood was upon me,—I was sorrowful yet not despairing,—and though I was not actually cognizant of any poignant remorse for all the evil I had wrought I was conscious of a faint, yearning desire to atone. The last little spark of my better nature had roused itself into a feeble glow, and it kindled within

[1] The most popular promenade in Paris.

me a sense of shame; a touch of late—and useless—penitence. I little knew how soon this nobler fire was to be quenched in darkness!—I little guessed what swift vengeance the wild Absinthe-witch can take on any one of her servitors who dares to dream of disputing her inexorable authority!

And by-and-by my laggard, faltering movements brought me to the familiar street,—the well-known stately mansion where I had so often been a welcome guest in happier days. The gates stood open,—but there was something strange about the aspect of the place that made me rub my eyes and stare in vaguely stupid wonder,—what dark delusion had seized upon me now? The gates stood open, as I said,—and the circumstance that awoke in me such dull confusion and amazement was, that the portals of the hall-door were also flung wide apart, and the whole entrance was hung with draperies of black, festooned with white; heavy draperies that trailed mournfully like drooping banners, down to the ground below. Again I rubbed my eyes violently—I could not believe their testimony—they had so often deceived me. Was this a spectral hallucination? I advanced hesitatingly—I ascended the steps—I approached those dreary black hangings and touched them;—they were real,—and the hall beyond them was dark and solemn, the gleam of a few tall candles sparkling here and there like tapers in a tomb. No one noticed me, though there were many people passing in and out—they were dressed in black and moved softly,—they pressed handkerchiefs to their eyes and wept as they went to and fro;—many of them carried flowers. Gradually the meaning of the sombre scene dawned upon me,—this was what is called in France a "*chapelle ardente*"[1]—a laying-out of the dead in state,—an opening of the doors to all comers, friends or foes, that they may be enabled to look their last on the face they loved or hated! A "*chapelle ardente*"—yes!—but for whom? Who was dead? The answer flashed upon me at once,—it was the widowed and unhappy Comtesse de Charmilles who had gone the way of all flesh,—of course!—it must be she! Bereft of husband and child, what more natural than that she should have wearied of life, and longed to join her lost loved ones!—and fresh tears sprang to my eyes as I realized the certainty that this was so. Poor soul!— I remembered her quiet grace and reposeful dignity—her charming manners,—her queenly yet sweet maternal ways—her invariable kindness and gentleness to me when I was her son-in-law in prospective. And now she was no more,—she had sunk down, broken-hearted, to the grave,—and in her death I felt that I too had the most cruel share!

---

[1] French for "chapel of rest."

"Wretched man that I am!" I thought, as I leaned feebly against the great staircase, up and down which the visitors were going and returning. "I am accursëd!—and only Héloïse can free me of my curse!"

Mastering my emotion by an effort, I addressed a maid-servant who passed me at the moment.

"She is dead?" I asked in hushed accents.

"Alas, yes, monsieur! She is dead!"

And the girl broke into tears as she spoke, and hurried away.

I waited another minute or two,—then gathering up my strength, I ascended the stairs slowly with the rest of the silent, tiptoe-treading mourners. The smell of fresh incense, mingling with the heavy perfume of lilies, was wafted towards me as I came nearer and nearer the chamber which was now turned into a high altar for death's service,—a glimmer of white hangings caught my eyes,—white flowers,—all white! Strange!—white, pure white, was for those who died young! And the pretty phraseology of an old French madrigal passed through my memory involuntarily;—

"Comme la rose quitte la branche du rosier
La jeunesse quitte la vie;
Celles qui mourront jeune,
On les couvrira de fleurs nouvelles;
Et du milieu de ces fleurs
Elles s'élèveront vers le ciel,
Comme le passe-vole du calice des roses!"[1]

Another step,—another—hush—hush! What beauteous still-faced angel was that, pillowed among pale cyclamens and tranced in frozen sleep?...

I dashed aside the silken hangings,—like a madman I rushed forward ...

"*Héloïse!*" I shrieked. "*Héloïse!*"

★ ★ ★ ★ ★

---

[1] Source unknown. "As the rose leaves the branch of the rose bush / Youth leaves life; / Those who die young, / Will be covered with new flowers; / And from the centre of these flowers / They will rise towards the sky / Like the passe-vole of the calyx of roses." The word "passe-vole" in the last line of the stanza is obscure.

Dead—dead! Grovelling on the ground in wild agony, I clutched handfuls of the flowers with which her funeral couch was strewn—I groaned—I sobbed—I raved!—I could have killed myself then in the furious frenzy of my horror and despair!

"Héloïse!" I cried again and again. "Héloïse! Wake! Speak to me! Curse me! Love me! Oh God, God! you are not dead!—not dead! Héloïse!—Héloïse!"

The fair face seemed to smile serenely. "I am safe!" was its mute expression. "Safe from evil—safe from sorrow,—safe from love—safe from *you*! I have escaped your touch,—your look—your voice—and all the bitterness of ever having known you! And being now grown wise in death I pardon—I pity you!—Leave me to rest in peace!"

Shaken by tearless sobs of mortal agony, I gazed distractedly upon that maiden image of sweet wisdom and repose;—the loose gold hair, unbound to its full rippling length, caught flickers from the sunlight through the window-pane,—the fringed white eyelids fast closed in eternal sleep were delicately indented as though some angel's finger-tips had passed them down caressingly,—the waxen-hands were folded meekly across the bosom, where a knot of virgin lilies wept out fragrance in lieu of tears. Dead—dead! Why had Death taken her?—why had God wanted her—God, who has so many saints—why could He not have spared her to the earth which has so few! Dead!—and with her had died my last hope of good,—my last chance of rescue! And I buried my head again among the odorous funeral flowers and wept as I had never wept before,—as I shall never have sufficient heart or conscience in me to weep again!

Suddenly a hand touched me gently on the shoulder.

"Señor!"

The voice was that of a stranger,—the accent Spanish—and I looked up in sullen wrath,—who was it that dared thus to intrude upon my misery?... A man stood beside me,—a lithe, dark creature with soft brilliant brown eyes,—eyes that just then were swimming in tears; his whole mobile face expressed emotion and sympathy—and in one hand he held—a violin.

"Señor"—he again murmured gently. "Let me entreat of you to restrain your grief! It alarms the people who come to render their last homage—it unnerves them! See you!—we are alone in this room—the others are afraid to enter. Pray, pray do not give way to such distraction!—she was happy in dying,—her health had declined for some time and she was glad to go,—and her death was beautiful,—it was the quiet falling asleep of innocence!"

His look, his words, his manner bewildered me.

"You saw her die?" I muttered confusedly. "You—you——"

"*Hélas! pauvre enfant!*[1] she passed away with her hand in mine!" he answered softly, and as he spoke, he took up a cluster of flowers from the couch, and, kissing them, laid them again in their former position.

I rose to my feet trembling violently, a sombre wrath gaining possession of my soul.

"And who *are* you?" I said. "Why are you here?"

"I am Valdez, the violinist," he replied,—and then I recollected,—this was the very "*maestro*"[2] about whose performances Héloïse had used to be so enthusiastic. "I came hither because she sent for me," he continued. "I travelled all the way from Russia. She wanted me,—it was to give me this, before she died."

And he touched the violin he held,—her violin!—her chiefest treasure!—and she had bestowed it upon *him*!

A sickening suspicion arose in me and almost choked my utterance. What bond had there been between her—the dead Héloïse,—and this man, the musical puppet of a mob's capricious favour? What if she had not died innocent after all!...

"Were you her lover?" I demanded breathlessly.

He drew back amazed, with a gesture of mingled pain and hauteur.

"Her lover?—I? You can jest in the presence of death, monsieur?... I love art,—not women."

I stared at him in dubious anger. The dead girl before us held some secret hidden behind her closed eyes and set, smiling lips,—a secret I feverishly craved to fathom!

"But she," I said. "She must have loved you—to have given you *that*!" And I pointed to the violin.

His dark face lightened into a grave smile,—a new and sudden interest flashed in his eyes. But he was otherwise unmoved.

"I do not see that at all"—he murmured. "She knew I would value such a gift,—that it would be more precious to me than to any one else in the world,—and that is why she was so anxious I should have it. Still, ... she may have loved me,—secretly, as many other women have loved me,—I never thought of that!—yet—it is possible! It was her music I cared for,—she played divinely!—and her violin, *this* violin—is a treasure beyond price! Ah! what sounds I will invoke from it! I laid it by her

---

[1] French for "Alas! poor child."

[2] From the Italian for "master." A great musical composer, teacher, or conductor.

side to-day,—I had a fancy that some message from the other world might steal into it from her dead presence, and make its tone more deep, more thrilling, more absolutely perfect and pure!"

I advanced upon him in rough haste,—something in my eyes must have startled him for he recoiled slightly—but I went close up and laid my burning hands upon his shoulders.

"Be silent!" I gasped hoarsely. "Is this the place or time to talk your art-jargon? Have you no soul, except for sound? She loved you!—I feel it,—I know it—I am sure of it!—she loved you!—yes!—you never knew it I dare say,—men never do know these things! But see what she has done for you!—she has left her spirit with you—there—in that violin you hold!—her graceful fancies, her noble thoughts, her tenderness, her sweetness—you have it all imprisoned there,—all to come forth at your bidding! When you play, she, Héloïse, will speak to you, caress you, teach you, help you, comfort you!—and I—I hate you for it—I hate you! For now I know she never would have pitied me,—never would have loved me again as she loved me once,—for in dying, she had no thought for me—she only thought of you—you, on whom Fortune smiles from day to day! Judge then how I hate you!—how I cannot do otherwise than hate you!—for she has given you all—and left me nothing! Nothing!... my God!—nothing!"

And with a savage cry I flung him from me and rushed from the room, not daring to look again on the white angel-face of that dead woman who smiled with such triumphant sweetness, with such indifferent coldness, on my desperate despair! I saw people make terrified way for me as I ran,—I heard some one exclaim that I was mad with grief!—but I paid no heed,—whether I was recognized or not I neither knew nor cared! Out into the street I plunged, as it were, into the thick of the passers-by ... could I not lose myself, I wildly thought!—could I not obliterate myself from sight and sense and speech and action?—was there not some deep wide open grave into which I could fall swooningly and there be covered in before I had time to suffer or struggle? Oh, for a sudden death without pain!—oh, for a swift cessation to this scorching bitterness in my blood—this heavy aching of my heart! Sick to the very dregs of misery, I raved for days in feverish agony,—agony that was blind, desperate, hopeless, helpless, cureless! What spectres stood beside me then!—what horrid voices shouted in my ears!—how strange and loathly the half-formed creatures that followed me and mouthed at me, gibbering in uncouth speech scarcely intelligible!—how the murdered man Silvion came and looked at me as at some foul thing!—

how Pauline, fair and pale, with a dying sweetness in her smile, drifted by me, finely fairy-like as a fleecy cloud in summer-time!—and, ah God! how the soft large eyes of Héloïse beamed piteous wonder and reproach upon me like bland stars shining solemnly on a criminal in his cell! Those eyes—those eyes!—they tortured me,—their mildness chilled me!—their pure and unimpassioned lustre shamed me!—they were angels' eyes, and their holy innocence scared and shook me to the soul! Oh, that horrible time!—oh those dreary, wild dark days and nights of utter loss and blank wretchedness!—that frightful space of torment in which every nerve in my body seemed torn and wrenched by devils!—how I was able to live through it, I cannot tell!

And when, like all other things, it wore itself out at last,—when I grew calm, with the dreadful calmness of sheer stupefaction and exhaustion,—then—then I realized it all, and my Absinthe-witch gave me a clue to the whole mystery! *There was a God!*—yes! actually a God!—a great, terrific, cruel, unforgiving, awful Being, and He in all His omnipotence had set Himself against me! He whose proud Will evolved the growing Universe,—He had arrayed His mighty forces of Heaven and Hell against one miserable atom of earth!—and the Titanic wheels of Life, Time and Eternity were all whirled into motion to grind me, a worm, down to destruction! One would think it a waste of power on God's part!—but He would seem to be most particular in trifles. Note how carefully he tints the rose, from deepest crimson to tenderest pink!—how recklessly He drops the avalanche on a village full of harmless souls asleep! What infinite pains he has bestowed on the burnish and hue of the peacock's plume,—all to make of a useless bird with a harsh voice, a perfect marvel of colour and brilliancy!—and what a deaf ear he turns to the shriek of the murderer's victim! Who will account for these things in Nature's plan? It is useless for any good pious folks to tell me that my miseries are my own fault. What have I done, I pray you, save drink Absinthe? I have poisoned my brain and blood!—well—but how ridiculously small the seed from which such grim results have sprung! *I* am not to blame if the Creator has done His work badly,—if He has made the brain so delicate and the spirit so volatile that its quality and comprehension vanish at the touch of—*Wormwood.* Nothing but wormwood,—it is a plant as well as a metaphor,—and God made it! God gives us plenty of it in our lives, as well as in our liquor!—and the preachers tell us bitterness is very wholesome! Everything is God's work—even evil,—and when, with the aid of my life's elixir, I grasped this fact thoroughly, I saw it was no use offering any more resistance to fate. For I was left without the smallest vestige of hope,—the little spark of penitence in me had been revived too late,—and throughout the whole drama, no one had thought of *me*! Silvion Guidèl had died thinking of Pauline,—Pauline had drowned, with the name of her lover on her lips,—and Héloïse, even Héloïse, had bestowed her last word, her last looks, not on me, but on a comparative stranger—a mere musical virtuoso! God's meaning was made plain! I was left to my own devices,—it was shown me distinctly that my life was without interest to any one but myself. I accepted the hint. As it was decreed, so it must be,—and I did as André Gessonex had done before me,—killed the last vestige of my flickering conscience in me with a final blow,—and became—*what I am*!

★　★　★　★　★

L'ENVOI

And what am I? My dear friends, I have told you,—an *absintheur*! *Absintheur, pur et simple!—voilà tout!*[1] I am a thing more abject than the lowest beggar that crawls through Paris whining for a sou![2]—I am a slinking, shuffling beast, half monkey, half man, whose aspect is so vile, whose body is so shaken with delirium, whose eyes are so murderous, that if you met me by chance in the day-time, you would probably shriek for sheer alarm! But you will not see me thus—daylight and I are not friends. I have become like a bat or an owl in my hatred of the sun!—it shone gloriously when Héloïse was lying dead,—I have not forgotten that!... At night I live;—at night I creep out with the other obscene things of Paris, and by my very presence, add fresh pollution to the moral poisons in the air! I gain pence by the meanest errands,—I help others to vice,—and whenever I have the opportunity I draw down weak youths, mothers' darlings, to the brink of ruin, and topple them over—if I can! For twenty francs, you can purchase me body and soul,—for twenty francs I will murder or steal,—all true *absintheurs* are purchasable! For they are the degradation of Paris,—the canker of the

---

[1] French for "Absintheur, pure and simple!—That's all!"
[2] French unit of money worth five centimes.

city—the slaves of a mean insatiable madness which nothing but death can cure. Death!—that word reminds me,—I have the means of death in my power and yet—I cannot die! Strange, is it not?... A little while ago I came upon one of my class in dire distress,—he had been a noted chemist in his day,—but he is nothing now—nothing but an *absintheur*, who suffers grinding physical tortures when he has no money wherewith to purchase what has become the emerald life-blood of his veins. I found him in a fit of rage, rolling in his garret and howling imprecations on all mankind—he was just in the mood to do what I asked of him. It was a trifle!—a mere friendly exchange of poisons! I gave him the *Absinthe* for which he craved so desperately,—and in return, he prepared for me a little phial of liquid, crystal-clear as a diamond, harmless-looking as spring-water,—a small draught, which if once I have the courage to swallow, will give me an instant exit from the world! Imagine it!—I shall not suffer I am told,—first a giddiness—then a darkness,—and that is all. I take it out often—that little glittering flask of death,—I look at it,—I wonder at it,—for it is the key to the Eternal Secret,—but I dare not drink its contents! I dare not, I tell you!—I am afraid—horribly afraid!—any condemned criminal is braver than I! For the longer I live, the more I realize that this death is not the actual end,—there is something afterwards!—and it is the Afterwards that appals me. Life is precious!—yes, even my life, surrounded with phantoms, darkened with delirium, enfeebled by vice and misery as it is, it is precious! I know its best and worst,—its value and worthlessness;—I can measure it and scorn it,—I can laugh at it and love it!—I can play with myself and it as a tiger plays with its torn and bleeding prey!—and knowing it, I cling to it—I do not want to be hurled into what I do *not* know! Some day perhaps—when a blind, dark fury overcomes my brain,—when spectres clutch at me and sense and memory reel into chaos, then I may drink the fatal draught I bear about with me;—but I shall be truly mad when I do!—too mad to realize my own act! I shall never part with life consciously, or while the faintest glimmer of reason remains in me,—be sure of that! I love life—especially life in Paris!—I love to think that I and my compeers in Absinthe are a blot and a disgrace on the fairest city under the sun!—I love to meditate on the crass stupidity of our rulers, who though gravely forbidding the sale of poisons to the general public, permit the free enjoyment of Absinthe everywhere!—I watch with a scientific interest the mental and moral deterioration of our young men, and I take a pride in helping them on to their downfall!—I love to pervert ideas, to argue falsely, to mock at virtue, to jeer at faith, and to instil morbid sentiments into the minds of those who listen to me;—and I smile as I see how "*La revanche!*" is dying out, and how content the absinthe-drinker is to crouch before the stalwart, honest, beer-bred Teuton! It is a grand sight!—and we are a glorious people!—just the sort of beings who are constituted to caper and make mouths at "*perfide Albion*"[1]—and capture mild English tourists in mistake for German spies! All is for the best!—Let us drink and dream and dance and carouse and let the world go by! Let us make a mere empty boast of honour,—and play off sparkling witticisms against purity,—let us encourage our writers and dramatists to pen obscenities,—our painters to depict repulsive nudities—our public men talk loud inanities—our women to practice all the wiles of wantons and *cocottes*![2] But with this, let us never forget to be enthusiastic when we are called upon to sing the "Marseillaise." How does it go?—

"Amour sacré de la patrie
Conduis, soutiens nos bras vengeurs,—
Liberté, liberté chérie
Combats avec tes defenseurs!
Sous nos drapeaux que la Victoire
Accoure à tes mâles accents
Que tes ennemis expirants
Voient ton triomphe et notre gloire!"[3]

Just so! Let us always glorify Liberty, though we are slaves to a Vice! Lift up your voices, good countrymen, in chorus!—

"Aux armes, citoyens! Formez vos battaillons!
Marchons! qu'un sang impur abreuve nos sillons!"[4]

Bravo!—Only let us roar this loudly enough, with frantic tossing of arms and waving of banners,—with blare of trumpets, with tears and

---

[1] "Perfidious Britain or England." A phrase attributed to Napoleon. The phrase alludes to England's alleged treachery to other nations.

[2] French word for "prostitutes."

[3] Last verse of the French anthem. "Sacred love of the homeland / Guide and support our avenging arms / Liberty, dear liberty / Fight with your defenders / Under our flags so that Victory / May rush to your manly strains / So that your dying enemies / See your triumph and our glory."

[4] Chorus of French national anthem. "To arms, citizens! Form your battalions! / March on! [So] that an impure blood may water our fields!"

emotional embraces, and we shall perhaps by noise and *blague*,[1] if by nothing else, convince ourselves if we cannot convince other nations, that France is as great, as pure and as powerful as she was in her Lily-days of old! We can shut our eyes to her decaying intelligence, her beaten condition,—her cheap cynicism, her passive atheism, her gross materialism,—we can cheat ourselves into believing that a nation can thrive on Poison,—we can do anything so long as we hold fast to the Marseillaise and the Tricolor![2] Mere symbols!—and we scarcely trust them,—but nevertheless they are our last chance of safety! France is France still,—but the conqueror's tread is on her soil!—and we—we have borne it and still can bear it!—we have forgotten—we forget! What should we want with Victory?—We have ABSINTHE!

THE END

---

[1] French word meaning "tall stories" or "bunk."
[2] Nickname for the French flag, which is composed of three colours—red, white, and blue.

Appendix A: Translations of French Poems and Songs in Wormwood

1. Charles Cros, "L'Archet," *Le Coffret de santal* (1873), translation by Wilbur Underwood, *M'lle New York* 2.1 (1898)

Of the lady's hair there was no dearth;
Gold as the grain in Autumn's girth
It rippled down unto the earth

Her strange, low voice you need must hark,
It seemed the voice of a Serapharch;
Her eyes looked out from lashes dark.

He never feared a rival more
While he traversed vale and shore,
Bearing her on his horse before.

For on all those of that cont'ree
She had looked full haughtily,
Until him she came to see.

And love's strength smote her with such dole
That for smiles and mockings droll,
A sickness crept upon her soul.

And mid her last caresses there:
"Make a bowstring of my hair
To charm your other ladies fair."

Then with a long, sweet kiss of woe
She died; and straight the knight did go
And of her hair he made a bow.

Like a pauper blind and lone,
On a viol of Cremone
Played he, begging alms with moan.

And all who heard those sobbing strings
Were drunk with joyous shudderings;
The dead lived in their quiverings.

The King was charmed and favored him;
He chanced to please the dark Queen's whim,
And fled with her in the moonlight dim.

But each time that he touched it, so
To play unto the Queen, the bow
Reproached him mournfully and low.

And at the sound of that death strain
They died half-way adown the plain;
The dead took back her pledge again.

Took back her hair that knew no dearth,
That, gold as the grain in Autumn's girth,
Rippled down unto the earth.

2. Anonymous, "Le Pauvre Clerc," an old Breton song, translation by Kirsten MacLeod

I have lost my boots and torn my poor feet,
Following my sweet one in the fields and in the woods;
Rain, sleet, and ice,
Are no obstacle to love!

My sweet one is young like me
She is not yet twenty;
She is fresh and pretty
Her looks are full of fire!
Her words charming!
She is a prison
In which I lock my heart.

I do not know what to compare her to:
Could it be to the little white rose that is called Rose-Marie?
Little pearl of young girls;

Lily among flowers;
She opens today, and she'll close tomorrow.

In courting you, my sweet, I have resembled
A nightingale perched upon a hawthorn branch;
When he wants to sleep, the needles prick him, so
He rises to the top of the tree and begins to sing!

My star is fatal,
My state is against nature,
I have had nothing in this world
But troubles to endure.
I am like a soul in the flames of purgatory,
Not one Christian in the world wishes me well!

There is no one who has suffered as much
With respect to you as I have since my birth;
So I beg you on both knees
And in the name of God to take pity on your clerk.

Appendix B: Letters from Corelli to George Bentley about Wormwood

[These letters from Corelli to Bentley are part of the Marie Corelli Collection, General Collection, Beinecke Rare Book and Manuscript Library, Yale University.]

1. From letter dated 15 October 1889

[First mention of *Wormwood* to Bentley; praises Bentley as publisher]

Your novel—I call it yours,—is well on its way, though only *begun* once I came home! I *was* writing another,—but a strange and terrible phase of the present life of the Paris people, presented itself to me in such forcible colours, that I set the first-commenced book aside, and flung myself into this, heart and soul—it promises to be much more powerful than "Vendetta!"[1] This is *your* book;—for naturally I [could not?] desire to work for a pleasanter friend or a more honourable house ... I do not think it is possible to find in all London a better house than yours—every author who publishes with you has by this fact alone attained a certain dignity, *selon moi*,—and this is precisely why I want you to have the best I can do.... I know already how you will like the new book I am preparing for you—terrible though the story is, it is (alas! for the French!) ... more than ... absolutely *true*.

2. From undated letter (1890)

[Description of *Wormwood*; contemporary accounts of absinthism]

I often wonder what you will think of the *absinthe* story! I have followed the man's career from early promise to early destruction, with a curious intensity of interest myself—, feeling that I have watched him through a sort of spyglass, as he has stepped down rapidly, hurried on by the green drug which is at once his delight and his despair. I read only yesterday an amazing chronicle of crime just compiled by a learned doctor in Paris, who traces all the cynical hostility of his fellow-citizens to this same most fatal passion. No novel can ever come up to the *truth* of the matter.

---

[1]   Corelli's second novel.

3. From letter dated 24 July 1890

[Cites Charcot on Absinthism]

I am glad you like my story as far as you have read—of course the close of
the first volume is the close of my hero's *respectable* career! Now listen to
an extract from a volume recently published in Paris by Dr. Charcot.[1]—

Twenty percent of the **incurable** cases of idiotcy and **savage mania** in
the asylums of France**, are owing to absinthe,** and a nearly equal percentage of *crime* committed *apparently for the most trifling causes,* can be traced to
the same vicious habit. **Unless the drinking of this pernicious drug
be forbidden by the State**, or some other stringent measures be adopted,
**the next generation of the French will be composed of a huge
majority of idiots and monomaniacs.**

[font in bold denotes text underlined in red in original letter]

4. From letter dated 5 August 1890

[Corelli's wishes concerning advertising and physical appearance of
Wormwood]

The story only wants its title page which I will send in the last thing and
a "Preliminary Note"—too short to be called a preface, to explain one or
two facts concerning the "drama" which will cause critics to meditate and
readers to think!...
    One little stipulation I venture to make!—and this is, that about a fort-
night *before* publication, advertisements should appear worded thus,—

In Preparation
A NEW NOVEL by Marie Corelli
author of "Ardath"—"A Romance of Two Worlds" etc
The Title will be announced in due course
I know that this will cause a little stir and excite the *Libraries.* How widely,
widely different my next book will be to this "bitter" one!—it makes me
smile to think of it!...
N.B. The covers of the book should be *pale green,* the colour of Absinthe,

---

[1]   French physician (1825-93) who specialized in neurological disorders and hysteria.

with the title running zig-zag across it in black letters—an adder or serpent twisted through the big *W*. Don't you think so?

5. From letter dated 6 August 1890

[Defends her artistic decisions to Bentley]

I am sorry you find the morgue tiresome in two instances,—but I did these *two scenes in the same place on purpose*. First, that the two lovers Pauline and Silvion, should be laid one after the other on the same slab,—2d because it was impossible Pauline if drowned could be taken *elsewhere* in Paris,—3d because the *absintheur* had to *feel* the wish that she might be thrown into the *fosse*, without a name .... I have more reasons even than these—but it would take too long to write them, and I could have spoken them in a few minutes. It would be inartistic to allow so sweet a girl as Héloïse to meet such a wretch as Gaston Beauvais at night *anywhere*—and you cannot see drowned bodies floating in the Seine ... below the Pont Neuf. They are all caught in the Morgue nets. The whole thing has been worked out with *precision* and *extreme care*, and though I know how kindly your criticism is meant, I cannot, my dear friend, alter it in this particular. With regard to the "can-can" I was quite prepared for your observation, and I will, if you wish, soften one or two of the more intense expressions. *Where* I got as vivid a description, I shall state in the "preliminary note"—so that will be made correct. As for critics!—I have learned enough to care nothing for anything they may say....

I cannot alter a scene that has been worked up to through the whole book, to please even the best of publishers or the most snappish of critics,—to myself rests the whole blame or praise—on *myself* the responsibility—. Absinthe is a frightful craze,—an absintheur a most pitiable object,—and as a matter of *art*, things are seen in the book *through* the spirit of absinthe. Hence it is lurid—it must be so—but I know its very power will do something to check the horror of it in France—it will excite comment and set people *thinking*....

[in a P.S. Corelli writes]:

The only thing I claim about it is that the *sequence* of events is *perfectly natural* and as it would inevitably happen.

6. From letter dated 28 August 1890

[Contemporary accounts of absinthe addiction; defence of her novel]

I do no think you need be in the least "afraid" of the new book. It is a subject that however repulsive, *would have to be done* and powerfully done, some day or other. And it is odd how often events march in the wake of the romancist who is a little bit courageous,—courageous enough to face and grasp some of the evils of our time. For example,—since I have been abroad the Paris "Temps"—"[1] is full of the most hideous details of a "tragedy"—due to absinthe—in which a man and woman came to the conclusion that life, as God meant it, was not good enough for them— therefore they prepared to leave it. And how? By using a small penknife to open each other's veins by *slow degrees*, and drinking absinthe in the course of the operation! What novelist could exaggerate the horror of such a scene! At Berne, a medical man at the *table d'hôte* got into conversation with me, not knowing I was a writer, and as chance would have it, got on the subject of Absinthe. "It is the curse of Europe"—he said,—"Three years ago, the Swiss had not taken to it,—but now they are always at it,—and the cases of mania and idiotcy are as a consequence on the increase. It is cheap,— and it deadens the intelligence, destroys the perception, and creates a brutish indifference to good or evil; it is a pity some powerful writer does not take the horror of it as a study for his pen. It might do good."

I agreed with him!—but of course said nothing. Oh, if this so "lurid" story will only *rouse* some few to think of the deterioration they are bring- ing on themselves and their children, I shall be infinitely rewarded! This is why it would have been impossible to treat such a subject in *faint* outline,— it had to be firmly, almost fiercely done, or not at all. It was work for a man to have done,—but the men write effeminately sometimes à la William Black,[2]—and the times we live in are not, (though they *seem*) effeminate. It is an age when the most strong and complex passions are at work,— suppressed, like the fires of Vesuvius,—but none the less felt. And with all humility, I believe, that when these passions are touched by the romancist or the poet, then and then only will the public heart respond. My dear friend, that great heart is so full of multitudinous aches and pains that I ache and burn with it!—and out of that close and intense sympathy, I write. It was this, I believe, that made the success of the "Romance" and

---

[1] A Paris newspaper.

[2] Scottish journalist and novelist (1841–98).

"Ardath"[1]—because I know instinctively in this period of rush and infinite weariness and cynicism, the multitude crave for something higher and more lasting—and ask to have their feelings *put into words.*

7. From letter dated 8 September 1890

[Condemns the press and her "sister" authors; defends *Wormwood*]

One paragraph in your last letter I *must* answer—you say; "I sincerely hope that the Press will not seize this opportunity to come down on you. Your sister authors are sure to do so and some of those wild pens on the press. The public however may forgive you—" etc. etc.

Now, my dear friend, has the "Press" ever lost an opportunity to "come down" on me as it is? Was not the "Romance" [described] as "*a farrago of nonsense*"—"Vendetta" as "*a brutal compound of villainy and immorality*"—"Thelma"[2]—as a "*ridiculous heroine*"—"Ardath" as "*an outrageous compound of venal sentiment and blasphemy*"—? After this,—after such wilful abuse and gross misunderstanding of my work, can you think for a moment that I *care* for press opinions? The press that deifies a "Rudyard Kipling"[3]—and hovers between fits of ecstasy and opprobrium over Zola and Tolstoi[4] and Ibsen,[5] is such an utterly worthless thing now-a-days to sway an author's fame one way or the other. The "public" is a different matter. *That* has forgiven me my sins always,—and I hope and believe it will understand my motive in having struck the key-note of *French morbidness,*—the partial secret of a national decay. The absinthe *trail* is over all France,—it helps to make French literature obscene, and French art repulsive,—and if I had not trusted it as powerfully as I have done, my work would have been no avail. My hero talks of the Creator in the way that shocks you, *because* it is precisely the way *every* Parisian thinks proper to talk now-a-days. And taking the whole subject altogether, let me remind you of "Père Goriot" by Balzac.[6] The power of this book is simply incontestable,—it is by some considered Balzac's masterpiece,—and yet no one can call it otherwise than repulsive in *every* way. I do not approach Balzac in anything, except in reverent admiration of his genius,—but as an *artist* I think it would be foolish

---

[1] Corelli's first novel (*A Romance of Two Worlds*) and her fourth.
[2] Corelli's third novel.
[3] English novelist and poet (1865–1936).
[4] Count Leo Tolstoy (1828–1910), Russian novelist and moral philosopher.
[5] Henrik Ibsen (1828–1906), Norwegian playwright.
[6] See this edition, page 62, note 4.

to paint a lurid subject in soft colours. And here we come to your allusion to my "sister authors—"! Do I not know them?—have they not hurt me, while I was yet weak enough to be hurt? Have they not taken my hand and kissed my lips, and then gone away to write abuse of me afterwards?— Yes indeed—over and over again,—and I have never paid them back in their own coin—I *could* not do so. I have never had a moment's jealousy of any other living writer, male or female. The principal thing my "sisters" grudge me is the "man's pen"—that one amiable critic allowed I possessed;—I do not write in a "ladylike" or effeminate way, and for that they hate me. Over and over again I have suffered a great deal in absolute silence,—more sorry for the littleness of my sex than for anything else,— and I am sorry to say I have found men-critics quite as spiteful. However, *now* I am hardened,—let the whole Press [turn and rend?] me, I shall not feel it! "Ardath" was my last touch-stone,—had they given me *true justice* for that book which they *never did*, I might have still cared a little,—but the "Savile Club"[1] knows me not,—and Andrew Lang of sixteen newspapers detests me,—and *now that I know how criticism is done*, I care not a jot for it! See how they paragraph Rudyard Kipling!—Andrew Lang's[2] work again!—what *can* one care for such publicity!...

Do not be anxious about the sentiments expressed in "Wormwood"— a brief explanatory word or two by way of preface, will make it clear that these are not *my* thoughts but the *imagined* thoughts of the absintheur. So far, I know I have kept to strict *art*.

8. From letter dated 26 October 1890

[Defends *Wormwood*]

Whether the public find the story repulsive or not I do not care. If they can stand Tolstoi's "Kreutzer Sonata"—they can stand anything. Mrs Grundy[3] is full of caprices—she has fits of morality and laxity,—and one cannot stop to study her changeful humours. A Major in the English army was here on Thursday night, and saw the title-page of my book—*he* told me I had done a "noble" thing in choosing such a subject; he has seen 500 men in the French ranks die in the space of 3 months from the effects of Absinthe. Well—I have done my poor best to show up its horrors,—but justice I do not expect from anyone except the Divine Ordainer!

---

[1] A London men's club, which consisted mostly of artistic and literary types.

[2] British folklorist, critic, and man of letters (1844–1912).

[3] A name personifying the tyranny of social opinion in matters of conventional propriety.

9. From letter dated 15 November 1890

[Complains about the reception of *Wormwood*]

Yes, dear Mr. Bentley—I saw the "critique" in the *Athenaeum*;[1]—it struck me as a strange one—and a more or less useless one, purposely arranged so *as to be* useless. However—what is the good of worrying over it! I feel that it is impossible for a woman writer to receive justice from *men*-critics, more particularly if she chance to show masculine power. If any *man* had written "Wormwood" there would have been a grand shouting over it both in the French and English press. I think it is not unnatural that one should feel disheartened at times; I am not disheartened as far as the Public are concerned because I have abundant proof that the Public is my friend, and as far as the purely material side of my success is concerned I certainly have nothing to complain of. But when I *know* and *feel* in my secret conscience that I have done a good piece of literary work, in pure nervous language, without showiness, without drag or *padding* or short of dramatic interest, I feel it a trifle hard that when others who do less good work can get high praise, that I should not also win a trifle of honest *recognition*. It would help me so much—it would bring out much better and stronger creations, and the world would not lose by it. As it is, discouragement sits on me like a cold night,—some would I know be perfectly happy with *material* success, with the money earned and the steady sale,—but all this does not help me so much as a few words of earnest encouragement. Well may I strive to be "masculine" in style!—I must also be masculine in endurance—for if I were weak-spirited I might sit down idly and weep, as I do sometimes when tired,—but I do not want to give way.

10. From letter dated 9 October 1891

[On the popular success of *Wormwood*]

[I]t is certainly a great help to my endeavours to find that I do not "go down"—even with such a terrific sort of story as the "*Wormwood*"—which seems to have had a surprising sale, to my astonishment. For you know you had your doubts as to the success of that particular horror! But the dear Public is a very capricious one—and it does'nt [*sic*] do to serve them always the same sort of dish. I want to keep in time with the various pulsations of the time—if I can do that—well and good!

---

[1]   A leading literary journal of the day.

Appendix C: Reviews of Wormwood

1. From *The Athenaeum* (15 November 1890): 661 (unsigned review)

"Wormwood" is a story of absinthe and the *absintheurs*—a grim, realistic drama. Marie Corelli has chosen her theme according to her knowledge and convictions—the scene Paris, the poison wormwood. Another might have taken London for a background and alcohol for the curse, and might have drawn an equally lurid and ghastly picture. And whatever the picture and its surroundings may be, neither absinthe nor alcohol would be the real possessing spirit of the human soul which falls a victim to it, but the abandonment, the despair, the loss of control and respect, which engulf a weak and self-indulgent nature. There is no degree of baseness and fury to which a nature abandoned to the slavery of drink is not capable of sinking. To overdraw the picture is impossible; the only question that nature asked is whether the painter has drawn it out of proportion, or in colours that distort the truth. What Marie Corelli has done—and it was necessary for the coherence and interest of her story—is to bring into the life of one man a sequence of events such as are constantly happening to different people. The effects of love, lawless passion, jealousy, hatred, insanity—all are grouped together round the lost *absintheur* whom the author has depicted.

2. From the *Pall Mall Gazette* (27 November 1890): 3 (unsigned review)

"My drama," says Miss Corelli, "is a true phase of the modern life of Paris. There is no necessity to invent fables nowadays—the fictionist [*sic*] need never torture his brain for stories either of adventure or spectral horror. Life itself as it is lived among ourselves in all countries is so amazing, swift, varied, wonderful, terrible, ghastly, beautiful, dreadful, and withal so wildly inconsistent and changeful, that whosoever desires to write romances has only to closely and patiently observe men and women as they *are*, not as they seem—and then take pen in hand and write—the truth." Excellent doctrine, this, for "fictionists" to follow, yet Miss Corelli's practice differs widely from her theory; to use her own words, it is so wildly inconsistent and changeful. Her book is a tract to teach us all that absinthe-drinkers must be damned. It is dedicated to the *absintheurs* of Paris; it is tied up with red ribbon, presumably in imitation of the stoppers of absinthe bottles, while a text from Revelation about the star called Wormwood is printed within a broad red border on the fly-leaf. So all that could possibly make such a sermon impressive has been done. Gaston Beauvais, "the unhappy hero," tells his own story in hysterical prose, and we are gradually shown how his desire for love begot desire for absinthe.... None of the characters are real, or interesting, or pleasant; ...A Frenchman with a taste for absinthe should be forgiven much in the way of bad words, so if Gaston writes "dumbfoundered," "dumbly," "favorite," "overwhelment," and even "frissonement," of course it is not Miss Corelli's fault. Nor can we reasonably rebuke her for such a piece of simmering stuff as this: "She looked at me straightly, her eyes full of a mournful exaltation, her breath coming and going rapidly between her parted lips. I met her glance with an amazed scorn—and hurled the bitter truth like pellets of ice upon the amorous heat of her impetuous avowal." As the book is "a drama of Paris," such untranslatable expressions as *mon ami, bon jour, allons, vraiment, au revoir*, abound, but, with the aid of Ollendorff,[1] no doubt the patient reader will master them. The impatient reader will surely be deterred from drinking absinthe by the awful thought that, like Gaston Beauvais, he may one day be impelled by the insidious drug to write his own autobiography in forcible-feeble prose. So this novel with a mission may achieve its purpose after all.

3. From *The Graphic* (29 November 1890): 624 (unsigned review)

Miss Marie Corelli displays her usual courage in three volumes eccentrically adorned by the binder, with scarlet ribbon, and by the printer with a startling effect in blood colour, and entitled "Wormwood: A Drama of Paris" (Bentley and Son). This prodigious narrative professes to be the confessions of an *absintheur*, or absinthe-drinker; through whom Miss Corelli delivers, concerning things and people in general, fierce and furious remarks which, she is careful to explain, are not to be taken as her own. The style can only be described as frantic; but no doubt this has, at any rate, the merit of being appropriate to the homicidal maniac whom she has made his own biographer.... We have always recognized in Miss Corelli exceptional gifts of imagination; and "Wormwood" in no way modifies our estimation either of her fancy or of her courage.

---

[1]   Named after H.G. Ollendorff who devised a system for learning foreign languages. Ollendorff guides were popular foreign language manuals in the nineteenth century.

4. From *The Academy* (29 November 1890): 500-501 (written by J. Barrow Allen)

Miss Marie Corelli's latest work is not so much a novel as a psychological study, and might have been entitled "Confessions of an Absintheur." However, *Wormwood* will do well enough; and Gaston Beauvais, the victim of absinthe, who relates with a fiendish sort of pride the stages of ever-increasing brutalisation that mark his downward career, ought to be sufficiently terrible a warning to banish all inclination for indulgence in the vice. Of course the author is by no means the first who has dealt with the subject in a work of fiction; but no one has treated it in more powerful style and with greater wealth of burning language. Like many others, Miss Corelli attributes much that is flippant, heartless, and immoral to "the reckless absinthe-mania which pervades all classes"; and, like many others, she makes the mistake of attributing to the whole French nation the vices that are mainly characteristic of Paris. But, so far as she is condemning this particular vice of the Parisians, her language is worthy of all encouragement; and especially is she to be congratulated upon having refrained from meddling with the secrets of the unseen world, and upon having taken grave realities for her subject. As she most truly observes, "There is no necessity to invent fables nowadays; the fictionist need never torture his brain for stories of adventure or spectral horror." Life as it is lived, presents plenty to write about; and so long as Miss Corelli wields her trenchant pen and employs her undoubtedly great talents upon matter of this kind, she has our heartiest wishes for her success.

5. From a review in *Kensington Society*, qtd. in *Academy* (13 December 1890): 554

Few modern writers have a greater command of eloquently vigorous language than Miss Corelli. It flows through the greater portion of the present thrilling work in lava torrents of bitter passion and pitiless revenge. The reader is whirled about like a leaflet amidst lurid flashes and wild gusts of maddened invective, almost blinded by the effort he or she makes to realise the tempest which rages through the man possessed of the "liquid fire."

6. From *Literary World* (17 January 1891): 21–22 (unsigned review)

Et le nom de cette étoile était ABSINTHE! Such is the startling cry of denunciation, taken from the Apocalypse as a motto, to arraign the vice of Paris. This strong romance, by Miss Marie Corelli, is a study—extremely realistic, yet saved by the honest and clean mind of the author from needless offense—of the horrible demoralization and the reversion to brute types of the modern Parisians, caused by the absinthe habit. The pallid green liquor, that seems like the soul of a serpent, establishes its power almost immediately, and leaves the victim a witch-dance of brilliant and diabolical illusions, terminating in lesion of the brain, a fixed idea, idiocy, and death.

Miss Corelli has handled her terrible theme with true vigor and efficiency, together with artistic reserve and moderation. Even to the fallen hero of the story, Gaston Beauvais, it is impossible to deny our interest and compassion; a deadly wrong done him by his friend had made the world totter around him, and left him an easy prey to the sophistries of a devotee of absinthe. "The green fairy," having driven from his brain the instincts of human rectitude, peopled its cells with demons, and the poor Beauvais goes running toward his death. The characters are drawn with strong dramatic contrast: Gaston, at first the type of the best Parisian youth—a type which is not yet extinct; Pauline, like a lily that retains its whiteness under the filth beaten upon it by a storm; the fathers of these two, delicately differentiated individuals of the class of *père noble*; and the priest, Silvion Guidèl, with his great error. The scenes are saved from sensationalism by the excellent art with which they are expressed, and by the firm purpose which animates the book.

Miss Corelli has written nothing superior to *Wormwood*, and the moral of this story is not alone for Paris or for France, but for every other nation where the curse of absinthe enters, either in its direct form, or in its more widespread and subtle secondary phase—the corruption and debasement of literature and art. Because a novelist or poet on the Boulevards spurs his jaded wit by absinthe, a crowd of imitators copy, and even highten [*sic*], his false and evil effects in art, with the hope of appearing expert and brilliant. There is, for example, a little group of New York fictionists (quite apart from the real and excellent *littérateurs* there) who have busied themselves with offering to the public the rinsings of the absinthe-glasses of their Parisian masters. It should not be difficult for these men to reform a habit which, it is to be hoped, exists in them as harmlessly as in the mirrors of the absinthe shops, a mere reflection of the attitude without the actual imbibing of the liquid. Perhaps, if one only knew how to look for it, there is a physiological cause for every literary phase. Seek for the nerve, excited or atrophied—and you may find the formula of difference between Baudelaire and Dr. Watts![1]

---

[1]   Charles Baudelaire (1821-67), French poet renowned for his dissolute lifestyle; Isaac Watts (1674-1748), English theologian and hymn writer.

Miss Corelli's preface should be noted, in which she sets right, in her lively fashion, several injustices done to her by pirated editions, with their hasty proof-reading and 'maddest misprints,' especially of Italian idiomatic phrases. She does well to warn the readers, who are to trace with her the destruction of a soul possessed by absinthe, against the misapprehension which awaits a writer who paints to the life indefensible personages and scenes—that the author is represented by the dramatic utterances of those characters, or has witnessed the details which are described. In *Wormwood*, Miss Corelli has scored a real success, employing to a worthy end an art in the line of the most popular French writers.

7. From *The Times* (23 January 1891): 13 (unsigned review)

"The fictionist," we are told by Marie Corelli, in an eloquent preface, "need never torture his brain for stories, either of adventure or spectral horror. Life itself, as it is lived among ourselves in all countries, is so amazing, swift, varied, wonderful, terrible, ghastly, beautiful, dreadful, and withal so wildly inconsistent and changeful, that whosoever desires to write romances has only to closely and patiently observe men and women as they are—not as they seem—and then take pen in hand and write—'the truth.'"[1] With all its feminine redundancy of adjectives, a very excellent plea for "Realism," if only all of us could be as cocksure as Marie Corelli that what seemed to us to be reality was not in reality mere seeming. But ought a "fictionist" who deals in nothing but verities to palm off upon her readers lurid descriptions of a *café-chantant* orgy without having been there? Is it not a trifle shabby to father her glowing picture upon a respectable English tourist, whom the "fictionist" (*vide* again the preface) perceived from his dress to be "of some religious persuasion," and whom she overheard enthusiastically commending the can-can to a younger companion, yet did not withdraw suffused with blushes, but "took calm note thereof for literary use thereafter?" At first, we felt inclined to say, with a Sheffielder in a certain play, "I know that tourist!" But upon other evidence we have decided to exonerate Marie Corelli from a suspicion which, one would have thought, a student of life as it is lived would have been in no hurry to repel. The evidence which satisfies us that Marie Corelli has never set foot in one of these naughty places is comprised in a single sentence:—"There are lovely women at the *cafés-chantants*; ... women as delicate as nymphs, and dainty as flowers." ... However, this is a tale not so much about *cafés-chantants* as

---

1   A quotation from Corelli's "introductory note."

about *absinthe*, which the fictionist has discovered at first-hand (not through listening to the conversation of tourists on steamboats) to be sapping the mental, moral, and physical fibre of Parisians of all classes. It is no stray tourist this time, but eminent doctors who have told this profound observer of things as they are all about it; how the "light green witch" completely strips the *absintheur* of all finer feelings, numbs his faculties, inverts his morality, and leaves him subject to accesses of sensual or homicidal mania. The tale of the descent of Gaston Beauvais, as related by himself, is a series of tedious and exaggerated soliloquies, relieved by tolerably dramatic, but repulsive, incidents. "Wormwood," we fancy, is not likely to be famous or even popular. This opinion we do not venture without diffidence. As the "fictionist" warns us, the "Public itself is the supreme critic now,... its unwritten verdict declares itself with such an amazing weight of influence that the ephemeral opinions of a few ill-paid journalists are the merest straws beating against the strong force of a whirlwind." That is Marie Corelli's modest way of announcing that her books have been known to find their way to railway bookstalls.

8. From *The Spectator* (28 February 1891): 312–313 (unsigned review)

Wormwood [is] a book which is made all the more disagreeable by an introduction from which we are evidently intended to draw the inference that the author has been actuated solely by a grave concern for the interests of national and personal morality. We recognised in November, 1886, when reviewing *Vendetta*, in the strongest way, Miss Corelli's great powers, and especially her force of imagination; but this book is to us exceedingly repulsive. Miss Corelli believes that England is becoming largely infected by French depravity; that French depravity in its most shameful manifestations is due to the rapidly spreading mania for the drinking of *absinthe*; and that, accordingly, it is her duty to write the fictitious autobiography of an irreclaimable *absintheur*, omitting none of his drunken drivellings, his maudlin moralisings, his diseased visions, his devilish cruelties and crimes. In portions of several of her previous works, Miss Corelli has treated some of the baser aspects of human nature with what seems to us an unwholesome elaboration; but in *Wormwood* we are allowed no relief,—no escape from the hateful prospect of the lowest deeps of depravity. We are, of course, acquainted with the usual apology for this kind of thing,—that "Vice is a monster of such hideous mien," &c.; but surely no ordinary Englishmen, to say nothing of English women, will believe that their virtue is fortified by their being made sharers in the hideous knowledge of a Parisian night-policeman or prison doctor. *Wormwood* is, in short, a book for the existence of which there is no sufficient justification, either ethical or artistic.

9. From a review in *County Gentlewoman*, qtd. in *Academy* (11 July 1891): 26

What a stir Marie Corelli's new book, *Wormwood*, has created. Everyone is talking about it. Never before, I should say, has the subject of absinthe-drinking in Paris been gone into so thoroughly and all its effects laid bare.

10. From Kent Carr, *Miss Marie Corelli* (London: Henry J. Drane, 1901) 109–110

[*Wormwood*] has its own purpose writ large; but in some inexplicable way this purpose becomes the vital part of a great artistic creation. Her delineation of the wretched absinthe drinker is the most consistently powerful piece of work Corelli has yet done. The story marches from horror to horror till the very crescendo of human devilry is reached. We follow the hero's grisly career till our very blood runs cold with loathing. We watch him brand the child-bride with open shame on her marriage morning and shudder at each further step of his fiendish revenge. And yet, with the tragedy at its height, there is no situation which could not safely challenge criticism as being absolutely right and inevitable. To borrow a famous expression—it is like realizing the absinthe-mania by flashes of lightning.

Appendix D: Corelli on Literature and Art

1. Marie Corelli, letter to George Bentley, 11 March 1887, Marie Corelli Collection, General Collection, Beinecke Rare Book and Manuscript Library, Yale University

[Corelli on authorship]

But I came away [from the Incorporated Society of Authors dinner] with the notion that the authors generally seemed pretty well disgusted with their lot, and all on very bad terms with one another, so that is was almost a pity they had taken to the profession at all. Amid all their grumbles and universal discontent, they seemed entirely to forget the ... joy of their art,— I mean the intense delight they find or *ought* to find in writing! The *art* appeared as nothing in their discussions—the "filthy lucre"—everything. Surely this is the wrong way to look at it? I could have arisen in my strength and spoken if my thoughts would have consented to form themselves into speech—but I am not a "blue"[1]—and am unaccustomed to public speaking so I sat silent and smiled placidly at the growling lions. I felt really sorry for them all—they seemed to find everything *so* hopelessly wrong! Now I am so thoroughly *happy* in writing,—so utterly absorbed in it and so fond of tenderly touching up my characters and descriptions, that I feel I should *have* to write on for my own pleasure, if no one would take pity on me at all to the extent of publishing what I wrote,—and as for "strained relations"—and "secret understandings" I cannot imagine what Mr. Besant[2] means. The most amiable publisher in the world cannot make *every* author popular,—it is too much to expect of him. When I have resigned a work of *mine* into *your* hands I always feel satisfied that you will do the best you can for both me and it,—and I should be sorry indeed to have anything to do with the "Incorporated Society" whose prospectus I send you by way of amusement. It is a mere wasp's nest of grumbles—and will *never do*!

---

[1] A blue-stocking, a woman having or affecting literary tastes and learning. In Corelli's day the term was often used in a derogatory fashion.

[2] Walter Besant (1836-1901) was the founder of the Society of Authors, a society which protected the rights of authors. Besant was particularly critical of publishers' treatment of authors.

2. Marie Corelli, letter to George Bentley, 6 April 1887, Marie Corelli Collection, General Collection, Beinecke Rare Book and Manuscript Library, Yale University

[Corelli on authorship]

I think no author ought to judge of another. After all literature is the edifice, and authors are only the working masons—if each one can add a fresh brick or stone to the building, that is something—and the builders should be too intent on the whole architecture to pause for an instant to criticize each other. Such is my feeling about all art, whether it be music, literature or painting;—and the only thing I sometimes long for is *fraternity* among all the followers of Art—a bond of joyous and sympathetic union should by right, exist among them,—or at least such would be *my* dream.

3. From Marie Corelli, "'Imaginary Love,'" *Free Opinions, Freely Expressed* (London: Archibald Constable and Co., 1905) 164–165, 167–168

[In this essay, Corelli describes "imaginary love" as an "elevating" emotion, an "uplifting of the heart and yearning of the senses." Yet it may also be, she points out, a "deceptive" emotion that may lead to disillusionment because though "it glitters before us, a brilliant chimera, during our very young days ... on our entrance into society it vanishes, leaving us to pursue it through many phases of existence, and always in vain." It is the yearning for and continual pursuit of this love that, for Corelli, is the basis of "all the greatest art, music, and poetry in the world."]

If we [artists] had to do merely with men as they are, and women as they are, Art would perish utterly from the face of the earth. It is because we make ourselves "ideal" men, "ideal" women, and endow these fair creations with the sentiment of "imaginary" love, that we still are able to communicate with the gods. Not yet have we lowered ourselves to the level of the beasts,—nor shall we do so, though things sometimes seem tending that way. Realism and Atheism have darkened the world, as they darken it now, long before the present time, and as defacements on the grandeur of the Universe they have not been permitted to remain. Nor will they be permitted now,—the reaction will, and must inevitably set in. The repulsive materialism of Zola, and others of his school,—the loose theories of the "smart" set, and the moral degradation of those who have no greater God than self,—these things are the merest ephemera, destined to leave no more mark on human history than the trail of a slug on one leaf of an oak. The Ideal must always be triumphant,—the soul can only hope to make way by climbing towards it. Thus it is with "imaginary" Love,—it must hold fast to its ideal, or be content to perish on the plane of sensual passion, which exhausts itself rapidly, and once dead, is dead for ever and aye.

With all its folly, sweetness, piteousness and pathos, "imaginary" love is the keynote of Art,—its fool-musings take shape in exquisite verse, in tales of romance and adventure, in pictures that bring the nations together to stand and marvel, in music that makes the strong man weep. It is the most supersensual of all delicate sensations,—as fine as a hair, as easily destroyed as a gnat's wing!—a rough touch will wound it,—a coarse word will kill it,—the sneer of the Realist shuts it in a coffin of lead and sinks it fathoms deep in the waters of despair....

Happy, and always to be envied, are those who treasure ["imaginary love"]. It is the dearest possession of every true artist. In every thought, in every creative work or plan, "imaginary" love goes before, pointing out wonders unseen by less enlightened eyes,—hiding things unsightly, disclosing things lovely, and making the world fair to the mind in all seasons, whether of storm or calm. Intensifying every enjoyment, adding a double thrill to the notes of a sweet song, lending an extra glow to the sunshine, an added radiance to the witchery of the moonlight, a more varied and exquisite colouring to the trees and flowers, a charm to every book, a delight to every new scene, "imaginary" love, a very sprite of enchantment, helps us to believe persistently in good, when those who love not at all, neither in reality nor in idealization, are drowning in the black waters of suicidal despair.

4. From Marie Corelli, "The 'Strong' Book of the Ishbosheth," *Free Opinions, Freely Expressed* (London: Archibald Constable and Co., 1905) 245–246, 246–251

... "Strong" ... used to mean strength. It means it still, I believe, in the gymnasium. But in very choice literary circles it means "unclean." This is very strange, but true. For some time past the gentle and credulous public has remained in doubt as to what was really implied by a "strong" book. The gentle and credulous public has been under the impression that the word "strong" used by the guides, philosophers, and friends who review current fiction in the daily Press, meant a powerful style, a vigorous grip, a brilliant way of telling a captivating and noble story. But they have, by slow and painful degrees, found out their mistake in this direction, and they know now that a "strong" book means a nasty subject indelicately treated. Whereupon they are beginning to "sheer off" any book labelled by the inner critical faculty as "strong." This must be admitted as a most unfortunate fact for those who are bending all their energies upon the writing of "strong" books, and who are wasting their powers on discussing what they euphoniously term "delicate and burning subjects"; but it is a hopeful and blessed sign of increasing education and widening intellectual perception in the masses, who will soon by their sturdy common sense win a position which is not to be "frighted with false fire."[1]...

"Art," says a certain M.A., "if it be genuine and sincere, tends ever to the lofty and the beautiful. There is no rule of art more important than the sense of modesty. Vice grows not a little by immodesty of thought."[2] True. And immodesty of thought fulfils its mission in the "strong" book, which alone succeeds in winning the applause of the "Exclusive Set of Degenerates" known as the E.S.D. under the Masonic Scriptural sign of ISHBOSHETH[3] (laying particular emphasis on the syllable between the "Ish" and the "eth,") who manage to obtain temporary posts on the ever-changeful twirling treadmill of the daily press. The Ishbosheth singular is the man who praises the "strong" book—the Ishbosheth in the plural are the Exclusive Set who are sworn to put down Virtue and extol Vice. Hence the "strong" cult, also the "virile." This last excellent and expressive word has become seriously maltreated in the hands of the Ishbosheth, and is now made answerable for many sins which it did not originally represent. "Virile" is from the Latin *virilis*, a male—virility is the state and characteristic of the adult male. Applied to certain books, however, by the Ishbosheth it will be found by the discerning public to mean coarse—rough—with a literary "style" obtained by sprinkling several pages of prose with the lowest tavern-oaths, together with the name of God, pronounced "Gawd." Anything written in that fashion is at once pronounced "virile" and commands wide admiration from the Ishbosheth, particularly if it should be a story in which women are depicted as the lowest kickable depth of drab-ism to which men can drag them, while men are represented as the suffering victims of their wickedness. This peculiar kind of turn-coat morality was, according to Genesis, instituted by Adam in his cowardly utterance: "The woman tempted me," as an excuse for his own base greed; and it has

---

1 From Shakespeare's *Hamlet* 3.2.271.
2 Unknown source.
3 Biblical name meaning "man of shame."

apparently continued to sprout forth in various of his descendents ever since that time, especially in the community of the Ishbosheth. "Virility," therefore, being the state and characteristic of the adult male, or the adult Adam, means, according to the Ishbosheth, men's proper scorn for the sex of their mothers, and an egotistical delight in themselves, united to a barbarous rejoicing in bad language and abandoned morals. It does not mean this in decent every-day life, of course; but it does in books—such books as are praised by the Ishbosheth.

"I don't want one of your 'strong' books," said a customer at one of the circulating libraries the other day. "Give me something I can read to my wife without being ashamed." This puts the case in a nutshell. No clean-minded man can read the modern "strong" book praised by the Ishbosheth and feel quite safe, or even quite manly in his wife's presence. He will find himself before he knows it mumbling something about the gross and fleshly temptations of a deformed gentleman with short legs;[1] or he will grow hot-faced and awkward over the narrative of a betrayed milkmaid who enters into all the precise details of her wrongs with a more than pernicious gusto.[2] It is true that he will probably chance upon no worse or more revolting circumstances of human life than are dished up for the general Improvement of Public Morals in our halfpenny dailies; but he will realize, if he be a man of sense, that whereas the divorce court and police cases in the newspaper are very soon forgotten, the impression of a "strong" book, particularly if the "strong" parts are elaborately and excruciatingly insisted upon, lasts, and sometimes leaves tracks of indelible mischief on minds which, but for its loathesome influence, would have remained upright and innocent. Thought creates action. An idea is the mainspring of an epoch. Therefore the corrupters of thought are responsible for corrupt deeds in an individual or a nation. From a noble thought—from a selfless pure ideal—what great actions spring! Herein should the responsibility of Literature be realized. The Ishbosheth, with their "strong" books, have their criminal part in the visible putrescence of a certain section of society known as the "swagger set." Perhaps no more forcible illustration of the repulsion exercised by nature itself to spiritual and literary disease could be furnished than by the death of the French "realist" Zola. Capable of fine artistic work, he prostituted his powers to the lowest grade of thought. From the dust-hole of the frail world's ignorance and crime he selected his olla-podrida of dirty scrapings, potato-peelings, candle-ends, rank fat, and cabbage

---

[1] Allusion to *The History of Sir Richard Calmady* (1901) by Lucas Malet (Mary St. Leger Harrison, née Kingsley).

[2] Allusion to Thomas Hardy's *Tess of the D'Urbervilles* (1891).

water, and set them all to seethe in the fire of his brain, till they emitted noxious poison, and suffocating vapours calculated to choke the channels of every aspiring mind and idealistic soul. Nature revenged herself upon him by permitting him to be likewise asphyxiated—only in the most prosy and "realistic" manner.[1] It was one of those terribly grim jests which she is fond of playing off on those who blaspheme her sacred altars. A certain literary aspirant hovering on the verge of the circle of the Ishbosheth, complained the other day of a great omission in the biography of one of his dead comrades of the pen. "They should have mentioned," he said, "that he allowed his body to *swarm with vermin!*"[2] This is true Ishbosheth art. Suppress the fact that the dead man had good in him, that he might have been famous had he lived, that he had some notably strong points in his character, but *don't* forget, for Heaven's sake, to mention the "vermin"! For the Ishbosheth "cult" see nothing in a sunset, but much in a flea.

Hence when we read the criticism of a "strong" book, over the signature of the Ishbosheth, we know what to expect. All the bad, low, villainous and soiled side of sickly or insane human nature will be in it, and nothing of the healthful or sound. For, to be vicious is to be ill—to commit crime is to be mentally deformed—and the "strong" book of the Ishbosheth only deals with phases of sickness and lunacy. There are other "strong" books in the world, thank Heaven—strong books which treat strongly of noble examples of human life, love and endeavour—books like those of Scott and Dickens and Brontë and Eliot[3]—books which make the world all the better for reading them. But they are not books admired of the Ishbosheth. And as the Ishbosheth have their centres in the current press, they are not praised in the newspapers. Binding as the union of Printers is all over the world, I suppose they cannot take arms against the Ishbosheth and decline to print anything under this Masonic sign? If they could, what a purification there would be—what a clean, refreshing world of books—and perhaps of men and women! No more vicious heroes with short legs; no more painfully-injured milkmaids; no more "twins," earthly or heavenly[4]—while possibly a new *Villette*[5] might bud and blossom

---

1   Zola was accidentally asphyxiated in his home by poisonous gases emitted from a stove with a faulty pipe.

2   Unidentified source.

3   Walter Scott (1771-1832), Scottish novelist and poet of the Romantic period; Charles Dickens (1812-70), English novelist; Charlotte Brontë (1816-55), English novelist; George Eliot (Mary Anne Evans, 1819-80), English novelist.

4   Reference to Sarah Grand's (Frances Elizabeth McFall's) *Heavenly Twins* (1893).

5   An 1853 novel by Charlotte Brontë.

forth—another *Fortunes of Nigel*,[1] another brilliant *Vanity Fair*[2]—and books which contain wit without nastiness, tenderness without erotics, simplicity without affectation, and good English without slang, might once again give glory to literature. But this millennium will not be till the "strong" book of the Ishbosheth ceases to find a publisher, and the Ishbosheth themselves are seen in their true colours, and fully recognized by the public to be no more than they are—a mere group of low sensualists, who haunt Fleet Street bars and restaurants, and who out of that sodden daily and nightly experience get a few temporary jobs on the Press, and "pose" as a cult and censorship of art. And fortunately the very phrase "strong book" has become so much their own that it has now only to be used in order to warn off the public from mere pot-house opinion.

---

[1]   An 1822 novel by Sir Walter Scott.
[2]   An 1848 novel by William Makepeace Thackeray.

Appendix E: British Views of Naturalism

1. From W.S. Lilly, "The New Naturalism," *Fortnightly Review* (August 1885): 241–256

[W.S. Lilly (1840–1919) was a barrister and man of letters who wrote on philosophy, theology, and literature. Lilly was a frequent contributor to the *Fortnightly Review* and other prominent periodicals of the day. In "The New Naturalism," Lilly summarizes the tenets of the Naturalist school while revealing his own bias against it. His views on Naturalism are very similar to Corelli's.]

M. Zola and his disciples unquestionably constitute the most popular school of contemporary French fiction.... English fiction too, if it has produced nothing which can rival M. Zola's compositions, has at least shown more than a tendency to imitate them from afar. And translations of that author's most characteristic works have been published in periodicals which, I am informed, are largely read....

The great aim and object of the New Naturalism, according to M. Zola, is a return to nature. The novelist, the dramatist, he says, ought to be the photographer of phenomena. Their business is to study the world—to observe, to analyse humanity as they find it. But this is best done in its most vulgar types.... The artist in experimental fiction is, apart from questions of style and form, merely a specialist, a *savant* who employs the same instruments as other *savants*, observation and analysis. His domain is that of the physiologist. Only it is more vast. To be master of the mechanism of human phenomena, to exhibit the machinery (*les rouages*) of intellectual and sensual manifestations, as physiology shall explain them, under the influences of heredity and environment, then to show the living man in the social order which he has himself produced, which he daily modifies, and in the bosom of which he undergoes a constant transformation—such is the theory of the experimental novel.... So too the language must be real—the language of the street—*un morçeau de rue*. The old notion of a style differing from that of common life, more sonorous, more nervous, more highly pitched, more finely cut, is an abomination to M. Zola, and it must be allowed that he scrupulously avoids it. With equal care he eschews idealism and poetry, which he calls lyricism, and of which, he tells us, literature is "rotting." Invention must be used as sparingly as possible and confined to the plot, which, however, is to be scrupulously kept within the limits of every-day life. The rest he will have to be mere copying—a transcript of facts. Formerly the greatest compliment you could pay to a novelist or playwright was to say, "He has a great deal of imagination." If such a speech were addressed to M. Zola he would regard himself as a very ill-used gentleman.

...There is nothing new in M. Zola's contention that the novelist, the dramatist, and the worker in all other arts must conform to nature. Art is nothing but the minister, the interpreter of nature; its function to create the image and symbol of that which is....

The Old Naturalism is at one ... with the New in proposing conformity to nature as its great law. Where the two differ is in the meaning which they set upon the words "conformity to nature." Formerly men looked upon phenomena as the visible expression of an invisible reality.... The conviction that behind the world of form, of colour, of extension there is a reality of which phenomena are the shadows was the life of the Old Naturalism. And the function of art was conceived of as being the union of spiritual substance and material symbol.... But art was held to be life, to be idealised creation.... So much as to the difference between the Old and the New Naturalism. The one was poetical, and in dealing with the commonest of realities was "quick to recognize the moral properties and scope of things,"[1] using sensible forms to body forth their inner significance. The other claims to be scientific, and declining to recognise in nature anything which cannot be analysed, or dissected, or vivisected, proposes as its object the study of the human animal—*la bête humaine*—subject to the action of its environment, the compulsion of heredity, the fatality of instinct. The one is dominated by the ideal, and in a true sense is, and cannot help being, religious. The other is strictly materialistic and frankly professes atheism.... [Zola] cast[s] aside ethical considerations. You have nothing to do with them he tells his disciples.... Your aim should be to produce a composition—he might have written decomposition—which logically classifies and correctly values facts....

.... M. Zola holds ... that the time in which we are living is essentially a New Age. Its spirit is "scientific." ... Everywhere there has been a return to nature, to reality. In politics it has assumed the form of Democracy; in metaphysics of Positivism; in art of Naturalism. You may call it generally the Naturalistic Evolution. It means everywhere the banishment of sentiment, of imagination, of empirical doctrines, of poetic idealism; the recognition of facts cognisable by the senses, which are the only facts; and the adoption of the experimental method. Analysis and experience, the study of environment and

---

[1]   Quotation from Henry Glassford Bell's (1803-74) poem "Mary, Queen of Scots."

mechanism—such is everywhere the course to be followed. The new demo-cratic society is merely a collection of organised beings existing upon earth in certain conditions—of *bêtes humaines*, who know that they are human beasts, and do not pretend to be anything else, who are well aware that the old religious conceptions which regarded them as something else are cunningly devised fables. The Republic as it happily exists in France, is the best type of human government—*le gouvernement humain par excellence*—rest-ing, as it does, upon universal suffrage, determined by the majority of facts, and so corresponding with the observed and analysed wants of the *bêtes humaines*, who make up the nation.... the New Naturalism supplies the fitting literature for this government, since it is the expression, in the intellectual domain, of the causes of which the Third Republic is the political and social outcome. Yes, he assures us, literature must become pathological or it will cease to exist.... M. Zola has devoted a long, and I must say, a very ingenious, essay to prove that the writer of fiction must follow the latest methods adopted by the student of experimental medicine. Art must disappear from the novel and the drama. The science of the vivisector is to take its place....

....And what shall we say of M. Zola's attempt to shelter himself and his method under the name of Balzac. He tells us, "Balzac was the great master of the real." True; the greatest certainly in the literature of France. But there is all the difference in the world between M. Zola's unimaginative realism and Balzac's imaginative reality. Balzac is no mere copyist from the streets. To him, as to every artist worthy of the name, the living model is a means, not an end; and he was, primarily and before all else an artist, ever work-ing in the spirit of his own dictum that art is idealised creation. An artist is one who reproduces the world in his own image and likeness. And in the *Comédie Humaine* we have a colossal fresco in which the society of the first half of the century is painted for us with pitiless accuracy and terrible pathos as by the brush of Michael Angelo—a Titanesque work ... Like the great Florentine, Balzac was indeed an anatomist, and owed his vast tech-nical skill to dissection; and, like him, he parades his science too much. But where the scalpel has destroyed, his brush recreates; and with what accu-racy of detail, what forces of conception, what depth of colour, what prophetic divination! His figures present that almost perfect union of type with character which is the highest note of the poet. They are instinct with life; they become to us, as they were to him, more real than the men and women of the phenomenal world; and no wonder, for genius holds of the noumenal. I know, and I by no means seek to extenuate, the blots which disfigure the work of this incomparable master. The ideal with him too often falls into the mud. King as he is among French artists in romantic fiction, his royal robes cover a cancer at the heart. M. Zola is wholly eaten up by that cancerous taint....

... the especial value of the writings of M. Zola and his school seems to me that they are the most popular literary outcome of the doctrine which denies the personality, liberty, and spirituality of man and the objective foundation on which these rest, which empties him of the moral sense, the feeling of the infinite, the aspiration towards the Absolute, which makes of him nothing more than a sequence of action and reaction, and the first and last word of which is sensism. Now, I am far from denying that this view of humanity may be presented—as a matter of fact it often has been—with great literary skill and adorned with graces not its own. M. Zola has done us this service; he has reduced it to its ultimate, its most vulgar resolution. He has supplied the most pregnant illustration known to me in literature that "the visible when it rests not upon the invisible becomes bestial."

... [The New Naturalism] eliminates from man all but the ape and tiger. It leaves of him nothing but the *bête humaine*, more subtle than any beast of the field, but cursed above all beasts of the field. It is beyond question—look at France if you want overwhelming demonstration of it—that the issue of what M. Zola calls the Naturalistic Evolution is the banishing from human life of all that gives it glory and honour: the victory of fact over principle, of mechanism over imagination, of appetites, dignified as rights, over duties, of sensation over intellect, of the belly over the heart, of fatalism over moral freedom, of brute force over justice, in a word, of matter over mind.

2. From H. Rider Haggard, "About Fiction," *Contemporary Review* 51 (February 1887): 176, 177

[H. Rider Haggard (1856-1925) was a popular novelist of the late-Victorian period, a writer of gripping adventure novels directed at a mostly male readership. Like Corelli, he was an opponent of Naturalism.]

Then ... there is the Naturalistic school, of which Zola is the high priest.... Here are no silks and satins to impede our vision of the flesh and blood beneath, and here the scent is patchouli. Lewd, and bold, and bare, living for lust and lusting for this life and its good things, and naught beyond, the heroines of realism dance, with Bacchanalian revellings, across the astonished stage of literature. Whatever there is brutal in humanity—and God knows that there is plenty—whatever there is that is carnal and filthy, is here brought into prominence, and thrust before the reader's eyes. But what becomes of the things that are pure and high—of the great aspirations and the lofty hopes and longings, which *do*, after all, play their part in our human economy, and which it is surely the duty of a writer to call attention to and nourish according to his gifts?

Certainly it is to be hoped that this naturalistic school of writing will never take firm root in England, for it is an accursed thing. It is impossible to help wondering if its followers ever reflect upon the mischief that they must do, and, reflecting, do not shrink from the responsibility.... "But," say these [Naturalist] writers, "our aim is most moral; from Nana[1] and her kith and kin may be gathered many a virtuous lesson and example." Possibly this is so, though as I write the words there rises in my mind a recollection of one or two French books where——but most people have seen such books. Besides, it is not so much a question of the object of the school as of the fact that it continually, and in full and luscious detail, calls attention to erotic matters. Once start the average mind upon this subject, and it will go down the slope of itself. It is useless afterwards to turn round and say that, although you cut loose the cords of decent reticence which bound the fancy, you intended that it should run *uphill* to the white heights of virtue.

3. From the National Vigilance Association, *Pernicious Literature* (1889): 5,6,7

[The National Vigilance Association was a social purity group formed in 1885. Initially the group involved itself in campaigns against prostitution but it soon became very concerned about the sale and distribution of what it regarded as indecent literature and photographs. Included among those writers considered obscene by the National Vigilance Association were Balzac, Zola, Boccaccio, and Rabelais. *Pernicious Literature* was a pamphlet circulated in 1889 which contained a transcript of a Parliamentary debate on "pernicious literature," excerpts from newspapers concerning pernicious literature, and a transcript of the trial of Henry Vizetelly, a publisher charged with publishing the "obscene" literature of Émile Zola.]

Debate in the House of Commons, May 8, 1888

Mr. S. Smith (Flintshire) said, he rose to call attention to the Motion which stood in his name, and which was as follows:—

"That this House deplores the rapid spread of demoralizing literature in this country, and is of the opinion that the law against obscene publications

---

[1]   Zola's courtesan heroine from the 1880 novel of the same name.

and indecent pictures and prints should be vigorously enforced, and, if necessary, strengthened." He assured the House that nothing but an imperative sense of duty had led him to take up so painful and so disagreeable a subject—nothing but the knowledge that there had of late years been an immense increase of vile literature in London and throughout the country, and that this literature was working terrible effects on the morals of the young. Such havoc was it making that he could only look upon it as a gigantic national danger ...There was nothing that so corroded the human character, or so sapped the vitality of a nation, as the spread of this noxious and licentious literature, and he believed it was at the bottom of that shocking state of the streets of London, of which they were continual witnesses.... [H]e believed [M. Vizetelly] to be the chief culprit in the spread of this pernicious literature ...

... Of the character of these works [Mr. Smith] would say that nothing more diabolical had ever been written by the pen of man. These novels were only fit for swine, and their constant perusal must turn the mind into something akin to a sty. *The Saturday Review*, a short time ago—

"Directed the attention of the police to the fact that books which no shop dare expose in Paris, or even in Brussels, are to be seen in windows in London. Books which have only escaped suppression in France through the astounding laxity which has allowed some parts of Paris to become nearly impassable to decent people—on the showing of Parisian papers themselves—are translated and openly advertised."

Some hon. members might say that *The Saturday Review* was something of a purist, but no one would make such an accusation against *Society*, one of the society papers. This paper said, on the 21st of April last—

"But of late has come a brutal change over this spirit of not too innocent fun, and the name of the worker of this transformation is Realism, and Zola is his Prophet. Realism, according to latter-day French lights, means nothing short of sheer beastliness; it means going out of the way to dig up foul expressions to embody filthy ideas; it means not only the old insinuation of petty intrigue, but the laying bare of social sores in their most loathsome forms; ... In a word, it is dirt and horror pure and simple; and the good-humoured Englishman, who might smilingly characterize the French novel as 'rather thick,' will be disgusted and tired with the inartistic garbage which is to be found in Zola's *La Terre*. Yet Messrs. Vizetelly, of Catharine Street, Strand, are allowed with impunity to publish an almost word for word translation of Zola's bestial *chef d'oeuvre*. In the French original its sins were glaring enough in all conscience, but the English version needs but a chapter's perusal to make one sigh for something to take the nasty taste away." ...

Now, [Mr. Smith] asked, were they to stand still while the country was wholly corrupted by literature of this kind? were they to wait until the moral fibre of the English race was eaten out, as that of the French was almost? Look what such literature had done for France. It overspread that country like a torrent, and its poison was destroying the whole national life. France, to-day, was rapidly approaching Rome in the time of the Caesars. The philosophy of France to-day was "Let us eat and drink, for to-morrow we die." ... Such garbage was simply death to a nation. Were they to wait till this deadly poison spread itself over English soil and killed the life of this great and noble people?

Appendix F: Nineteenth-Century Degeneration Theories

1. From E. Ray Lankester, *Degeneration: A Chapter in Darwinism* (London: Macmillan, 1880) 58–62

[Lankester (1847-1929) was a biologist, a professor of zoology, and a director of the Natural History section at the British Museum. A follower of Darwin, Lankester wrote a number of popular science books.]

The traditional history of mankind furnishes us with notable examples of degeneration. High states of civilisation have decayed and given place to low and degenerate states. At one time it was a favourite doctrine that the savage races of mankind were degenerate descendents of the higher and civilised races. This general and sweeping application of the doctrine of degeneration has been proved to be erroneous by careful study of the habits, arts, and beliefs of savages; at the same time there is no doubt that many savage races as we at present see them are degenerate and are descended from ancestors possessed of a relatively elaborate civilisation. As such we may cite some of the Indians of Central America, the modern Egyptians, and even the heirs of the great oriental monarchies or pre-Christian times. Whilst the hypothesis of universal degeneration as an explanation of savage races has been justly discarded, it yet appears that degeneration has a very large share in the explanation of the condition of the most barbarous races, such as the Fuegians, the Bushmen, and even the Australians. They exhibit evidence of being descended from ancestors more cultivated than themselves.

With regard to ourselves, the white races of Europe, the possibility of degeneration seems to be worth some consideration. In accordance with a tacit assumption of universal progress—an unreasoning optimism—we are accustomed to regard ourselves as necessarily progressing, as necessarily having arrived at a higher and more elaborated condition than that which our ancestors reached, and as destined to progress still further. On the other hand, it is well to remember that we are subject to the general laws of evolution, and are as likely to degenerate as to progress. As compared with the immediate forefathers of our civilization—the ancient Greeks—we do not appear to have improved so far as our bodily structure is concerned, nor assuredly so far as some of our mental capacities are concerned. Our powers of perceiving and expressing beauty of form have certainly *not* increased since the days of the Parthenon and Aphrodite of Melos. In matters of the reason, in the development of the intellect, we may seriously inquire how the case stands. Does the reason of the average man of civilised Europe stand out clearly as an evidence of progress when compared with that of the men of bygone ages? Are all the inventions and figments of human superstition and folly, the self-inflicted torturing of mind, the reiterated substitution of wrong for right, and of falsehood for truth, which disfigure our modern civilisation—are these evidences of progress? In such respects we have at least reason to fear that we may be degenerate. Possibly we are all drifting, tending to the condition of intellectual Barnacles or Ascidians. It is possible for us—just as the Ascidian throws away its tail and its eye and sinks into a quiescent state of inferiority—to reject the good gift of reason with which every child is born, and to degenerate into a contented life of material enjoyment accompanied by ignorance and superstition. The unprejudiced, all-questioning spirit of childhood may not inaptly be compared to the tadpole tail and eye of the young Ascidian: we have to fear lest the prejudices, pre-occupations, and dogmatism of modern civilisation should in any way lead to the atrophy and loss of the valuable mental qualities inherited by our young forms from primaeval man.

There is only one means of estimating our position, only one means of so shaping our conduct that we may with certainty avoid degeneration and keep an onward course. We are as a race more fortunate than our ruined cousins—the degenerate Ascidians. For us it is possible to ascertain what will conduce to our higher development, what will favour our degeneration. To us has been given the power to *know the causes of things*, and by the use of this power it is possible for us to control our destinies. It is for us by ceaseless and ever hopeful labour to try to gain a knowledge of man's place in the order of nature. When we have gained this fully and minutely, we shall be able by the light of the past to guide ourselves in the future. In proportion as the whole of the past evolution of civilised man, of which we at present perceive the outlines, is assigned to its causes, we and our successors on the globe may expect to be able duly to estimate that which makes for, and that which makes against, the progress of the race. The full and earnest cultivation of Science—the Knowledge of Causes—is that to which we have to look for the protection of our race—even of this English branch of it—from relapse and degeneration.

2. From Gina Lombroso-Ferrero, *Criminal Man According to the Classification of Cesare Lombroso* (London: G.P. Putnam's Sons, 1911) 31, 32, 32–33, 82–3, 84–85, 85, 142–43

[Cesare Lombroso (1836–1909) was an Italian criminologist, one of the founders of the science of "criminal anthropology." Lombroso maintained that criminals had distinctive physical and mental characteristics which distinguished them from ordinary people. Lombroso attributed these differences to degeneration and atavism. Gina Lombroso-Ferrero, who was Lombroso's daughter, worked with her father and carried on his work after his death. The following excerpts of Lombroso's account of "criminal man" accord very well with Corelli's characterization of Gaston Beauvais, demonstrating the widespread circulation of Lombroso's theories.]

Part 1 "The Criminal World"

Chapter 1: "The Born Criminal"

Cynicism. The Strongest proof of the total lack of remorse in criminals and their inability to distinguish between good and evil is furnished by the callous way in which they boast of their depraved actions and feign pious sentiments which they do not feel....

Sometimes, indeed, a criminal realises dimly the depravity of his actions; he rarely judges them, however, as a normal person would, but seeks to explain and justify them after his own fashion....

... Others ... think themselves excused by the fact that many do worse things with impunity ...

The constant perusal of newspaper reports leads criminals to believe that there are a great many rogues in higher circles, and by taking exceptions to be the rule, they flatter themselves that their own actions are not very reprehensible, because the wealthy are not censured for similar actions.

... Criminals [then] are not entirely unable to distinguish between right and wrong. Nevertheless, their moral sense is sterile because it is suffocated by passions and the deadening force of habit.

Chapter 3: "The Insane Criminal"

Special Forms of Criminal Insanity

Alcoholism

Psychic Disturbances—Hallucinations. The most frequent and precocious symptoms are delusions and hallucinations, generally of a gloomy or even of a terrible nature, and extremely varied and fleeting, which, like dreams, in nearly every instance arise from recent and strong impressions. The most characteristic hallucinations are those which persuade the patient that he experiences the contact of disgusting vermin, corpses, or other horrible objects. He is gnawed by imaginary worms, burnt by matches, or persecuted by spies and the police.

Apathy. Another characteristic almost invariably found in inebriates who have committed a crime, is a strange apathy and indifference, a total lack of concern regarding their state ...

Contrast between Apathy and Impulsiveness. This apathy alternates with strange impulses, which, although strongly at variance with the patient's former habits, he is unable to control, even when he is aware that they are criminal....

Part 2: "Crime, its Origin, Cause, and Cure"

Chapter 1: Origin and Causes of Crime"

Illnesses, Intoxication, Traumatism

... [B]esides the crimes of violence committed during a drunken fit, the prolonged abuse of alcohol, opium, morphia, coca, and other nervines may give rise to chronic perturbation of the mind, and without other causes, congenital or educative, will transform an honest, well-bred, and industrious man into an idle, violent, and apathetic fellow,—into an ignoble being, capable of any depraved action, even when he is not directly under the influence of the drug.

Appendix G: Clinical and Artistic Views of Absinthe

1. Findings of Dr. Legrand as cited in *The Times* (4 May 1869): 12

There are two classes of absinthe drinkers. The one, after becoming accustomed to it for a short time, takes to imbibing it in considerable quantities, when all of a sudden delirium declares itself. The other is more regular, and at the same time more moderate in its libations; but upon them the effects, though necessarily more gradual, are none the less sure. Absinthe drinkers of the former class, are usually noisy and aggressive during the period of intoxication, which, moreover, lasts much longer than drunkenness produced by spirits or wine, and is followed by extreme depression and a sensation of fatigue which are not to be got rid of. After a while the digestive organs become deranged, the appetite continues to diminish until it is altogether lost, and an intense thirst supplies its place. Now ensues a constant feeling of uneasiness, a painful anxiety, accompanied by sensations of giddiness and tingling in the ears; and as the day declines hallucinations of sight and hearing begin. A desire of seclusion from friends and acquaintances takes possession of the sufferer on whose countenance strong marks of disquietude may be seen; his mind is oppressed by a settled melancholy, and his brain affected by a sort of sluggishness which indicates approaching idiocy. During its more active moments he is continually seeing either some imaginary persecutor from whom he is anxious to escape, or the fancied denunciator of some crime he dreams he has committed. From these phantoms he flies to hide himself, or advances passionately towards them protesting his innocence. At this stage the result is certain, and dissolution is rarely delayed very long. The symptom that first causes disquiet to the habitual absinthe drinker is a peculiar affection of the muscles, commencing with fitful contractions of the lips and muscles of the face and tremblings in the arms, hands, and legs. These are presently accompanied by tinglings, numbness, and a distinct loss of physical power; the hair falls off, the countenance becomes wan and sad-looking, the body thin, the skin wrinkled and of a yellowish tinge—everything, in short, indicates marked decline. Simultaneously with all this lesion of the brain takes place; sleep becomes more and more disturbed by dreams, nightmares and sudden wakings; ordinary illusions, succeeded by giddiness and headaches, eventually give place to painful hallucinations, to delirium in its most depressing form, hypochondria, and marked impediment of speech. In the end come entire loss of intellect, general paralysis, and death.

2. From an article on absinthe in the *New York Times* (12 December 1880): 6

A French physician of eminence has recently declared that [absinthe] is ten times more pernicious than ordinary intemperance, and that it very seldom happens that the habit, once fixed, can be unloosed. The same authority says that the increase of insanity is largely due to absinthe. It exercises a deadly fascination, the source of which scientists have vainly tried to discover, although they have no trouble ascertaining its terrible effects. Its immoderate use speedily acts on the entire nervous system in general, and the brain in particular, in which it induces organic changes with accompanying derangement of all the mental powers. The habitual drinker becomes at first dull, languid, is soon completely brutalized and then goes raving mad. He is at last wholly or partially paralyzed, unless, as often happens, disordered liver and stomach brings a quicker end.

3. Charles Cros, "Lendemain," *Le Coffret de santal* (Paris: 1873)

Avec les fleurs, avec les femmes,
Avec l'absinthe, avec le feu,
On peut se divertir un peu,
Jouer son role en quelque drame.

L'absinthe bue un soir d'hiver
Éclaire en vert l'âme enfumée,
Et les fleurs, sur la bien-aimée
Embaument devant le feu clair.

Puis les baisers perdent leurs charmes,
Ayant duré quelques saisons.
Les réciproques trahisons
Font qu'on se quitte un jour, sans larmes.

On brûle lettres et bouquets
Et le feu se met à l'alcôve,

Et, si la triste vie est sauvé,
Restent l'absinthe et ses hoquets.

Les portraits sont mangés des flammes;
Les doigts crispés sont tremblotants...
On meurt d'avoir dormi longtemps
Avec les fleurs, avec les femmes.

★ ★ ★

With flowers and with women,
With absinthe and with fire,
We can divert ourselves a while,
Play our role in some drama.

Absinthe drunk on a winter's eve
Lights up in green the sooty soul,
And flowers, on the beloved
Grow fragrant in front of the clear fire.

Then, kisses lose their charms
Having lasted several seasons.
Mutual betrayals
Mean we must part one day, without tears.

We burn letters and bouquets
And fire begins in our alcove;
And, if sad life is saved
There remains absinthe and its hiccups....

The portraits are eaten by flames;
Tense fingers tremble ...
We die from having slept so long
With flowers, and with women.

4. Arthur Symons, "The Absinthe-Drinker," *Silhouettes* (1892; London: Leonard Smithers 1896) 32

Gently I wave the visible world away.
Far off, I hear a roar, afar yet near,

Far off and strange, a voice is in my ear,
And is the voice my own? the words I say
Fall strangely, like a dream, across the day;
And the dim sunshine is a dream. How clear,
New as the world to lovers' eyes appear
The men and women passing on their way!

The world is very fair. The hours are all
Linked in a dance of mere forgetfulness.
I am at peace with God and man. O glide,
Sounds of the hour-glass that I count not, fall
Serenely: scarce I feel your soft caress,
Rocked on this dreamy and indifferent tide.

5. Ernest Dowson, "Absinthia Taetra,"[1] *Decorations* (London: Leonard Smithers, 1899) 47

Green changed to white, emerald to an opal: nothing was changed.

The man let the water trickle gently into his glass, and as the green clouded, a mist fell from his mind.

Then he drank opaline.

Memories and terrors beset him. The past tore after him like a panther and through the blackness of the present he saw the luminous tiger eyes of the things to be.

But he drank opaline.

And that obscure night of the soul, and the valley of humiliation, through which he stumbled were forgotten. He saw blue vistas of undiscovered countries, high prospects and a quiet, caressing sea. The past shed its perfume over him, to-day held his hand as it were a little child, and to-morrow shone like a white star: nothing was changed.

He drank opaline.

The man had known the obscure night of the soul, and lay even now in the valley of humiliation; and the tiger menace of the things to be was red in the skies. But for a little while he had forgotten.

Green changed to white, emerald to an opal: nothing was changed.

---

[1] Latin meaning "abominable absinthe."

Select Bibliography

Biographies of Corelli

Bigland, Eileen. *Marie Corelli: The Woman and the Legend*. London: Jerrolds, 1953.

Carr, Kent. *Miss Marie Corelli*. London: Henry J. Drane, 1901.

Coates, T.F.G, and R.S. Warren Bell. *Marie Corelli: The Writer and the Woman*. Philadelphia: George W. Jacobs and Co., 1903.

Masters, Brian. *Now Barabbas Was a Rotter: The Extraordinary Life of Marie Corelli*. London: Hamish Hamilton, 1978.

Ransom, Teresa. *The Mysterious Miss Marie Corelli, Queen of Victorian Bestsellers*. Thrupp, UK: Sutton, 1999.

Scott, William Stuart. *Marie Corelli: The Story of a Friendship*. London: Hutchinson, 1955.

Vyver, Bertha. *Memoirs of Marie Corelli*. London: A. Rivers Ltd., 1930.

Critical Works on Corelli

Adcock, A. St. John. "Marie Corelli: A Record and an Appreciation." *The Bookman* (May 1909): 59-78.

Casey, Janet Galligani. "Marie Corelli and Fin de Siècle Feminism." *English Literature in Transition* 35:2 (1992): 163-78.

Federico, Annette. *Idol of Suburbia: Marie Corelli and Late-Victorian Literary Culture*. Charlottesville, VA: UP of Virginia, 2000.

Felski, Rita. "Love, God and the Orient: Reading the Popular Sublime." *The Gender of Modernity*. Cambridge, MA: Harvard UP, 1995. 114-44.

Kershner, R.B. "Modernism's Mirror: The Sorrows of Marie Corelli." *Transforming Genres: New Approaches to British Fiction of the 1890s*. Eds. Nikki Lee Manos and Meri-Jane Rochelson. New York: St. Martin's Press, 1994. 67-86.

Kowalczyk, Richard L. "In Vanished Summertime: Marie Corelli and Popular Culture." *Journal of Popular Culture* 7 (1974): 850-63.

MacLeod, Kirsten. "Marie Corelli and Fin de Siècle Francophobia: 'The Absinthe Trail of French Art.'" *English Literature in Transition* 43:1 (2000): 66-82.

Samuel, Horace B. "The *Weltanschauung* of Miss Marie Corelli." *Modernities*. New York: Dutton, 1914.

Stuart-Young, J.M. "A Note Upon Marie Corelli by Another Writer of Lesser Repute." *Westminster Review* 166: 6 (1906): 680-92.

Background Reading

Altick, Richard D. *The English Common Reader: A Social History of the Mass Reading Public, 1800–1900.* 2nd. ed. Columbus: Ohio State UP, 1998.

Anderson, Rachel. *The Purple Heart Throbs: The Sub-Literature of Love.* London: Hodder and Stoughton, 1974.

Conrad, Barnaby. *Absinthe: History in a Bottle.* San Francisco: Chronicle, 1988.

Feltes, N.N. *Literary Capital and the Late Victorian Novel.* Madison: U of Wisconsin P, 1993.

Freedman, Jonathan. *Professions of Taste: Henry James, British Aestheticism, and Commodity Culture.* Stanford, CA: Stanford UP, 1990.

Griest, Guinevere L. *Mudie's Circulating Library and the Victorian Novel.* Devon, UK: David and Charles, 1970.

Keating, Peter. *The Haunted Study: A Social History of the English Novel 1875–1914.* London: Fontana, 1991.

Lanier, Doris. *Absinthe: The Cocaine of the Nineteenth Century: A History of the Hallucinogenic Drug and Its Effect on Artists and Writers in Europe and the United States.* Jefferson, NC: McFarland and Company, 1995.

Leavis, Q.D. *Fiction and the Reading Public.* 1932. London: Pimlico, 2000.

Pick, Daniel. *Faces of Degeneration: A European Disorder, c. 1848–1918.* Cambridge: Cambridge UP, 1989.

Pykett, Lyn. *Engendering Fictions: The English Novel in the Early Twentieth Century.* London: Edward Arnold, 1995.

Showalter, Elaine. *Sexual Anarchy: Gender and Culture at the Fin de Siècle.* New York: Viking, 1990.

Tuchman, Gaye, with Nina E. Fortin. *Edging Women Out: Victorian Novelists, Publishers, and Social Change.* New Haven: Yale UP, 1989.

West, Rebecca. *The Strange Necessity.* London: Jonathan Cape, 1928.

394 lb(s) de Rolland Enviro100 Print
100% post-consumer

Environmental savings
Based on the products you selected
compared to products made of 100% VIRGIN FIBERS
of the industry are:

 3 trees

 3,260 gal. US of water
35 days of water consumption

 412 lbs of waste
4 waste containers

 1,071 lbs CO2
2,031 miles driven

 5 MMBTU
25,403 60W light bulbs for one hour

 3 lbs NOx
emissions of one truck during 4 days